ALSO BY OMAR TYREE

Just Say No!
For the Love of Money
Sweet St. Louis
Single Mom
A Do Right Man
Flyy Girl

LESLIE

A Novel

OMAR TYREE

Simon & Schuster

New York • London • Toronto • Sydney • Singapore

SIMON & SCHUSTER
Rockefeller Center
1230 Avenue of the Americas
New York, NY 10020

SIMON & SCHUSTER and colophon are registered trademarks
of Simon & Schuster, Inc.

Designed by Dana Sloan

Manufactured in the United States of America

ISBN 0-7432-2866-9

All she ever wanted
was to see the sunshine outdoors
where the blue sky met with white clouds;
to hear the chirps of birds in the morning
after the soothing silence of the night;
to taste the satisfying explosion of bacon,
eggs, grits, and toast with jam;
to smell the roses and brown bark
of maple-filled trees;
and to touch the soft lips and warm body
of a loving man.

—Omar Tyree, "The Five Senses of Humanity"

urban (er´ben) *adjective:* characteristic of or belonging to a city or town

horror (hor´er) *noun:* **1** a painful emotion of fear or abhorrence; an intense aversion **2** that which may excite terror; something frightful or shocking

LESLIE

THE
FAMILY

Life I

The Chocolate Crew

New Orleans, Louisiana. The view of a handheld video camera widened. The date on the small view screen read THURS JAN 11–01. The color was vivid and clear with the sun still up at 3:36 P.M. The picture enlarged to capture the full front view of the light-blue-painted two-story house. The paint job was bright and striking, with white trim that outlined the windows, the roof, and the one-car garage. There were three new wooden steps that were still unpainted, which led to a light-blue-and-white front porch. Four plastic white chairs sat out on the porch for lounging. And a white screen door shielded the heavy, light blue front door, which led into the house.

"This is our home, sweet home, or at least for the meantime."

The camera zoomed in on the pleasant brown face of a college girl. Her hair was done in tight shoulder-length braids. She spoke right into the lens of the camera with poise and confidence as the focus locked in and followed her.

"Okay, that's the outside. Now we'll walk inside to meet my girls. They're also my housemates."

The girl smiled wide for the camera with bright white teeth and smooth skin.

"We call ourselves 'the chocolate crew' because we're all chocolate brown. But it's not like we planned it that way, like we had color favoritism or anything. That's just how it happened.

"But anyway, let's walk inside . . ."

The lens zoomed in as the camera moved forward and followed her through the front door. The view widened again inside the living room. The room had a plain white paint job, with no artwork or family portraits on the walls. It was a rented student house with a marble fireplace and shiny hardwood floors that were covered by large Oriental rugs. Two girls sat on the sofa to the left, with a third girl sitting inside the dining room that was straight ahead.

"Okay, let me introduce myself first, since I'm giving the tour here," the host in braids spoke into the camera. She was excited and straightforward with her introduction.

"My name is Bridget Chancellor, and I'm from Ann Arbor, Michigan. I came here to Dillard University to enroll in the nursing program while experiencing the city of New Orleans."

"It's *N'awlins,* girl. Not *New Or-leans.* You don't know that by now? You've been here over a year already. Get that proper shit out ya' voice."

The camera angled left to the two girls who sat on the sofa. The first one, who was closest to the camera, was plump, with short pressed hair that was curled at the edges. She hid her face to laugh when the bright light of the camera focused on her.

The second girl, who had interrupted Bridget, wore a black bandanna around her head, with twisted hair that poked out in twenty different directions. She had all of the mouth in the world, and she hid it from no one.

Bridget grinned and said, "That's Yula Frederick and Ayanna Timber."

The camera zoomed in on Ayanna Timber, with the twisted hair and loud mouth. She responded accordingly, with her hands swaying, head bobbing, and mouth running to her own beat.

"Yeah, I'm the *A-to-the-Y-A-double-N-A,* and if you wants to play, then don't swing *my* way, 'cause I'll send you to a grave like a thug from the boulevard for trying to act *hard.* So don't pull my card unless you're ready to *go,* blow for blow, flow for flow, and now you *know.*

"So who you wanna *step* to with your *weak-*ass crew, it ain't the *A*-to-the-*T* from the *chocolate* girl crew, you'll get your ass spiced *up* like a Leslie stew."

Laughter filled the room, including a grin from the fourth housemate, who sat alone in the dining room, before Bridget took control of the camera again.

"Anyway, Ayanna's from Houston—"

"The southwest si-i-ide!" Ayanna hollered.

"—and I forgot what she's supposed to be studying because she changed her major three times already," Bridget continued.

Ayanna said, "It's sociology."

"Whatever," Bridget said. "You need to keep your mind on your work instead of your rapping."

"Shit, B, you need to keep your mind off your little Creole boyfriend who be over here every other night."

The camera angled left and right to keep up with their rapid conversation. When the view stopped on Bridget, she looked embarrassed. Ayanna was giving unscripted information.

Bridget said, "Well, at least I still get my work done. And he doesn't call himself a Creole."

She faced the camera to explain things further. "Um, Ayanna didn't mean B like in, you know, a *B* or anything like that. She just meant it, like, *B* for Bridget."

Laughter filled the room again.

Ayanna said, "Girl, stop trying to explain everything. You need to be a damn anthropologist or something with the way you always try to explain shit. Some things ain't meant to be explained."

"And some words are not meant to be used all the time," Bridget responded. "Well, anyway," she said, moving on, "Yula Frederick is from Mobile, Alabama, and she's a nursing major like I am. That's how we met in our first semester, freshman year."

"Why don't you shut up a minute and let Yula introduce herself?" Ayanna snapped.

Bridget sighed and didn't say another word. What use was it? Ayanna was unruly. She was a disruptive force, where Bridget was raised on civility.

The camera zoomed in and focused on Yula's wide frame while she sat on the sofa. She watched it apprehensively. Then she dropped her reservations. She said, "Well, you know, we're the chocolate girl crew or whatever, but it's not just because we're brown; it's also because we're tasty."

They laughed again. The camera zoomed out and focused on the fourth housemate, sitting alone at the dining room table. She was doing homework. She looked up from her book and shook her head, above the playfulness.

The camera angled back to Yula. She said, "I can't speak for everyone else, but I know I gets mines." Yula had no shame, and she liked to shock people, like at that moment.

Bridget stopped the tone of the conversation. "No one asked you that, Yula. You don't have to share that. I mean, keep some decency."

Ayanna said, "Girl, she can say she gets her man if she wants to. What's wrong with that? I know I get mine."

"Yeah, you hang out with enough of them," Bridget responded.

Ayanna frowned and said, "Bridget, don't try to act like you don't be gettin' yours. Don't even front for the camera like that. Be real about it."

Yula agreed with Ayanna. "I know. She's trying to be all Goody Two-shoes up in here."

Finally, the fourth housemate spoke up from the dining room table. "Y'all all in here tellin' y'all business. You don't even know what she's gonna do with this stuff."

"That's what I'm trying to say," Bridget added.

"It's a documentary on the life of college students, right?" Yula asked.

Bridget said, "Yeah, but still . . ."

"A documentary for *who?*" the fourth housemate questioned.

The camera zoomed in on her dark brown face of symmetry. Her eyes, nose, lips, and chin were all defined in smooth arcs and were lined up perfectly. Her long, straight black hair was pulled back in a ponytail and held in place with a red scrunchie.

Bridget said, "That's Leslie Beaudet. She's from New Orleans, and she tells us what time it is down here. Go ahead, Leslie, say something for the camera."

The camera didn't budge from her while she sat calmly at the table. It zoomed in closer to her. Leslie's face filled up the screen. The stillness of her eyes was just as perfect as everything else about her. They peered straight ahead with serious intent.

Leslie asked them, "What do you want me to say?"

"Say anything," Ayanna told her. "Tell us something extra about N'aw-lins. Talk about that voodoo shit down here. Speak in French, L. Do *anything,* girl. Anything!"

Everyone laughed but Leslie. There was no playfulness left in her. She was mature beyond her years, and the calm focus of her eyes on the camera told you everything . . . and nothing.

She turned from the camera and declined to speak, with a simple shake of her head and a hum, "Mmmpt mmm." And that was it.

"Come on, Leslie, just tell us how you like to cook, and about your aspirations in school and stuff," Bridget complained in the background.

The camera refused to move from Leslie. It loved her stillness, the shine of her long black hair, and the value of her sparse movements. Nothing was wasted with her. And not another word was spoken from her mouth.

≈

Bridget apologized to her camera-holding friend when they walked outside together.

"I'm sorry about that, Kaiyah. I mean, Leslie knew what we were doing. She even agreed to be here for it."

The sunlight had faded by the time they had all told their individual stories. All except for Leslie, who continued to listen while doing her homework.

Kaiyah asked, "Is she usually tight on conversation like that?" She was a tall, medium-brown girl wearing a green-and-white sweatshirt from Tulane University.

Bridget nodded. "I'm afraid so. But sometimes she talks. I mean, we couldn't have become friends without it, right?" She forced herself to grin. "I mean, she'll come around. She just needs to be comfortable in front of the camera, that's all."

Kaiyah returned her nod. "Well, as long as she keeps it real with herself. You don't want her to act outside of herself. Documentaries are supposed to capture people just how they are in everyday situations. So she did good by just being herself."

Bridget asked, "Well, do you think they'll still decide to use us in the documentary?"

Kaiyah couldn't promise her anything. Even the question bothered her. She liked the chocolate crew. They would have added the needed flavor to the documentary of college students that she and a handful of Tulane classmates were working on. However, Kaiyah also understood the racial politics of America. Blacks were often not included in popular American culture, and she didn't want to set Bridget and her housemates up for a letdown.

Kaiyah took the safe road. She said, "Well, we'll have to wait and see. I mean, since you guys all live here in the same house, that would make it easier for us to stay in contact and film all of you."

"That's what I'm saying. We would be perfect for it, like MTV's *The Real World,* right?" Bridget joked.

Kaiyah smiled, but she still made no promises. "I'll see what happens and call you."

Bridget sighed. It was out of her hands. She would have to be patient and await the outcome. She refused to hide her disappointment from her friends when she reentered the house.

"Oh well, now we have to just wait and see," she told them in dejection. Bridget looked forward to her college life being documented. She wanted to stand out and be special.

Yula looked at Ayanna, and Ayanna looked over at Leslie. Leslie looked up from her work again but didn't comment. No one wanted to blame her, but they all thought about it. They all wanted to be special and to stand out. Who didn't? Maybe it would have been best if Leslie had not been home and they had left her out. However, Bridget remained optimistic. Leslie would come around. Besides, they couldn't come down on the New Orleans homegirl too hard if they still wanted to eat well. Leslie was the best cook in the house. She was the best cook that any of them had ever known, including their mothers and extended family members. Leslie could outright "throw down" with exotic meals. Cajun food. Creole food. Soul food. Haitian. You name it!

Ayanna broke the stale silence in the room and asked, "Well . . . what's for dinner tonight . . . Leslie?"

The room was filled with laughter again. Even Leslie chuckled at it from the table.

She said, "Don't worry about it, I'll hook it up like I always do."

"Yeah, and I don't even need the names," Ayanna joked. "I can't pronounce most of that shit anyway. Jambalaya. Etouffé. Whatever, just hook that shit up, L. *I* still love you."

Leslie had a joke herself. "Seven dollars a plate," she told them.

Ayanna stopped and looked at Bridget.

"You still giving her a discount on the rent for her cooking?"

Bridget looked embarrassed again. She looked at Leslie and shook her head in disgust.

Yula said, "Wait a minute, I can cook too. What kind of discount do *I* get?"

Leslie said, "You can cook tonight then."

Ayanna frowned. "Oh no she can't. I'm too hungry tonight for that experimentation shit. I'll fuckin' go to Popeyes' for all of that."

Yula said, "Don't even try it, Ayanna. My cooking is *not* that bad."

Leslie flashed an eye of reprimand at Bridget before she responded to Ayanna. "Popeye's cook some of the same stuff that I cook anyway. Maybe you should eat there every night."

Ayanna stopped the joking. She realized that Leslie was pissed about her big mouth.

She said, "Leslie, don't even get like that. I'm not sweatin' that rent thing. You deserve a break on the rent. I mean, *you* get most of the groceries."

"Well, why you bring it up then if you not sweatin' it?" Leslie asked her.

Ayanna felt trapped and guilty. She looked for a way out.

She said, "Well, Bridget told me about it. Maybe she got problems with it."

Bridget raised up her hands and closed her eyes. Ayanna's mouth was unbelievable!

Bridget said, "Ayanna, you are just too damned petty!"

"Whatever, as long as I eat tonight. I pay my damn rent. Or my mother pays it, 'cause I ain't got no money like that." She looked at Bridget and said, "But your father does. I don't know why you sweat any of us for real, Bridget. You know how hard college is on us."

Bridget snapped, "Ayanna, you knew how hard college was going to be on you financially before you ever met me. So don't even play that. That's just plain foul. And you know it."

Ayanna chuckled and said, "You can't blame a girl for trying."

Yula continued to feel left out of the argument.

"I can cook and buy groceries too," she protested. "*I* need a damn break on the rent."

Leslie took a deep breath and let it all slide. She got back to her schoolwork.

≈≈

Hot spices sprinkled into the simmering pot that Leslie stirred with a long wooden spoon that night. She stood in front of the stove inside the kitchen, wearing a full apron. She no longer needed to measure her ingredients. Her cooking had become a precise rhythm. Time and practice had made it perfect. As she cooked, she looked expectantly every few minutes or so at the white telephone that hung on the kitchen wall near the refrigerator.

Leslie could feel the phone before it would ring sometimes. Her ears could zone in on it before it made a sound. It would be another call from her family. They were always calling her. By age nineteen, in her sophomore year of college, she was used to it. Her family needed her. So she had learned to expect their calls while in the middle of anything.

As she watched the phone, anticipating its ring, she noticed the abused telephone cord that had been stretched out of shape, dangling almost to the floor, twisted and deranged, and twirling without reason. Yet they still managed to use it.

Leslie watched that phone cord bouncing up against the wall and wondered. What would her life be like if she had more control over it? Or perhaps . . . if she had control over others, so that she might unravel herself and break free from their grip. She wanted to fall to the ground and unshackle her feet from the past, so that she could run away and feel . . . *alive* again, like when she was younger. She wanted to be exempt of responsibility. But as she was, they still managed to use her—her loyal stability, her levelheaded dignity, and her high regard for duty—against herself, while they ignored her, the telephone cord stretched out of shape, dangling almost to the floor, twisted and deranged, and twirling without reason. Maybe she should have left and traveled far enough away from home to avoid the entanglement. If such a thing were even possible for a woman. Freedom from family and friends was sacrilege. A woman was the root of things, and Leslie felt every one of her roots. They were holding her down instead of allowing her a chance to grow and extend her branches toward heaven . . . and toward the sunshine. But instead of receiving a phone call from her family, Bridget snuck into the kitchen to apologize to Leslie for her indiscretions.

She placed her right hand on Leslie's shoulder. "I'm sorry about that, Lez."

Leslie brushed it off with a shrug. "That's all right." Only it wasn't. It was never all right. Leslie had always gotten the short end of the stick, and she had found a way to make do with it. But that didn't make it all right. Why did Bridget feel a need to express their private agreement to Ayanna in the first place?

"If you want me to pay the full rent, just tell me," Leslie commented. She remained focused on her pot and the spoon that stirred it.

Bridget apologized a second time in a lower tone. "Leslie, I'm sorry. I didn't mean it like that. I don't need you to pay the full rent. I mean . . . I understand your situation."

Leslie asked her curiously, "What situation?" She was unmoved by the apology and tired of its ritual. She didn't want anyone's pity. She wanted respect for all that she had done and would continue to do.

Bridget felt ashamed of her assumptions. She stammered and said, "Well, I . . . I mean . . ."

"You mean what? That I don't have as much money as you do?" Leslie asked her.

Bridget did not understand her situation. It was about more than just money. It was about having peace of mind. Bridget had peace of mind. And her father's income as a physician allowed her to be able to do things that Leslie could only dream about.

"Well, I'm starting over at zero, Leslie. It's not like it's my money," Bridget reasoned. "I mean, I'm using it right now to help all of us. And my father knows that. But I can't let it be like a free ride on me. We still have to work for it. Everybody has to work for it. That's what we go to school for."

"And I'm not working for it?" Leslie asked her, spoon in hand in her apron at the stove.

Bridget sighed and said, "How many times do I have to say that I'm sorry?"

"Until you remember not to do that shit again," Leslie told her. "Because you can't just buy my acceptance of an apology, you have to work for it."

Leslie turned away from her and went back to her cooking.

Bridget only looked and shook her head. She still didn't know how to figure Leslie out, but she never stopped trying. She wanted to be there for Leslie as a true friend whenever she would need it.

Leslie felt the stare on her back and added, "Dinner'll be ready in ten minutes."

Bridget responded with a nod. "Okay. And thanks for everything. I really appreciate all that you do, Leslie. And I mean that."

Leslie met her friend's eyes with hers and nodded back to her for a truce. However, when Bridget had left the kitchen, Leslie smiled to herself and thought about her words, "starting over at zero."

That girl don't know what "zero" means, Leslie thought to herself. *Let me start at zero from her house.*

When they all sat down at the dining room table to eat, Leslie felt good about the absence of her usual phone calls. She didn't let on to it, though. She held that small semblance of peace to herself and kept busy to lessen her anxiety about it. How long would it last?

"L, why don't you sit down and stop moving around so much?" Ayanna complained. She noticed Leslie's diligence around the table. She joked and said, "Let Y do some of that shit. She could use the exercise."

Bridget grimaced and shook her head from behind her plate at the table.

Yula said, "Don't pay her no mind, y'all. I don't even think about that girl. Because if she really bothered me, I would just toss her tomboy ass on the floor and just sit on her."

Bridget said, "She has no respect for anyone." At the same time, she thought to herself, *Why is she even here with us?*

Ayanna responded to Bridget's statement and thoughts on her.

"I mean, I love y'all and everything, I'm just keepin' it real. And I'm that nigga to say what needs to be said," she responded with candor.

Yula looked around the room and raised up her hands. "Well, there you go. That's why I don't pay her no mind. She's that nigga, and niggas *will* say anything out their mouth."

Bridget said, "But I thought that we were here in college to learn how *not* to be niggas, and bitches, and hoes, and all that other negative shit."

Ayanna's eyes popped open at the table from behind her own devoured plate of food.

She said, "Did you hear that shit, L? B just said 'niggas,' 'bitches,' 'hoes,' and 'shit,' all in the same sentence. Oh my God! I must be having a bad influence on this girl."

She continued joking and said, "Bridget, don't be like me. Okay? Be better than me. Be yourself. Okay? Because I don't want your father to disown you. That would fuck it up for all of us. I like this house. I really do."

The room filled with laughter again.

Ayanna added, "To be honest about it, though, B, you never *was* a nigga, you just a brown American. But you came to N'awlins to be *around* niggas, so don't even front. That's why you like me. I know you like me. 'Cause I'm raw like that with no seasoning. But see, Y and L know what being a nigga is all about. They know what I'm talking about. *We* know."

Leslie said, "Don't put me in that."

Yula agreed with her. "I know. She acts like it's a badge of honor or something, and it ain't. I came to college to get away from that nigga shit just like Bridget said."

"Well, how come y'all all didn't go to a white school then, since y'all want to get away from 'nigga shit' so much?" Ayanna asked them. When the response didn't come quickly enough, Ayanna concluded, "That's what I thought. Everybody's in here frontin' but me. I'm the only one keepin' it real."

Yula smiled and said, "I wanted to feel comfortable around other educated black people, but not niggas."

Leslie answered, "Those white schools cost too much anyway, unless you're on a full scholarship." Leslie was on a partial academic scholarship at Dillard, with off-campus employment and student loans. Ayanna and Yula were attending school on straight tuition, student loans, and work-study programs. And Bridget . . . was another story.

"So what's your excuse, B? Go ahead, spit it out," Ayanna told her. She knew that it wasn't a money thing with a doctor's daughter.

Bridget answered, "Like Yula said, to be around other educated black people."

"You could have gone to Xavier for that. You could have been down like Brandy over there at Xavier with your little Creole friend, Eugene. Why you choose Dillard?" Ayanna pressed her.

Bridget snapped, "Does it matter? Would you be better off if you never met me?"

Ayanna thought about it and came out grinning.

"Nah, girl, you my dog. I'm glad you came here," she responded with a chuckle.

Bridget said, "And I'm not your dog, Ayanna, I'm your girl. That sounds a lot better to me. Stop talking like these rapper guys so much. And stop sweating Eugene, too," she added. "You act like you're jealous."

Ayanna denied it. She said, "That boy ain't even my type."

Leslie smiled at it. Ayanna was lying. She *was* jealous of Eugene. Secretly, Leslie figured that Ayanna wanted her own light-skinned, wavy-haired friend. Ayanna wanted more than what she felt she deserved, and she envied Bridget for going for it. Leslie even wondered if her Houston friend would fall for her older brother, Pierre. He didn't have the light skin but he had the dark wavy hair. A head full of it.

Yula looked at Bridget and frowned at her choice of words.

She joked, "You're her girl, Bridget?"

Ayanna caught on to it and started laughing.

"Oh, I don't get down like that. I gotta have the wood after the tongue. The real wood."

Leslie laughed and shook her head. Ayanna was a trifling fool! But she was harmless, as long as you never took her too seriously. However, the self-assured remarks from Bridget kept Leslie on her guard, joke or no joke. Bridget understood that she was privileged, and she was secure in her wealth. Leslie envied that security. She had toiled every single day of her life to earn any and every thing that she had, and it was never secure. Yula coveted Bridget's slim, trim waistline, although she would never admit it. Yula had learned to live with what size she was given. So they all envied Bridget. Bridget could afford to be confident and optimistic. She was rich beyond income. She was rich in mind, body, and in spirit, the most important wealth.

"Anyway," Bridget told them, "I'm glad that we're all here with nowhere to go tonight, because I always wanted to play this thing with you guys."

She stood and rushed over to the coat closet. She pulled out a white bag from the bottom and hurried back to the dining room table, tugging out a brand-new Ouija board.

Yula took one look at it and said, "I know that ain't what I think it is."

Bridget smiled, all giddy about it. "Yeah, it's a *wee-gee* board," she confirmed.

Ayanna grinned and said, "Every time I see that word, I think, How come it's not pronounced *ou-jah* board, or just spelled differently?"

Leslie smiled and said, "*O-u-i* is pronounced *we* in French and it means 'yes.' And *ja* or *gee,* spelled *j-e-u,* means, like, a game. So it basically means a yes game, or an answer board." She began to clear their plates from the table and added, "It's like witchcraft, where you call out the spirits for answers."

"Is it anything like voodoo?" Ayanna asked.

Yula looked back and forth at them with large eyes.

Leslie continued to smile while shaking her head. "I don't know why you keep asking me about voodoo. I don't know much about that. You probably know more than *I* do, as much as you like to talk about it."

"I mean, it's just interesting to me, that's all," Ayanna explained. "And with you being from New Orleans and knowing French and Creole and everything, I just figured that you would know."

Leslie shook her head. "Well, I don't."

She had often asked her father about voodoo as a child, out of her own curiosity. And her father would never talk about it. But she had never asked her mother.

Bridget asked them all, "So is everyone willing to play it?" It was slightly after eight o'clock.

Leslie nodded her head and grabbed the last of the food to put away.

"I'm willing," she said, moving swiftly to the kitchen.

Ayanna said, "Yeah, count me in, girl."

But Yula was uninterested, and that was an understatement.

She said, "Aw, hell naw! I'm not playing that shit. *Hell no!*" she hollered.

Bridget opened up the box over the dining room table.

"Come on, Yula, it'll be fun."

Yula shut her eyes and refused to even look at the game.

Ayanna said, "Oh shit! You got a glow-in-the-dark one?"

Bridget said, "I figured it would be more fun to play it in the dark."

Yula started to get up and walk off, with her eyes still closed.

In the kitchen, Leslie shoved the leftover food into the refrigerator and tossed the dirty plates into soapy water in the sink to wash later. She began to pray that the phone didn't ring. She even thought of ignoring it if it did. She had some serious questions to ask the spirit world. She had never come face-to-face with an actual Ouija board before. She had only heard and read about it, along with palm readings, numerology, tarot cards, and everything else that was deemed mystical, including the often talked about voodoo.

Ayanna tried to keep Yula from leaving the room as Bridget read the instructions.

"Come on, Yula, stop acting stupid. It's only a damn *game*. That shit ain't real," Ayanna insisted while yanking Yula's arm.

Leslie sat and helped Bridget with the instructions while picking up the message indicator, a raised, triangular-shaped pointer with an open eye at the center. The Ouija board sat out under the dining room light to effect a strong glow while in the dark. It was labeled with the twenty-six letters of the English alphabet in a downward arc, with the ten basic counting numbers from one to nine and then zero below. Above the alphabet, and in opposite corners of the board, were the answers YES and NO. And at the very bottom was the written message GOOD-BYE.

"So, this is supposed to point to something as we hold on to it?" Leslie asked Bridget, referring to the message indicator.

Bridget answered, "Yeah. But it looks more complicated than I thought. How are we supposed to actually *spell* stuff with it? That seems like it'll take a lot of time. And we only have thirty minutes until the glow starts to fade."

"I guess we start with simple words first," Leslie suggested. She smiled and said, "Maybe we'll ask it what kind of grades Ayanna will get this semester."

Ayanna yelled, "I heard that," while still struggling with Yula. "Come on, y'all, help me to get Yula back to the table. She's acting all paranoid and shit."

Yula said, "Girl, I'm not messin' with that witchcraft stuff. I know I didn't come to college for that. So y'all can just leave *me* the hell out of it!"

Leslie told Ayanna, "Let her go, then. We'll just ask it whether or not she'll be able to sleep tonight without having nightmares."

Everyone laughed but Yula. Yula froze in her stance, immobilized. Then, with a desperate heave, she freed herself from Ayanna's grip and flung her to the floor. The panic of fear had strengthened her.

She said, "That shit ain't funny, Leslie. It's not. I don't play with that kind of stuff. Y'all just need to leave that damn thing alone. I'm serious, y'all. Put that thing away."

Bridget smiled at her overzealous friend and paid her no mind. She was eager for a new experience, and Yula was acting childish about it. Yula reminded Bridget of far too many Southern stereotypes and slave films, where black actors and actresses responded to everything that moved. Their eyes would widen comically while they ran about in circles, hands raised to the sky, wearing ragged servants' dresses and farmers' overalls. And those embarrassing images of America's past perceptions of the "Negro" made Bridget more determined to ignore Yula's misguided fears. But how could she explain it to her friend without offending her?

As Bridget thought it over, Leslie glared at Yula from the table and asked her, "Why? What is this Ouija board gonna do to us that people can't?"

Good question. They all looked toward Yula for the answer.

"I don't know, I just don't want to fool with that thing," Yula answered.

Ayanna looked back to Leslie. Leslie seemed excited while in a game of willpower.

"Well, go to bed, then," she told Yula. "You wanna be afraid of things just because you've never experienced them before? Go to bed."

They waited again for Yula's response.

"There's gonna be a lot of things that you've never experienced before, Yula," Leslie told her. "You need to get over that shit. Just face it head-on. Be a woman about it. This here ain't nothing but a game. And we're all friends in here."

Leslie pointed with her right finger toward the front door. "But that shit out there," she continued, "is real. So what are you gonna run from out there? Or who are you gonna run from?"

Yula took a deep breath and calmed her nerves. "That's different, Leslie."

"How so?"

"I mean . . . like you said, that's real life. But I don't have to play with no game if I don't want to."

"Well, just say that, then, instead of acting all scary," Ayanna jumped in on her.

They all waited there for Yula. Would she step up and face her fears, or would she back down and crawl away to safety?

Yula took another look at Leslie and decided to defy her. She wasn't going to bed like some kid afraid of a damn game board. She was bigger than that. And she would prove it to them.

Yula flicked her head in defiance and said, "I'll play the damn game, then," and strutted back over to the dining room table to join them.

Leslie grinned, slyly. Yula had done exactly what she wanted.

Ayanna recognized the game and laughed to herself. *I don't believe Yula fell for that shit,* she thought to herself. *That's the oldest trick in the book. She stupid!*

Once they were all seated at the table and surrounding the Ouija board, Bridget took control again. After all, it was her idea. Bridget had all of the ideas, or most of them. She snidely considered herself to be the leader of the group.

She said, "Okay, the first question I want us to ask is if this thing really works or not, before we even take it seriously."

Ayanna chuckled and said, "Yeah, because it looks like a kiddie toy with those happy-faced moons on it."

Leslie said, "Wait a minute. Let me turn off all the lights."

Yula's heart damn near jumped in her throat. "You don't have to turn off *all* the lights, Leslie."

Ayanna started laughing again. Bridget chuckled at Yula herself. But Leslie went about her business with urgency. She clicked off the lights and returned quickly to the table.

They were all seated and ready to play the game of fate, questions, and answers. Yula composed herself, taking several deep breaths. The last thing in the world that she wanted was to put an evil spell on herself while in the middle of getting a college education, friends or no friends. Yula had always stayed away from getting too involved with things. She tried to make herself invisible, so that she could sneak her way into a nice life. But on occasion, she would appear and reveal something extra from deep down in her soul. Something that she had been holding back. So there she was, trying to be brave with her college friends, pushing herself to stick it out with them, and to test her fate with her foot placed heavy on the gas instead of selecting cruise control.

They were all gathered at the dining room table in New Orleans.

Bridget smiled, Ouija board set out in front of her, glowing lime green in the dark. She took a breath and said, "Well . . . okay . . . here we go."

Ouija Board

Leslie said, "So, what's the first question that we ask it?"

Ayanna grinned and answered, "Let's ask it if Yula is scared as shit right now."

Yula looked at her and took another breath, keeping her composure.

Bridget said, "Let's just ask it if it really works."

"All right. Ask it, then," Leslie told her.

"Okay. We're supposed to put our fingers gently on the pointer and let it move by itself."

Yula wasn't touching that thing. Watching it was enough, especially in the dark.

"Y'all don't need four hands on it. That thing ain't big enough for the four of us anyway."

So Leslie, Bridget, and Ayanna placed their fingertips on the pointer while Yula watched them.

Bridget smiled at the center of attention and said, "Mighty spirit world, show us your stuff."

Ayanna looked at her and frowned, sitting directly across from her.

"Girl, would you shut up with that wack shit and just ask the question? You sound like a damn white girl movie. O mighty spirit world," she mocked her.

Leslie and Yula laughed, sitting to the left and right of Bridget.

Bridget ignored Ayanna and got back to the questions.

She asked, "Do you really work? Can you really tell us what we want to know?"

Yula took another deep breath from the right. She was ready to hyper-ventilate and leap from the table as soon as that pointer thing moved. So they waited. And waited. And . . . nothing happened.

Ayanna asked, "Are you sure we're not supposed to push it a little bit to get it started?"

Bridget agreed to it. "All right. Well, do I ask it another question, then?" She was baffled. Had the first question been forfeited? What were the rules?

Ayanna answered, "I don't know. You read the damn instructions, right?"

Yula grinned, finding an opportunity to relax her nerves. Maybe the thing didn't even work. But Leslie grew impatient with them. They were not taking it seriously enough.

She said, "Let me ask the questions. Y'all not really concentrating on it. It said to concentrate."

Bridget don't know what the hell she's doing anyway, Leslie thought to herself.

She stood up from her chair on the left and said, "Bridget, let me sit in the middle."

Bridget looked up and hesitated. It was her idea.

Ayanna noticed her reluctance to move and snapped, "Bridget, get your ass up and let Leslie sit there. You don't know what you doin'. Leslie *knows* this shit."

Bridget rose slowly and swapped seats with Leslie.

Leslie sat down at the center of the Ouija board and wasted no time with it. She said, "Okay, everybody concentrate for real now."

They placed their fingers back on the pointer, with Yula abstaining again. Why was Leslie so damned pressed about it? Yula would rather that Bridget were still asking the questions.

After a minute or two of concentrating in silence and darkness, Ayanna grew impatient herself.

"When are you gonna ask the questions, Leslie?"

Leslie answered, "I already have."

Bridget looked and opened her mouth to comment but was beaten to the punch.

Ayanna asked, "Well, when were you gonna let us know? That ain't how you're supposed to play."

Leslie smiled it off, which was a rarity. She said, "Y'all don't need to know the questions. All y'all need to do is concentrate. I'll ask it the questions."

Yula frowned and said, "Leslie's crazy, y'all. Let Bridget ask the questions again."

Bridget said, "Well, what did you ask it, Leslie?"

Leslie paused. All eyes were on her.

Should I tell them? she asked herself. She looked at her college friends all surrounding her at the table. They were hungry, helpless, and begging for her revelation. They were on her time, and in her control. Leslie found power in that, the fear of the unknown. So she decided not to tell them.

She nodded her head and said, "Okay, I'll ask it out loud, then."

Bridget was hip to Leslie's sidestep answer. She said, "The same question that you just asked it? I want to know what you asked it the first time."

But Leslie refused. She said, "Don't worry about it. It didn't work anyway."

Ayanna smiled and kept her thoughts to herself. *Leslie's trying to pull some wicked shit on us. I gotta keep my eye out on her.* Yula was thinking the same thing. Leslie wasn't to be trusted.

Leslie asked her next question out loud for them all to hear and ponder over the Ouija board: "Are humans really in control of their fate in this world? Or are we born into situations that we can't control?"

"That's two questions, Leslie," Ayanna told her.

Bridget said, "I thought we said we were gonna ask it the easy questions first."

Yula said, "I know. You can't ask that thing questions like that."

"Why can't I?" Leslie asked them. When no one answered fast enough, Leslie added, "You just have to believe in it."

Yula sat there and thought to herself, *Leslie's up to something. I can see that now.*

In the middle of their thoughts and counterthoughts, the pointer slid toward the upper left-hand corner of the Ouija board, toward the YES answer.

Yula shoved herself away from the table and hollered, *"Oh shit! It moved!"*

Ayanna sucked her teeth and said, "Leslie pushed that thing, girl. Calm your big ass down. You gon' break the chair."

Leslie didn't comment. It was an accident when she pushed it. Or was it meant to be pushed? Were accidents really accidents?

Bridget wondered the same. "Maybe that's the right answer, though," she responded. "It's not as if Leslie meant to push it in a certain direction."

Ayanna looked at her and frowned. "Aw, girl, if we're gonna play it that way, then we can all ask it questions and shove the thing around the board to see where it stops. That's not how it's supposed to work either."

Bridget said, "Well, you sure know a lot about the rules, for a bystander. Why don't you tell us how to play it, then?" Bridget was putting Ayanna's big mouth on the spot.

Leslie broke in and said, "What difference does it make if y'all not gon' take it seriously?"

Yula eyed Leslie again and responded, "You told me that it was only a *game,* Leslie. Now you want us to be all serious about it. Make up your mind."

Leslie eyed Yula back. "Are you ready to play for real without jumping up and acting scared?"

Ayanna said, "Yeah, let's stop fuckin' around and do it."

"Well, first, I think we need to analyze this answer," Bridget commented.

Ayanna asked her, "What answer?"

"The first answer to Leslie's question."

"That don't count, girl. Leslie pushed that thing," Ayanna insisted.

Bridget said, "So what? Let's discuss the answer anyway."

Ayanna looked around the table, attempting to find someone to second her thoughts of moving on, but Leslie agreed with Bridget.

"She's right. Let's talk about the answer."

Ayanna was bored with that idea. She wanted to see if the Ouija board would work on its own.

She said, "I thought you said we only have thirty minutes before this thing stops glowing."

Bridget ignored her and went on. She said, "So, a 'yes' would mean that we *do* have control over our fate as humans, Leslie."

"But a 'yes' to the second question would mean that we can't really change things either," Leslie countered.

Yula nodded her head. She was open to participate in the discussion of human fate as long as they were not fooling with that damn Ouija board again. However, Ayanna felt cheated.

"Aw, that's corny. Y'all don't really want to play this thing. We can discuss fate on our own."

Leslie looked at Ayanna and snapped, "Why don't you shut up a minute? You're always acting a damn fool. That's why you never get shit done."

A hard silence poisoned the air in the room. Bridget dropped her eyes at the table, feeling the burn in her lungs. Yula took another deep breath, suffocating in the thickness and expecting . . . anything.

Ayanna looked back at Leslie, although not as fixedly as Leslie stared at her, and she commented, "I can say whatever the fuck I wanna say, and when I wanna say it."

With that she rose up from the table, not for a confrontation, but for a tactical retreat.

"Fuck this game. I gotta make a phone call anyway," she huffed.

Leslie smirked and thought, *Yeah, you go make that phone call.*

Bridget and Yula didn't say a word. Ayanna had always run her mouth, and Leslie had always carried herself with a jagged edge. So their response to each other was normal.

Ayanna strutted away from the table and headed for the stairs, while mumbling underneath her breath, "Bitch don't tell me what to do. I'm not Yula or Bridget."

When Ayanna arrived at the black cordless phone in Yula's room upstairs, she found that it had been turned on and left off the hook.

She frowned and cursed, "That damn Yula is forever hanging the phone up wrong." She hung it up correctly and got a dial tone before making her call. Before she could get a good conversation going, the second line buzzed. She was tempted to ignore it, but she didn't.

"Shit. Hold on," she told her friend.

She clicked over to the second line and answered, "Hello."

"Hey, is Bridget in?"

"Who is this, Eugene?"

"Yeah."

Ayanna told him with no hesitation, "Call her back in thirty minutes."

He said, "Well, just tell her that I'm in the neighborhood."

"Yeah, aw'ight, I'll tell her." *Horny ass,* she thought to herself. *They always fuckin'. Then Bridget tries to act like she's still a virgin. She needs to kill that Britney Spears noise.*

Ayanna clicked the line back over to her own conversation. "Anyway, like I was saying . . . Eve's flow is all right on some songs, but on other songs, she just—"

The phone line buzzed again.

"Shit!" Ayanna snapped. "Yula done made the phone a damn hot line, keeping it off the hook like that. Hold on again."

She clicked over a second time and asked with more irritation in her voice, *"Hel-lo?"*

There was a slight pause on the phone. "Umm . . . can I speak to Leslie?" It sounded urgent. Babies were crying in the background.

Ayanna paused herself. She had plenty of hesitation on that call. She took a deep breath and thought it over, coming up with the only sane conclusion.

"Hold on a minute."

She clicked back to her conversation and said, "I'll call you back."

She returned to Leslie's phone call and began a slow, torturous walk down the stairs toward the dining room table. She wanted to show Leslie that she was not afraid of her, but that she was civil enough to know when to call a truce. Family was family. Ayanna understood that. So she strolled up to Leslie with poise, as her housemates continued to sit at the table with the Ouija board out. They were still discussing life and human fate even after the glow of the board had faded.

Ayanna looked Leslie in her eyes and said, "It's your sister," and handed her the telephone.

Leslie nodded, acknowledging Ayanna's maturity. She gently took the phone in her palm and said, "Thank you."

Little Sister

Leslie excused herself from the table.

Her sister was telling her over the phone line, "I've been callin' you for hours, Lez. What was wrong wit' y'all line?"

Leslie looked back toward Yula and said, "The phone must have been left off the hook. You called around seven the first time, didn't you?" *While I was cooking,* she thought to herself.

"Around there. Yeah," her sister answered.

Ayanna squeezed out a grin. They may have been beefing, but Leslie was on point most of the time. Ayanna had to admit that to herself.

When Leslie's stressed-out sister, a teen mother twice over, began to shout at her crying kids in the background of their phone conversation, Leslie reprimanded her in French. *"Ça suffit!"*

Her puzzled housemates had no idea what she had just said, but they all felt the impact of it. Leslie was pulling rank again. From what they could see, Leslie didn't take any shit from anyone. But her roommates didn't realize the full weight of her struggles.

Leslie's sister whined, "I just need a break tonight, Lez. Jurron out there runnin' the streets again with this new girl he started hollerin' at, and these kids are always cryin'. All fuckin' day long, Leslie! All damn day! I'm just tired of this shit, man.

"Shut up!" she yelled to the kids in the background again.

Leslie wanted to shout back at her sister in French or in English, *You think I'm not tired of fuckin' baby-sittin' for you? And all the other shit that I have to do in my fuckin' life?! You should have never gotten your ass pregnant by him and dropped out of school to be his sex slave!* But she couldn't say it. The love she had for her sister went deeper than that. Much deeper. So she calmed her nerves and gave in . . . like she always did.

Leslie looked down at her watch. It was past nine-thirty and closing in on ten o'clock.

She responded to her sister in French again, *"Je serai chez toi vers onze heures."* I will be over there at eleven.

"Thank you, Lez. I love you, girl. I love you so much."

Leslie returned the love: *"Je t'aime aussi."*

When she hung up the phone, she told herself, *I guess I won't ever have peace of mind from thinking about my family.* It was her first Ouija board question, the unrevealed one.

Leslie handed the phone back to Ayanna and thanked her a second time.

Ayanna blew it off. "Don't worry about it. As long as you do the same for me when my peoples call."

Leslie nodded and said, "You know it," before she ascended the stairs to gather her travel bag.

Ayanna turned to Bridget and smiled. She said, "Your man Eugene called, too. He said to tell you that he was in the neighborhood."

Bridget hesitated. Why did he have to tell Ayanna that, of all people? But she still had to call him back. She just hated for things to be so damned . . . obvious.

Yula looked and grinned at her, realizing Bridget's façade of innocence.

"Aw, go 'head, girl. You know you wanna call 'im," she teased. "Ain't nobody payin' you no mind in here. Go ahead and get yours."

Ayanna offered Bridget the telephone.

Bridget stood up and took the phone while heading toward the kitchen for privacy.

Ayanna shook her head. She said, "That girl a trip. She know she jonzin' for that nigga."

Yula chuckled, still seated at the table. She said, "I know." Then she thought to herself with a grin, *You like him, too, Ayanna. I know you do. But he is cute. I just ain't never been into light-skinned guys like that. I mean, what's the point? Them light-skinned guys are all whores anyway. They're nothing but sleazy-ass heartbreakers.*

≈

As Leslie prepared herself for an all-night baby-sitting job of her two nieces, Bridget snuck beside her again, this time in Leslie's back room upstairs.

"Are you going out again, Leslie? It seems like you rarely ever get a chance to rest."

Leslie ignored her. Obviously, she didn't have the luxury of rest. Leisure time was most affordable to the rich, who no longer *had* to work hard, or the dirt poor, who no longer *cared* to.

Leslie looked at Bridget and asked her, "Can I borrow your jacket again?"

Bridget said, "Whatever's mine is yours, Leslie. Anytime."

Leslie turned away from her and took another breath while closing her eyes to meditate. Bridget said the silliest damn things. If only humans could trade places like they did so much in the movies.

"I'll just remember that you said that," Leslie told her friend.

Bridget smiled, feeling useful and satisfied with herself.

"You want me to drive you anywhere tonight?"

Leslie shook her head. "No, I'm all right. Maybe another time."

"Okay. Whenever you need it."

Leslie headed for the front door with her bags and said her good-byes to her housemates, who were all healed and friendly again. What were friends for?

"All right, Lez!" Yula yelled to her.

When the front door swung open for Leslie to leave, Bridget's friend Eugene was just about to ring the doorbell.

He caught Leslie on her way out and said, "Oh, hi." He observed her loaded bags and asked her, "You're heading out for the night, hunh?"

Leslie barely looked at him. She answered, "That's what it looks like," and walked on by. She headed down the three wooden steps of the patio to reach the sidewalk. Then she turned left and headed down the block with pep in her step.

Eugene Duval, lean and agile, with olive skin and dark, wavy hair that shined under the patio light, looked back at Leslie for a whole minute, frozen by the cold shoulder that she gave him.

He asked himself, *What the hell is her problem?* She was the only one in that house who failed to pay him his just respect.

Leslie headed briskly down two blocks toward the bus route on North

Broad Avenue. As soon as she arrived at the corner stop, the bus pulled up and opened its doors to her. She stepped on board, paid her fare, and sat in the first seat available. She was on her way to the infamous Desire housing project, located in the far northeast corner of New Orleans, a secluded island of poverty and despair. It hadn't started off that way. None of the projects started off the way they ended up in America. They were all brand-spanking-new at one time, housing proud, unsuspecting working people. When the projects actually worked, they were able to move up those fortunate few who were economical enough to save for a down payment on their own homes, secure a rental property, or move into a private apartment complex of more social status and elevation. But when the projects failed, they left behind those who were unfortunate, through whatever circumstances had let them down or held them back from their goals, including, in far too many American cases, the level of melanin in their epidermis. So in the year two thousand and one, the majority of American projects had become nothing more than four-cornered islands of human treachery for brown people who strained to see sunshine through the rain.

Leslie's eyes told the whole story, if you cared enough, knew enough, or asked yourself enough honest questions to read them. Her melanin-heavy father had been broken before Leslie could reach a normal level of maturity, and she had been forced to come face-to-face with the horror of poverty ever since.

When she changed buses at Louisa Street, the hard reality of the Desire project smacked her harshly in the face. Even the bus driver looked doomed. Few drivers wanted a shift on the Louisa route that cut through the projects. But a job was a job, and somebody had to do it.

The young and restless males at the back of the bus jumped into full clown mode as soon as Leslie stepped aboard.

Someone yelled out the catchy street anthem of impoverishment mixed with wayward hormones: *"I want a PROD-JECT CHICK! One who don't GIVE AH FUCK!"*

The careless laughter from the back of the bus transformed the vulgarity into fun. It was entertainment at the expense of morality, as well as a blatant disrespect for the elders who rode the bus with iron ears that had become immune to the everyday debasement that went on.

Leslie took another seat at the front of the bus, among the young, stressed-out mothers and the tired but determined grandmothers who traveled with their children and grandchildren. Even at close to midnight they traveled. Travel proved that they were alive, and that they still had places to go. Then they would return home to somewhere. Anywhere. To wherever they had to call a home.

"Hey, girl!" someone yelled from the back of the bus. "You lookin' good up there. Why don't you come back here and holla at me? I got *beaucoup* lovin' to give. Just tell me whatchew need. I'm only on the bus right now 'cause my li'l car got totaled.

"Never let a drunk nigga drive your car, girl," the young man continued. "That's for true! So come on back here and holla at me. My car in the shop right now. We ain't gotta ride no buses."

His audience laughed from the back while Leslie maintained her normal breathing and refused to budge. One young girl looked at Leslie to read her response. She understood the disrespect but not how to disregard it. So she searched Leslie's eyes, awaiting something to happen, until her gray-haired grandmother nudged her to stop staring.

"Turn around and sit on your behind, girl. Be still!"

You were always told to "be still" in the ghetto, and at the same time that other people acted a complete fool. It was only a matter of time before the children riding at the front of the bus with their mothers and grandmothers would eventually act a fool their damn selves, unless they were the strong ones who learned the technique of ghetto yoga. You had to flat out ignore all of the bullshit that surrounded you to survive it. Otherwise . . . you would be likely to go insane. And there would be plenty of nonsense engulfing you every single day to drive you there . . . into insanity.

But Leslie was a strong one, a ghetto yoga master. She taught the curious young girl who continued to stare at her to remain above it all. So Leslie continued to be still, while showing no visible pain or concern. Because if she moved . . . and she responded to it . . . then they would succeed in breaking her abstinence to absurdity, and there would be no one there to pick up her pieces and aim her back into a direction of tranquillity. They were all too busy picking up their own fragments of a shattered dream of humanity to care. And few of them believed in the straight lines of progress anymore. They had never had much solid direction to begin with. They had learned to believe in only the jagged scribbles of misery.

The young girl eventually turned away from Leslie and was impressed by her focus. She could take it. She was indeed strong. Or maybe . . . she would have appeared stronger if she responded and told those boys to shut the hell up and leave her alone. The young girl was still confused about that. Her grandmother surely responded to her when she did the wrong things, or hurt people's feelings with shows of disrespect. But those mean boys at the back of the bus were out of her grandmother's range of authority. She was helpless to effect change with them. Not even the bus driver spoke up about it. He just wanted to make it back home that night to his own family without being shot at. It was just a damn job that paid the bills. Why risk his life for it?

All the while, the young fool at the back of the bus kept right on talking: "Come on, girl, holla at me!"

One of his friends finally spoke up to silence him by adding lethal venom of his own: "Yo, you betta leave that girl alone, man. She look like the type of girl that'll kill you. Dem black ones be da ones. Ya heard me? Dem black ones."

His friend howled, "Dat's for true, nigga! Dat's *for true!*"

And boy did they laugh back there, as if they were all that much lighter than Leslie was. And they were not. But they were males, and that gave them the only edge that they had to stand on and spit from.

The young girl's eyes nearly popped out of her head at the front of the bus when she looked to stare at Leslie after that diss. How would she respond, or not respond to *that?* Even the girl's grandmother was stirred by it. She slowly shook her head and grunted, "Mmpt, mmpt, mmpt!"

Calling a girl black in the ghetto was the worst sin in the Bible! The color black had become the most terrible thing in the world for a woman to be. All that Leslie did in response was turn away and look out of the window. She couldn't face the girl's stare with that. She succeeded in holding it all in, but she didn't want anyone to read her eyes at that moment. They had no idea how much wrath Leslie had been holding back from herself over the years.

Triflin'-ass, no-good, ignorant, no-job-havin', stinkin', raggedy, dirty-ass motherfuckers! She cursed them in her private thoughts. *I hate this shit! I fuckin' hate it! I hate coming over here! The things I do for my fuckin' little sister!*

But on the outside . . . Leslie remained as calm as freshly cut green grass, the kind that few poor people ever got a chance to walk on. There wasn't much grass in the ghetto. You had to find it, steal it, and hide it to keep it. But then you would need water, sunshine, and consistent care for it to grow.

One of the older men, riding in the middle of the bus, found enough bravery in his ailing heart to say something.

"Hey, ah . . . ah . . . why don't y'all show some respect in here?"

They looked at the tattered-clothed old man as if he were crazy. Then they mocked him.

"Ah . . . why don't you shut the fuck up and buy yourself some new shoes?"

The laughs just never stopped from back there. Even when they tried to correct themselves, they only succeeded in dropping more napalm on a flaming forest.

"Aw, you wrong, man. You wrong," another young male said through the laughter at the back of the bus. Then he added, "That nigga could be somebody father in here."

"I thought he was your daddy? He look like you, nigga."

"Aw, hell naw, that motherfucka ain't my father. My father live in Pittsburgh."

The old man stammered, "Y'all, y'all all know y'all all goin' to hell, right? All of you."

"Yeah, we'll see ya' ass when we get there, then. It look like you goin' first."

"For true!" another one hollered, validating their collective thoughts. How much worse could hell be than the hell that they were all raised in on earth? And if they could, they would yank the devil by his stringy red tail and wrap his ass around the high telephone wires like they did with their old tennis shoes. Then they would practice their aim while hurling his pitchfork at him as he swung there upside down.

What a relief it was when those fools finally climbed off of the bus two stops before Leslie's. That's when everyone began to breathe and talk freely again.

"Dem damn boys don't make no sense," a young mother commented with her two sleeping toddler sons stretched out across her lap. "None of 'em do. And then they gon' go right ahead and get somebody pregnant. Probably already got kids."

"Mmm, hmm. Now that is the truth," someone agreed.

Leslie arrived at her stop at Abundance Street in the middle of the set-aside acreage called Desire, where scores of dilapidated three-story rectangles of brick held its brown tenants. But what was so *desirable* about the dark, where the night-lights had been knocked out for months at a time before being fixed or replaced? What was so *desirable* about the jobless men and aimless boys who stood posted by the corners every night and day, taking extended and unearned breaks from responsibility to their community and family? What was so *desirable* about all of the young mothers there who were too immature to be mothers, and who had no income or satisfactory education, along with their limited self-dignity and lack of motivation?

What was so *desirable* about all of the drug-addicted aunts, uncles, and friends who only lived to see the next supply of high, while they sold their souls to the rationalizing drug dealers who called themselves "businessmen"? What was so *desirable* about the stench of sewage waste compounded by the filth of loose trash? What was so *desirable* about the rats that ducked in and out of the crevices between the separate buildings? And what in the world was so *desirable* about the unexpected violence that would set things off there quicker than a pack of firecrackers on Independence Day? Whose independence was it anyway?

Where was the independence for the ghetto, the freedom to feel free without the weight of poverty bending you over and breaking your back?

A million questions ran through Leslie's mind as she trekked toward her sister's apartment on the second floor of her dark building. The building right beside it had been evacuated after a fire there a month ago. Another one bites the dust, until eventually there would be none. Then where would the unfortunate live? And how?

They just move on to the next poor area or housing complex and live the same damn way, Leslie answered for herself. It had happened to her own family, moving from one bad situation to another.

Leslie had always asked and attempted to answer her own questions that way. She would walk sometimes in a daze as if she were a stranger, an alien to planet Earth. Her serene detachment from the turmoil of poverty had its roots in the private conversations and lessons that she had received from her father. He was a proud Haitian immigrant, who had allowed her an opportunity to see things as he saw them and to break them apart as he would. He had a clear, outsider's vision of the psychology of urban American distress, a vision that he had passed down to Leslie, along with his French and his love of cooking.

Leslie was not at all like her American-born mother, who accepted the destitution and helplessness of impoverishment at face value. Nor was she like her older brother and younger sister, who chased the chaos of the 'hood, addicted to its entertaining gamble of mortality. They would blow their dice daily, hold them in their hands, toss them up against the walls of the ghetto, and then hope for a seven. But Leslie wanted more than just a lucky roll of hope. She wanted freedom for real, like her father. But what price would she be willing to pay for it?

Leslie's sister, Laetitia, was standing in the doorway of her apartment when she reached the top of the dark stairway of the project building.

"It took you long enough," she complained.

She was dressed in all lime green, ass poked out and ripe breasts. Bearing two children had given her fuller body parts than Leslie's.

Leslie walked by her and into the apartment with her bag of things without a word. It was typical behavior of her sister to forget that she had selflessly traveled there through the night just to baby-sit her kids free of charge. There was no sense in complaining about it. Laetitia just didn't get it. She was used to being spoiled by her loving older sister.

When they stepped into the living room, Leslie's two nieces, Renée and Anna, were watching a loud videotape on a twenty-seven-inch color television set. It was the Harlem-based film *Sugar Hill,* starring Wesley Snipes.

The nieces jumped from the sofa and tried to climb up their aunt's legs as soon as they spotted her.

"Calm y'all asses *down,* dammit!" Laetitia snapped at them.

Leslie gave her a look. She said, "They shouldn't even be up at this time of night. Especially watching this kind of a movie. And it's loud. Turn that damn thing down."

Laetitia went to lower the volume. She said, "They wouldn't go to sleep, Leslie. Once I told them that you were coming, it was just *on* for both of 'em. You know how they get around you."

Leslie bent over to kiss them and was met by a whiff of funk that exploded up her nose from a soiled diaper that had gone unchanged.

She immediately raised her nose to a safe distance and responded, "Shit!"

Laetitia looked at her sister and laughed. She said, "That's Anna's ass stinkin' like that."

"And you didn't change her?"

Laetitia looked offended by the question. She answered, "Naw, girl, she did that shit right after I finished doin' my nails." She held up her shiny green fingertips. "I mean, you said you was comin'."

Leslie shook her head and carried her niece into her room to be changed. Her nieces were a year apart, with Renée, the older, turning three right before their mother would turn eighteen.

Laetitia followed Leslie into the girls' room to talk while the big sister changed the diaper.

"That girl take shits like a grown-up. She must get that shit from her father," Laetitia joked. "*I* don't even take shits like that."

Leslie smiled and went on about her business of changing the soiled diaper. She asked her sister, "What are you waitin' on? Go ahead and go out. Where are you going, anyway?"

Laetitia let out a long sigh. She said, "Girl, I don't even feel like goin' now. You know what this damn fool told me, Lez? He gon' sit up there on the phone and tell me, 'Um, I don't really *feel* like goin' out or nothin'. Let's just *chill* at my apartment and watch movies.'

"That motherfucka must think I'm stupid," she said. "He just wanna get some. So I told his ass, 'I can watch movies at my own damn house. I just got a brand-new twenty-seven-inch TV for Christmas.'"

Leslie thought, *Yeah, a brand-new TV while still living in the same filthy-ass neighborhood!*

Laetitia continued and said, "But he know his ass can't come over here, because Jurron would kill his ass if he caught him try'na holla at me. Talkin' 'bout, 'Meet me at the corna of your block.' I ain't thinkin' 'bout that damn boy no more."

Leslie reasoned, "So why go out with him? He knows you live with your babies' father, right?"

Laetitia snapped, "Yeah, Jurron lives here with me, but he gets to do whatever the hell he wants to do, anytime he wanna just up and chase some new pussy around."

Leslie looked at her two nieces and back to her sister. "Your mouth, girl, your mouth" is all she told her.

Laetitia said, "I know, but all of this is stressful on me, Lez. I mean, I ain't even eighteen yet."

Leslie looked at her sister and back to the children. Whose fault was it that Laetitia was in her situation? And why should the kids have to suffer through generations of irresponsibility?

Leslie looked on the bright side and said, "Well, at least y'all all still a family in here."

Laetitia frowned at her. "If you wanna call the shit that," she said and walked out of the room.

≈≈≈

Leslie took a while to put the girls to bed. She liked to read to them, translating the English words into French. She kept herself sharp that way, while introducing her nieces to their heritage.

She expected Laetitia to be gone when she walked back out to the living room, but she was not. Instead, her sister was wiping off her brown foundation makeup, revealing the blotches of lightened skin around her nose, lips, and eyes from the skin ailment called vitiligo. And in the light,

Leslie could see the faded melanin in between Laetitia's fingers.

Leslie sat down on the sofa beside her without any words. They had said everything to each other before. They were sisters.

Laetitia smiled and said, "I'm glad you read to them in French like Daddy used to do with us."

Leslie nodded and kept her thoughts to herself.

Laetitia read her thoughts and felt guilty about them. She could do that. They were sisters.

She said, "I mean, I could try to teach them French, Leslie, but I don't wanna mess up."

Again, Leslie kept her thoughts to herself, but Laetitia read them again.

"Leslie, everybody can't be smart like you. I mean, I was havin' enough problems trying to do my regular homework, instead of try'na learn all that French stuff," her sister pouted.

Leslie took a breath and responded against her better judgment.

"Spanish families don't have a problem with being bilingual."

Laetitia reasoned, "But that's because they have to, Leslie. A lot of their parents don't even speak English. And a lot of them can't read it and write it like you can with French."

Leslie wanted to leave it alone, but Laetitia wanted the argument.

"Daddy was always around *you* more with it anyway."

Leslie could see where that argument was going, and she wanted to cut it off at the head.

She said real calmly, "Laetitia, you chose to be around Mom because you knew that she wouldn't sweat you to do anything that you didn't want to do. You and Pete. So don't even try it."

Laetitia paused, defeated for the moment by the truth. She had been afraid of her father's seriousness, just like her older brother, Pierre, had been. In fact, Laetitia took her cues from her brother instead of from Leslie. And she and her older brother had both become horrified by their father's sense of urgency. He meant what he said and with no escape clauses. There was just no way around, over, under, or through him, until . . . he had been broken. And then they just wanted him to love them. That's when he had clearly chosen . . . Leslie.

Laetitia took a sobering breath and looked at Leslie's long, black hair. It was like their mother's hair, only Leslie's hair was thicker, stronger, and healthier than their mother's. And Leslie's skin was the most beautiful dark brown tone that Laetitia had ever seen. Leslie could easily pass for a model, the type that American magazines were finally beginning to showcase inside their fashion spreads, the radiant and beautiful dark-skinned sisters. And she could cook like a born chef!

Leslie had everything. She was "the one," the lucky one, the number seven.

Leslie read Laetitia's silence and knew what it meant. She was self-loathing again. She confirmed it when she reached out and stroked Leslie's hair.

"Renée has hair closer to yours. I guess it always comes to the oldest," Laetitia commented.

Leslie thought fast and said, "Mom's not the oldest."

"Yeah, but Mom's whole family has that kind of hair. That black *Indian* grade."

It only took a few more seconds before Laetitia expressed her insecurities out loud. Leslie could feel it coming while she tried to ignore it with the distraction of the television.

"I wish I had it," her sister told her anyway.

Shit! Here we go again, Leslie thought to herself. There was nothing that she could do about Laetitia's insecurities. She couldn't cut her hair off and give it to her sister, no more than she could trade her skin, temperament, or determination with her. If there were such things as fairy godmothers to make it happen, Leslie would do it in a heartbeat. But all that she could do was love her sister, sympathize with her, be there for her, and watch her children whenever Laetitia would fall under too much of the weight to bear. Leslie had never shared the weight of her own story with her sister. Only Pierre and their father knew it. Laetitia didn't need to know. Nor did their mother.

Laetitia mumbled, "Some of us are just . . . unlucky in life, Leslie."

Leslie shook her head, attempting to deny it. She looked into her sister's eyes and said with conviction, "Life is what you make it, Laetitia. And we may not all start in the same spot, but you determine your own finish."

Laetitia shook her head, denying Leslie's position. She said, "Everybody ain't like you, Leslie. I mean, you were born that way. Mom told me. She said you had the most of Dad in you. And me and Pete . . ."

Laetitia didn't have to say it. It had come up before. Their mother was perceived as the weak link. Leslie had always felt guilty about that, because she had never bothered to respect her mother.

Leslie looked away and said, "Mom did what she could. She supported Dad. But then when he got sick . . ." Leslie paused. She hated to think about how America had broken her father, and what he had to do for her. He had been so strong and passionate when they were little. Leslie loved to think back to her father when they were still the *Bo-day* girls, the correct French pronunciation of their name. They lived in a clean white house on Treme Street, pronounced *Tra-may* in French, at the bottom of New Orleans's Seventh Ward, and in walking distance from downtown.

Jean-Pierre, their father, was a determined Haitian cook, destined to have his own restaurant in the famous French Quarter, where blacks could not even eat at one time. And Anna-Marie, their mother, was a soft-spoken black Indian woman, with smooth, dark skin and long, dark hair.

The *Bo-days* had been special at one time. They were more exotic than even the light-skinned Creole of New Orleans, because they were dark, beautiful, proud, and their father spoke real French, served real Creole recipes, and he knew the original Creole culture of Haiti, "the first *free* Af-frican nation of the New World," he had told his family in his accented English.

Those were the memories of her father that Leslie refused to let go.

Laetitia broke her sister out of her daze. She asked, "Leslie . . . do you think I'm stupid for being dedicated to Jurron? I mean . . . he's the only guy I've ever been with."

Leslie thought before she answered. She said, "That's the way it used to be. But now, with the way that people break up and stuff . . ." She shook her head and never finished her sentence. She didn't need to.

Laetitia knew what Leslie was saying. After soiled relations with their men, women often became lonesome and loose. And after the next one . . . they got even looser. Until they were all over the place, with no rules or regulations over their temples. Leslie knew. Their own mother had gotten loose. She was lonesome and needy because her man had been broken and deserted her.

Laetitia suddenly smiled and felt proud of herself. Jurron had been her only man, and he had fathered both of her children. Her daughters even had his last name, Chesterfield.

"Jurron's all right," she said. "I mean . . . he don't hit me or force me to do nothin', like a lot of other guys try to do with their girls. He give me money when I need it." She stopped to correct herself, "Or when he got it, you know."

She chuckled, thinking about her sweet, real thing of a man before she continued: "I mean, I can't get mad at him for wantin' somethin' . . . different every once and a while."

Leslie looked at her, and Laetitia looked back at Leslie.

She rushed to explain the situation, convinced by her own logic. "I mean, he told me that he uses protection wit dem *other* bitches, and *I* got his kids, Leslie, so . . ."

Leslie wanted to shake her head and speak on it, but she didn't. Laetitia had always been the pacifist, just trying to get along with everybody and find someone to love her and to be friendly with. But the ghetto kids didn't want to hear that *friendly* shit! No one was going out of their way to befriend them. So when the *Bou-det* family, their name mispronounced in English, moved away from their clean white house on Treme Street and into the poorer section of the Seventh Ward, on the other side of Claiborne Avenue, Leslie was forced to kick much ass for her sister. The ghetto kids teased Laetitia because of her skin disease, and then because her father was Haitian, causing her to feel the opposite of the specialness that they had when they lived on *Tra-may*. So Laetitia began to hide her French. She no longer wanted to be special. She just wanted to fit in with the rest of the poor kids who were their new neighbors. She wanted to relate to them, and to the sweet pain of poverty. Being poor had a certain soul to it. Because when you lived in the ghetto, you were all poor there together, and that sense of togetherness drowned out Laetitia's insecurities and her feelings of lonely isolation. And then . . . she met Jurron.

So who was Leslie to deny whatever . . . happiness her little sister could steal in her microcosmic world of acceptable satisfactions? Or whatever Laetitia chose to call it. Because if Laetitia wasn't happy . . . then guess who else would be forced to suffer in her misery?

So Leslie held her tongue again, in protection of the mental health and welfare of her two nieces, as well as to safeguard her own sanity from a little sister who seemed to be born to want, and too willing to compromise.

Laetitia looked hard into Leslie's calm face and read her big sister's thoughts again. She said, "Jurron is the only thing I got, Leslie. I mean . . . I don't know what I would do without him."

Leslie sat there inside the Desire project and nodded her head, accepting who her sister was for about the hundredth time. She told herself, *Laetitia can't help it. She's just like Mom.* Then Leslie felt guilty again for not showing her mother the same sympathy that she showed her sister.

Big Brother

Pierre Beaudet sat between a girl's legs as she parted his long, dark, wavy hair with a comb and began to braid it from front to back.

"Tell me if I pull it too tight. Okay, Pete?" the girl told him with a smile.

"Aw'ight," he grunted to her, unconcerned with the pain. He could take it.

She said, "Okay," and continued smiling. She liked having him there in between her legs. She was having fantasies about him. She would braid Pierre's hair for free if she didn't need the money. He was a dream nigga, dark-skinned, with "pretty hair," a straight nose, nice height, and he wasn't overly mean like the rest of them. The boy even had a French name and could speak it.

Oooh, gir-r-rl! she thought to herself. She was damn near ecstatic while she schemed on how to get Pierre in between her legs again, the sweet way.

"Aw, dat nigga know he wanna scream like a bitch. Stop frontin', nigga," Pierre's friend Coup commented from the chair across the room. They called him Coup, short for *beaucoup,* the French word meaning "a lot," because the boy had always found a way of getting his hands on some money, stolen goods, easy women, and whatever else you needed. Coup was a stone-cold hustler. A ghetto survivor. He was the kind of guy that the American rap performers loved to brag about. But Coup was the real thing, he just wasn't that good looking.

The girl frowned and said, "Fuck him, Pete. He's just jealous 'cause you a *pretty* nigga."

Coup stared and grinned at her. She was right. But Pierre was his lackey anyway. Pierre's pretty face and hair made it easier for Coup to outsmart people who got distracted by his sidekick's attractiveness. And on Pierre's side, Coup was a respected ghetto general, who gave him plenty of protection. They had a partnership of convenience that worked well for both of them.

However, Coup couldn't let some homely hair-braiding bitch get the last word on him. So he took another look at the girl. He said, "Pierre twice as pretty as your ass. And you a girl. So what dat mean?" he asked her. Then he started laughing.

The girl stopped braiding Pierre's hair for a second and looked back at Coup. "Fuck you, nigga," she spat. But she didn't mean it. Coup gave her plenty of greenbacks to braid his own hair.

Pierre began to shake from laughter while still sitting in between her legs. That was the closest she would ever get to him. She *was* rather homely. Pierre wouldn't touch that girl with *Coup's* dick. But on the down low, Coup had already had her. What the hell? Sex was unavoidable in the ghetto. There was far too much proximity there to escape it, and the pleasurable feelings of human friction made life worth living. When it felt too good, girls with the good shit ended up pregnant, over and over again. It wasn't always the pretty ones with it either. However, the more headstrong girls protected themselves better. They were fortified enough in their game to only give it up to the top-notch "ballers," what the hustlers called themselves at the maximum levels. Or if the game didn't play out as they had planned it, they would cop enough money from fools on the side to end things with repetitive abortions.

Pierre was hip to all of the game, and he hadn't gotten one girl pregnant in all of his twenty-one years. Some of the desperate, love-lustful girls in the 'hood would beg and plead for that pretty French nigga to unleash his genes on them, while they dreamed of pretty babies, as if prettiness alone would give them and their children a get-out-of-the-ghetto free pass. Pierre knew that wasn't the truth. He had caught hell for half of his life from down-on-their-luck kids who wanted to kick his ass just for making them feel three times as ugly as they already felt. Prettiness surrounded by ugliness was a dangerous thing to have. It tended to heighten the superficiality of the physical. Even white people were crazy about blond hair and blue eyes, as if the lack of melanin made that much of a difference in human survival. But in reality, you were what you perceived yourself to be, or what you had

been seduced into believing you were from the opinions of others. So
humans had all gone crazy! And Pierre wanted to abstain from the madness
of it. He wasn't even that sexual. A girl had to damn near talk him into it.
All of the hype about his exotic black looks had turned him off.

When Pierre's hair was braided, Coup looked at him and smiled.
"Aw'ight, nigga, ya' shit is tight, now let's go make some money. These girls
paged me for some weed, like, an hour ago."

Pierre stood up, grabbed his jacket, and nodded. "Let's go, then."

The girl had already been paid, but she wanted something extra. She
spoke up on it with a grin.

"Hey, um, Pete, if you need me to tighten 'em up if they get too loose,
just call me. All right?"

Pierre faced her and nodded with six large twists of neatly braided hair.
He thought nothing of it. She was just being cool. But Coup sucked his
teeth at her and read her comment the real way.

He said, "He don't wanna fuck you, girl. Stop sweatin' this nigga. Go
on witcha ugly ass."

The girl grimaced at him and thought, YOU wanted it. Only she
couldn't say so. She realized that Coup's money was worth more than her
small ego. She knew she was supposed to keep her mouth shut. That's just
how it went when you were at the bottom of the pecking order.

They walked outside to a black-and-tan Navigator SUV and hopped in,
with Pierre on the passenger side. Coup turned on the stereo system extra
loud, blasting the latest hip-hop CD from the Brooklyn, New York, rapper
Jay-Z. Then they sped down the street of New Orleans's Seventh Ward,
heading east to the Ninth Ward on business.

Coup nodded his head to the music and began to sing along with the
chorus: "I need a gangsta gir-r-rl who can ri-i-ide in my passenger see-eat / I need
a gangsta gir-r-rl for my gang-sta fam-milee . . ."

Pierre grinned, nodding his own head to the smooth pulsation of the
bass line over thick drums.

Coup suddenly remembered something and turned the music down.
"Hey, man, you know who I saw out here on the bus stop this morning?"
he asked Pierre excitedly.

"Who?"

"Your sister Leslie," Coup answered with pleasure. He liked Leslie. He
said, "She was out here early in the mornin', man, with a big-ass bag over
her shoulder, when I was coming back from my li'l creep run out here. I
was ready to offer her a ride, but she got on the bus."

Pierre nodded and left it alone. However, Coup kept going with it.

He asked, "Who your sister know out here, man?" referring to the far side of the Ninth Ward.

"She was probably over my baby sister house," Pierre answered him.

"Who, Laetitia? Where she live at?"

Pierre didn't even want to say it. He hated talking about his sisters. "Desire," he mumbled.

Coup looked at him hard to make sure that he heard him right. "Desire? Desire projects?"

Pierre was ashamed of it. He remembered the well-to-do beginnings of his family all too well. He tried to forget them, but he couldn't. They were a part of his dreams, and the only good dreams that he had.

"Fuck your sister livin' there for?" Coup asked him with all seriousness. "You don't give your sister no money, man? I mean, you ain't makin' what I'm makin', but damn! How you gon' let your baby sister live in the projects like that?"

Coup had made sure to take care of all of his family members, or as many as he could afford. Looking out for family was a strong show of honor.

Pierre sighed, not wanting to get into that kind of a conversation. His family history was a long and complicated story. He shortened it as much as he could.

"Man, she fell in love with some nigga at fourteen. She got pregnant and had a baby by him. And she wanted to live with him, and that's what he had to offer," he answered. *So what the fuck can I say about it?* he thought to himself.

Coup just stared at him. He said, "Y'all never heard of an abortion before? Man, that same shit happened to one of my li'l sisters, right when she was 'bout to graduate from high school. And the ma-fucka who did it started try'na play her, right, like niggas will do. I guess he ain't know who the fuck he was dealin' wit! So I caught up to his ass and beat the shit out of 'im. I took my li'l sister to an abortion clinic to take care of business. And I told her ass, 'The next time this shit happen, I'm gon' whip *your* ass. You choose a ma-fucka that's gon' do you right!'"

He stopped and said with full conviction, "And I *meant* that shit, man! So my li'l sister in college now, just like Leslie. She go to SUNO." Southern University at New Orleans.

Coup shook his head and said, "I ain't playin' that shit with my family. That's how niggas be takin' so many setbacks. And I may have to do this shit that I'm doin' out here to survive, man, but I don't want all my family involved in this shit. Fuck that!

"A li'l sister need protection out here, man! Ya heard me?" he concluded.

Pierre agreed and tried to look away, feeling effeminate, like his father had often referred to him. Pierre had never been able to protect his sisters. Every time he even thought about them he felt guilty, and with Leslie in particular. They had an ugly and secret history together.

Adding insult to injury, Coup smiled at him and started talking about her. "Shit, a li'l sister like Leslie, I wouldn't mind gettin' her pregnant my damn self. She look good, man. Ya heard me?"

Pierre took a breath, smiled it off, and tried his luck at sticking up for her. "Come on, man."

Coup ignored him and went right ahead talking shit about her. "Leslie got that no-bullshit attitude, man. She da type that'll put it on you when you get it. I can see it now . . ." He was grinning his ass off, and having a good time with it.

Pierre tried again to plead for some respect for his dear sister. Leslie had been through so much already, and Pierre's chapter had been a major part of her life's painful book.

He said, "Come, on, man. Stop that shit."

Coup did stop, just to stare at him again. He said, "What dat mean?" with hard eyes.

Pierre couldn't take the heat from the stare. He averted his eyes and said weakly, "I'm sayin', man . . . come on, dat's my sister." He paused and forced himself to use some bold logic. He met Coup's eyes again and said, "You wouldn't let me talk about one of *your* sisters like that."

Coup started laughing at him, mocking him in his face. Pierre was nothing but a pretty boy lackey. He was not even a foot soldier. He was a toy nigga of the worst kind. He got no respect!

Coup said, "Boy you wouldn't even think to say no shit like that about one of my sisters. I should smack you in your head for even sayin' that shit to me."

Pierre's heart started racing like it had always done. Why couldn't everybody just get along? *Why can't we?* he had always wondered.

But the hard world of the streets had no sympathy for talk of peace and harmony. Coup thought to himself and decided to pull his rank as general. You couldn't afford to slip with your power in the 'hood, or your underlings would start to get courageous ideas about their own ambitions.

Coup nodded to himself, agreeing with his thoughts on the matter.

He said, "Matter fact, bend your head over here, man."

Pierre just looked at him. He was too baffled and afraid to speak. He didn't want to say the wrong thing or even say the right thing in the wrong way.

Coup pulled over the Navigator SUV and hollered, "Nigga, I told you to bend your head over! Now don't make me have to get the fuck out this car on ya' ass!"

Coup was taller and thicker than Pierre, so Pierre decided to do as he was told. As soon as he leaned forward in the passenger seat, Coup reached out and smashed his head into the glove compartment. He then turned the music back on and began to sing along with the chorus again as if nothing had happened: *"I need a gangsta gir-r-rl who can ri-i-ide in my passenger see-eat . . ."*

He looked over at Pierre intently, as if sending him a message that he was no more than a punk who could be smacked down and disrespected at any moment.

"I need a gang-sta gir-r-rl for my gang-sta fam-milee . . ."

When they arrived at their destination, without many new words spoken between them, Coup turned off the ignition and looked over at his sidekick.

He said, "Seriously, though, Pete. From one big brother to another, man . . . you supposed to be willing to die for your sisters, man. Ya heard me? 'Cause if you won't die for your mom and your li'l sisters in this world, then who the fuck else you gon' die for? For me? And *this* shit?" he asked, referring to the luxuries of a lucrative street family.

Coup shook his head and said, "It don't work like that, man. I tell everybody like this, 'If you not man enough to die for ya' *blood* family, then it's no fuckin' way you gon' join mine.' Ya heard me?

"So let this shit be a lesson to you, Pierre," he told him. "You let no mafucka disrespect your mom and ya' sisters. Now you got somethin' you wanna get off your chest about this shit?" he added.

Coup started to take off his jacket right there inside of the SUV.

Pierre looked and immediately shook his head. "Nah, man. I feel you."

Coup paused before he put his jacket back on.

He said, "You sure you ain't got shit you wanna get off ya' chest?"

Pierre shook his head again. "We cool."

Coup put his jacket back on and said, "I know you feel me, motherfucka! I'm just try'na make you a propa' soldier out here. And we cool for now, just don't put ya'self in a situation that's gon' make it otherwise."

They climbed out of the car and met up with a group of three eager girls.

"What's up, Coup? We paged you a while ago. What took you so long to holla back at us?" the lead girl asked him. She wore a yellow bandanna around her head, like the other two girls.

Coup looked back at Pierre and smiled before he responded to the girl. "This ya' world, I'm just a squirrel out here. Everything revolves around your crew."

The girl caught on to his obvious sarcasm and laughed a bit.

She said, "All right. My bad, you had other business to tend to."

Coup nodded to her and asked, "So, what's up?"

She spoke in a low tone. "We wanna buy ah ounce of weed?"

Coup frowned and said, "That's all? An ounce?" Their urgency made him feel that they were talking much stronger business.

"I mean, we just gettin' started, you know. We try'na get our hustle right first," she explained.

Coup looked at her two nervous girlfriends and smiled. They were all fronting their roles, trying to play harder than they were. Coup could tell from their eyes and their aimless energy. They moved too much and were too easily distracted.

He figured he'd run them through his sucker test.

"Aw'ight, y'all got a hunnet?"

"A hundred? For an ounce? We thought it'd be, like, *sixty-five*?"

Coup looked and said, "Tell 'em, Pierre."

Pierre said, "We got the best shit you can buy. Straight from the islands. And we pack our shit tight. So if y'all wanna get in the game, you myz well start at the top. Once y'all get rid of this ounce and order more weight, we can cut y'all a better discount."

One of her girlfriends spoke up to haggle with them. "But I'm sayin', we just try'na *start* our hustle. We wouldn't even make no money off of that."

Pierre said, "Nobody make no money when they first start. Y'all just basically settin' up y'all customers. That's how it is in any business."

He smiled and added, "Y'all ain't gon' make no money until you flip it, like, the fourth time."

The lead girl looked at Pierre's face and hair real hard and said, "You know who he remind me of? Like, a dark-skinned Ginuwine, the singer."

Her girls looked and chuckled. "Yeah, he do look like him a li'l bit."

Coup chuckled at their distraction and decided to toss out his big bait to the little fishes in the pond. Not that he would make any money off the chump change they were haggling over; he was just keeping his game tight to snag a much bigger fish later.

He gave them some hustling advice and said, "Yeah, well, when y'all get this weed, don't try to sell it to no guys. Y'all be better off sellin' it to girls, or to some of these college students, so y'all don't get taken for y'all money. But don't go lookin' for no college niggas wit shit on you. You just let folks know that y'all got that, and you let them come lookin' for you."

The second girlfriend said, "I know that's for true. Guys be try'na get over."

Coup started walking back to the car.

"Aw'ight. I'ma have my team come around wit it in a few."

Pierre gave the girls another look and said, "Aw'ight now. Y'all be safe." It was his hook line. Coup had trained him to say it. He wanted everyone to like Pierre. It gave people an easy-on-the-eyes face to connect to.

"You too, honey," the lead girl said with a chuckle. Her girlfriends joined her in the flirting.

"Y'all come back real soon. Especially you," the third girlfriend said under her breath.

They laughed to themselves while Coup and Pierre climbed back into the SUV.

Coup told Pierre immediately, "See that shit right there? That ain't make us no fuckin' money, Pete. But it's good community relations and shit. You show up in person, let people see ya' face, you take care of 'em, show 'em respect and all lat, and them ma-fuckas'll look out for you, dawg. Ya heard me? That's how you work the streets."

He said, "Now, I'll never drive over here for this petty shit again, but if I see them somewhere, I'll stop and say hi and shit, or whatever, and even-tually they'll talk good about me. But see, some other ma-fuckas like to get too big, and then they don't wanna fuck wit da small people no more, and that shit is a mistake. Because then the street ain't gon' have no love for you. And when you fall off . . . that's it. Nobody'll give a fuck.

"So I always remind myself to stay street wit it and make new friends . . . *and* enemies when I have to," he added. "'Cause see, everybody ain't gon' wanna be ya' fuckin' friend. So you gotta know the difference. You feel me on that, Pete?"

Pierre nodded his head. "Yeah, I feel you."

Coup shook his head and started laughing hard, all out of the blue. He said, "You see how dem 'hood rats were sweatin' you like dat, nigga? Boy,

you like the sweetest candy in the world for these hoes. I need to start sellin'
ya' ass. I'd fuckin' charge these rich-ass housewives, like, five hunnet an
hour for you when their husbands out of town on business trips gettin'
theirs, and shit. Then I'd charge six hundred if they want you to eat that
shit. And seven hunnet if they want you da start talking that French shit
while you fuckin' 'em."

He laughed at his new hustle idea and added, "I'd make another million
in a couple of months off ya' ass."

Pierre smiled and kept his mouth shut. At least Coup wasn't disrespect-
ing his sister this time.

Coup made a cell phone call and told his underlings to make the drop
and pick up from the girls in the Ninth Ward while he and Pierre drove
westward and south, back toward the Seventh Ward.

"Yo, and if dey try da talk you down on the price, I want y'all to fake a
phone call to me and give it to 'em for eighty. And make sure y'all tell 'em
it's because I said I like them. Okay? Holla at me later."

He hung up his cell phone and nodded to Pierre, who was smiling at
Coup's cunning.

Coup acknowledged the respect and responded, "Pierre, real business is
twenty-four hours a day. 'Cause even when you sleepin', if you got a good
rep and tight game about ya'self, ma-fuckas stay talkin' 'bout you. And I
mean wit good things *and* wit bad things. So a big-time nigga can never
really sleep. Ya heard me? Somebody always got you up at night."

Pierre's pager went off just as Coup finished his last sentence. He read
the number and pass code under the pager's light. It was his mother calling
him with an emergency.

He looked at Coup and said, "Yo, I gotta make a run for my mom,
man. That's her paging me now." He had had enough of Coup for one day
anyhow. He needed to get away from him and wash the funk of fear off
himself. Sometimes his protection felt more like a hostage situation than
being a comrade. Pierre's remaining threads of manhood could only take so
much of Coup each day before he would lose all of it. And then what
would Coup do to him? What would the world do to a young man who
had lost all of his natural . . . testosterone? If it's a world still ruled by the
violence and territorial boundaries of men, then it would turn that young
backboneless man into a pussy. A bitch! A girl! Just ask the other men of a
thousand nations.

Coup looked at Pierre and grinned, knowingly. He said, "You act like a
momma's boy, too. That's what fuck up a whole lot of niggas. You get raised

by your mom, and you end up all . . . emotional and shit. Don't know how to control your manhood right.

"I mean, I ain't have my pop around when I was young either, but my uncles took me under their wing, to make sure that I understood shit right," Coup continued. "I had football coaches. Baseball. I was around a lot of men when I was coming up, to help me see shit straight. But some niggas, man . . ."

Pierre didn't want to cut him off, but he did want to get the hell out of Dodge. Pronto! Coup had something to say about everything, and he spoke as if he was right about all of it. He was used to being a general. And as they say, power corrupts, and absolute power corrupts absolutely. So as soon as Coup paused in his thoughts, Pierre let him know that he wanted to be excused from his lecture on manhood. He had heard enough of that "be a mahn" shit from his father years ago.

"Yo, you can let me off right here, man. I can jump on that bus right there and ride it on down to my mom's crib," Pierre told him.

Coup paused and thought, *What, this nigga don't want me da give him a ride there? . . . Fuck it, just let him go. Bitch probably gotta go change his tampon.*

Coup smiled and nodded to him. "Aw'ight, man, I'll see you t'mar, den."

Pierre jumped out of the car as swiftly as a freed house cat and said, "I'll holla at you."

Coup yelled through the window, "And make sure you gi' ya' sister some money in them projects, nigga! Fuck wrong witchu?"

Lonely
Momma

Pierre made sure that Coup's Navigator was out of sight before he
crept inside a nearby fast food restaurant. Then he searched and
found a telephone near the rest rooms to call his mother.

Pierre had always talked to his mother, even when he had run away
from home. But he couldn't stand to see her anymore. Not with how she
had become so . . . damaged and unhealthy. Her spirit had been worn down,
and her sunken face, thinning hair, and diminutive stance all showed her
defeat. Although Pierre still loved her dearly, his mother seemed less of a
woman to him now. She had become genderless, and was not as distinctively
featured as he had pictured her in his youth. She had been so beautiful
before. Proud. Radiant. She had been powerful with the fewest of words, or
at least she was to Pete, as she had nicknamed him. And her little Pete had
always wished that he could have his own woman to love one day, one who
would be just like his mother was in the beginning: beautiful, kind, giving,
loving, soothing, infinity. So he desired to hold that more spirited, womanly
picture of his mother in his mind and frame it there.

When his mother answered his call from the pay phone, Pierre greeted
her in French, *"Bonjour, Madame Beaudet!"*

At her place, not far away from him in the Seventh Ward, Anna-Marie
Beaudet cradled the telephone in her right hand and held it up against her
ear. She now lived in a shotgun house, a rectangular-shaped dwelling that
ran from front to back and was used to house qualified low-income resi-
dents of New Orleans. She began to smile, hearing the French of her first-

born. But then she descended from her quick high and responded, *"Comme ci, comme ça!"*

Although she had grown accustomed to the many references in French as a native of Louisiana (a French purchase of the North American states that still held bountiful French ties, culture, and history), Anna-Marie Cooke had not learned French as a youth. But when she married Jean-Pierre Beaudet, a Haitian man who was fluent in French and determined to teach the language to his American-born wife and their three children, Ann (as her friends called her) was forced to learn as much French as she could.

Back at the restaurant, her son began to frown at her response. She was never doing well anymore, and Pierre had failed to cheer her. He even asked himself on occasion, *What's the use in even trying? My mother is just unhappy.* And she had reason to be. Her family dream had turned into a living nightmare.

"So, what's up, Mom? You need anything?" Pierre asked her. His pockets were wide open for her. He liked to drop gifts off at the house and surprise her with them when she was not at home, or mail her things with a card of appreciation. But mothers know their kids. Pierre had been avoiding her presence.

"It'd be nice to see you sometime, Pete. Are you embarrassed of me now?" she asked.

He denied it. "Nah, Mom, that's crazy."

"Well, what is it, then?" She had illusions of family get-togethers and dining again at nice restaurants. *Their* restaurant, where she would smile and laugh until she teared, like she used to do. She wanted to feel proud of her family again . . . and before she would die.

Ann imagined that her death would come soon. She just hadn't bothered to tell anyone yet.

She asked her son again, "What is it, Pete? Why won't you come see your mother like you used to do?"

Then she listened carefully to her son's sad excuse of an answer. Her firstborn: "Mom, I'm sayin', I'm just out here try'na to do some things, that's all. I just get busy."

Not good *things,* Ann told herself. She had rarely been one to complain about how people chose to live their lives, not even her own children. People were going to be who they were. Live and let die. But now that she was dying, Ann wanted more than what she had usually asked for.

"Well, I can't see how you gon' get so busy that you can't even see your own mother," she huffed at her son before she coughed. It was a dry, painful cough that had not gone away despite the many cough medicines that she used. She coughed harder whenever she became irritated.

Pierre dodged her complaint and asked her, "Are you all right, Mom?"

"Does it sound like I'm all right, Pete? What do *you* think?"

She didn't use to snap at people before, either. Pierre had enough of that attitude from his father. Then from the kids in the neighborhood. And then from Leslie. And now from Coup. Pierre didn't need it from his mother too. He needed her to be beautiful and understanding again. But she wasn't. It was just wishful thinking on his part.

Pierre frowned and said, "I'll see what I can do," without committing to anything.

"Well, if you talk to Leslie, you tell *her* to come see me then," his mother shot back at him.

He said, "You'd prob'bly catch her over Laetitia's house. She be over there a lot now."

"I said I want *you* to tell her. I don't wanna call her at Laetitia's," Ann snapped. "I'm sick right now, and I don't need to be around them kids with it."

Pierre grinned at his mother's insinuation. Laetitia would try and leave her kids with any family member who even called her. He told his mother, "Well, why don't you call her at her college house, Mom? You know the number. What you need me to do it for?"

Ann was being a curious instigator. For some reason, ever since Pierre had come back home from running away in his early teen years, he seemed to avoid contact with his sisters, particularly with Leslie. He barely even said her name half of the time.

Ann said, "I just called her a few days ago and I don't feel like leaving another message. I don't wanna bother her too much while she's doing what she needs to do. So I want you to tell her that 'our mother's' been asking to see her. Since *you* won't come by and see me."

Pierre broke down and said, "Aw'ight, I'll come see you, Mom. You wanna see me t'night?"

Ann looked bewildered as she continued to talk to her son over the telephone. She asked herself, *What in the devil is going on with him and Leslie?*

So she decided to ask him, "Is there any particular reason why you've been avoidin' your sister for so long? What did she do to you? What did *I* do to you?"

Pierre was already shaking his head. He didn't want any family job dealing with Leslie. He *was* trying to avoid her. He owed her too much. And he had no idea how he would ever repay her.

He answered, "She didn't do nothin' to me. I'm not avoidin' her. I just can't see why you can't call her yourself."

"Because I just told you why!" his mother shouted at him. She started coughing again. She used that to her advantage. "Now do what I told you to do before I die. Can you just do that for me, Pierre? Pierre Beaudet. My first and only son. Tell Leslie that I want to see her before I die. I wanna see you, too." She thought about it and added, "Together."

Pierre shook his head on the pay phone again. His mother was being melodramatic. She wasn't dying. She just needed to think more positively and get herself healthy. Maybe she needed a new man or something. That always seemed to cheer her up in the past. Or at least for a little while, until the new man was no longer there for her. So Pierre didn't plan to respond to his mother's talk of dying. It was all an act to have her way with him. Mothers would do that with their sons sometimes. Just like they would often do with their husbands; make them feel guilty to have their way. And the husbands and sons would do the same to their mothers and wives. It was all a human board game of emotions, and Ann had won this round.

Pierre sighed and conceded to her. "Aw'ight, Mom. I'll tell her." But he added, "I don't know if I'm gon' be there with her at the same time, though."

"Why not?" Ann asked him.

A recorded message came on over the pay phone: "Please deposit twenty-five cents for the next three minutes!"

Ann huffed, "Pay the phone, boy."

Pierre took out two quarters and slid them into the coin slot. Then he commented on his mother's new mean streak. "You've been actin' real mean lately, Mom."

She said, "I know. Because you've gotten used to me not sayin' nothin' to you. 'Everything gon' be all right, Pete. Everything gon' be all right,'" she mocked of her sweeter, happier years.

Then she snapped, "Well, I ain't sayin' that shit to you no more, Pierre. And everything ain't gon' be all right. And it ain't *been* all right for *years* now. So ain't no sense in me lyin' to myself or to you, or to nobody else. Not no more. Unt, unh. I'm gon' be honest before I die, dammit!" she confessed to herself. "I'm gon' be *honest* before I die!"

Pierre said, "Mom, you're not dyin'. Okay? You're not dyin'!"

Ann paused and thought for a moment. Pierre would just have to find out when it happened. But Leslie had to know. Leslie was a whole different story. She could handle the truth. However, Pierre had always run away from it, just like her husband had told her. She had turned their son into a . . . momma's boy. A passive dreamer.

Ann took a slow, painful breath and said, "You don't know nothin', boy. Just tell Leslie that I said to come see me. That's all I'm askin' of you."

When she hung up the phone with her son, Anna-Marie sat alone in her house and thought about her oldest daughter. What would Leslie say? What would Leslie think? How would Leslie feel? And what would Leslie do when she told her daughter, face-to-face, that she was dying of AIDS?

Ann wasn't certain of it yet, but she had many of the signs and symptoms: tiredness, body aches, coughs, appetite and weight loss, and an inability to stay healthy. She had taken the blood test a few weeks ago. The results would be back any day now. A call from hell.

Nevertheless, there was no sense in waiting for hell to come claim her. Ann still had friends. She still liked to go out. She wanted to at least act like everything was still normal. So she got dressed to go out, and called up a cab to take her to where everybody would know her name, a dance bar for oldies, where all of the blues people hung out. There were at least two of them in every black ghetto in America. After all, soul people had to have something to keep them alive. *Anything.* And the blues kept them hanging, tugging, pulling, and climbing themselves back out of bed every day because they knew that everybody had them. It was normal to feel blue while wrapped in brown skin in America. So they accepted it, and moved on with their lives.

As soon as Ann climbed out of the cab to show her face up in the place, she was greeted warmly and was stirred by the groove. It was Friday, soul night, where the DJ played up-tempo dance grooves, and Aretha Franklin was on, singing *R-E-S-P-E-C-T*: "*What you need / you know I got it / all I'm askin' for / is a little respect when ya come on . . .*"

Ann's friends saw her step in the joint, baby-dolled up in a red sequined dress, cut right above the knees with a scoop neck, and they started acting foolish in there. They were already filled up on the liquor from the bar at the left side of the dance floor.

"Chillld, who man you in here to steal t'night, Ann? It betta not be mine! We be fightin' in here, girl. We be fightin'!"

Ann smiled it off and did a slow spin to show off her dress. "Which one is he, girl? I'll go get 'im," she teased. "He still got all his teeth on 'im, don't he? 'Cause I don't want 'im if he ain't got no more teeth. I'll throw *that* nigga back.

"You can have 'im ya'self," she continued joking. "All by ya'self."

"Whuuu, gir-r-rl!" they howled in there, clowning through the soul music.

"My man got teeth. He ain't got no money, that's what he ain't got."

Ann said, "Well, den, what makes you think I wanna steal a man wit no money? I can stay my ass at home and get a hot stiff one in me. All I need is a telephone."

"Whuuu, gir-r-rl, you ain't lyin'! Mr. Telephone Man, where you *at* t'night? And make sho' ya bring all ya' tools witcha!"

Ann looked around and said, "Some of dese niggas up in here look like dey ain't got no damn tools. Musta pawned dem at the Chink store for dat fake-ass jur'ry dey got on."

"Whuuu, gir-r-rl, you mean t'night! And I likes it when you mean, Ann. I like it a lot!"

"Ann came in here and said, 'I'm pullin' out my goddamn claws on 'ese niggas t'night!'" her girls yelled and hooted. Humor was a must, the nastier the better. Black folks were professionals at it. The men and the women.

One of the guys overheard the riffraff talk from the women in there and responded, "Well, sense you all in here talkin' so much shit, which one ah y'all know how da dance? Dat's all *I* wanna know."

He was a short man in a black derby hat with a couple of shiny gold-capped teeth up front.

Ann stepped out at him and asked, "What you want from me?" and started rocking her hips.

Her partner caught right on to her groove and led Ann out onto the dance floor, while Roy Ayers slid on and pumped through the speakers, singing "Pretty Brown Skin": *"Pret-ty brown skin I'll be tru-uuu / pret-ty brown skin I love you-uuu . . ."*

The bass line and drum kick were bouncing and thick as Ann's girls flowed onto the dance floor to join her with the men. Then they all started laughin', and swingin', and twistin', and bobbin', and steppin', and dippin', and twirlin', and screamin', and yellin', and grinnin', and wooin', and flirtin', while the men were just smilin', and plottin', and gamin', and stalkin', and drinkin', and smokin', and schemin', and sweatin', and fantasizin' on hot sex on a platter as they all danced their asses off.

James Brown started wailing next, singing "Down and Out in New York City": *"So you try hard, or you die hard / and no one gives a good damn . . ."*

They sure didn't give a "good damn" in *that* place! They were all alive, and living their lives however they had to. They were soul people moved by something deeper than the stress.

Next up was Maze, celebrating "Joy and Pain" as they all clapped along with the snare on the downbeat. Then Tina Turner asked them all, "What's Love Got to Do with It?"

The women started yelling, *"Sing it, girl! Sing it! Ay-men ta that shit there! Who needs a heart?"*

By the time the Ohio Players came on with "Fire," they were already *on fire* and in there, dancing as if there were no tomorrow. The DJ just wouldn't let up as their overheated bodies continued to work up a sweat on the dance floor. Evelyn "Champagne" King kept them going with the pulsating bass riff of her hit song "Betcha She Don't Love You": *"And I bet'cha she don't luuuv—youuu / like you know I luuuv youuu . . ."*

When the DJ followed that up with Sly and the Family Stone's "Family Affair," Ann began to think that she may die right there on the dance floor.

"Ya can't cryyy-eee . . . / but ya cryin' anyway because you're all broke down . . ."

Ann looked toward the DJ booth in the back corner and thought to herself, *What is this nigga trying to do up in here? Where da damn break song at?* He was playing too many hits to stop yourself from dancing. Soul music was the emperor, and to step away from it was high treason.

The DJ finally let them off of the hook when he played Phyllis Hyman's slower-tempo "Betcha by Golly, Wow": *"You're the one that I've been waiting for . . . for-evv-ver . . ."*

Ann took a few deep, painful breaths and nearly fell out as she tried to make her way back to the bar area to have a seat. Her partner caught her by the waist right before she fell over.

"Shit, girl, I'm ti'ed too," he told her. "But you set it *off* in here! Let me get you ova' dis bar and get you ah drink."

Ann huffed, "As long as I ain't payin' for it."

He looked at Ann as if he was offended.

"Aw, nah, I gotchu. I gotchu right here in my arms." Flirting big-time with her.

Ann smiled and said, "Thank you." He had no idea how much of a help he was at that moment. Ann thought to herself, *Maybe this shit here wasn't no good idea. I hope I make it da hell back home t'night before I keel over and die up in here. My Jeezus!*

Ann hadn't gotten a chance to go out and dance at all with her husband, Jean-Pierre. *Jahn,* which was how the French pronounced it, didn't dance. He was thirty-four and twelve years Ann's senior when they first met down in the French Quarter nearly twenty-three years ago. He had told her before that when he witnessed grown black American men tap-dancing for nickels and dimes on the street corners of the French Quarter downtown, it turned his stomach to see them degrade themselves in such a way. He had had enough degradation of black skin in his homeland of Haiti, and he had not come to America to become a part of their buffoonery. His aim was to be a respected chef, and to own his own restaurant . . . in the French Quarter, of all places.

So he told Anna-Marie, "I am *not* a dan-sing fool," and that was that. Jean didn't waste words with his accented English or with his French.

Ann sat there on the bar stool and began to daydream about her husband while Phyllis Hyman continued to sing her heart out. All the while, her short dance partner in the black derby hat and gold teeth was steady trying to gain her attention with his flirting.

He said, "I bet you was ah fine li'l thing when you were younger, hunh? 'Cause you still as fine as cherry wine right now. Mmpt, mmpt, mmpt," he hummed at her.

Ann smiled in his face, took the drink that he had ordered for her, held it to her dry lips for a sip, and went back to daydreaming about her husband. Jean was such an intelligent and dignified man. He had presence about him. He was the kind of man who could walk into a crowded room, and you could just feel him there, white or black. Jean could intimidate people with just a stare. Ann had seen him do it more than a few times. She even began to chuckle, imagining Jean walking into that bar and scaring the little man who she sat with half to death.

Her dance partner looked at her sideways and asked, "What I say dat was funny?"

She took another sip of her drink and shook off his question.

"It's nothin', just keep talkin', I hear you. I'm tipsy. I get a li'l silly when I drink."

He smiled and said, "Oh. Okay." Then he thought to himself, *Shit, she barely drank anything. I wonder what she gon' do when I really get some liquor in her behind.* He nodded to himself and thought, *This here look like it's gon' be a good night! She on the thin side from what I like, but dem small girls can ride it for hours! They seem like they got more energy sometimes. Or maybe dem big girls wear me the hell out too fast, I don't know.*

He was thinking ahead of himself about how the night would end, but Ann was having no such thoughts. All that she could think about was Jean-Pierre and how America had . . . broken him.

The DJ changed the slow record and put on another classic, this time from Minnie Riperton. She was singing the seductive, adults-only song "Come Inside Me": *". . . we should be one . . . / do you wanna come—in-si-i-i-ide my luh-ahhhvvvv . . ."*

Ann listened to the lyrics and nodded her head. She told herself, *That's the kind of shit right there that got me inta trouble in the first damn place,* before she coughed hard into her drink.

"Damn, baby, you gotta cold or something?"

Ann looked into the little man's face and was tired of holding back the truth. So she told him, "You don't even wanna know," and coughed again into her fist.

That caused him to nod and lean his head away from her to sip his own drink. *Maybe this ain't gon' be no good night,* he told himself. *I don't want her coughin' on me with that shit. Whatever the hell it is she got. I've had enough damn diseases in my life.*

Suddenly, her short dance partner turned into Samuel, an evil-spirited man who had done Ann in years ago. Samuel had been very talkative and candid with her, right after Jean had moved out of their home and went elsewhere to rekindle his damaged pride.

Samuel said to Ann back then with foul intent, "I guess that Haitian nigga finally came around and realized that America ain't gon' let him have no damn black restaurant in the French Quarter."

Samuel took a sip of his drink and chuckled into his glass, the devil re-incarnated.

"Nigga musta thought he was Superman," he told Ann, with another laugh of mockery. She was still a beauty queen back then, and healthy. But she was in distress, and lonely. The man that she had grown to love until death had gotten up and walked away from her . . . and their kids, which was a rarity for a Haitian.

Samuel looked into Ann's tearful eyes on their fateful night and said, "See, that's the problem with them foreign niggas, Ann. They come over here and talk all that shit to us, as if the white man brought us niggas over here to run the damn country instead of being slaves in this motherfucka." He looked at her and asked, "What da hell dey think we been doin' over here all these damn years, Ann? Havin' a gotdamned picnic?"

His cigarette seemed to appear in his hands from nowhere, with smoke surrounding him as if it was leaking out of his body. But Ann didn't care that night. Samuel was the only one who even attempted to make sense of it all for her. He had been plotting on her for years, just waiting for an opportunity to make her his prey. He knew that Jean would break sooner or later. Jean was just too hardheaded about how things went down for black men in America.

Samuel nodded and continued: "Now all that Haitian nigga had to do was buy a nice building where the rest of us niggas lived, and he could of had his restaurant up and runnin' years ago. And you know this, Ann. You know it as well as I do.

"But no, that nigga didn't wanna be around us!" Samuel spat. "He too gotdamned good for the rest of us niggas! He want white folks' money, as if they just gon' open up their pockets and give it to 'em. In the gotdamned French Quarter!

"This ain't no damn Haiti! That nigga was out of his damn mind!" Samuel insisted to Ann that night. "Motherfucka too damned proud to even know how to Uncle Tom dese white folks. What, he ain't know nothin' about Louis Armstrong? Motherfuckin' Satchmo. He knew how to Uncle Tom dese white folks, and they still love his ass for it.

"He got a park named after his ass right here in N'awlins," he added. "And I bet that Haitian nigga of yours didn't even wanna to know about 'em, did he? And Louis Armstrong is a gotdamned legend. He got plenty of white folks' money. But he knew how to get it."

Ann finally stopped his berating of her husband with tears falling from her eyes.

"Please . . . no more."

Samuel looked into her eyes and went soft on her, just like Satan would. "Oh, I'm sorry, baby. I didn't mean to upset you with all of this, Ann. But I'm upset right now," he told her. He touched her hand and said, "Here you are, a beautiful young woman, with three beautiful kids, and you've been supportin' this . . . this man's big-time dreams for years. And look where it gotchu?"

He looked into her eyes in her moment of weakness and concluded, "But I'm still here for you, Ann. I'm still here. Because I understand things. And that nigga don't." He shook his head defiantly and repeated, "He just don't. And that's how it is wit dem . . . foreigners."

Ann couldn't remember everything that she was thinking that night. She especially couldn't remember how she allowed herself to backslide and tumble face forward into the gates of hell. All that she knew was that she ended up in Samuel's filthy bed that night, naked and pleading for him to give it to her as hard and as long as he wanted. And he did. And the pain was sweet, just like the ghetto. It was sweet misery. So Ann continued to sneak out and into hell at night, looking for Samuel for more of the same, while knowing damned well that he was no good for her!

"Motherfucka!" she snapped, back to her senses in the year 2001. Ann stared at the little man in the black derby hat and gold teeth, who still sat next to her at the bar.

He asked her, "Who you talkin' to?" with a raised tone of offense. "Are you all right in here? Maybe you need to put that drink back down."

Ann took a breath and gathered herself at the bar. She didn't need to be there anymore. It wouldn't help a damn thing! There was nowhere to run and hide from her misfortunes. So she got herself together to return home to her shotgun house.

The little man reached out to grab her arm as she began to walk away from him.

"Hey, girl," he said to her, as if she were a child in need of a reprimand.

Ann snatched her arm out of his grasp and shouted, *"Look, motherfucka, getcha goddamned hands off of me!"* as if she were talking to Samuel. But Samuel had already passed away to his grave three years ago. And Ann hoped that he had returned straight back to hell! But where would she be going when she died? She was dying from the same curse that Samuel had died of, acquired immune deficiency syndrome. Or better known as AIDS.

The scene that Ann made at the bar sent her friends and the bartender to her rescue.

"Are you all right, Ann? What's gotten into you t'night?"

None of them knew. Only Samuel's ass knew, and that motherfucker was dead already! So who could Anna-Marie Beaudet run to for sympathy?

She shook it off and headed for the door. "I'm just goin' home now," she told them all. "I'm just goin' home." And she walked out to find a taxi.

But on the way home in the cab, Ann broke down and started crying. Hard!

The taxi driver asked her, "Are you all right, ma'am?" He looked back at her from the driver's seat, up front. He was a middle-aged white man who seemed at peace with himself. But at that moment, everything and everyone represented the devil to Ann.

She snapped at him and said, "Look, just take me da hell home. I gotcha damn money. I can't run from you if I wanted to."

The taxi driver looked shocked. He responded, "Ma'am, I wasn't assuming anything like that, I was just askin' ya because you seemed—"

She cut him off and repeated, "Just take me the hell home. Okay? Just drive! Or I'll catch another damn taxi." She even moved for the door to climb out.

The taxi driver said, "Wait a minute, I'll take ya for free if I have to. I just don't think you need to be out on the street right now. So let me go on and take ya home."

The woman didn't seem to be in her right frame of mind, and the driver felt that it would stay on his conscience if something happened to her that night that could have been avoided.

But the woman snapped, "Well, good! Drive, den! And I'm payin' you my damn money. Because I don't need no goddamned white man's sympathy! You ain't sympathize when you motherfuckers were killin' us, and hangin' our baby boys from trees for lookin' at your ugly-ass women! So don't sympathize wit me now!"

The middle-aged white man took a deep breath, shook his head, and was glad when they arrived at her destination. Then she threw the money at him up front and shouted, "And you can keep the goddamned change!" as she climbed out.

The taxi driver watched her stumble up to her steps and pull out her house key to open the door before he drove off. He thought to himself about whether or not he would pick up the next black person late at night who didn't look to have it all together. But how could he even tell what was on each black person's mind when they would approach his taxi at night? They were not a part of his world.

Proud Daddy

Monday morning, Anna-Marie Beaudet finally received her phone call from NOMHC, New Orleans Medical and Health Center. "Ms. Cooke, we need you to come in for your test results," the nurse told her over the phone.

Ann hadn't used her married name. She didn't want her husband or children implicated in what she had done. She didn't see her misfortunes as their fault. Nor did she blame herself. Not really. It was just all in the intangibles of life. Shit happens . . . and then you die.

Come in for what? Ann asked herself. "Just tell me over the phone," she responded to the nurse. What was the use in getting up, getting dressed, and traveling just to receive bad news in person? There wasn't any cure for it. And treatment cost money, which she did not have.

The nurse hesitated a moment. "That's against our policy," she said. "We have to have exit consultations."

Exit consultation? Ann repeated to herself. *Does that mean that I'm not positive for AIDS?*

"I'll think about it," she responded.

The nurse insisted. "Ah, Ms. Cooke, we really need you to come in as soon as possible."

Ann's heart rate increased, revealing her fears. The urgency in the nurse's voice had given her the information that she needed. She nodded her head and said, "I have it then? I have AIDS?" She just wanted to get it over with. *Tell me now, goddammit! Right now!*

She coughed into her small fist again and grabbed at her constricting chest to help herself breathe. Things had gotten worse after Friday night's party.

But the nurse refused to confirm the test results over the telephone. It was against policy. They needed to speak to their patients eye to eye about what steps to take next.

"Ms. Cooke, this is our normal procedure in all cases," the nurse responded with emphasis.

Ann took another painful breath and conceded. "Okay. I'll make it in there as soon as I can."

"Thank you," the nurse told her.

Ann hung up the phone and slowly nodded her head. *This is it,* she thought to herself. *I'm dyin' . . . and there's not a damn thing I can do about it.*

She struggled up from her seat in the darkness of the house, with only a dim light on. But before she took a step away from her chair to pace the room and to cry out loud again, she decided to call her husband at the Open Arms Homeless Shelter off Saint Claude Street in the Ninth Ward. Jean-Pierre had worked and lived there for the past six years, and Ann just wanted to hear his voice.

She took another breath and paused before she picked up the phone to call the number.

"Open Arms," a woman's voice answered.

Ann hesitated a second before she forced herself to ask for her husband.

"Can I speak to Jean-Pierre Beaudet, please?" They could still *talk* to one another. He still sent her money. And legally, they were still married, without ever filing for a divorce.

However, the woman at Open Arms was reluctant to go looking for Jean. He was out and about while cleaning up the place as he usually did on Monday mornings. The weekends, as one can imagine, were very busy. There was plenty of cleaning to do on Monday mornings.

"Ah, who's callin'?" she asked politely enough.

However, Ann figured it was none of her business who was calling. She didn't need all of the formalities, she just wanted to speak to her damned husband!

"Is he available?" she asked, instead of giving her name.

The woman hesitated. "Not at the moment," she answered. "I can take a message for him and have him call you back."

Ann shook her head against it. She just wanted to get Jean with her on the phone. She'd rather call back ten times than to wait around all day for him to get back to her. She had already done enough waiting with the AIDS test result.

So Ann responded, "Never mind. I'll just call him back later," and hung up the telephone before the woman could utter another word to her. But Ann needed to talk to Jean. She could hardly breathe without talking to him. Leslie had not called her. Nor did her son, Pierre, bother to visit her that weekend. But Laetitia called. And when she did, Ann didn't share too many words with her. She spoke briefly to the children and gave her second daughter the cold shoulder to stop her from even thinking about Nanna baby-sitting some-damn-body. Laetitia needed to realize that a woman was expected to take care of her own children. Only . . . Laetitia was far from having the maturity of a woman. Nevertheless, her daughter's simplemindedness was the least of Ann's problems at that moment. And after not being able to talk to anyone, she broke down and cried again, with enough sorrow in her heart to fill a bucket with her tears. In her moment of extended loneliness, she was forced to make another desperate phone call while grabbing at her chest.

Anna-Marie dialed 911, and as soon as someone answered the line, she told them, "This an emergency. I'm dyin' of AIDS." She forced out her words through her tears and the pain that she felt in her chest. "I can't breathe right now," she told them. "I can't breathe!"

≋

Jean-Pierre walked into the small and shabby office where a receptionist worked the telephones at the homeless shelter. He was a midnight brown man, with steady dark eyes, a tall, wiry frame, and only sprinkles of gray hair on his head. He wore a sky blue jumpsuit, while pushing along a white mop pole that stuck out of hot, soapy water from the metal bucket with wheels he used to clean the filthy tile floors with.

The receptionist looked up at Jean from her tiny desk chair and was ready to give him the phone message that he had missed. But from who? The woman said that she would call back. Jean had work to do anyway. And he was the kind of dutiful man who didn't like to be bothered whenever he was at work. So the receptionist responded, "Hi, Gene," and left it at that.

Jean nodded to her and hummed, "Mmm, hmm." He thought to himself, *When will they eva' pro-nounce my name right in this place? It's pro-nounced Jahn!*

However, he had learned to keep his thoughts to himself around Americans. They became offended far too easily by the things on his mind that he had often shared with them. They didn't seem to want to hear the truth on many matters. And they did not accept the truth well. In fact, many Americans seemed adversely childish and misguided in their logic. They often expressed far too many opinions based on too little fact. So Jean had forced himself to mind his own business when around them. Only he could not. Because Americans consistently discussed subjects of interest to him with their . . . small-mindedness, and Jean felt a compulsive need and a desire to enlighten them.

They were at it again, bright and early that Monday morning, while inside the recreation room. They sat in front of a small color television set, where a couple of broken-down Ping-Pong tables and an old, worn pool table surrounded them.

"I think we'd be a lot better off if we took them damn sports out of the school systems."

That was Freddie talking. He was fifty-four years old, with a rounded beer belly and frisky gray hair all over his head and face. He was sitting in one of the lounge chairs in front of the television.

"If they did that, we'd end up with a lot of kids who wouldn't even go da school. Some of these kids only go dere to play sports."

That was Ray, a much younger man than Freddie at age thirty-eight. He was leaning against the cement column that stood behind the lounge chair that Freddie sat in.

"You got *that* right! Especially wit dese boys. I wouldn't na went ti' school if it wanent fi' baseball. And I had to wait all year long till springtime to play. But I knew it was comin'."

That was Clarence, sitting in the lounge chair across from Freddie's. Clarence was forty-five.

Freddie countered the two younger men with passionate candor.

He said, "Well, I think them damn sports are fuckin' up a lot of our kids' minds out here! All they wanna do now is play basketball. I see some of these boys out here on the basketball courts up till two o'clock in the damn mornin'! The gotdamn lights ain't even on out there at the playground, and they still out there playin'. Like them young niggas got night vision."

"And then you walk ova' to 'em and ask 'em, 'Look here, boy. Now I know you can play basketball. I can see that. But nigga, did you do your homework after school today? That's what I wanna know. Nigga, didja do ya' homework?'" Freddie finished tartly.

Ray began to laugh at the truth of Freddie's comment, but Clarence had his own counter.

Clarence asked, "Freddie, what's gonna pay you fifteen million dollahs ah year—doin' ya' homework . . . or playin' basketball?"

Ray looked down at Freddie and nodded his head in agreement with Clarence's point.

"Now, he gotchu dere, Freddie," Ray said. "He gotchu dere."

Clarence exclaimed, "You gotdamn right I got 'im! 'Cause if doin' homework eva' could get a nigga fifteen million dollahs ah year like these basketball players get, den I woulda been one homework-doin' mother-fucka! I'll tell ya that! I'll tell ya that, right now!

"Shit, da white man ain't gon' neva' pay some nigga fifteen million dol-lahs for doin' some damn homework!" Clarence concluded.

Ray burst out laughing again. "Dat's f' true, Freddie. Dat's f' true!" Ray responded. "You can't argue wit 'im 'nere. You can't argue wit 'em!"

Jean-Pierre smiled slightly while he worked his broom and dustpan around the edges of the room's littered floor and listened in on the conver-sation. Jean never said that Americans were not humorous. They just had to learn when to separate the fun and games from the serious business of life. Yet in America, black men had found a way to elevate their self-degrading humor into riches. Black comedian movie stars had been making millions of dollars for decades!

However, Freddie, the elder of the conversation, was not done yet. He looked calm and determined in the lounge chair when he responded, "See, now that's what's wrong wit niggas now. You think the white man is givin' you somethin' when he's really taking it away.

"So he gives a few niggas fifteen million dollars a year, so that those nig-gas can mislead the other niggas into believin' that they actually gon' get some of it."

Clarence cut him short and said, "They do get some of it. You think these basketball players don't share da wealth? Shit, when ney get rich, everybody get a new house and a car!"

Ray didn't agree with that one. He said, "I don't know about that right there, man. There's too many cases of dese basketball players not paying for their own kids to believe that. And some a dese ballers got, like, three and four kids from different women dat dey don't be payin' for."

Clarence looked at Ray and shouted, "That's bullshit! They pay for them damn kids. Some of 'em payin' up ta five thousand dollahs a month!"

Freddie said calmly from his chair, "See now, that's just more miseducation. So the white man is systematically lettin' everybody know that you can give a nigga money and take him out the ghetto, but if his mind ain't right, he still gon' act like a nigga. Can't even keep his women right."

Ray started nodding his head again. He said, "Yeah, that's f' true, man. That's what it is. That's it, right there."

Jean-Pierre was just itching to get inside of the conversation and add some of his thoughts on it. He agreed with Freddie, and they were in the same age range. So Jean began to move slower and slower, distracted in his work, and started missing some of the dirt on the floor. The other homeless men in the room had heard it all before and were tired of hearing it. All of the talk never changed anything. So they continued about their own business of watching television, playing pool, Ping-Pong, and daydreaming about beautiful white boats on the long journey to heaven in the afterworld. It had to be many times better than this place they lived on called earth, that's for sure!

Clarence had shut his mouth for a minute with no reasonable comeback, so Freddie took the opportunity of the open floor. "See now, after the American Civil War, and during the Reconstruction era, the black man had a lot more skills in this country outside of playin' football and basketball."

Clarence cut him off again and complained, "Here he goes wit damn American history shit again. Nobody wanna hear that shit in here, Freddie. Nobody wanna hear that."

Freddie finally lost his cool and said, "Well, we need to hear it," and rocked forward in his chair to take a more assertive position.

Jean stopped cleaning altogether to listen. *I would like to hear this,* he thought to himself.

Freddie said: "See now, you have to remember that American slavery was about work. And if you had slaves who didn't have any skills to help you make more money, then you traded and sold his ass for something else, just like they do now wit dese damn sports teams. So ain't nothin' changed. Ain't nothin' changed!"

He said, "But during the Reconstruction era, when freed black men were allowed to go into business for themselves, you had niggas who were masons, carpenters, shipbuilders, cooks, doctors, everything! And at that time, this country wasn't all that white. We were probably more like sixty-forty in this country, and eighty-twenty in the South!"

"So the white man looked around and said, 'We betta get some more white boys over here to help us run this motherfucka, or these free niggas could take over the whole gotdamn country!'

"And that's why the white man put up the Statue of Liberty in New York, and told the rest of them white boys in Europe, 'Give us your tired, your hungry, your poor,' and all that other bullshit, when it was all about keepin' American niggas in check, see."

At that point, Jean couldn't help himself any longer. He nodded his head in agreement with Freddie and spoke up in support of his historically based hypothesis.

Jean said, "A-meri-ca has not opened her pearly white gates so readily to my Haitian brothers and sistahs, nor to the non-white Hispanic communities of this country."

Clarence looked over at Jean and immediately became defensive. He never liked Jean too much.

He said, "Yeah, but you motherfuckas still sneak over here, and den start lookin' down on us like everybody else do. Haitians, Africans, Jamaicans, all of 'em. As if we ain't been catchin' hell over here already from all these white boys!"

Jean raised up his palms in peace. He said, "I unda-stan' our disputes. How-eva', let's us not allow our diff'rences in cul-ture to misdirect the his-story that this country has had with all peoples of color. In par-ticular, its his-story with dark brown peoples."

Freddie nodded his head, and was open to Jean's views on the subject. Even Ray was listening.

Ray responded, "Go 'head, Gene, whatchu got ti say about this?"

Jean said, "I must ad-mit that when I first came to this country and to the city of New Or-leans in Louis-ee-ana, I was full of de-termination and dreams about owning my own restaurant in the French Quarter downtown. In par-ticular because I was fluent in French, the official language of my native land in Haiti."

Clarence started laughing out loud, rudely, before Jean could finish his point.

Clarence said, "You thought you were gonna have a Haitian restaurant in the French Quarter, hunh? Well, who you thought was gonna eat there? Because it ain't that many Haitians here. And if you had to charge the same prices to niggas that you would have to charge dem white folks to be able to pay rent in the French Quarter, niggas'll look at you like you crazy.

"'Cause see, let me tell you somethin', Gene, niggas don't pay the same prices for black shit that they'll pay for white shit," Clarence explained. "And them white folks ain't gon' support ya' ass down there in the French Quarter in the first place! So evidently, you had a whole lot to learn comin' over here to America, thinkin' you just gon' do whatever you wanna do," he snapped at Jean. "'Cause see, from where I'm sittin', you about three shades blacker than me, and the white man don't care what language you speak, as long as he can see ya' black ass comin'!"

Ray looked away from Jean and had to hold in his laugh. But the other men in the room didn't stop from laughing. All eyes were on Jean, and he had been quickly reminded of why he chose to stay out of the conversations with them.

However, Freddie didn't laugh. Freddie commented, "He's just showin' his ignorance, Gene. That's all. He don't know no damn betta."

"I don't know betta?" Clarence asked. "Well, tell me what I said that was wrong. Hunh, Freddie? Tell me what I said that was wrong."

Freddie didn't have a fast enough answer. So Clarence said, "You know damn well, dem white folks don't care nothin' about no French-speakin' nigga from Haiti in the French Quarter. Unless Gene got some voodoo dolls he wanna sell down nere. Oh, they'll buy that crazy shit! They got stores full of that shit down in na French Quarter!

"Now if you wanna explain somethin' to me, Gene, then you tell me what that voodoo shit is about in Haiti," Clarence barked at him.

Freddie shook his head. "Don't even pay him no mind, Gene. He ain't got no damn sense."

But Clarence insisted. "Nah, Freddie, if he know so gotdamn much, then let him explain what that voodoo shit is about. Fuckin' dancin' around wit decapitated chicken heads, and stickin' dolls wit' needles and shit."

Ray continued to hide his laughter. He wasn't too sure about Jean. He feared him. Jean didn't seem to be the kind of man that you could fuck with like that and get away with it. But Clarence didn't give a damn! And when Jean actually opened his mouth to answer his question, even Freddie was shocked by it.

Jean said, "The Haitian religion of Vaudou is misunda-stood in America, and it has been turned into a pa-gan religion like all other religions of peoples of color."

Clarence cut him off again. He said, "Well, what the hell is all this nonsense about chicken blood and shit?"

Ray looked at Clarence and couldn't believe that he was being so bold about it. But Freddie waited for the answer, along with a few of the other homeless who listened in on the conversation.

Jean calmed himself and answered, "In the Bible, A-braham was told to give a sac-crifice to his God. And at first, he was told to offer up the life of his son, Isaac. And A-braham, in his loyalty to his God, was willing to sac-crifice the blood of his own son."

Clarence cut him off a third time and said, "What da hell does all of that have to do with the chicken blood I asked you about?"

Freddie cut Clarence off and said, "Let 'em get to it. He's gettin' to it."

Clarence was getting in the way with his impatience.

Jean continued: "But before A-braham could murder his son, his God was honored by his loyalty, and he told him to look behind a rock, and there he would find a calf to offer him instead."

Jean stopped and noted, "Now I say this because in the Haitian religion of Vaudou, as well as in most religions of the world, in-clud-ing the three major Western religions of Christi-anity, Is-lam, and Ju-daism, humans have always given offerings to their God and to their ancestors."

Freddie nodded his head and put two and two together.

"So, the slaughterin' of the chickens is just the offering to the ancestors?"

"That is cor-rect," Jean answered him. "You offer what you can af-ford and what would be respectable to the ancestors that you are there to honor."

Clarence said, "Well, why you gotta dance and shit when you do it?"

Obviously, Clarence had watched many American films on the subject.

Jean loosened up and smiled before he answered. "As a child, I did not want to dahnse. I had no int'rest in dahn-sing at tall. When I came to A-meri-ca, and saw the black mahn and his sons dahn-sing for nickels and dimes on the street corners, I forbid my children and my wife to dahnse."

He said, "But as I have grown olda and matured, I now rea-lize that dan-sing is as much a part of being a black mahn," he said, turning his dark hands outward to them, "as having brown skin. And in every cul-ture where there is brown people, they will danse in their spirituals and in their ceremonies as a part of the living, and of the dead."

Ray caught on with a nod and said, "That's f' true, man. We known for dancin'. And the white man can't dance a lick? Them muthafuckas count numbers ti dance."

Clarence, though, was still unimpressed. Foreign blacks had always tried to make things seem so . . . simple. And it insulted his intelligence to even hear that simple explanation shit!

He said, "And what about these gotdamn voodoo dolls all over the place? You gon' try da explain that shit away too, right?"

Jean continued to smile. Clarence had lost the pepper in his tone, and Jean knew that he had soothed the rough waters of his American brother. He explained, "In the Hin-du religions of the East, they speak of the human essence of kar-ma."

Ray nodded and jumped right on board with him again. "Yeah, what comes around goes around. So don't fuck me if you don't wanna get fucked right back," he joked.

Jean-Pierre laughed with them and went on with his explanation.

He said, "The two English words to explain this be-lief in my home-land of Haiti is 're-ci-procity' and 're-demption.' The likeness of every human be-ing can be repre-sented in a doll, just like with a photo-graph or with an il-lu-stration. And each doll can be viewed as a represen-tation of a person's spirit, good or bad. Howeva', that does not mean that you can stick a needle in that doll and cause an ac-tual person harm, living or dead.

"So you see now, that A-meri-cans have made the Haitian religion of Vaudou into something viewed as witchcraft, simply because we were a free nation of black people who had main-tained much of our Af-frican ancestry."

In his words and clear explanation, Jean had made all of the American talk of voodoo as witchcraft seem ludicrous. It was all a misappropriation that had been used for entertainment and for profit. It was another Dracula. Frankenstein. An invisible man. A mummy. The werewolf. And a wicked witch, flying through the night on her broomstick. And the homeless black men of the Open Arms facility were satisfied with Jean's sound logic. They were even proud. Jean had explained his Haitian roots, while stripping it of the spookiness that African-based religions had acquired not only in Amer-ica but throughout the Western world. Jean allowed the black American men to breathe a little deeper now, knowing that their shared African her-itage was not an abomination to humanity. And they had less of a reason to feel . . . embarrassed by their Haitian brother or by their own African roots.

However, Clarence remained unsatisfied. No Haitian man was going to show him up and shut his mouth on any subject. So Clarence opened his mouth again, and smiled wide, with confidence.

He said, "Well, tell me something else, Gene. Since you so gotdamned smart, how come you here with us in a homeless shelter? And Haiti may be free, but how come y'all so motherfuckin' poor? And how come so many motherfuckers got AIDS down nere in Haiti? Hunh? Explain that shit! Nigga!"

The recreation room turned into an icebox of emotions. Everything just . . . stopped. Only a white Ping-Pong ball moved, as it bounced off of the table and hit the floor, unreturned by a paddle. They were all frozen and waiting for Jean's response, as if it would be fatal.

Jean answered, "I'm making myself useful here." And he went back to sweeping up the floor, while he inhaled and exhaled in meditation to stop himself from murdering Clarence.

≈

When Jean left the room, Ray started to breathe again.

He looked at Clarence and said, "Man, are you crazy?! Gene cooks the food in here. You gon' fuck around and die of food poisonin', Clarence. You mark my words."

Clarence shouted defiantly, "Well, bring it on, then!" He added, "And if he wants us to call his ass *John,* then he needs to spell dat shit the right damn way!"

Freddie sat still in his chair and shook his head. Clarence was fucking with fire! Anytime you take shots at the surviving threads of a man's dignity, you do so at your own risk.

However, Jean kept right on going with his business of cleaning up the shelter that Monday morning. He cleaned and disinfected the bathrooms, swept and mopped the hallways, and collected all of the trash to dump out back in the horrible-smelling trash bins. And then he just stopped, surrounded by the stench of compiled waste, and thought back to the misfortunes of his life.

Jean had suffered dearly, and all in unison, starting with the loss of his position as a skilled cook in the French Quarter. Had he never lost his job and been blackballed by the fraternity of empowered white chefs of New Orleans, who did not appreciate his pride or his show of superiority in the preparation of foods, Jean and his family would have never been forced to move into the impoverished sections of the Seventh Ward. None of the property owners in the French Quarter would agree to sell Jean a space in which to build the dream of his own restaurant. Nor would the American banks offer him the loans that he would need to establish one. So Jean found himself on his own, a dark brown–skinned immigrant with a family to provide for. And in the fading away of his dreams and aspirations as an American, he was forced to empathize with the feelings of insignificance that his black American brothers had been dealing with, the everyday use, abuse, and abandonment of their humanity.

The stress involved in Jean's internalized failures accelerated a previously undiagnosed condition of hypertension, or high blood pressure. And the high blood had shrunken his kidneys, resulting in kidney failure, to the point where Jean needed dialysis, an expensive procedure to flush out the impurities that had built up within his body. That's when the doctors advised him to try and reduce the suppressed rage and hostility that he held. He was told that his feelings of anger and resentment to whomever or whatever would only add to his failing health. To survive it, he would need to take daily medications and involve himself in behavior modification, to change his usual ways of doing and responding to things.

Not particularly a religious man, Jean had prayed on it. What had he done to deserve such misfortune? When he was given no clear answer, Jean-Pierre chose a new direction, to empower his children and family with love, commitment, and education. And in his new zeal for life, Jean became driven to make sure that his children would remain special, even while his first son, Pierre, and his second daughter, Laetitia, tried their hardest to reject his eager teachings.

And then . . . right in the middle of Jean's progressive reevaluation of life, his beautiful first daughter, Leslie, the one who showed the most potential, with the most understanding and the strongest temperament to succeed, had been violated by undesirables of Seventh Ward poverty. Who did the *Bou-dets* think they were, anyway? Everyone could be touched in the ghetto. Everyone!

Jean nearly cried to himself for the thousandth time as he remembered his daughter's torturous words to him in French, *"Je suis triste, papa."* I am feeling sad, Father.

When he asked his daughter why, she calmly explained that some neighborhood boys had forced her into an abandoned home and made her perform vile acts with her mouth on their penises. She added that the same boys had often bullied her older brother, Pierre.

Jean looked at his daughter incredulously. Leslie was eleven years old, and he could not believe the amount of calm in which she had explained things to him. Her eyes and reactions remained steady and logical, which in her situation was illogical. However, Jean was not calm!

"Zut!" he cursed in French. *"J'ai mal partout! Qu'ai-je fait pour mériter tel malheur?"* I ache all over. Who or what have I done wrong to?

This time Jean-Pierre was consumed by his misfortunes! But when he looked into his daughter's dark eyes and read them, he felt soothed, as if her calm held the answers to his pain.

Leslie then spoke to her father in English. "I'm okay, Daddy. But Pierre," she mentioned with a pause, "he doesn't know what to do about these boys. They're bigger than him."

Jean nodded his head and took a deep breath. Then he told himself with conviction, *Someone is going to die for this. There will be redemption.* And there was.

Jean remembered the pleading fifteen-year-old boy who he had captured within the Seventh Ward. The whites of the boy's wide eyes in the darkness of the abandoned home where Jean had dragged him popped vividly into his mind. And the boy's begging voice pierced his ears anew: "Please, mister. I'm sorry. I didn't mean to do it. I didn't mean it."

Jean waited long enough to hear the boy mumble his last words. But he felt no sympathy for the boy. He was there to do what he had to do.

"Stand up against the wall," he commanded the boy, so that he could measure his young neck for the swing of his sharpened machete knife.

The boy shivered in fear and stood tall, up against the wall in the silence of the dark. His tears were barely visible as they poured down his face, followed by the hot piss that exploded in his pants and raced down his left leg to the floor. The piss of fear had done the same with Pussy Pete, the pretty Haitian boy, who the impoverished kids of the Seventh Ward loved to torture. And with one swift chop to the neck, Jean ended the boy's life. Then he proceeded to hack at the rest of him—arms, legs, and torso—cutting the boy's limbs into small enough pieces to stuff inside several heavy-duty trash bags.

With the precision of his blade and the decisiveness of Jean's chops, the bloodletting was minimal, leaving little evidence of the massacre that had taken place there in the dark of the abandoned home. Then Jean discreetly discarded the bags of human body parts into an oversized trash dump to be taken away . . . and forgotten.

And he had gotten away with it, the calculated murder of an American black boy. Or at least he had gotten away with it in the eyes of the American law, because in the eyes of the universal spirit, Jean was forced to pay for it. How could he ever retain a sane mind and good health with murder on his conscience? And he wondered if he would have to do it again.

Yet . . . after he had redeemed his daughter, Jean and Leslie began to have a certain understanding of things. And in their understanding, they became closer.

Jean told her, "You have nothing to fear, my child. And with all of my love, and my soul, I will pray to the an-cestors that you will sur-vive any-thing in this world, and in the world after this one."

Leslie nodded back to her father and told him, "I will," with the assur-ance of a goddess.

And they walked together, alone, where the father shared his knowl-edge with the daughter on all that he knew. Or all that he could reveal to her in her youth. And they traveled together in distance, time, space, and in mind, where only they could understand each other.

So Leslie understood when her father told her that he could no longer stay with them as a family. Because it would kill him. He could not success-fully modify his behavior while feeling that he had failed his wife and fam-ily. It was the doctor's orders to make himself feel . . . useful again. And although the doctor did not intend for Jean's behavior modification to include subtracting himself from his wife and family, Jean knew that he would meet an early grave if he was to look daily into the hopeless eyes of Anna-Marie, Pierre, and Laetitia. However, there was no greater joy in Jean's heart than the private time that he shared with Leslie, and the elation that he felt when he looked into her eyes of unconquerable will.

Jean nodded his head at the back of the homeless shelter in the now time, and he was still surrounded by the stench of the trash. But yet he smiled to himself. Thoughts of Leslie's strength had always given him strength. And to hell with Clarence! He would meet his maker on his own account. Jean wanted to make certain that he would remain a free and untroubled man to see the day when his first daughter would graduate from college, like she had done with honors from high school. And then one day . . . Leslie would establish her own international restaurant, and allow her wise and experienced father to become the head chef there for as many nights of life that he would have left in him.

Jean walked back inside Open Arms Homeless Shelter to continue with his work, while humming the American soul song performed by the Temp-tations that he had learned to love and to share with his daughter: *"I-I-I gues-s-s you-u-u say / What can make meee feel this way? / My gir-r-r-rl / I'm talkin' bout, my-y-y little girl . . ."*

The Debts
of Men

Leslie inspected the final presentation of two hot, ready-to-be-served plates of bayou curried shrimp and mango chutney while in the kitchen area of Hot Jake's restaurant. The aroma of the strong curry spices, steamed jasmine rice, toasted coconut, and hints of mixed-in pineapple attacked the senses. It was a wonder the employees didn't all pig out in the kitchen, seduced by the arousing scents of every new order of the prepared meals. Some of the specialties at Hot Jake's were even old recipes from Leslie's father, Jean. Although he would never reveal them all. It was a master chef's creed to carry his favorite recipes nearly to the grave with him.

Leslie had been working at Hot Jake's as a cook ever since she had turned sixteen, for four and sometimes six days a week. The restaurant was conveniently located on Gentilly Boulevard, not far from Dillard University, where Leslie could walk to work from school.

She gave her nod of satisfaction on the food preparation, and when she looked up she spotted Jake, the burly and good-natured owner, strutting through the swinging kitchen doors with the cordless telephone to his ear. He was full of laughter in his conversation.

"Nah, I'm not working her too hard. But she already runs the kitchen. The only thing more she got in here to do is my job," he was saying.

Leslie smiled, knowing that Jake thought highly of her ambitions. She also knew that he was speaking to her father. They went back some years on the New Orleans food scene. Jake was one of the few friends her father had held over the years. Their connection had gotten Leslie a job there. However, Jean had always wanted his own place, and for Leslie to eventually have hers.

Jake laughed hard and said, "I'm sure she will. She'll make the top five restaurant list in whatever city she's in. But all right, she is right here," Jake said, handing the phone to Leslie.

She answered, *"Bonjour, papa."*

"Bonjour, ma chérie," Jean-Pierre responded. *"Comment ça va à l'école?"* How is your schooling?

"Les nouveaux cours vont bientôt commencer. Je suis sûre de réussir." New classes are beginning. However, I am sure to do well.

Jean chuckled with pride and stated, *"C'est bon d'entendre."* Yes, that is good to hear.

Jake listened to Leslie speaking French to her father before he went on about his business. He had always been impressed with Leslie. She had needed little guidance or pep talks to maintain her passion for the job. She was a dream employee! Jake only wished that he could have more employees like Leslie there to work for him, young and old.

When her father asked if Leslie had spoken to her mother lately, she paused. She had been thinking about her mother after visiting Laetitia and her nieces, but she hadn't called to speak to her.

She answered, "No, I haven't."

Her father said, *"Tu lui diras que j'ai demandé de ses nouvelles."* You tell her that I asked for her.

Leslie paused again. She no longer wanted to play the role of the interloper between her parents. Nevertheless, she did need to speak to her mother. So she agreed to her father's demand.

"Oui, je lui dirai." Yes, I will tell her.

Jean went on to honor his daughter about how proud he was of her, and how much joy it brought his heart to know that she was doing so well with everything despite the hardships that their family had been through. Then he told her that he loved her dearly, as always.

"Je t'aime, papa," Leslie told him back.

Jean hung up the telephone slowly and began to think of his estranged wife. He still loved his wife as dearly as he loved his daughters and his only son, Pierre. Things had just gotten . . . complicated between them all. Blood was thicker than water, but the flow of water down a stream was a hell of a lot simpler to explain than the pulse of family blood through delicate veins.

Anna-Marie Cooke had fully believed in Jean, like a good wife should.

And he had been consistent with her, like a good husband should. And when he looked into her face and told her that she was the most "beau-ti-ful" woman that he had "eva' eyed" in his life when they first met down in the French Quarter, Jean meant every syllable of his accented English. When he told her that he would cook her the best meal that she had "eva' tasted," he did. Then he told her that he would marry her and make her the proud madame of a beautiful white house, with children, in New Orleans. Ann believed in him, with each of his declarations revealing the truth of his hard work and honor for her. And she built enough confidence in him to spurn her family members who questioned her love for an older, immigrant Hai-tian man with big American dreams.

And when the dreams fell apart with his wealth, his health, and his family esteem, Jean could remember his faithful wife—faithful to everything that he was bold, brave, and manly enough to stand for in America—as she pleaded with him in her newly learned French:

"Je t'en prie, chéri! Ne laisse pas tomber tes rêves! Nous y arriverons ensemble!"
Don't you give up your dream! We will make it together!

But Jean only smiled at his wife's desperate attempt to push him forward. He even kissed her on her lips and was impressed with her French. Although her pronunciation was rough, Ann had learned the language much quicker than he expected her to. Yet . . . he had no positive response to her plea that evening. All he knew was that the white immigrant owners and chefs of the fine restaurants in the French Quarter were all conspiring to shut him out.

Jean's blood began to boil anew as he thought back to the dismal day of fate in which he was pushed out of his job at Le Château. The new manager said that it was a decision handed down from the top. There was nothing that he could do about it. He was simply following orders. The owner had new menus that they were to begin serving. And they wanted to replace many of the old cooks, not just Jean. But Jean took it personally.

He argued, "Why not give us the chance to learn these new menus?"

It was a fair argument, but the response was less than fair. The new management dug up Jean-Pierre Beaudet's résumé of years ago, and noticed that he had not been accredited by any of the major cooking schools that they desired in their new employees.

When the slight of accreditation was brought to Jean's attention, he responded with the fervor that made a lot of the white men of the French Quarter kitchens averse to him.

"I have been a pro-fes-sional cook of ex-quisite recipes and food preparation for more than eight-teen years! I could teach all of these ah-mateur cooks that you have hired here right now!"

Jean failed to realize that brown-faced men in America claiming superiority over white men in anything other than sports, rhythm, and the mythology of sex and the long cock was definitely unacceptable. And although Jean was factual in his assessment of his cooking skills, the word traveled fast that he was a showboat who needed to establish his own restaurant somewhere else, rather than be hired on a staff where he may assault and insult the agreements of cooking hierarchies.

However, Jean did not journey to America to include himself within a subservient culture of black Americans. He had come to America to become an American, a full one, and to receive the same liberties that white immigrants were afforded. Italian, German, French, and white Spaniard immigrants were allowed their dreams within the French Quarter, so why not he? They were not asked to find their own restaurants elsewhere. So Jean refused to accept the affront.

Nevertheless, he had mouths to feed and a mortgage to pay. And it was not Ann's job to do those things. Jean was to be the provider. He would not allow himself to accept anything less than his duty, nor would he accept a job that was less than his qualified skills. However . . . now that he was wiser and years removed from the embarrassing onslaught of his ego, Jean thought that if he had had an opportunity to do it all again, then maybe . . . he would have responded differently.

So he felt shameful, ashamed that he had not been able to live up to the promise that he had given his wife. And no one knew it . . . but Jean cried for Anna. He cried a lot for her, while he prayed on a way to somehow, someway return the support that she had so firmly given to him. But how could any man repay a woman for her heart, a heart that beat with unconditional love, and for life's sake alone? How could a man repay a woman for the sharing of her womb to bear children, and then to feed, nurture, and love them until the grave and after? How could he repay her for the warmth that she gives to a home? And how could a man ever repay a woman for the trust that she endows in him from the moment that her heart skips a beat and becomes heated inside her chest at his sight, at his breath, and at his touch?

The debt was bottomless. Jean had felt its weight, attempting to drown him. Millions of men had died all around the world ten, twenty, and thirty years before their wives, trying their damnedest to repay them for their selflessness, their humility, and their deeds. And Jean found himself penniless at his wife's feet, choosing to flee from the heavy bond of her love to conserve his own life, while he and his family all suffered from the consequences of his abandonment . . . like a million other fatherless families have suffered.

≋

Back at Hot Jake's restaurant, Leslie phoned her mother while she still had the cordless telephone in hand, but there was no answer. She hung up without leaving a message, and reminded herself to call again later.

When Leslie walked out from the kitchen area to return the telephone to Jake, he stopped her and asked how her father was doing.

"He's doing fine. We're all just trying to make sense out of life, that's all," she told him. Then she smiled, performing the perfect role. She wanted to head off Jake's questions about her family before he got started with them. It was easy for outsiders to try and simplify someone else's life, and Leslie didn't want to hear it.

Jake read her busy demeanor and allowed her to get back to work.

"All right, well, if there's anything I can do," he said, leaving his support open for her.

Leslie smiled a second time and said, "You can give me another raise if you want."

Jake looked at her and began to chuckle to himself. Leslie was a hard cake to ice. She had too many layers to deal with. She was a chip off of her father's block, only she was more . . . subtle with it, which made her intellect more powerful and elusive.

Jake read her crafty message and decided to leave her and her family alone.

"Go on back to work, Leslie," he responded to her with a grin.

Leslie returned to cooking and supervising the new orders inside the kitchen, while her fellow employees watched her with awe and with envy. Some of the jealous newcomers even fancied Leslie as a lucky-behind college girl with the right connections. How little they valued all of her hard work. And how little they knew or cared of her hardships. But Leslie never paid their stares or conceptions any mind. She had work to do and places to go in her future. And as they pondered the talents and opportunities that she had been given at such a young age, Leslie thought of much higher goals, goals that they could not even conceive for themselves. International ownership, world travel, and all of the heights of real human wealth were thoughts that allowed Leslie the strength she needed to levitate above the pettiness of human insecurities.

While she continued to work and meditate on her future, Jake interrupted Leslie's peace with a second phone call. "You got the family hot line in here tonight," he joked.

Leslie took the phone from his beefy hands again, and forced herself not to become irritated by the disruptions.

"Bonjour, ma jolie sœur." Hello, my pretty sister. It was her brother, Pierre.

Leslie smiled immediately. It was an automatic response of love for kin, especially kin who didn't bother you too much. Pierre had always respected Leslie's need for space.

She gave her brother some N'awlins English in her response. "Whassup, hunh?"

Pierre laughed and said, "Nuntin', man. Nuntin'. Whassup wit you?"

"Nuntin'. But um, I jus' saw Tee an' nem Thursdee," Leslie responded in a Southern drawl. "I stayed ova' dere f' da night, an' ney doin' aw'ight. You know."

"Dey doin' aw'ight, hunh?" Pierre answered.

Leslie said, "Yeah, man. Dey aw'ight ova' dere. I gay' Tee sum my cheese, and she ate it up like a rat, man. Ate it all up!"

The cooks and employees inside of the kitchen all looked at Leslie as if she had just lost her mind! Or at least those who didn't really know her. The people who knew her better found it comical. Leslie was much more versatile than one could imagine.

Pierre laughed over the telephone and asked her, "I bet they lookin' at you over there like you crazy, ain't dey? Probably thought you were some old, snotty college girl."

Leslie laughed out loud with her brother and responded to him in French, *"Tu as raison!"* You're right! *"Je l'aime bien comme ça."* I like it that way. *"Ils ne me connaissent pas de toute façon."* They don't know me anyway. *"Je suis profonde."* I'm deep.

Pierre responded, *"Oui, tu es profonde."* Yes, you are deep. "But um, I just called to tell you that Mom wants to see you. And she been actin' funny lately."

"Comment?" How? Leslie asked him.

"I don't know, she jus' . . . she jus' been actin' mean lately."

Leslie smiled. She thought to herself, *Pierre is such a fuckin' baby! God! Mom can't express her feelings when she wants to? Pierre needs to just grow up!* She went to straight English and said, "I'm planning on calling her tonight when I get off from work."

"Cool. I gotta get over there to see her myself," Pierre commented. Then he hesitated before he asked his sister, "Are you doin' all right?"

Leslie nodded with the phone to her ear while she looked over the incoming orders.

She answered, "Yeah, I'm fine." She was upbeat about it.

"Okay, so . . . nobody bothering you at school or anything?"

When Pierre asked her that, Leslie froze for a second.

She answered, "No. Why you ask?" Pierre had never asked her anything like that before. He kept his conversations brief with Leslie, ever since he had . . . allowed her to be violated inside an abandoned project house when they were younger.

Leslie had blocked out the memory of it, so that she could move on with her life. But it was always there in the back of her mind. And now she remembered it. The scene flashed into her mind as she became speechless. She still had never forgiven Pierre for his cowardice.

Why is he doing this all of a sudden? Why? she asked herself.

Pierre took a breath over the phone and answered his sister's unspoken question right on cue.

"I'm just try'na to look out for you, Leslie. That's all."

Leslie's joy of talking to her older brother turned into a sharp pain as quickly as a finger snap. *Look out for me? Who the fuck are you kidding?* she cursed him.

She decided right then to end their phone conversation before things got ugly. She didn't mind showing her fellow cooks and employees her versatile language, but she didn't want them to witness her losing her cool. She didn't want to give them the satisfaction of knowing any of her personal struggles. Leslie was private that way. She had always been private.

So she addressed her brother hastily, "Yeah, I'm fine. But I got work to do. I'll call her when I get home tonight," she said, eager to hang up the phone with him.

Pierre said, "Leslie. Wait a minute."

"Quoi?" What? his sister snapped in French.

Pierre responded slow and meaningfully, *"Je t'aime."*

But instead of giving the love back to him, Leslie nodded and said, "Okay," before she pressed the off button to hang up the phone on him. However . . . the damage had already been done. Pierre had forced her to remember.

"You okay, Leslie?" one of the cooks asked her there in the kitchen.

Leslie had briefly lost track of her consciousness. She was in a standing daze, daydreaming. But she shook it off quickly enough.

"Oh, no, I'm all right, I just got some . . . things on my mind," she responded. "Could you do me a favor and take this phone back to Jake? I have to use the rest room."

"Oh, no problem, girl. I got it. Go on."

Leslie headed for the small rest room area at the back of the kitchen where all of the cooking staff went. She hustled in and locked the door behind her. She walked into the stall, closed the door, and sat there on the toilet seat just to think things through. And she couldn't fight it. The reality of the past had always haunted her:

"Hey, Lez-lee! Hurry up! Dey got ya' brother!" a boy from the Seventh Ward shouted to her.

"Who?" Leslie asked the boy, while she searched for her brother in the neighborhood.

"Bernard and Kelsey."

Leslie's eleven-year-old face lit up in horror as she raced after the boy and into an abandoned house, all gusto and ready to throw down for her family. She was afraid of no one. Why couldn't those boys just leave Pete alone anyway? He had never bothered any of them.

"There she go, man," Kelsey told Bernard. They were standing well inside the abandoned house, where no one could see them. Leslie immediately searched her surroundings for grown-ups, but she couldn't spot any fast enough to help her.

"Don't even think about screamin' t' nobody, girl," Bernard warned her. "I'll kill 'im right now if you scream!" That's when Leslie spotted the small black gun in his hand. He was pointing it at the back of her brother's head and behind his ear.

Poor Pete looked as if he had cried a river down his face already.

Kelsey said, "Tell her to come here, man, before we shoot you."

Kelsey was fourteen and Bernard was fifteen. Pete was only thirteen that summer, and he was still wiry and lightweight compared to the rugged stock of the other boys. Nevertheless, Leslie was up for their challenge. She was fearless, and had been born with it.

They probably don't even have bullets in the gun, she reasoned. She told her brother cleverly in French, *"Il n'y a pas de balles dedans."* They don't have fire.

Pierre exclaimed, *"Si, il y en a!"* Yes, they do have fire!

Kelsey looked confused and said, "Hunh? Y'all betta talk English in here! Tell her to come here in English, man. In English!" They were punking Pierre because they knew that they could.

So Leslie told them defiantly, "No! Let him go!"

Kelsey said, "Girl, you think we won't hurt 'em," and punched her brother in the stomach, sending Pierre to his knees. Kelsey's goal in life was to be one of the baddest little niggas in the 'hood, which he surely couldn't become by letting some little girl bluff him. She was about to get her brother hurt!

"You betta tell 'er to come here," Bernard reiterated to Pierre as they yanked the frail, pretty boy back to his feet to stand between them.

Leslie was still unmoved by it. She looked to the younger boy, who had led her there. He was still standing in the doorway. She told him, "Go tell somebody."

"James, you betta not tell nobody, boy!" Kelsey hollered at him.

James shook his head eagerly and said, "I'm not."

"Den watch the door, den!"

James was a puppet on a string. "Aw'ight," he told Kelsey. The boy just wanted to belong to somebody. His momma didn't give a damn about him, and rumor had it that James could have had any of six different men as his father, because his mother was a known whore.

So Leslie had no one to turn to. However, Bernard looked into her eyes and began having second thoughts about it.

Man, this damn girl ain't even scared, he told himself. He didn't want to kill anyone. He and Kelsey just had some freaky thoughts on their minds after sneaking a long peek at some white people porno movies they found around the house. Kids get into anything their parents, aunts, uncles, or older cousins may have. Even when they would try to hide it. So the boys got to thinking, with a stolen gun they figured no one would miss until they had played with it out in the street for a while, and up walked happy Pierre Beaudet, Pussy Pete, with a chocolate ice cream cone in his hand. The boy had a pretty, long-haired sister, too. Her name was Leslie. And many of the teenaged boys in the Seventh Ward only wished that Leslie was a few years older.

Nevertheless, Bernard and Kelsey had ideas right now, and they didn't want to wait. They didn't feel that ghetto girls had any protection anyway, especially with a punk-ass brother like Pussy Pete around. They didn't even stop to think about her father. Many fathers were not around to protect their daughters. They were either MIA (missing in action), drunk and stinking, or too busy chasing around young girls themselves to lie down with to forget their own shortcomings.

However, these boy didn't realize how strong Leslie's dignity was. Bernard wanted to cop out. He just couldn't say it. So he forced himself to be bold about things. He just had to stand up and do it, like . . . a man. Men did what they wanted to do. Then some of them would die and go to jail for it. That was just the harsh reality of the 'hood. Nobody could change it. It was the rules of life there. Or the only rules that they knew. You live, you eat, you shit, and you die.

Bernard decided to be as bold and as defiant as little Leslie was being. He gripped the trigger of the gun in his hand and said, "I'm just gon have to kill 'im, then, if she ain't gon' come."

That's when Pierre started bawling in terror, "Leslie, pleeeease! Pleeease!" He let go of his urine in his shorts, shooting down his left leg.

Leslie remembered herself moving forward as if she had no legs. *I have to save my brother,* she could remember thinking. She felt that she had somehow floated across the dirty old floor to meet them there inside of the abandoned project house. Her thoughts were crystal clear in her mind.

They will never leave Pierre alone unless I help him.

Bernard was even bold enough to pull out his thing in her face, and tell her to suck it, while Kelsey traded places with him and held the black gun to her brother's head.

And Leslie . . . did what he had asked her. All the while, she thought to herself, *It'll be over soon. It'll be over. And then they'll all get theirs! Every last one of them!*

Kelsey began to laugh, as sick as he wanted to be, and couldn't wait to get his turn. Even James got excited and left guard at the door to check in on what they were doing in there.

"Getcha' ass back at the door!" Kelsey yelled at him.

Leslie could feel the boys around her, watching her and enjoying their sickness as she closed her eyes. She also knew that her older brother was there, standing weak and helpless. And she vowed that she would never be like him. She would rather die first. But since she loved him . . . she would help him.

All that Pierre could do was close his eyes and pray that he was only having a foul nightmare in his bed. *This is not happening,* he told himself. *This is not happening! Why can't somebody help us? Help us, somebody! HELP US! PLEEEEEASE!*

But Pierre didn't make a sound . . . and nobody came to their rescue. So before Leslie could tell their father what had happened, her brother ran away from home, guilt-ridden and confident that his father would kill him for what he allowed to happen to his little sister.

≋

Boomp, boomp, boomp!

"Leslie, are you all right in there?" someone called from outside the rest room door at Hot Jake's.

Leslie shook her head, smacked herself in the face with both palms of her hands, and pulled her thoughts together inside of the stall. She stood up and flushed down only water.

"I'm coming out now," she yelled toward the door. She unlocked the door and walked back out whispering, "It's that time of the month, you know," with a sly grin.

"Child, you crazy. Go on and handle your business."

"I already did," Leslie said and kept walking. She sucked it all in and went back to work. Misfortune had been the topsoil of her life, and there was nothing that she or anyone else could do about it but to keep growing.

Leslie spared her brother's life by never telling their father of Pierre's role in her violation that day. Otherwise, the father may have murdered the son. Or maybe the son would have gotten hit in the street by a speeding car and been crippled in his mind and body for the rest of his life, like James had been. And even if Pierre had stayed away from home at their cousin's house, or had run farther away, he would have eventually gone insane, haunted by his deeds to die a young, lonely death, like Kelsey did of a heroin overdose in Shreveport at age seventeen.

And now . . . out of the blue . . . Pierre wanted to become a new protector of his sister. Maybe that's how he saw fit to repay her for his life?

"S'il te plaît," Leslie told herself, while looking over more new orders of spicy foods. "Mon frère n'a pas de culot." My brother does not have the courage.

She continued to ignore those who stared at her in awe, as well as those who envied her high self-regard and her level of skill, because they would never know what it took for her to maintain her sanity . . . after all that she had been through, and all that she continued to struggle with.

Revelations

Anna-Marie Beaudet breathed deeply and carefully while lying on the elevated, white-sheeted bed downtown at Charity Hospital. Her head was propped up against two pillows, with an IV tube attached to the vein of her left arm. A respirator machine stood at the right side of her bed, with a heart monitor behind it. A box of surgical gloves sat nearby for the doctors and nurses to handle her with.

Ann was running out of time, and it was useless to even cry about it anymore. Tears would not heal her, and she had only had a few wishes on her mind to even hope for before she died.

"Is there anything more that I can do for you?" the young white nurse asked her.

Ann looked at the blond-headed nurse and responded, "Outside of you giving me your clean blood to live with, what else can you do for me? You ain't got no cure for this shit, do you?"

The nurse smiled embarrassingly. She didn't know what else to do. She was not experienced enough to know how to handle a testy patient who was dying of AIDS. At least cancer was looked at with some form of pity. But AIDS? AIDS was the worst form of mortality to die of, because it included the baggage of moral judgment. So Ann figured why in hell should she be nice when she knew that she was being judged? By everyone!

"Well, you can get me the telephone, if anything," Ann snapped at the nurse. "I need to call my damn daughter down here to see me."

The nurse got her the phone and was anxious to leave the room. Who wants to be whipped on for no reason? It was unfair to her. But she also understood that no one wanted to die, no matter what the circumstances were. So she couldn't honestly blame the dying woman for her spitefulness.

"You dial nine and then the number," she told her patient.

Ann snatched the phone from her hands. "Yeah, yeah, I know, just gimme da damn phone."

She waited for the nurse to respond to her uncivilly so that she could give the young white woman a bigger chunk of her mind. But the nurse was smart enough to ignore the temptation.

Ann dialed the phone number to her daughter's place near Dillard University's campus on purpose. She realized that Leslie was more than likely at work at Hot Jake's restaurant, and working as hard as she had trained herself to do. Nevertheless, Ann wanted to stir things up and make her daughter's visit that night more . . . confrontational. Leslie had a chip on her shoulder that needed to be knocked off before Ann had lost all of her physical strength and her voice to do it with. She had named her daughter Leslie in the first place, simply because she liked the name. And it seemed to fit her first daughter to a T. "Lez-lee," the mysterious one.

At the blue-and-white house of college girls, Bridget was the first to reach the telephone.

"Hello," she answered with her normal pep. She had everything in the world to be thankful for, to the point where she looked for things to make her life feel more soulful. She wanted substance and struggle in her life, the stuff that poor people seemed to have so much of. Bridget felt that she had missed out on that soul while growing up in the suburbs of Ann Arbor, Michigan, among thousands of well-to-do white Americans who lived by the precision of wealth.

"Who is this?" someone asked her over the phone. The woman was not asking her nicely either. However, Bridget assumed that she recognized the voice, so she answered respectfully.

"This is Bridget."

"Well, Bridget, is my daughter Leslie there? I need to talk to her."

I knew it, Bridget thought to herself with a smile. *It's Leslie's mother.*

"She'll be back in after ten. She's at work right now," she answered. "You need the number?"

"I *have* the damn number. I had that damn number before you even knew my daughter, girl. You think I don't know where Leslie works? What the hell is wrong with you? You think only college girls got brains?" Ann snapped at her.

Bridget went dead silent on the phone and didn't know what to say or think.

Leslie's mother continued: "Now what I need y'all to do to is call Leslie at that damn restaurant and tell her ass that her mother is in the hospital. And it would be nice to see her before I die in this damn place." Then she coughed . . . and coughed again.

Bridget was stunned into obedience. She didn't know Leslie's mother too well, and she had never met her in person. But one thing that Bridget did know was that Leslie wouldn't want all of them aware that her mother was in the hospital. They all realized that Leslie was fiercely private.

So Bridget walked farther into the kitchen, where she had answered the telephone, away from earshot distance of Ayanna and Yula, who sat in the other rooms. She responded to Leslie's mother in a near whisper, "Okay. Which hospital are you in?"

"Charity Hospital downtown. And tell her that I used my maiden name."

When Bridget hung up the phone, she felt excited to be involved in a life-or-death issue. She gathered her thoughts together before she walked out of the kitchen. She headed straight for the closet to grab a light jacket to wear.

"Where you goin', Bridget?" Yula asked her.

Bridget shook her head and answered, "I'm just making a quick run."

Ayanna grinned, knowing better. "Mmm hmm, she prob'bly on her way to meet Eugene somewhere," she insinuated. "You ain't foolin' nobody, Bridget."

Bridget smiled. "You're right. I just can't get enough of him." And she walked out the door.

She got in her dark blue Acura Integra in the private driveway next to the house, and she immediately drove toward Gentilly Boulevard, headed for Leslie's job at Hot Jake's.

I can't believe this, she told herself as she drove. *Has Leslie been trying to avoid her mother or something? Why didn't her mother call her job herself if she knows the number? What's going on with them?*

Bridget had no idea of any rift between Leslie and her mother, but she was game to find out. When she arrived at the restaurant where Leslie worked, she made sure to be as discreet as possible when she asked one of the waitresses for her.

"Ah, excuse me, I'm Bridget, Leslie *Bo-day*'s friend from school, and I really need to speak to her if I could."

The waitress nodded. It was not a problem. "Okay. I'll go get her."

"Thank you very much," Bridget told her politely.

As soon the waitress made eye contact with Leslie inside the kitchen, Leslie knew that she was about to be interrupted again.

"Hey, Lez, some girl named Bridget from school is out there to see you."

Leslie took a breath and thought to herself, *What the hell is going on tonight?*

"Did she say what she wanted?"

"You want me to go ask her?"

Leslie thought better of it. "No, I'll go see her."

She began to undo her apron, figuring that she could use a short break. But when she spotted Bridget wearing a face of concern while waiting for her at an empty table inside the dining room, Leslie concluded that she wasn't about to have a break. It looked serious.

"What's wrong?" she immediately asked, before taking a seat across the table.

Bridget told her calmly, "Your mother called tonight. And she said to tell you that she was in the hospital."

Bridget expected a dramatic response of some sort. However, Leslie just stood there and stared at her without a word. It wasn't as if she was not concerned about the health or well-being of her mother; Leslie was simply pacing her emotions. There had always been events in her life to get dramatic about. Overreactions only served to push her closer to the edge of sanity. One could never control the amount of stimuli in their lives, but Leslie could control her responses to them. So she remained calm and logical, again using the ghetto yoga technique of emotional withdrawal.

Bridget became confused by her friend's lack of a response. She asked her, "What's going on with you guys? Your mother acted as if you didn't want to speak to her or something."

Leslie responded, "Why are you whispering?"

Bridget looked at her and was more confused. She couldn't seem to figure Leslie out.

She answered, "Well . . . I didn't think that you would want everyone to know."

Leslie nodded her head and sat down at the table. *This is going to be another one of those long-ass nights for me.*

Bridget reached out to hold her hand across the table. "What are you thinking about right now?" she asked.

Leslie faced her and said, "Why?" as she slid her hand away.

Bridget was at a loss for words for a second. She was trying everything she could to reach out to Leslie, while Leslie continued to reject her support. But they were supposed to be friends. Friends opened up to each other. Friends shared each other's pains. Friends trusted one another.

So instead of answering Leslie's question, Bridget said, "I didn't tell Ayanna and Yula what was going on. I knew you wouldn't have wanted me to. But your mother sounded as if she was really . . . ticked off at something."

Leslie looked away and couldn't help her slight smile. She actually liked the idea of her mother being reactive for a change. Maybe she should have had a stronger attitude about some of the things that went on in their lives a lot sooner. Leslie had always felt that her mother was a pushover, especially when it came to Pete. Leslie had even used their mother as bait to talk Pierre into coming back home after he had run away.

"Mom is worried about you, Pete. I didn't tell Daddy. I won't. I promise you. Okay? So come back home. Mommy misses you," she remembered telling her brother over the phone. He had been staying at their cousin's house in the nicer section of the Ninth Ward, near Lake Pontchartrain.

In response to Leslie's plea, Pierre wailed, *"Je suis désolé! Je suis désolé!"*—I'm sorry! I'm sorry!—before he finally decided that it was safe enough to return home. Yet . . . Leslie had never told him that she forgave him. Nor did she tell her brother that their father would handle things in his own way. All that Pierre knew was that those mean boys had suddenly disappeared, as if it was . . . magic. Their mother, Ann, and sister, Laetitia, never knew a thing about any of it. They were both too fragile to know.

"Leslie? What are you thinking about?" Bridget asked her friend a second time.

Leslie seemed to have floated away for a minute. She shook her head and raised her fingers to her temples to give herself a brain massage.

She answered, "I don't know, girl. I just need a fuckin' break from everything right now. So what hospital is my mother in? Charity?" she asked Bridget. Charity was the only hospital where her mother could be. It wasn't as if the poor people of the Seventh Ward had that much of a choice. Charity was their local hospital, accepting most patients.

Bridget nodded and answered, "Yeah. Do you need me to drive you over there? I don't mind. If you need to talk about it with someone, then I'm here for you."

Leslie looked into Bridget's eyes to read if she could trust her. Bridget took in her stare and didn't budge from it. So Leslie nodded to her and gave in.

"Okay," she said with a long sigh. "Let me go get my things and leave early, then."

Bridget was too excited to contain herself.

"Thank you so much, Leslie. I just feel a need to be there for you. Anytime."

Leslie smiled at her as she climbed to her feet. *This girl is too pressed,* she told herself. Then she went to inform Jake that she needed to leave early for the night. Obviously, there was too much going on that night for her to be able to concentrate on her work.

≈

"Do you trust me at all, Leslie?" Bridget asked inside her car as she drove her friend toward Charity Hospital downtown.

"Why do you need me to trust you so much?" Leslie asked her back.

"Because we're friends. Aren't we? I mean, *I* trust *you.*"

Leslie asked her, "Do you really?" She doubted if anyone told the whole truth and nothing but the truth. Humans all carried too much baggage to be that open and honest with each other.

However, Bridget responded to her question immediately. "Yeah, I do trust you. I would let you borrow my car or anything."

"Yeah, but it's not like you can't get a new one if I fucked it up," Leslie reasoned with a grin.

"But that's not the point," Bridget told her. "I wouldn't let Ayanna borrow my car, because she's not responsible enough. She might have a bunch of thugs and weed smoke all in my car. But I know that you would be more responsible with it, whether you got into an accident or not."

Leslie decided to humor herself. She said, "What if the accident was my fault?"

Bridget looked at her and asked, "What do you mean?"

"I mean, what if I was in the wrong, like I ran a stop sign or something? What would you say then?"

Bridget shook her head and smiled it off. "You wouldn't do that."

"Why wouldn't I?" Leslie asked her. *You don't know me that well,* she told herself.

Bridget searched her eyes. "I mean, why would you do something . . . on purpose like that?"

Leslie broke out laughing. She said, "I can't believe how you have this . . . this big innocent view of the world like that. Everything ain't just . . . nice out here like that, Bridget. How many times do I have to tell you that?"

Bridget got bold and asked her, "Well, what has happened in your life to make you feel so skeptical of people like you do?" It was as if Leslie believed that the whole wide world was after her for some reason. What had she done, or what had happened to her and her family to make her feel that way? Bridget really wanted to know.

Leslie shook her head and looked away, out of the passenger-side window, declining another opportunity to reveal her pains.

She said, "If you don't know by now, then you wouldn't understand it if I told you." Then she faced Bridget and said, "Ask Ayanna. She knows. She talks about it all the time."

Bridget said, "Ayanna just acts that way because she thinks that that's how black people are supposed to act, as if we can't have any high culture or dignity about ourselves. But Leslie, you know better than that. I know you do. I mean . . . I admit it, Leslie . . . I kind of look at you like . . . a queen. And I mean, you just have so much going for you, that's it's really messed up for you not to feel that you can't be more open about who you are and just be more . . . I don't know, appreciative of what God has given you. I mean, a lot of people would love to have all of the talents that you have."

Leslie sighed and snapped, "Girl, please! People would rather have your money over my shit any day of the week. Are you crazy?! Go on somewhere with that."

Bridget felt slighted and hurt by it. She fell silent. She thought to herself, *I wish I had your talents. Sometimes I feel like my father's money is the only thing that I'm good for.*

They reached the hospital entrance much faster than Bridget expected. She still wanted to talk about things. Yet she figured they would have more time for talk afterward.

"Do they have good parking here?" she asked Leslie.

Leslie looked at her and frowned. She said, "You don't have to park. I'll just see you later on at home."

"You don't want me to come in with you?" Bridget asked her.

Leslie looked at her as if she had lost her mind. "Come in for what?"

"I mean, you know, to be with you. To give you support."

Leslie wondered how she had dropped her guard like that, but it was definitely back up again. She gave Bridget a stare and told her in French,

"Ma fille, tu commences à me taper sur les nerfs."

Bridget asked, "What does that mean?"

"It means that you're starting to get on my nerves, girl. Now go on back home. This is *my* business." *I don't know why my mother called the house with this shit in the first place,* she told herself. *She knows where I work!*

Her roommate was shocked by it. Leslie still had that edge about her, so Bridget backed off.

She said, "Well, your mother told me to tell you that she's listed under her maiden name."

Leslie eyed her again before she thanked her. *"Merci."* Then she climbed out of the car and walked toward the hospital entrance . . . alone.

Bridget sighed, feeling so close and still so far away. Then she drove off . . . disappointed.

≈≈≈

Leslie walked into the intensive care unit of the hospital and spotted her mother lying in her bed, and rapid thoughts began to race through her mind. What did it all mean? Was it the end for her mother? Was it the end for their family? Or did Leslie need to apologize to her mother to have everything return back to normal? Or what they viewed as normal, which had been a normal hell among the living. Or maybe her mother was being shown mercy by being allowed to escape from it all, and to slip away into the afterworld.

Ann had a respirator mask affixed to her nose, and a clear IV tube was feeding the vein in her left arm. She looked at peace, as if she had accepted her fate with courage. Until she saw her first daughter standing beside her at the bed. Then she got excited again.

Ann took the respirator mask off her face so that she could speak to her daughter, even if it would be the last breaths of her life.

"So you came, hunh?"

Leslie took a seat beside her bed and asked, "Why wouldn't I come?"

"Because you had other things to do," her mother answered. Leslie had often avoided their mother-daughter conversations by claiming to be too busy for them.

She nodded her head and admitted it. "I'll always have other things to do."

Ann stared at her a minute, admiring her daughter's beauty, the length of her hair, the perfection of her dark skin, and the focus of her eyes. Leslie seemed impenetrable, just like her father had seemed long ago. But now Ann knew better. Anyone could be broken. Even Leslie.

So Ann responded to her daughter with spite. "Well, that ain't gon' change nothin', Leslie. And you can work all you wanna work, but if you ain't *meant* to be rich, you ain't gon' *be* rich. You don't know that by now?"

Leslie looked at her mother with the calmness of a monk and said, "I guess I don't."

Ann didn't like that answer. Leslie refused to be broken, even on her mother's deathbed. And the truth was . . . Ann had always envied that in her daughter. It was that . . . unbreakable determination that had attracted her to Jean.

Ann nodded her head and smiled. She said, "You're just *like* that man. Just *like* him," and she began to laugh. But when she laughed, she began to cough again, and the nurse returned to the room to tell her to put her respirator mask back on.

Ann pushed it away and said, "Can't you see I'm talking to my daughter here? You know I'm gonna die anyway. Let me just talk to my damn daughter without that thing on my face."

Leslie looked into her mother's fiery eyes, and turned to the nurse. "Just for a minute, please."

The nurse hesitated, but what was the use? The daughter looked as defiant as the mother was. So the young nurse walked back out of the room.

Ann looked at Leslie and asked her, "Did they tell you what I was dying of in here?"

Leslie answered, "No." She didn't believe her mother was dying anyway. She was just depressed if anything, depressed and unhealthy because of it.

"Good," her mother told her, "because I wanted to be the one to tell you." She looked into Leslie's eyes and said, "I'm dying of full-blown AIDS, Leslie," with every bit of strength that she could still muster in her frail body.

And Leslie didn't . . . budge. But she did take a deep breath, deeper than usual. Because she immediately thought of her father, and of Haiti, and of Africa, and how the international AIDS epidemic (viewed initially as the gay white man's disease) now seemed to haunt black people, and entire families, just like slavery did, and poverty, and despair, and the countless deaths of tribal warfare for the remnants of fleeting power that were left from the carnage. And in her mind, Leslie wanted to kill for it, to annihilate, to murder, all for the redemption of her people, and of her father, and of her mother, who she still loved.

But . . . who would she kill? And how? And when? And . . .

Leslie dropped her head into her hands, and the nerves in her body began to twitch until tears welled up in her eyes. And when she cried, it was not softly, but in big tears, with loud sobs. She could not help it.

It's unfair, she told herself. *It's UNFAIR! What did we do? What did we DO?*

Her mother didn't expect that from her. She wanted it. She did. Ann wanted to show her daughter that everyone was vulnerable. And she realized that Leslie had always viewed her with disdain and with pity, as if *she* could have done a better job as the mother of the house. As if *she* could have held the family together with a stronger bond, and with stronger leadership. So now that Ann was dying, Leslie would get her chance to prove it. It was what Ann had wanted on her deathbed, proof from the daughter that she could handle what the mother could not.

Nevertheless, Ann figured that Leslie would meet the challenge head-on, like the strong-headed Aries child that she was, and like her father would, another Aries. They knew it all, and they could do it all, so Ann wanted Leslie to prove it. She just never . . . expected her daughter to cry.

"I'm sorry, Mom," Leslie told her through her tears. "I'm sor-reee." She stood up to hold her mother in bed, and to cuddle with her, becoming a little girl again, and melting Anna-Marie's coldness to her. Coldness had never been her way in life, and it wouldn't be her way in death.

Ann was a warm person, and a mother to the end. So she began to cry with her daughter, and she became afraid again.

She whispered, "I don't wanna die, girl. Lord knows I don't. But there's nothing we can do about it now." She kissed her daughter's forehead.

"And I'm sorry too, baby," she told her. "I didn't mean to hurt you this way. But I've been hurt, Leslie. *J'ai mal, très mal.*" I hurt, very badly.

"Je sais, Maman. Je sais." I know.

Then the mother smiled with happier memories on her mind.

"You should have seen how happy your father was when he saw that I could pick up the French. I was surprised by it my damn self," she commented with a chuckle.

"But once you all started speaking French around the house, it came easier for me. It was like the words just . . . formed in your mind after a while. *Pierre, mets tout de suite les poubelles dehors.*" Pierre, you take out the trash right now!

Ann chuckled calmly, and with no cough.

She said, "But no one spoke as fast as you did. I had to slow you down to speak to you," Ann remembered. "That's when I first began to feel that you thought you were . . . smarter than me."

Leslie said, *"Je ne suis pas plus intelligente que toi."* I am not more intelligent than you. *"Et tu es très courageuse."* And you are very strong. *"A ta place, je n'aurais pas pu survivre."* I would not have been able to survive what you have.

Ann responded, "You were stronger than me from the moment that you were born, girl. You were just born that way. And was always curious about everything, with those big old eyes of yours," she shared with her daughter.

She looked into Leslie's eyes and said, "But you grew into 'em once you got older. They don't look so big now. But they were. Some people say that big eyes on a baby means that they'll be able to see more in life. You know, like they have innate wisdom or something."

Ann started to cough again, but she was right in the middle of her memories, so she continued to talk despite her health.

"Your father told me once that your eyes reminded him of his grandmother on his mother's side." She began to laugh for some reason and coughed harder.

Leslie was just about to stop her, and tell her to return to the respirator mask, but Ann was on a roll and refused to stop.

She said, "Your father told me that she was a Vaudou priestess in Haiti. He never used the word 'voodoo,' you know. He said 'voodoo' was an American word. But he also told me that he was scared of that grandmother."

Ann's memory of the conversation became crystal clear in her mind. It seemed relevant at that moment for Leslie to hear it. And once Leslie had heard the word "priestess" spit forward from her mother's lips, she became alert, and was eager to listen. Because a priestess was powerful.

Leslie sat back on her chair to pay her mother her full attention. She had never listened to her mother more intently in her life! But now . . . she was saying something of value to her.

"The reason why I guess I'm remembering all of this right now . . . is because your father told me that the last time he saw his grandmother in Haiti, she was on her deathbed. And he said that there was a lot of different family members in the room, but that she seemed to be looking at him more than anyone else in there."

Ann finished her story and nodded. "And he said that . . . your eyes reminded him of her."

Leslie heard her mother's words and was shocked, in a good way. She felt uplifted! Energized! And purposeful!

A priestess! A priestess! she repeated to herself. Then she wondered, *What about me? Is it in my blood? Am I a priestess too? I've always felt extra things in my life.*

Suddenly her pain began to make sense. Leslie could feel it! It all made sense now.

But then Ann lost control of her cough and started gagging for air.

Leslie forced the respirator mask back onto her mother's face.

"Nurse! Nurse!" she yelled in a panic.

The young white woman ran back into the room and made sure the mask had been affixed correctly. Then she checked the oxygen to make sure that she could stabilize her patient's labored breathing.

Leslie breathed slowly and deeply along with her mother, the nurse, and the respirator machine, until they were all calm again. That's when the nurse gave the mother and daughter both a look.

"Please, keep the mask on," she told them, before she nervously walked back out of the room. *Why can't black people just cooperate with the rules like everyone else does?* she asked herself. *I have the most problems with them. All the time!*

Ann rolled her eyes at the woman's back as she left.

Leslie caught it and smiled. Then she became serious again. She told her mother in French, *"Papa ne m'a jamais raconté cette histoire."* Daddy never told me that story.

Ann nodded with the respirator mask still on. Then she responded, *"Il me l'a racontée une seule fois."* He only told me once.

AWAKENINGS

Life II

Housemates

Eugene Duval rowed his naked, olive-toned body into Bridget's chocolate brown while she dug her nails into his back and moaned. But then he stopped and whined to her, "Your *nails,* Bridget. You know I bruise easy. Why do you keep doing that?"

She looked up into his pleasing face from her pillow and apologized.

"I'm sorry. You just feel good, baby."

He said, "I know, but damn, girl. You gotta stop scratching me."

"O-*kay,*" Bridget whined back to him. She just didn't want him to stop. The pleasure of Eugene was heavenly. So she forced herself to dig her nails into the sheets of her bed instead of into his soft skin.

However, Eugene was becoming bored with their mundane sex life. He wanted more kinkiness, and Bridget continued to deny him what he wanted. So after he had pleased her, and then himself, he turned over on his back with his hands clasped behind his head and began to wonder.

"Hey, um . . . what's up with your girl, Leslie? How come she acts like she do? She barely says anything when I'm over here. She don't like me over here or something? What did I ever do to her?" he asked Bridget, with a lighthearted chuckle.

Bridget rolled over and nestled her head into his chest. "It's a lon-n-ng story. That's just the way she is, basically. That's just . . . the way she is."

"Well, how did you become friends with her, or housemates or whatever?"

"I mean, we kicked it in our freshman year and everything. She's cool.

She just doesn't . . . open up to people like that," Bridget answered.

"Well, how did she open up to you?"

Bridget thought about it. "Basically, she just talked about how she was from New Orleans and she could cook, and how she wanted to own her own chain of restaurants one day. And we all started hanging out together. Then she took us around to places in the French Quarter, and to Mardi Gras and stuff. So we all just decided to move into a house together for our sophomore year."

Eugene nodded his head and paused. He was about to get . . . risky. But as long as he kept it conversational, he figured that he could get away with it.

He asked Bridget, "Does she have a boyfriend or anything?"

Instead of becoming alarmed and jealous, Bridget laughed at the question.

"Why is that funny?" She confused Eugene with her laughter.

She told him, "Everyone asks me that. And I just think that it's funny, because she's focused on getting her work done right now. There's nothing wrong with that."

Eugene relaxed and said, "Oh." He was glad that Leslie was unattached. Having a boyfriend would have derailed his fantasies about her. But hearing that she was unattached . . . served to strengthen them. He was beginning to feel that anything would better than the same old missionary sex with Bridget.

They both lay there in silence until Eugene felt himself rising again. Bridget could feel it too, pushing up against her leg. But his thoughts were no longer on her. Eugene was thinking about Leslie and her long, natural hair, dark, almond-shaped eyes, and her deep ebony skin, as smooth and as sensuous as black silk and satin. Eugene could only imagine himself sinking into Leslie's interior parts deeply, deeper, and deepest, until she would engulf him. She would become a black octopus with her legs, arms, fingers, toes, and tongue, exploring him fully. Then when they would finish in their mating . . . she would become his mommy.

Bridget interrupted him in his exotic thoughts about her housemate.

"You're ready for round two already?" she asked him with a gentle squeeze of his erect tool. "That was fast," she added with a chuckle.

Eugene responded halfheartedly, "Oh . . . yeah. I guess so."

≈

That same night, at a New Orleans nightclub located on the west side of Xavier University, the thick drumbeats of hip-hop music pounded into the ears of nearly a hundred brown patrons. It was freestyle night on the open microphones, as the sound system moved the well-curved behinds of the young women there, who wore scanty, formfitting skirts and revealing blouses as they ground up against the loose, oversized blue jeans and pelvises of the testosterone-heavy guys. Pumping through the giant black speakers was the wildly popular song from local rap star Mystical, as he screamed his warnings of reckless heat and passion onto the dance floor: *"Dain-ger! Boomp, boomp, boomp! Dain-ger! Boomp, boomp, boomp! Get on the floorrr! Da nigga right cheeere! Sing it!"*

The energy inside the large, dark room was indeed explosive as they partied to the fullest. And as the DJ spun the records, he played the home-grown rap star Juvenile, telling the young women in the place to *"back that thang up,"* with the 504 Boyz expressing to the crowd who *they* were, right before he played the Big Tymers bragging about how much platinum, diamonds, and hundred-thousand-dollar cars they shined, and gleamed, and "blinged" in. Then he played the legendary Master P, asking the party people, *"Where my soldiers at?"* right before he spun the record of the Brooklyn, New Yorker, hustler Jay-Z, bragging about how big he was pimpin' the wanna-be fabulous ghetto girls. The DJ followed that up with Dr. Dre and Snoop, letting the hard-core streets know that they still had love for them.

Their songs represented the height of the new urban culture for the loyal fans and dedicated followers of hard-core hip-hop. Forget about the slow-moving blues of the old-timers in the community. Fuck the blues! This new generation of hip-hop had the drums! And they were no longer banded to the brown peoples of America. So they beat their drums wildly, while energizing their new life force, and healing themselves:

BOOM, BAP, BOOM-BOOM, BAP-BOMP
BOOM, BAP, BOOM-BOOM, BAP-BOMP
BOOM, BAP, BOOM-BOOM, BAP-BOMP
BOOM, BAP, BOOM, BAP . . .

Ayanna Timber was in heaven there! She lived for the drums, the thugs, the hustlers, and pimps, and players, and ballers, and guys who had rhyme skills like she had. She lived for it! There was no other place that she'd rather be than right there in the mix of the sweet poetry of mathematical noise. In a word, it was wizardry, as each master of ceremonies put a spell on the crowd, who were forced to rock to the rapid word cadences that rode the waves of the beat.

But Yula Frederick couldn't take it! There were just too many rowdy guys swarming in there for her taste. It was too dark and anxious in there. The music was too harsh and aggressive. And the women there were just too . . . accepting of all of it, including Ayanna. So Yula pulled her house-mate aside to let her know that she had had enough already.

"Look, I'm going back to the house, Ayanna. I'm just not feelin' this in here."

Ayanna nodded her head, barely acknowledging her. "Go 'head then. I'm all right."

And as the open microphone began to be passed around to those who were brave enough to freestyle, Ayanna pushed and shoved her way through their cipher just as the confident guys would do, while Yula made her way for the exit.

Ayanna made it up front where the action was, and waited in her blue Dillard University sweatshirt, with a matching blue bandanna wrapped around her head. Her oversize blue jeans hung loosely on her hips, and her black Timberland boots tapped steadily to the pulse of the beat. She stood ready to go to verbal and rhythmic war with the guys, while she breathed heavy and talked herself into it.

I'm going next! I'm going next!

The microphone was being rocked by the braggadocios and egotistical guys: *"Bitches fiend for the beast in my big jeans / they love to sweat me 'cause my dress code is clean / so they scheme / thinkin' they gon' get some green / but all they get is more dick / HUNH you know I'm mean . . ."*

The crowd of mostly guys laughed and hollered and nodded their heads in approval.

"Yeeaah, nigga! What!"

"What!"

It was a particularly raw night on the microphone as each guy tried to outmatch the vulgarity of the first: *"Last night I worked the walls of this nigga's baby momma / so now he wanna run his mouth wit da fuckin' drama / so I had to tell his ass with my gun that I'ma / put seven bullets in his ass real fast . . ."*

"Ahhhhh, nigga!"

"Yo, that nigga crazy, right dere!"

"Go 'head wit dat shit, dawg!"

Ayanna schemed out her plan, telling herself, *Okay, I know how I'm gon' rock it now. I know how I'm gon' rock it!* And before they could blink, she stepped up swiftly and seized the microphone in her hands before the next guy could grab it.

Once their eyes were all on her, there was no backing down. The beat was calling her bluff:

BOOM-BOOM, BAP
Ba-BOOMP, Ba-BOOMP, BOOM-BAP
BOOM-BOOM, BAP
Ba-BOOMP, Ba-BOOMP, BOOM-BAP . . .

Ayanna took a last quick breath with no time to waste and did her thing: *"It's a girl, so / I know you got your eyes on my thighs / you wanna rise / and meet me later for a little surprise / 'cause I'm a bitch and you a guy . . ."*
Sometimes, when the fraternity of hip-hoppers got really excited, they would interrupt the master of ceremonies before he—or she, as the case may be—could finish. That was the case with Ayanna's bold flow that night. Especially since she was a girl. That made it extra. The raw skills of rap were usually a guy's arena. Girls were only supposed to watch and listen, like pom-pom–carrying cheerleaders. But not tonight. The guys howled for a girl.
"Ohhh, she rockin' nat shit! She rockin' it!"
And Ayanna continued to ride the beat: *". . . and guess what / I like it rough / yup, I said I like it rough / I got a man in jail right now who's tough and all that stuff . . ."*
"Ohhh, shit! She fuckin' it up, dawg!"
". . . but how he gon' know / if I hit you off real slow . . ."
The cipher of guys exploded in unison, "Ohhhhh, shiiiiitttt!" Even the DJ was nodding and grinning. The girl was dope, establishing a lyrical high on their brains! And she wasn't finished yet: *". . . or we can speed up the flow / and just like on this microphone / I got the real blow. You wanna show and prove / make your move / and we can groove / but make sure you're bringing something big enough to soothe . . ."*
"Ohhhhhhhh, shit! She ripped all you ma-fuckers! She ripped all y'all!"
"Dat bitch bad as shit! She bad!"
"Who want it after her shit? Who want it next?"
Ayanna left the microphone smokin'! She didn't even care who went next. She had risen to their challenge, and they respected her for it. They gave her the love that she cherished from them.
"Yo, where you learn to rhyme like that? I know you ain't learn that shit from Dillard," a street general stepped up and asked her with a smirk.
Ayanna could tell that he was of high rank by how the crowd dispersed and waited their turn when he stepped up to her.

She grinned when she answered him. "I'm from Houston. We just *flow* like that."

He said, "Naw, I've been to Houston. Houston ain't all like that. Scarface and nem is tight, but your shit is extra, you know, for a girl and all."

Ayanna spoke up for her gender. "Why it gotta be all like that? It's plenty of girls kickin' it now. We goin' platinum faster than some guys do. Look at Lil' Kim and Foxy. And now Eve doin' her thing wit da Rough Riders."

He smiled at her and said, "Yeah, I know." Then he took a whiff of the girl, and was pleasantly surprised. "Damn, what's that shit you got on?"

"Ahhh, you like that shit, don't you? It's body oils," she told him. "But I can't tell you what kind. I don't want nobody coppin' my shit like that. People quick to bite ya' shit if it smell good."

The street general laughed, thinking his own thoughts about it. *Yeah, I'd bite ya' shit, aw'ight. And then I'd make you bite mine.*

However, Ayanna's eyes averted to his lieutenant, who stood slightly behind him with pretty, dark skin and braided hair to match.

Damn! Who da fuck is that? she asked herself.

"So, do you go to Dillard, or you just wearing the shirt?" the general asked her.

"No, I go there," Ayanna answered, and took another peek at his friend.

The general caught it and smiled, knowing the game. The girls could never seem to keep their eyes off his attractive sidekick.

He asked her, "You know some girl named Leslie?"

Ayanna looked into his face and decided to humor him. "I know about five Leslies at school," she lied. She only knew two, and the other Leslie was from Florida. She doubted if he was talking about her. He was a local, so he was more than likely asking about Leslie Beaudet, Ayanna's housemate from N'awlins. Then he confirmed it.

"Leslie *Bo-day*," he enunciated properly. "She a dark-skin, long-haired girl. She half Haitian and she speak French."

When he told her that, his friend tapped him on the arm and shook his head.

The general turned and smiled at him. "Be cool, man, I ain't gon' say nothin'. I'm just askin' 'bout her."

That made Ayanna curious. "Why, is she your girlfriend or something?" she asked the lieutenant. In a funny way, he looked like Leslie. Maybe she was dating her own type. Or maybe . . . he was related to her. Leslie did have an older brother.

But the pretty boy walked away before she could ask him anything. So she asked the general, "Is he related to Leslie? What's his name?"

The general shook his head, denying it. He wanted to redirect the conversation. "That's enough about that. I was jus' askin' t' be askin'," he told her. "Let's talk about you a li'l bit. They call me Beaucoup. What they call you?"

Ayanna smiled and said, "Beaucoup? That's French too, ain't it. You Hai-tian too?"

"Naw, we jus' all know each other from the neighborhood. We use a lot of French names and shit around here. That's just New Orleans for you. But it don't mean we all *speak* that shit.

"But anyway, you want a drink or something?" he asked her.

"Sure." And she began to walk with him toward the bar.

"What did you say your name was again?"

Ayanna smiled and said, "I didn't. But it's Ayanna."

"I-yahn-na?" he pronounced correctly.

"Yeah."

He nodded. "Cool. I like that. Ayanna."

≈

Yula made it back to the house and felt guilty about leaving her friend at the rowdy hip-hop club by herself. She needed someone to talk to about it so that she could fall asleep in peace. But when she walked upstairs, Bridget's door was locked. That meant only one thing; Eugene was over. And Leslie was nowhere to be found, as usual.

"Shit," Yula mumbled to herself. She couldn't decide whether to take her clothes off and call it a night or remain dressed in case Ayanna would need her in some way.

Dammit! I should have never gone there with her. Then it would just be her problem if something happened to her. But now, since I went with her . . . Yula felt that it was her responsibility to make sure Ayanna got back home safely.

Yula took a deep breath and decided to call up a taxi service to travel back to the scene of the crime. But as soon as she had made the phone call, Leslie walked in.

"Leslie, I'm so glad that you're here," Yula told her excitedly.

Leslie looked her over and asked, "Why?"

"Because I need to talk to somebody about this."

"About what?"

Yula cringed and said, "I left Ayanna at the club by herself."

Once Leslie heard that, she loosened up and smiled. "Please, don't worry yourself about that girl, Yula. She knows how to act in those crowds. You shouldn't have went there with her in the first place. You know she's not gonna want to leave until the end of it. And then she'll wanna get high with people. So you were gonna have to leave her eventually anyway."

Yula nodded, knowing that Leslie was right. "I know. I know," she admitted.

That was all that Leslie planned to say about it. She figured, to each her own. She was tired and more than ready for bed that night, but she still had reading to do. And she had far more pressing issues on her mind than Ayanna's penchant for hip-hop sociables.

Nevertheless, Yula wanted to talk about it. So she knocked on Leslie's bedroom door after she had sent the angry cabdriver away.

Leslie took a breath with a new book lying open on her lap. *Will I ever get any fuckin' peace?* she asked herself. "Come in, Yula," she told her house-mate, while hiding her new book under a pillow. It was her business alone.

Yula walked in smiling. She said, "I'm sorry, Leslie. I just feel guilty, man. I mean . . . how are you able to just . . . do what you need to do like that?"

Leslie stared at her for a minute. She said, "We're not getting any younger, Yula. Everybody has to just be themselves. You can't walk around trying to please people all the time. That just makes you mad when you realize that you haven't spent enough time thinking about *you*."

Yula nodded. Leslie had always made perfect sense. In wisdom years, she was a grandmother while the rest of them were toddlers.

Yula said, "I know. I should just go to sleep and see her in the morning, right?"

It was a rhetorical question, so Leslie didn't bother to answer it. Instead, she wanted to give Yula some added advice. She said, "You know what, Yula? If I had all the free time on my hands that you have, I would make nothing but straight A's. You don't have a thing in your way but you. But I always have other people to think about, and a lot of situations just seem to get in my way."

She said, "That's why I don't mess around when I have things to do. I rarely get any time to myself. But you? Yula, you need to just stop holding back on yourself. For real. I mean, you worry about petty shit."

Yula walked back to her room as if she had been spanked with a repri-mand. She knew that she rarely gave her all. And she wondered how long she would continue to bullshit herself. Success was for people who worked hard toward definitive goals. So how long could Yula live as if she had none? How long would she continue to play possum? And although many victorious people liked to talk about luck and good fortune, most of them had already put in the sweat of desire and commitment to become "lucky." Their successes were not by chance, they were by practice.

So Yula could not sleep that night, feeling guilty now about her own lack of effort.

Leslie's right, she told herself. *I should just go for everything I want and stop playing. I should just go for it! She's right!*

When Ayanna finally made it home that night, Yula was still up in her room, pondering her future. Ayanna barged right into her room and said, "You missed it, girl. I ripped that shit up tonight! They know my name now, Yula. They all know my name up in that camp."

Yula nodded and said, "I'm happy for you. I was just worried that you wouldn't make it back home safely."

Ayanna looked at her and frowned. "Okay, Grandma. I drank all my milk up, too," she joked. Then she got serious and said, "Shit, girl, if I was worried about that, I wouldn't have let you leave me. I know my way around by now."

"I see you do," Yula told her.

"And guess what I found out?" Ayanna asked her.

Yula couldn't help herself. Gossip was good. "What?"

Ayanna started to whisper, "Have you ever met Leslie's brother or a boyfriend or something, who looks like her?"

Yula squinted her eyes trying to figure out what Ayanna was getting at. "No. Why?"

Ayanna began to smile, tickled by her own little secret. She responded, "Naw, I ain't even gon' get into that. I don't know if it's true anyway. I just got a hunch. Leslie likes to play secrets, so I can play that game too. But I'm gon' catch her ass. You watch." That's when Yula sniffed the marijuana fumes that reeked from her friend's clothes.

Yula shook her head and told her, "Leslie's a good person, Ayanna. She just don't take no shit from nobody. *I* need to be more like that."

Ayanna sucked her teeth and insisted, "Naw, man, Leslie thinks she's slick. But I'm gon' show her ass that I know what time it is. Watch me."

Yula just shook her head again as Ayanna walked out of her room. She told herself, *I think you better leave Leslie the hell alone. She hasn't said anything to you that didn't need to be said. I just wish that I had the balls to say things sometimes. And I will. Watch me!*

≈

In the morning, Yula awoke at a quarter to nine and panicked. "Oh, shit!" Her first class at Stern Hall that morning began at nine, and it took her at least twenty minutes to walk to campus on an energetic day after she had gotten dressed and groomed. So technically, Yula was already late before she could even get started. The new question was, how late would she be?

She jumped out of bed, grabbed her clothes together, headed for the bathroom to take a shower, and kept up a rapid pace until she was dressed, groomed, and ready to go at ten after nine.

Bridget and Leslie were already on campus at their first classes by then. And when Yula rushed downstairs at the house, she disturbed Ayanna, who was still catching Zs on the pullout sofa where she slept in the living room.

Ayanna popped her eyes open just long enough to snap at Yula for making so much commotion going down the stairs.

"Damn, girl, break the fuckin' staircase while you're at it. Shit! People are still try'na sleep around here."

Yula ignored her and rushed out the front door, down the patio steps, and up the street, only to run out of breath long before she could reach the first corner.

She stopped and took a couple of deep breaths while just about keeling over. "Shit! I need to do some damn joggin'," she admitted to herself. She had never been a big fan of physical education, and she had hated gym class in high school. In fact, Yula's initial spurt of energy had taken so much out of her that her walk to campus became slower and more painstaking than normal.

When she finally arrived at campus, it was after ten o'clock, and Yula had missed her first class of nursing. Then she spotted Bridget all calm and smiling, while standing inside the hallway before their second class was to begin, at eleven.

"Why you all smilin' today?" Yula asked her tartly. She had become hot and sweaty in her rush to school that morning and she was not in a good mood.

Bridget told her, "Don't worry, I have all of the notes."

Yula snapped, "Well, how come you didn't wake me up this morning? You usually do."

Bridget caught on to Yula's attitude that morning and spoke up to correct her. "You mean, I usually *try* to. But I didn't have time this morning, Yula. I had to drive . . . Eugene back to school, and then make it back to class through rush-hour traffic. So I was out the house this morning before eight. And you know you wouldn't have wanted me to wake you up that early."

Bridget got irritated herself and added, "I'm tired of trying to wake you up anyway, Yula. You know what time our classes are. I'm not your personal manager."

Yula didn't want to hear it that morning. She was still feeling peppered about missing class.

She told Bridget, "Whatever. You too busy fuckin' that yellow boy all the time, and you need to give his ass a break."

Bridget was blindsided by it. They had classmates in earshot distance of them in the hallway. And you know they started looking.

Bridget lowered her voice to a whisper and responded, "I don't *believe* you said that to me. That's none of your business, Yula. And I don't appreciate you saying that, especially out in public."

Yula snapped, "I'll say what I wanna say. It's the truth. You always fuckin' that boy."

Bridget was beyond embarrassment! She wanted to just . . . disappear. Evaporate! She wanted to turn into a ghost right there on the spot. Or at least take back the hands of time to prepare herself for Yula's unprovoked wrath that morning. What had she done to deserve that from Yula? So when their eleven o'clock class started, Bridget made sure to sit on the other side of the room, while thinking terrible thoughts about her so-called friend. Real friends wouldn't do that to each other.

She needs to lose some damn weight! Bridget thought to herself. *That's what she needs to do! She's just jealous because she doesn't have a steady man. Maybe if she lost some damn weight, she could keep one. But no one wants to be seen with her big ass! That's why she's always getting those . . . on-the-down-low friends. Guys are embarrassed of her.*

To make things worse for Yula that morning, she was still tired. She had gotten only a few hours of sleep that night. So as the class began to take notes from their lecture, Yula began to fall asleep against her right hand, which was propped up on her desk. And she couldn't stop herself.

Damn! she cursed. *I gotta get some more sleep! I feel terrible. I'm all hot and funky . . . I don't even think my deodorant is still working after rushing out this morning. And now I'm too tired to pay attention.*

Then she looked over at Bridget sitting in the far right corner of the room.

That was wrong what I did to her, she admitted. *I need to apologize to her.*

All of a sudden, Yula felt a lump in her throat, heaviness in her heart, and guilt on her mind. And in a flash, she broke down and cried. She cried not only from the offense that she had caused Bridget, and not only from missing class that morning, and not only from hanging out the night before with Ayanna, but from the accumulation of the truth that Leslie had shared with her. Yula was simply not getting the job done for herself, and she had no one to blame for it but herself. She realized that many of her family members and friends back home in Mobile, Alabama, had never had a chance to go away to school. So she felt she needed to do more to make sure that she didn't waste that opportunity. And she became . . . disappointed with herself, as it all rained down on her head right there in the classroom.

"Ahhh, excuse me, Miss ahhh . . . ," their instructor stammered.

"Frederick," Bridget stood up and informed him. She was immediately on the case to comfort her friend in need.

"What's wrong, Yula?" she asked, with a hand on Yula's arm.

Yula was pouring out tears and weeping into her hands at her desk. She mumbled, "I jus' gotta apply myself more. I gotta dedicate myself. And I'm sorry, Bridget. I'm sorry 'bout what I said to you. I didn't mean that. I'm jus' really tired right now."

I knew something was wrong! Bridget told herself.

"Okay, I'll just drive you back home then," she said to her friend.

"But I need to be here in class," Yula refuted.

Bridget said, "Well, you'll get your rest today, and you'll start over tomorrow, that's all. Okay, Yula? Let's go." She wasn't giving Yula a choice. She was embarrassing herself now.

Yula said, "I can't!" She was determined to stick it out and get her own lessons for the day.

Bridget responded, "Well, you're just gonna have to. And you can start over tomorrow. Now come on." And she waited until Yula gave in.

When they sat in the car, Yula looked over at Bridget in the driver's seat and mumbled, "This won't happen again, Bridget. I promise you. This won't ever happen again."

Bridget nodded to her and said, "Okay. You just get your rest . . . and stop trying to hang out with Ayanna. Because . . . to tell you the truth, Yula . . . between me and you, I've just about given up on that girl. She needs to get her priorities straight."

Yula nodded, agreeing with her. "I know. But I gotta get *my* priorities straight too," she added.

Bridget swallowed hard and added her own confession to the mix. "You were right too," she said. "I probably do need to cut back on Eugene."

The Priestess

When Ayanna finally climbed out of bed, washed up, brushed her teeth, and pulled on another set of baggy jeans and a sweatshirt to make it back to Dillard's campus for class, she had already missed her first two courses of the day and was running late to her third.

She arrived on campus with her black canvas backpack hanging off her left shoulder. She was still on a minor high from the events of the night before, and she took in all of the campus scenery as she walked slowly.

This school reminds me of a damn missionary camp or something, she told herself while viewing the plain white campus buildings. They were all evenly spaced along the greenery of the front lawn of twisting tree branches and gray stone benches, where the students sat and conversed. *We need more color on this campus. And this place ain't never looked as phat as the brochures and shit they send out to you. They must've taken those campus pictures on the best damn day ever! Probably used airbrush or something,* she joked to herself.

Man, I can't wait till I blow up and get signed to a phat rap contract! It's like, only a matter of time now. And I'm out of here! she mused. *Then I can pay my mom back her money for sending me here.*

"Ayanna," someone called her.

Ayanna broke from her thoughts and turned to spot Leslie, walking toward her from her right.

"Oh, what's up, L?" she said before she waited.

Leslie appeared to be pleased for some reason. Usually she walked around with a poker face that was unreadable.

Ayanna noticed it immediately. She asked, "You in a good mood today, hunh, L?"

Leslie just smiled at her. She answered, "I just found out something."

Ayanna smiled herself. *I found out something too,* she thought.

"So, what you find out?" she asked Leslie.

Leslie paused to make sure that her revelation would hit Ayanna the right way. She was curious to see if there was any validity to her heritage. The setup was crucial.

"Can you keep a secret?" she asked Ayanna.

Sharing secrets was unusual for Leslie. And why would she share them with Ayanna of all people? Ayanna had the biggest mouth.

"What?" Ayanna responded hesitantly. Her jaw dropped open and the entire campus disappeared for a minute. It was just her and Leslie in the middle of an island, having a one-on-one conversation. And it felt eerie to Ayanna. What was going on?

Leslie said, "I found out that my Haitian grandmother was a *voodoo priestess.* And my father said that I look just like she did."

Ayanna asked herself, *Am I fuckin' still high, or what?* It occurred to her that she had seen and heard Leslie's revelation to her before.

I saw this! she snapped to herself. *Oh my God! It's déjà vu! It's déjà vu!*

But just like that, Ayanna's vision was over. Because déjà vu only lasted for seconds. However, those mere seconds were enough to spook her the hell out! Ayanna stood frozen in fear, while Leslie smiled wider than she had ever witnessed from her before. Was it all a game?

Leslie asked her, "Ain't that something, Ayanna? I couldn't believe it. But it all makes sense, though. Because all my life, it seemed like, whenever someone did something bad to me, something real bad would happen to them. Like, I had my own war angel watching over me."

Leslie stopped and asked again, "Ain't that deep, Ayanna?"

Ayanna was still speechless . . . and motionless.

She uttered, "Un hunh." But inside she was screaming, *Oh, shit! Get her away from me! Get her away from me!* But she couldn't budge to break away. That's when Leslie took her hand and began to walk across campus with her.

"And remember . . . this is just between me and you, Ayanna. Okay? It's our secret now."

Ayanna could see that they were moving from all of the white school buildings that they were passing. Only . . . she couldn't feel her legs. And as plenty of Dillard students walked by them, Ayanna continued to scream without being heard: *Get her off of me! Get her off of me-e-e-e!*

But no one moved to help her. She was on her own.

"Ayanna . . . Ayanna!" Leslie addressed her. They had stopped walking and were standing out in front of Leslie's next building for class.

Ayanna snapped out of her terrified haze and mumbled, "Hunh?" only to hear Leslie repeat the mad reality in a soft tone.

"This is just between me and you." Then she just . . . faded away, with her eyes still burning into Ayanna's consciousness.

It took a few more seconds before Ayanna could gather her bearings. Once she did, she dropped her backpack to the ground so that she could massage her temples with her hands.

Fuck! she exclaimed to herself. *I'm fuckin' trippin'. I'm trippin'! I gots to be!* She shook her head and told herself, *I gotta leave that smokin' weed shit alone. For real!*

Leslie was confused about the sensation herself, as she sat inside her economics class.

What was that all about? she asked herself of Ayanna's spooked-out reaction. She realized that it was risky business to test her like that, but Ayanna was the perfect subject for her. Yula would have flipped out and had a heart attack if she had revealed anything about . . . voodoo to her. And Bridget was already game for secrets, so the information would not have been a sufficient test with her. But with Ayanna's mouth, and her bring-it-on attitude, Leslie figured that if she could shut *her* up, it would be a real show of power. If she really had any. Yet . . . Leslie still didn't expect for the test to go over so well that morning. She couldn't even feel herself doing it all. It just kind of . . . happened. And she had no idea that her housemate had experienced déjà vu.

Hmm, Leslie wondered while taking notes in class. *I guess now we'll see if it's real.*

≈

Blrrrrrrrpp! . . . Blrrrrrrrrpp! . . . Blrrrrrrrrpp!

Yula struggled from her bed to answer the cordless telephone.

"Hello."

"Yes, may I speak to Leslie *Bo-day,* please?" The woman sounded urgent but calm. However, Leslie was still at school, and she had refused to carry a pager. None of her housemates could blame her for that, either. The girl had enough interruptions in her life as it was.

Yula answered, "Umm, she's still at class. Can I take a message for her?"

"Yes, could you please inform her to call Charity Hospital as soon as possible?"

Yula was wide awake after that. She paused and said, "Charity *Hospital*?" She calmed herself down and responded, "Okay. I'll tell her as soon as I catch up to her."

"Thank you," the woman told her. And that was it.

Yula stopped and thought for a minute before she shook her head with the phone still in hand. "Damn," she expressed out loud. She didn't know what was going on at Charity Hospital, but there was one thing that she did know: "Leslie got it, bad! She ain't even lyin'."

I feel sorry for her, Yula thought. "God knows I feel sorry for that girl," she said aloud.

She also knew that Leslie wouldn't want everyone in her business. So Yula climbed out of bed a second time for the day, and was determined to find Leslie alone on campus. But when she looked over at the clock, the time read five-thirty.

"Damn, I was sleepin'! Leslie's probably ready to go to work by now." Then she smiled mischievously. "I'm hungry anyway."

But when Yula made it over to Hot Jake's restaurant, where Leslie worked, on Gentilly Boulevard, the staff told her that Leslie had called out for the day.

Yula thought, *Damn. Now I gotta pay for my food here.*

≈

Leslie rode the bus down to Saint Claude Street on a mission to see her father in person at the homeless shelter for the bone that she had to pick with him.

I can't believe he never told me, she continued to think to herself. She had her own ideas as to why her father never told her. But she still felt, *He should know me well enough to trust me!*

The Open Arms building was rather new, and Leslie had never felt embarrassed to have to see her father there. She understood that life was complicated, and she had had little time to cry about it. Crying had never changed much anyway. If it did, then Leslie figured her sister, Laetitia, would have become a princess to live in a fabulous castle of a thousand rooms with the way that she had cried over the years. But Leslie had no time for the countless tears. She wanted answers.

She strutted into the office room and said, "I'm here to see *Jahn-Pierre Bo-day,*" all pronounced correctly.

The woman behind the desk showed Leslie immediate respect because of her serious diction.

"You must be his daughter," she assumed. "The one in college."

"Yes, I am," Leslie told her.

The woman stood in a hot second and said, "I'll go get him from the rec room."

"Thank you," Leslie told her as she left.

Jean received word that his daughter was there to see him, and he hustled into the room to greet her with a loving hug and a kiss on the lips.

"Bonjour, ma chérie. A quoi dois-je cette visite imprévue?"—What's brought you here unexpectedly?—he asked her.

Leslie answered, *"Par amour et aussi pour des nouvelles."* Love and information. She made it clear that she wanted to speak to him in private when she angled herself toward the front door.

Jean responded, *"Je vois,"* I see, and led his daughter out.

When they walked outside, Leslie immediately told her father in English, "Mom is dying."

Jean paused and thought about it. Then he nodded and proceeded to walk forward with his daughter on the sidewalk. He said, "Anna has been dying a slow death eva' since I left the family. We both have." It was a truth that Jean had known for years.

Leslie responded, "Yes, but you don't have what she has." She stopped to look into her father's face before she continued, "You don't have AIDS."

Jean froze in his tracks and asked, *"Quoi?"* What?

Leslie explained it to him. "She was lonely. And she said that you hadn't touched her . . . for years, Daddy. What was she supposed to do?"

Jean said, "We are more than just sex-ual be-ings on this earth, Leslie. I wish more people unda-stood that." *Like you do,* he thought to himself. He realized that his first daughter had been turned *off* to sex, where his second daughter had been turned *onto* it.

Leslie said, "Yes, but we are all born to it, Daddy. It's normal to want somebody. And Mommy loved you. She still does."

Jean snapped, "And *I* love her. You know that I do, Leslie. *"Qu'est-ce que tu me racontes là?"* Why do you say this to me? He thought that he and his wife had had a mature understanding about things. He had to leave, or he would have . . . died there.

However, Leslie answered her father tartly, "Because she's dying in the hospital and you haven't even visited her."

Jean said, "I did not know that she was in a hos-pi-tal! *Je vais aller la voir immédiatement!*" I will go to see her immediately!

Leslie said, "She told me something else, too. Something that *you* never told me."

Jean became calm in his . . . irritation. Leslie was his treasured daughter. So he calmed himself before he would become . . . irrational. But he did not like her tone.

He asked her civilly, "And what was that?"

Leslie then calmed herself, knowing her father's temperament.

She asked him, "How come you never told me, Papa?"

"Told you what?" he snapped at her. His excitement in seeing her had ended.

Leslie said, "That I reminded you of my grandmother in Haiti . . . the Vaudou priestess. Is it in my blood? Tell me," she demanded of her father.

Jean looked into his daughter's hard-pressed eyes and stood tall in his defiance. *"C'est du charabia!"* That is nonsense! *"Je ne crois pas à ces choses."* I do not believe in such things, he told her.

"So how come you never told me that I looked like her?" Leslie pressed him.

It was a complicated question. In fact, it was so . . . complicated that Jean began to look around him to see who might have been listening in on them.

"Parle-moi en français." Speak to me in French, Jean told her.

Leslie studied her father's avoidance of the issue and decided to be defiant herself. Why had he made her wait for so long?

"It is true?" she asked him, still speaking in English.

"This is not the place to dis-cuss this," he told her pointedly. He then led his daughter into an alleyway. He said, "There are still many things that I do not under-stan about the religion of Vaudou in my homeland of Haiti. And I could not tell you what I did not know."

In his private thoughts, he pondered to himself, *I have always unda-estimated my wife, Anna-Marie. I told her that story one time . . . and she re-membered it! Maybe because it was meant to be told. But why after so many years? Why now! What is the ans-ser?*

Leslie asked her father, "So, that means that you can't teach me, then?"

She viewed him as greater than he even thought of himself. After all, he was her root to the earth. And without roots . . . there would be no branches.

"Teach you *what?*" Jean responded. Leslie had her father on his heels, which her mother could never do.

She answered, "To be a priestess."

Jean looked at his daughter incredulously. She was a determined beetle, one of the strongest of insects. So he repeated to her in French, *"Je ne peux pas t'apprendre ce que je ne sais pas."* I cannot teach you what I do not know.

Leslie asked him, "Are you sure?" and searched his eyes before she continued. "Because I was reading a book last night that explained that I should call on Ogun to protect me, and to teach me how to stay strong. And it said that Ogun is the god of war, who protects with fierceness . . . and with iron."

She stopped herself a second before she added, "Like you've done for me."

Jean took a deep breath and nodded to her. He said, "My child, ev'ry father should be O-gun when he needs to be. There is nothing special about that. The white mahn has carried his guns and cannons for a lonnng time now. And he has de-fended his daugh-ters and his sons. Fiercely!"

"And then little Haiti fought him back and won her freedom," Leslie reminded her father.

Jean nodded slowly to his daughter. He grinned, and was proud once again of his country's early independence from oppression, and of his daughter's knowledge of the history.

However, he stopped smiling when he told her, "Be care-ful of what you read about in these books, Leslie. Books can only re-late what some people *think* they know."

He looked into his daughter's eyes and said, "But life, life is the real tea-cher of things that are unknown." He then held his head up high and added, "Only now am I wise enough to under-stan the truth of things. And there have been many books . . . that have lied."

Leslie listened to him and remained convinced that her father knew more than what he had said.

≈≈≈

Leslie rode the bus back to campus to continue with her life and with her studies, while her father rushed to see his wife at Charity Hospital for his own accounting of what his daughter had told him.

And on the way back to her home near Dillard's campus, Leslie thought about everything, including the revelation that she had shared with Ayanna that day. Now she saw how unwise it was of her to present tests, and how out of character she had been in revealing things. Leslie viewed it as a semblance of her youth and immaturity.

No wonder my father didn't want me to know, she thought to herself ashamedly. Because power and immaturity, of any kind . . . was dangerous. Leslie understood that now. But it was too late to undo her mistake. So dealing with Ayanna became the new pressing issue on her mind. But when she arrived at home, instead of finding Ayanna, she ran smack into Yula, who had been dying to speak to her.

"Oh, my God, girl! I've been try'na to catch up with you since five o'clock!" Yula exclaimed. Then she spoke in a lowered tone. "You got a call from Charity Hospital today. They said for you to call them ASAP?"

Yula asked, "What's goin' on, Leslie? What's going on? And what can I do to help you?"

Leslie looked into her friend's face of sympathy and answered, "Nothing." She knew before she even made the phone call to the hospital . . . that her mother, Anna-Marie Cooke . . . had passed away, and without her father getting a chance to make . . . atonement . . . like she had done the night before.

Anna-Marie's Mourning

Jean-Pierre was still disturbed by his daughter's visit that day as he rode a taxi toward Charity Hospital in downtown New Orleans. Leslie had been doing just fine with her schooling, and her new college friends, who all had solid aspirations. So why had she suddenly become so . . . interested in Vaudou? What exactly had her mother told her? And more important, how had Anna-Marie fallen victim to AIDS?

Jean shivered at even the thought of the fatal disease. He had not involved himself with any drugs, let alone intravenous ones, and he had always been careful with his sexuality. Jean was a late bloomer by choice because of the fear of being denied his destiny. He did not want to impregnate a woman or to start a family in Haiti before he had had a chance to chase his dreams in America. Nor had he desired to fall for the first American woman who would bat her eyelashes in his direction. But just as his daughter had called him her *Ogun,* Anna-Marie had become Jean's *Erzulie,* the goddess of love.

Ann had been the youngest of three Cooke daughters. Both of her older sisters had married well-to-do American men, who showed much less melanin in their skin. The Cooke family viewed those marriages as good choices for the futures of the offspring. However, Jean-Pierre's melanin level was at the opposite end of the chart, and Anna-Marie was dark brown already. So there would be no move up for their children, or at least in the eyes of the melanin codes of New Orleans. Nevertheless, Ann grew to love Jean, and she wanted to marry him despite the inhibitions of her family.

Jean had even joked of how her family name fit perfectly with his lifelong trade and passion. And now . . . the thought of how their dreams together had been ruined brought fresh tears to his eyes as he rode in the backseat of the taxi. America had become their nightmare.

Jean then reflected on the many stories that he had forgotten of Haiti. His daughter Leslie had reminded him of his lost roots. And roots were easily lost in America, where children flocked so eagerly to blend in.

Blend in to what? Jean snapped to himself as he thought it over. There was no such thing as a melting pot in America. He was wise enough to know better now. America, the land of opportunity, had become an illusion. The real America was all about uneven competition. And in their apparent failure to stay afloat, Jean, his wife, and their children had received a bowl of rotten stew that had been poured out in the middle of the barren streets called the ghetto, where you melted in to misery until you became used to it.

Jean-Pierre Beaudet knew better than the lie now. He knew better! And he was right not to allow his daughter to know her real power in such a land that rotted its seeds. Because rotten seeds . . . would only produce rotten fruit. So Jean was afraid of what his daughter might do with power.

He remembered how he had run from it himself, the entire culture of Vaudou. And although he could still understand the language, Jean had even spurned the native Creole of his lower-class family in Haiti. He vowed instead to learn textbook French, and then English, so that he could become more worldly. But the aristocrats of Haiti had always been hostile to those born of lesser fortune. It seemed that privileged children had become that way in every culture. And the educated mulatto (mixed-race) students of Haiti never bothered to befriend Jean when he had taken college courses briefly at the University of Port-au-Prince. However, in America, Jean believed, it would all be different. In America, he believed, hard work and skill would eventually make him rich.

He knew better now. And he realized that the ugliness of class and poverty was a worldwide epidemic, and it was as torturous to the human soul as dying of AIDS.

"That's twelve dollars," the taxi driver told Jean as they pulled up to Charity Hospital.

Jean gave the black man a ten and a five, and waited patiently for his change.

The taxi driver gave him three one-dollar bills in change, slowly. He did not want to let go of it. Or at least not all of it. He figured that he deserved a tip.

But Jean took all of the change in his hands and mumbled a gruff

"Thank you" before he climbed out of the cab. He couldn't afford to tip.

Jean walked into the hospital and over to the information desk. He wanted to remain as insignificant as possible. Everyone realized that something was amiss whenever you were visiting the hospital, unless it was for the recovery of a loved one or for the arrival of a newborn baby. Sometimes newborn babies were not even welcomed, particularly by far too many impoverished men, who seemed to desire children much less than their unmarried girlfriends.

Jean asked the woman standing behind the information booth, "Do you have an Anna-Marie . . ." He paused a second and said, "*Cooke* in your residence?" He knew that his wife would not want to bring shame to his name. She was regal in that way, a very respecting woman. They still had the dignity of their children to protect.

The information clerk checked her computer screen before she looked back up to Jean, glumly. He read her eyes and awaited her words.

She asked, "And you are?"

"I'm her husband," he answered without hesitation. There was no more time for pride and for complications. He needed to see her, feel her skin, and beg her for his forgiveness.

But the woman behind the information booth paused before she responded to him. She said, "I'll be right with you, sir." Then she picked up the telephone to call the doctor and a nurse . . . to explain the situation to the man . . . with care.

≈

Leslie had gathered up her sister, Laetitia, and her two nieces, Renée and Anna, and took a cab from the Desire projects to catch their father at the hospital before he would leave. She also paged their brother, Pierre, with a 911 message of urgency to meet them at Charity Hospital for their mother. And when Leslie had arrived there at the downtown hospital with Laetitia and her two daughters in their arms, they found their father sitting with a nurse inside the waiting room, where he was reluctant to take his hands down from his face, and away from his burning eyes that were full of tears.

Leslie saw her father sitting there and paused. At least *she* had gotten a chance to laugh with her mother again. But Jean had been . . . robbed of Ann's last smile. And her smile had always been a beautiful sight to see.

Laetitia began to cry before she was even told what was going on. Leslie did not offer to tell her sister yet, just in case their mother had pulled through with some kind of a miracle. But it was only wishful thinking. So when Laetitia saw her father crying as he was, she knew instinctively that something had gone terribly wrong. And when Laetitia cried, her youngest daughter, Anna, cried with her, while Renée, the oldest, searched her young soul for the proper reaction. It was not tears that she felt, but questions that she needed answered. *What is everyone crying for? What is going on?*

Pierre walked in on them a minute later, and surprised everyone. They had gotten used to him being AWOL, ever since the first time that he had run away.

Pierre looked at his father sitting there in misery and asked the question that everyone was wondering, *"Qu'est-ce qu'il y a?"* What is the matter?

Jean finally looked up to answer the voice and question of his son and first child. He was proud that Pierre was there with them. However, he was not proud of his answer.

"Ta mère est morte." Your mother has left us.

Laetitia translated the French, and began to cry even louder.

Pierre ignored his baby sister's wailing as he had always done, and questioned the nurse who remained at his father's side.

"Well, what did she die from?" *I didn't even get a chance to see her like I said I would,* he told himself. And of course, he felt guilty about it.

The nurse figured to lessen the blow when she answered, "Pneumonia."

But Jean would not allow it. The truth needed to be told and dealt with. So he countered the nurse's move of humanity and responded, "She died of AIDS . . . and of a lack of love."

When he finished his words, his eyes met a spot on the floor below him . . . and they did not move from it. And then they *all* felt guilty.

≈

The hardest part of preparing for Anna-Marie's funeral was telling the extended Cooke family not only that she had died but what she had died of. And instead of Leslie being given that added duty, Pierre volunteered himself to inform them. He had been more familiar with the Cookes anyway. Pierre had always sought out their comfort whenever he could not find it at home. To his surprise, after their initial anger had simmered, the Cooke family came together and offered to pay the cost of the entire funeral, which Pierre found to be peculiar.

Wait a minute, he thought to himself. *They wouldn't help my mom out all these damn years just because of my father, but now they wanna pay for a grand funeral with a fancy casket and tombstone. Ain't that some shit!*

However, Pierre was damn sure going to allow it! It was the least that they could do after so many years of spite and indifference that they had shown his mother while she struggled. Or maybe she had rejected their offers in her own show of dignity. Nevertheless, the recollections of it all did not settle well on Pierre's mind.

The funeral was a week after Ann's death. And Laetitia could not believe how ugly she felt there. Her mother's extended family was eye-popping attractive to her. They surrounded her and her daughters in every shade of pretty brown skin imaginable. Some of them had gone full American Creole, while a few of them could even pass for white. And in Laetitia's eyes, with her self-esteem permanently damaged through her skin disorder, and the ill will of tactless children who had teased her, she felt that everyone in the room was three times prettier than she was, including her big sister, Leslie. So she held on tightly to her daughters to use them as a buffer against any extended conversation with anyone in the room.

Leslie realized her sister's low esteem and her fragile ego. So she decided to use herself as a buffer as well, to protect her next of kin, and her two nieces. Because children remembered things.

However, no one seemed to be all that concerned with Laetitia, nor with her children and her personal problems. They seemed not to care at all about her. The Cookes were ignoring Laetitia, just as they had ignored her mother. The funeral became an extension of their ignorance. But on the other hand, they seemed to be extremely concerned about Leslie, the college daughter . . . and all of her aspirations.

"So, what are you studying in school, Leslie?"

Straight face. "International business."

Smile. "O-o-oh, that's nice. What year are you in?"

"My sophomore year."

Nod. "Do you still speak French fluently?"

Grin. "Yes."

Smile. "That's beautiful. I bet you're still getting good grades, too. Aren't you?"

Smile back. "I try my best, you know."

Observation. "And your hair and skin always looks so . . . beautiful. It's so . . . radiant."

Slight grin. "Thank you."

Politeness. "Oh, and you look nice today, too, Lah-tee-ya."

Huge smile. "Oh, thank you."

Leslie's correction. "It's Lah-tee-see-ah."

More politeness. "Oh, okay. Lah-tee-see-ah. And are these your two daughters?"

Still smiling. "Yes."

Pensive nod. "Oh . . . okay."

End of politeness. Back to the main subject. "So, Leslie, do you plan to stay in America, or travel the world, when you get out of school? International business sounds so . . . exciting."

Leslie didn't even know most of their names. They barely saw her. However, she could imagine plenty about them. She could read them. Leslie was a pro at reading people. It was her strongest mode of protection while living in the 'hood. Hard living had some advantages. And since the Cookes had always scorned the choice that her mother made in marrying her Haitian father, Leslie had never cared much for her American relatives.

Once everyone had settled down and filled into the aisles for the funeral to begin, inside the large church that many of the Cookes had attended, near Lake Pontchartrain (including Anna-Marie when she was young), her husband, Jean-Pierre, was still a no-show.

As the nuclear family of Beaudets sat in the front pews for the closest family members, Laetitia leaned and asked Leslie if she felt their father would come. After all, it was his wife's funeral.

Leslie was beginning to wonder about that herself. The Cookes had never liked Jean to begin with, and the Beaudets could all imagine how less they liked him now. Their viperous tongues were surrounding them, even while in church.

Leslie answered, "I don't know." However, she had read in her new book that in the religion of Vaudou, a ceremony of death was to be taken very seriously.

Pierre had his own doubts about their father attending. *I know I wouldn't want to be here if I was him,* he mused to himself. *It seems like they hate him in here . . . That's fucked up!*

Then he turned to his sister Laetitia. "I see that your boy, Jurron, didn't make it out here either, hunh?"

Laetitia had no comment. She was doing all that she could not to complain about anything. It was the only way she figured she could keep Jurron . . . in the long run. So she had learned to accept his short spurts of absence.

However, Leslie would not allow her brother to act as if he was innocent of inexcusable absences. "We all need to learn how to stick around when things get tough, Pete," she told him.

Pierre got the message . . . and he shut his trap as if Leslie was the oldest.

After everyone had viewed Anna-Marie's body—which was covered in white—and they had said their words, shared their tears, and mumbled their prayers, Jean-Pierre Beaudet made his grand entrance, wearing a spotless dark suit and a colorful tie of African kente cloth. He had gotten a close shave and an American haircut, long on top and close on the sides, that made him look fifteen years younger. But his late show at the funeral gave the viperous family members more of a reason to hiss and to shuffle in their seats when he walked in.

Jean ignored them, just as they had done with him, his wife, and their young children for so many years. He walked straight up to Anna-Marie's body, lying inside the fancy casket, and he leaned down to kiss her on the lips, with a proclamation in English, so that all of her extended Cooke family could understand him.

He said, "Anna . . . I love you to-day. I loved you yes-terday. And I will love you still tomorrow. And as you rest now . . . far a-way from this place . . . I will count the days until we are to-gether a-gain . . . and in each other's arms."

As he turned to walk out for a grand exit, he looked toward Leslie only briefly, and she knew exactly what to do.

Leslie stood up to stop the hissing while grabbing Laetitia's oldest daughter, Renée, and pulling her up and into her arms. Then she looked back to Laetitia.

"Let's go," she told her younger sister forcefully.

Laetitia wiped her tear-filled eyes, nodded her head, and stood up to leave with her second daughter, Anna, in her arms. Then Laetitia looked back at Pierre. "You comin'?" she asked him.

Pierre took a breath and looked around into the eyes of his disapproving aunts, uncles, and cousins. Then he stood to his feet defiantly and told himself, *Fuck it. This my family.*

The Beaudets marched out of the church together. Outside they found that their father had rented his own black limousine.

When they all had climbed inside and closed the doors, Jean smiled charmingly to his children and proceeded to pull out a doll from inside of his suit jacket, a doll that had been designed in the likeness of his wife, their mother, and his grandchildren's grandmother.

He said with the doll held up in his right hand, "Anna is smiling with us now. And don't worry. They can bury her bod-dee in the dirt on their own. The bod-dee is nothing but a form of dirt that we live in. But we have her soul . . . and we have her love. And she tells me that she will love us al-ways.

"Now," he told his children and granddaughters, "my old friend Jake has al-lowed me to cook my own meal at his res-taurant. And he has closed it down for the day, in honor of my wife, Anna. And we will all go there now and eat . . . as one family."

Laetitia grinned the widest. She was tickled by her father's young look, and by his spirited energy. She thought to herself, *This is the daddy that I used to know before he got sick from his kidneys . . . And I love him when he's like this! I'm just mad that I was so . . . afraid of him when I was younger. But he's a good man. He really is.*

Man
Problems

At Hot Jake's restaurant, Jean finished with his prayers, joined by his three children and two granddaughters, who all sat around him at a large table in the empty dining room with their heads bowed and their eyes closed.

"And may the great One, who we all know as the cre-ay-tor of all things, bless the food that we eat, and bless our one fam-milee to remain healthy and strong."

However, when his only son, Pierre, opened his eyes again, while sitting behind a hot plate of food, all that he could think about was the voodoo doll that his father had created in the likeness of his mother. It sat out on the table as they proceeded to eat. And Pierre had lost his appetite.

"Let me go to the bathroom," he said out loud to his family.

Jean looked over at Anna's doll and nodded his head in its direction.

He told his son, "Your mother excuses you."

Pierre looked at his father and grimaced. Then he looked around the room to make sure that Jake had not heard his father's comment from the kitchen.

Laetitia found it all humorous and began to chuckle, along with her daughters. And Leslie watched her brother, noticing his sour mood. Pierre didn't seem to be pleased with things.

"Aw'ight," he grumbled as he stood from the table and made his way to the rest room.

When Pierre strolled near the kitchen area on his way to the rest room, he spotted Jake chomping down on his own plate of Jean's food.

Jake grinned and mumbled, "Boy, your father can still cook his ass off. Goddamn he can cook! You need to take some lessons yourself, junior," he teased.

Pierre smirked and went on about his business. When he reached the bathroom, he looked into the mirror there and shook his head, knowing that he didn't have to go.

He mumbled to himself, "He out here acting crazy now, wit dis voodoo shit. Fuck is wrong wit him? Mom dyin' den took him over the edge. Shit!"

So Pierre waited there inside the bathroom, stalling for time. When he finally walked out, he bumped into someone and was startled, thinking that his father had followed him and had heard him in the bathroom.

"Shit!" he exclaimed as he jumped back. But it was only his sister Leslie.

She asked him in French, *"Quel est ton problème?"* What is your problem?

Pierre took a calming breath before he answered her. "Come on, Leslie, he's in here losing his damn mind." He looked at his sister intently and asked her in a whisper, "Whassup wit dis voodoo shit, man? Whassup wit dat?"

Leslie remained poised. It was halfway her fault for reminding her father of things.

She said, "He'll get over it. He just—"

"Naw, man, this is crazy," Pierre commented, cutting his sister off. "I'm not gon' sit out there to eat wit dat damn doll sittin' out on the table like that, man. What if Mr. Jake sees that shit?"

Leslie couldn't help but grin. Her brother was embarrassed by it. But then she stared at him and said, "You don't seem to be taking Mom's death all that seriously, Pierre. All she ever wanted was to have a dinner with all of us together again, like we are now. But everything is always about what *you* feel, or what *you* want.

"You are so selfish, Pierre," she snapped at him. "You've always been that way."

Pierre said, "Leslie, how you gon' tell me how I feel? What, you think *I* don't hurt just because I ain't cryin' like everybody else. I'm hurtin' too, man. I'm hurtin' too. But I ain't goin' crazy wit it, like . . . like he is."

Leslie continued to stare at him. Pierre had always been a runaway kid, and there was no way that she could miraculously change him now.

She said, "All I'm asking you to do is finish this dinner with us, Pierre. That's all I'm asking you. Do it for Mom," she told him. *And do it for me,* she told herself. *Because you still owe me.*

Pierre looked at his sister and calmed himself down. He realized that he was in debt . . . to everyone. So he had no choice.

"Aw'ight, man. I just hope he don't start talkin' to that damn doll no more."

Whatever, Leslie thought to herself. *As long as you do what you're supposed to do as a member of this family.* Then she told her brother out loud, "And it's *Vaudou* or *Vo-dou,* and not *voodoo.* That's America's *witchcraft* word."

Pierre turned to his sister and responded, "Whatever, man. We are American. We ain't never even been to Haiti." And he walked out on her, leaving Leslie there to assess his words.

Pierre made his way back to the dining table to try and finish his plate of food in light of his father's . . . distraction.

Leslie thought alone for a minute before she walked out to follow him. Her brother's words had struck a nerve. She told herself, *He's right. America is all that we really know. New Orleans. Or better yet, N'awlins, the black parts . . . So maybe I ought to go visit Haiti one day.* She nodded to herself and concluded out loud in French, *"Et je dois y aller." And I will go.*

When Leslie had made it back to the table, she watched her brother forcing down his food, while Laetitia and her daughters continued to enjoy their father's company.

Jean spotted Leslie on her way back to the table and said, "Hurry, Leslie, and take your seat to finish your meal. Your mother says that your food is get-ting cold now."

Leslie grinned and looked at Pierre.

Pierre stopped eating and shook his head with a frown.

Seeing that, Leslie decided to increase her brother's embarrassment. She spoke right at the doll and said, "Don't worry, Mom. We're all here together now, and we love you."

Then she sent her nieces into an uproar of laughter when she picked up the doll of her mother from the table and kissed its lips.

Their father nodded in approval. Laetitia began to laugh with her daughters. And Pierre turned up his nose in outrage.

Leslie thought to herself, *So what? Pierre is just gonna have to deal with who we are.*

≈≈≈

"So, how's the family taking everything, Leslie?" Jake asked her back in the kitchen area of his restaurant the next workday.

Leslie answered him while continuing to focus on her entrée preparations.

"We're still all hanging in there, you know."

Jake said, "Well, whatever your family needs, I'm here to help out in whatever way that I can."

Leslie nodded to him. "Okay. Thank you. I'll let you know."

As usual, she had a million thoughts that ran through her mind as she worked. She still had not had an opportunity to talk to Ayanna about . . . their secret. But since Yula and Bridget had not brought up anything to her about it, Leslie figured that Ayanna actually could keep her mouth shut for a change. Or maybe they were all giving Leslie some needed space and peace of mind after the loss of her mother . . . from cancer, as Leslie had told them.

Then she thought about her father, and wondered how long he would mourn their mother, and about how open he now was with them about the native beliefs of Haiti. As her brother, Pierre, had already mentioned, Leslie wondered if their father's thoughts on his wife's death would become a concern that she would have to keep a close eye on.

However, Pierre was still himself. He was as single-minded as he wanted to be, a born and practicing nomad. Leslie even shook her head and mumbled about her brother out loud, "That damn boy . . ."

Laetitia and her daughters had all had a great time with the family. Not that they didn't cry and feel sorrow about the loss. However, Leslie could not remember the last time that her sister had interacted with their father as well as she had done with him after the funeral. Leslie figured that it would be a good thing to push the two of them closer together. Laetitia, Renée, and Anna could all use a new understanding of fatherhood in their lives, in light of their situation. Leslie vowed that it was a great idea!

I should even stop by to visit Laetitia tonight, she thought to herself. *But then again, I don't want that damn boy of hers to know that I'm coming. I haven't been around him in a while. And I need to catch him at the house with Tee and the girls to see how he treats them.*

So when it was time to call it a night from the job, instead of going back to her shared college house to rest up for her classes the next morning, Leslie found herself on another bus ride to the Desire projects to see her sister, her two nieces, and her nieces' father, all unexpectedly.

And the same bullshit as usual went on with the juveniles who rode the back of the public bus that night. They were talking loud and ignorantly, while continuing to disrespect the elders and the children.

Even the bus driver that night had heard enough. He pulled the bus over to the curb, put it in park, and stood up to walk to the back where all of the commotion was.

The solidly built black man said real calmly in the middle of the aisle, "Now look . . . I've had about enough of this bullshit tonight. Ya hear me? Now the next time I stop this damn bus, I'm gon' call the cops t' take your asses home. Now try me!"

But no sooner than the bus driver turned his back to return to his driver's seat, one of the boys gave him the middle finger and launched his rowdy friends into mocking laughter.

The bus driver ignored it and went back to drive. He had a schedule to keep.

Just two more hours, he told himself. *Just two more hours.*

Someone said, "Dat ma-fucka mad 'cause he only a bus driver in life. He makin' bus fare to live."

That's when Leslie decided to face them from her seat. She was tired of ignoring their shit! So she asked them, "And what are you doing with your life? Any of y'all?"

"Mmm, hmmm." The elders on the bus backed her with their approval. Somebody had to say something to them. The bus driver had to drive.

The boys looked Leslie over and were turned on by her . . . audacity to raise her voice at them. And they were prepared to show her why people left them the hell alone.

"Nobody was talkin' to her black ass," one of them mumbled out of view.

Leslie said, "Well, *I'm* talkin' to you. And why you gotta hide when you say it? Punk!"

She knew the language of boys, and how to call them out.

So the boys looked around and started instigating. "Oooh, she called you a punk. I wouldn't take that shit, man. I wouldn't take that shit."

Leslie looked the instigator right in his eyes and said, "You a punk, too. Now what do you wanna do?"

Leslie thought, *Shit! I just lost my damn mom to this ghetto shit, and if I have to join her in the grave tonight, then I'm just gon' have to go there! Because I'm not gon' fuckin' live like this no more. Fuck that!*

She inadvertently stood up and undid her jacket as if she was ready to throw down immediately. But one of the older women on the bus touched her arm ever so lightly.

"They got the message, young sister. They got the message."

Leslie looked into the woman's wise, brown face, and calmed herself.

She took a deep breath and meditated on her peace of mind before she reclaimed her seat. And as soon as the boys began to respond to it, the older woman cut them short with perfect timing and tact.

She said, "Sometimes in life, we don't know who or what we're dealing with until it's too late, and I feel a need to stop something . . . before it happens. So I would advise you boys to let her be. Right now."

A sudden hush fell over them. No one dared to speak. Because the truth had been spoken. So the boys did nothing but wiggle their fingers and wait, until they felt safe enough to run their mouths again. That old woman didn't seem so normal to them anyway. She seemed . . . spooky. It was something about how she spoke and how she looked that made them obedient to her.

In the new silence of the bus, the older woman touched Leslie's shoulder from the seat directly behind her. She said, "Keep the *love* in your heart, young sister. Don't be pulled to the *other side*," she added, as if speaking in riddles. "There may be no way back from it."

Leslie responded to her without turning her head. "I'm trying," she said out loud. *And I think I'm losing,* she thought to herself.

The older woman said, "Well, you keep trying . . . This too shall pass . . . It all will."

Leslie nodded again, and faked agreement with the woman. But inside, she continued to think to herself in her young, urgent reality, *It's not gonna pass. And I'm tired of hearing that shit! So I'm not gonna ignore what I feel anymore . . . I'm not!*

≈≈

Leslie was exhausted by the time she reached Laetitia's dark project building. She could sense that she was losing her tolerance for everything. Her mental stamina was running out. Maybe visiting her sister at Desire that night was not such a great idea after all. Maybe she should have just . . . called her.

As Leslie ascended the stairs toward Laetitia's apartment, her bad instincts about surprising her sister that night were confirmed.

"Who in nare wit chall?" a drunken man was screaming into Laetitia's locked door. *"Well, where y'all mother at?"*

Leslie panicked at the sight of him and went into full drama mode. She yelled fiercely at him, "The *fuck* are you doin'?" and shoved the man away from the door.

He tumbled backward and fell into the dark hallway. He stuttered from the floor, while looking up in surprise at Leslie, "I, I, I wah, I wus jus' try'na help somebody out. Wha, wha, whatchew push me down for . . . girl?"

The man was reeking of alcohol. But Leslie had to ignore him and see what was going on inside her sister's apartment. That's when she heard her nieces screaming at the top of their lungs from behind the locked door.

"Mom-meeee! Mom-meeee! I want my mom-meeee!"

"Renée! It's Auntie Leslie! *Bonjour, ma petite nièce!*"—Hello, my little niece—Leslie said through the door. And she waited for the response.

"Bonjour, ma grande tante"—Hello, my big aunt—Renée answered her calmly. Fortunately, she was an early talker who learned fast.

"Bon-jour, ma grande tante," her sister, Anna, mimicked her.

Leslie became delirious. She was halfway between feeling pride that her nieces were learning French and outraged that her sister had left them there at home by themselves.

The drunken man rose to his feet inside the dark hallway and asked, "What language you speakin' di dem?"

Leslie answered, "French." Then she asked him if he lived there. She realized that she needed his help.

He said, "Yeah, I live here. I live in apartment two twelve. But my ol' lady locked me out tha' doe' right now. But I know she l'ah me," he offered with a nod. "She l'ah me! I know she do!"

Leslie nodded to him. "I guess you can't get back in the house, then. Does anybody have a master key to these apartments?" she asked.

"Ah . . . tha' superintendent. But he won't be back here till demar."

Shit! Leslie cursed to herself. She looked at the door and wondered if she was strong enough to kick it in, but it was double bolted to discourage those who had ideas of ill will, as well as to ward off the frequent robberies that went on inside the projects. Desire wasn't a place where people could expect to have their valuables voluntarily protected by their neighbors. Or not anymore at least. Nor were the city police around to protect property. They served only to lock people up, after things had gotten out of hand.

"I want my mom-meee," Leslie's nieces continued to whine. At least they were calmer now.

Leslie lied and told them, "Mommy's coming. She's on her way. OK, *ma petite nièce?*"

Renée answered, "O-K . . . *ma tante.*"

Leslie thought to herself, *I'm gonna whip Laetitia's ass!*

"Mom-meeee," Anna whined a second later. "Mom-meeee," she repeated more intently.

It was torture. Leslie slid to the floor with her back pressed up against the door and continued to breathe, using more of her ghetto yoga to remain calm.

"I'm here, Anna. I'm here," she told her youngest niece. "It's Aunt Leslie. I love you. OK? *Je t'aime.*"

"*Je t'aime,*" Renée responded for her sister.

The drunken man looked down and asked Leslie in amazement, "What ah . . . what chew gon' do? You just gon' stay down nere and talk dat French to 'em?"

Leslie looked at the man and asked him, "What else can I do?"

He was about to tell her to climb through the outside window. But then he said, "*I* know who she talks to. Ah . . . Lateesha, right? Dat's dare mother's name," the man remembered despite his inebriation. "She's da girl wit da . . . da spots on her skin. She got a skin disease, right?"

Leslie took another breath and was ready to scorn the man. She was fed up with people identifying her sister in that way.

She answered him anyway. "Yes, she's my sister." Talking to the drunken man had allowed her to maintain her sanity at the moment. She didn't know how she would act if he was not there. His presence created a support mechanism for her, or least until someone sober came along.

The man finally told her, "She's friends with Betty down the hall in apartment two twenty-eight. I'll go get her for you."

Leslie looked surprised for a second. A drunken man was going to her rescue. So what could she say but "Thanks" as she continued to wait on the floor, while calming her nieces through the door with her words.

Leslie told herself, *This is crazy! Ever since we moved into this . . . bullshit, I've always had some crazy shit to go through before the night was over. But if I never came over here . . . then what could have happened to my nieces if I was not here to calm them down? And how many times has Laetitia done this shit anyway?*

Leslie mumbled to herself out loud, "I'm gon' find out tonight. I swear to God I am!"

To her surprise again, the drunken man headed back in her direction with help.

"Oh my God! Did they wake up?" a wide-bodied woman in her thirties asked, covered in only a light blue nightgown. She had keys in her hands.

Did they wake up? Leslie exclaimed to herself before she responded uncivilly to the woman. She climbed back to her feet and allowed the woman to open the door with the keys.

The woman explained, "Laetitia told me to keep an eye out for them, but they were sleepin' when I left, and I didn't think that she would be gone for this long."

Leslie looked back toward the woman's apartment and noticed a man standing in the doorway. He wore nothing but boxer shorts, with a fresh cigarette in his hands.

Hmm, mmm, Leslie thought to herself. *She had to go on back and get her fuck on while watching after somebody's damn kids, right? That's some ghetto shit! That's just what I'm talking about!*

Leslie pushed her way inside the opened apartment and immediately hugged her nieces, kissing all over their wet faces of tears and snot.

"I'm here, babies. I'm here," she told them.

Her nieces hugged her for dear life, and wouldn't let go.

The woman with the keys in hand watched and nodded. She said, "Well, you got 'em now. So I'll jus' go on back to my place. And you're Leslie, right? Her older sister?"

Leslie answered, "Yes," with her nieces still in her arms.

The woman smiled and said, "I noticed you from the pictures. Laetitia always talks about you. You're even prettier in real life than in the pictures."

The drunken man heard that and grinned from the doorway where he stood.

"Unh, hunh, she, she sure do," he stuttered in agreement.

At the moment, Leslie was not amused by it. She asked the woman, "How many times has Laetitia left out like this? Your name is Betty, right?"

Leslie had never met the woman before, but the drunken man had mentioned her name when he went to get her.

"Unh hunh," Betty mumbled to her with a nod. She gave Leslie the respect of an adult. Leslie carried herself with a certain seriousness in her tone. And Betty realized that she didn't look too . . . responsible at that moment.

"And you keep a set of her keys in your house?" Leslie assumed, from how Betty held on to them.

"Yeah," she answered.

"So my sister does this a lot, then?"

Betty started to speak. "Well, she, ah . . ." She stopped in midsentence and looked back at the door. She said, "Mitch, could you excuse us for a minute? Now I thank you for coming to get me like you did, but this is gettin' personal now."

Mitch nodded his head and backed away from the open door.

"Oh, I unnerstan'. I'm, I'm, I'm jus' . . . glad I wus able da help out."

"Thank you," Leslie faced him and told the man again.

"Anytime," he told her as he smiled with stained teeth.

While Betty showed him away from the door, she looked up the hall-way toward her company for the night. "I'll be right there," she told him. "Wait one minute. Okay? Don't leave me. I'm comin'."

Leslie shook her head and thought, *She's pitiful!* before Betty could catch her frown.

"Now like I was sayin'," Betty started up again after she had shut the door back, "I have a set of Laetitia's keys, and she has a set of mine, just for emergencies, you know. But Mitch don't need to know all that."

"Well, what would have happened if he hadn't come to get you?" Leslie asked her.

She had Betty on the spot.

"Well, I would have checked back up on 'em eventually."

"After you finished getting your fuck on, right?" Leslie asked her tartly. She was getting tired of toning down her words, too, even while around her nieces that night.

Betty looked at her with a pause. *Did she just say what I think she just said?* she asked herself. She began to chuckle in embarrassment.

"I don't think it's funny myself," Leslie commented to her.

Betty stopped laughing. She explained on the defensive, "Well, your li'l sister's been havin' man problems. And she's been out here chasin' around that li'l . . . nigga of hers, and ain't been takin' care of the children right." She stopped herself momentarily and said, "And excuse my French, but since we havin' a candid, adult discussion in here—"

Leslie cut her off and said, "First of all, the word 'nigga' is not French. Second of all, if you're speaking about somebody my nieces know too well, then I would advise you not to call him that in their presence, whether he is or not. It's a general respect thing."

Betty looked confused. She responded, "Well, he ain't showin' ya' sister no respect."

"And how much respect are you getting?" Leslie snapped at her.

Betty just happened to be in the wrong place at the wrong time with the wrong person, while being caught doing the wrong damn thing on the wrong damn night!

She said, "Well, you know what . . . I think it's time for me to go," and started marching toward the door. "And you can keep these goddamned keys of hers!" she added, and pulled them off her key chain ring to throw on the floor at Leslie's feet.

The last word was dangerously important for some people. So Leslie stood there with her nieces still in her arms and thought, *Go ahead. Call me a bitch. So I can fuck your fat ass up! I need a fight right now!*

However, Betty played it safe that night and kept on walking.

Leslie waited at the doorway until the pissed-off woman had reached her apartment and slammed her door with her company in tow. Leslie then picked up the keys and locked Laetitia's door before taking her nieces to bed. They had suffered from the sins of enough grown-ups for one night. Or pretend-to-be grown-ups. And the girls needed to rest, and to dream of nicer things.

So Leslie washed them up, changed them into fresh, clean clothes, and sang to them in their beds, a song that someone had sung to her, when she had been young and distressed.

"I-I-I gues-s-s you-u-u say / What can make meee feel this way? / My gir-r-r-rls / I'm talkin' 'bout, my-y-y little girls . . ."

Visualization . . .

As soon as the girls fell asleep in their room, Leslie waited on Laetitia's living room sofa until 1 A.M., and then 2 A.M., before she fell asleep at nearly three o'clock in the morning.

Laetitia eased her way in the door well after three and was pleased that everything was quiet, safe, and sound, until she noticed her sister, Leslie, resting on her sofa.

"Shit, Leslie! What are you doin' here? You scared the hell outta me!"

Leslie opened her eyes calmly and said, "The question is, what are you *not* doing here?"

To Laetitia's good fortune, Leslie had exceeded her energy limit for the night and was now reserved to get the plain facts of the matter rather than to whip her sister's ass, like she planned to do at eleven, twelve, one, and even two o'clock that night.

Laetitia took a seat next to her big sister and answered, "This new bitch is trying to take Jurron from me. So I had to go find out some information on her. 'Cause I might have to hurt her ass."

Leslie looked her sister in the face and knew better. Laetitia had been afraid of fighting her entire life. She was too busy trying to be . . . loved by someone. And Leslie told her so.

"Tee, you're not gonna do a damned thing to that girl, and in the meantime, you out here leaving my nieces with some woman who was pressed to get her little . . . screw on."

Laetitia smiled. "Who, Betty?" Then she frowned and asked, "She had somebody in here?"

Leslie answered, "No, but she locked your daughters in here while she went back to her own place to fuck. And the shit is not funny. So I had words with that woman. And I never even met her before, but she had my nieces in here, crying and banging on the door for you, and I didn't appreciate that shit.

"Now what's going on with you?" she asked. "You wanna lose your two kids now?. We just lost Mom."

Laetitia took a breath and looked defeated. "I don't know what to do anymore, Leslie. I mean . . . I love Jurron. And after being with Daddy after the funeral and all, I jus' . . . I jus' wanted to get my own family in order. So that's when I started tryin' to find out who this girl is, because Jurron's not even comin' back home now."

Leslie paused and pondered the situation. "What did you find out?" she asked.

Laetitia got excited. She said, "I got her phone number. I know where she works. And she lives right over in the Florida projects."

Leslie thought, *Damn! He's gonna up and leave my sister for another project chick? What the hell is the use? I don't understand these guys sometimes.*

She asked her sister, "What she look like?"

Laetitia frowned at the question. "You know, typical light skinned, fat ass . . . you know what guys like." Then she looked at Leslie again. "They like you, though. You know, 'cause you special lookin' for a dark sistah."

Leslie huffed, "Look, these ignorant assholes out here still call me black." But then she redirected the conversation. "So, what do you want to do to this girl?" she asked Laetitia.

Laetitia paused and started smiling wider than she should.

She answered, "Umm . . . maybe I can work up some of our voodoo stuff on her."

Leslie looked and asked, "What do you mean, our voodoo stuff?"

Laetitia began to whisper. "You know . . . we're Haitian, Leslie."

Leslie maintained her poise and showed her little sister nothing more than a poker face. Laetitia was far too immature to know anything. And Leslie damn sure was not planning on leading her anywhere in their conversation but to a dead end.

She said, "We're American, girl. Daddy's Haitian. And we don't know shit about it. Ain't even been there before."

Laetitia sucked her teeth and said, "I know, but I was just . . . thinkin' about it, you know."

Leslie became curious. She asked her sister, "So, what would you do with it if you had it?"

Laetitia smiled again. She answered, "I'd scare the fuck out of her at first, to make her leave my man alone. And if that don't work, then I'd put a curse on her ass or something to make her look real ugly. Or make her go crazy or something."

Leslie couldn't help it. She laughed out loud. "Girl, you're the one who's crazy!"

But Laetitia didn't laugh at it. She said, "I'm serious, Leslie. I've been thinkin' about it."

That's when Leslie got serious. She thought, *Obviously, Daddy pulling out that doll of Mom like he did after the funeral must've had an effect on this girl.*

She asked, "How long have you been thinking about this?" to make sure.

Laetitia surprised her when she answered, "I've been thinkin' 'bout it for years. I mean, wouldn't it be the shit if we had like . . . some power to make people do what we want? I always thought about that. I jus' never told nobody."

Damn! Leslie thought to herself. *And I thought that I was the only one.* However, she maintained her calm logic with her sister.

"Everybody thinks about stuff like that, Tee. But that don't mean we can do it. So you might as well get that shit off your mind," she told her.

Laetitia looked at her and became frustrated. She said, "I gotta do *something,* Leslie. This girl fuckin' wit my life. Jurron is all I got."

Leslie said, "He is not all you have. And you need to stop saying that shit. That's why he gets away with all the shit he does now!" she exclaimed. "You need to stop that shit, Laetitia. Jurron is just one fuckin' guy!"

Leslie had found new energy in their argument, and she was rapidly losing her cool again.

Laetitia teared up and yelled, "He is all I got! I'm not in school like you, Leslie. And people don't like me like they like you. And you know how much I love Jurron," she whined as fresh tears rolled down her face.

Leslie pitied her sister, but she was growing tired of the sympathy game too. She said real coldly, "Laetitia, you've made up excuses your whole fuckin' life, and you don't do nothing but dig yourself deeper and deeper into every fuckin' hole, and then try to act like somebody owes you something. Well they don't! And I understand that you've had it bad because of your vitiligo and everything, but I'm a tell you something, I ain't had no fuckin' Barbie doll house, either! And it's a lot of shit that I go through every day that you don't know about. But you don't care about me. Nobody gives a fuck about what I'm going through!" she spat at her sister in a tirade. "And I don't ask for this drama shit like you do, nor do I fuckin' cry about it all the time!"

Laetitia took it all in and broke into heavy tears like she was used to doing.

She whined, "Why you talkin' to me like this, Lez-leee? All I want is my maannn back."

Leslie stood up from the sofa and yelled into her sister's face, "That boy ain't the fuckin' world, girl! God, you just like Mom!"

When Laetitia curled into a ball and hid her face of tears behind her hands on the sofa, Leslie looked up to the ceiling and realized that it was no use.

She thought, *If I don't get this boy back for this girl, she gon' ruin Renée and Anna's lives, and fuck up mine, too, when I can't stop worrying about them. And I need to be concentrating on school! But this shit is all gonna fall in my lap if I don't handle it. And this girl is gonna bring me down with her.*

Shit! Leslie cursed herself. *I should have just buckled down and kicked Laetitia's ass a long time ago for all of this weak whining and shit! But now she's about to drive me crazy!*

≈≈≈

Leslie barely got a full hour of sleep that night. She sat still on Laetitia's sofa in the dark, long after her sister had gone to bed. All that Leslie could think about was her mother's angry words to her from her hospital bed: ". . . you can work all you wanna work, but if you ain't *meant* to be rich, you ain't gon' *be* rich."

And there she was, sitting up in the projects, no less, with her sister and her nieces, while she had classes to attend in just a few hours.

Leslie shook her head and continued to defy her mother, even from the grave.

"I'm not like you," she told herself out loud. "And I'm gonna do whatever I need to do to survive . . . Whatever I need to do," she insisted.

Then she spotted the folded piece of paper that her sister had left on the coffee table. Leslie picked it up, opened it, and read the name, "Phyllis."

Is this the girl? she thought to herself of Laetitia's adversary. Then she did the unthinkable. She picked up the telephone and dialed the handwritten phone number after five o'clock in the morning!

As the phone rang, she read the rest of Laetitia's notes on the paper, which listed the girl's job location at Popeyes, the bus she caught to and from work, and even the building that she lived in at the Florida projects.

I guess Laetitia was serious, Leslie thought to herself. Then someone answered the phone, an irritated woman.

"Hel-low."

Leslie maintained her poise. "Can I speak to Jurron?"

There was a slight pause. "Who the hell is this?"

"I just need to speak to Jurron."

"Do you know what fuckin' time it is?"

"I know that Jurron has a family. Do you know that? When is he coming home to his kids?"

"When he fuckin' gets ready, like any other grown man."

"So, you do know that he has a family, then?" Leslie asked her.

"And . . . so does the fuckin' president," the woman snapped. "Look, who the fuck is this? If you want to discuss this for real, then you can call me during daylight hours. Because this shit here is childish!"

"And what do you call taking somebody's father at night?" Leslie countered.

"I call it mindin' my own fuckin' business! And if he wasn't supposed to be here, then he wouldn't be!"

Leslie said real civilly, "Look, Phyllis, I'm just trying to get you to do what's right. So have your fun with Jurron or whatever, stay protected if you need to, and then you send him back home to his family."

And Phyllis . . . laughed at Leslie's logic. She said, "I like your motherfuckin' nerve. Shit, ain't nobody out here did me those kind of favors. So I'm gon' do whatever I need to do to get what I want, jus' like everybody else does."

"But it's not always about what you want. I mean, don't you come from somebody's family? This is about respect," Leslie reasoned with her. She was surprised that the woman had even remained on the phone that long.

Phyllis responded, "Look, li'l girl, because you're obviously immature, so let me explain something to you. A man is gonna do what he wants to do. And if he was satisfied at home, then he would stay at home. So evidently, this here is not my problem, it's *your* problem. So get a fuckin' grip!" And she finally hung up the phone in Leslie's ear.

Leslie let the dial tone linger in her ear before she hung up the phone. She looked around her sister's apartment in the coldness of the living room and thought to herself, *Laetitia's right for a change* . . . Then she mumbled out loud, "I'm gonna have to kill this damn girl."

Either that, or she's gon' end up killing us, she pondered. *Because we can't sit around and take no more of this ghetto shit!* So Leslie studied the information on Laetitia's sheet of paper. And she folded it back to place it where she had found it . . . as if it had never been touched.

≈≈

Time could not move fast enough for Leslie. First she needed to see the girl. So she showed up to order a Popeyes chicken dinner at the location where Phyllis worked. And there she was, wearing the name tag PHYLLIS and standing front and center, while she asked Leslie for her order.

Leslie prepared her camouflaged speech and went to work on her mark, while wearing the homeliest clothes that she could find in her closet, with a baseball cap to hide her long hair under.

"Gimme, umm, dat umm, umm, chicken wit da number, umm, three."

Phyllis looked up at the order board and asked, "The tenderloins dinner?"

Leslie studied her face. She wasn't all that pretty, just light skinned, with bruises and blemishes on her face from hard living. Her nose was even crooked and out of line with her forehead and chin. And her lips were too dark for her face, as if she had done too much smoking, sucking, or both.

Leslie figured from the first sight of her that she couldn't touch Laetitia. If only Laetitia could feel more . . . secure about herself, she would realize that she could still put many girls to shame, even with her skin disease, including this Phyllis chick.

Leslie went to answer her question by changing her order. "Nunt unh, umm, I umm, I umm . . . change my orda'. Can you gimme dat umm, et-tu, et-tu . . . Hi' you panounce dat?"

Phyllis began to smile. *This damn girl needs to take a public-speakin' class or somethin'. God!* She answered, "Etouffée?"

"Ahh, yeah, dat. But umm, iz-zit any good, doe, for true? 'Cause umm, I'on wan'nit if it's nasty. I hate nasty food! It be givin' me da runs."

By then, the cooks and the other cashiers were beginning to laugh at the odd girl.

Phyllis chuckled herself and said, "It's good. So you want that?" to rush the order. She was losing her patience, the little that she had.

Leslie nodded and said, "Yeah, gimme dat."

"You want anything to drink wit it?" Phyllis asked her.

Leslie looked at her and asked, "Y'all sell Ol' English Eight Hun'nit in here?" with a straight face.

The staff began to laugh even harder, but Phyllis was no longer amused by it. This girl was just holding up her damn line.

So she snapped, "Look, we don't sell that here. If you want that, you go up the street and get it. It's plenty of liquor stores down the street."

Leslie backed away from the counter and nodded again. She said, "Okay, den. I ain't even hungry no moe' anyway," and walked out the door. But before she left, she checked the store hours on the door to see what times they closed.

"Hell was wrong wit dat girl?" Phyllis asked out loud. She was filled with nothing but spite, while the rest of the staff continued to laugh, even in the presence of other customers. Then Phyllis mocked her, "I umm, I umm, I umm . . ."

"Stop, Phyllis, that's wrong," one of the cashiers warned her with a grin of her own. "Some people just ain't got it all together."

Phyllis said, "Well, she need to get it together, because she got problems. Can I take your order?" she asked the next person in line.

≈

"Have you seen Ayanna lately?" Leslie asked Yula. She was back at her college house and was dressed in the normal gear of a conservative college girl, with your typical blue jeans and a sweatshirt, with her hair back out.

But Yula barely looked at Leslie from the dining room table, where she concentrated on her schoolwork.

"Like you told me, Lez, I can't worry about what she's doin'. I got other things to think about," she answered. It was late, and Ayanna was still nowhere to be found.

Leslie looked at Yula and was proud of her friend's answer, and her actions.

She said, "That's good."

Yula offered, "You wanna study with me?"

Leslie declined. She had other issues on her mind at the moment.

"Not right now, but maybe another time."

Yula nodded and said, "Okay." As Leslie began to head for the staircase, Yula added, "And Leslie . . . thanks for settin' me straight like you did. I appreciate that."

Leslie stopped and said, "Don't worry about it. That's what friends are for."

When she reached her room upstairs and toward the back, shut her door, and crashed on her bed to think things through, she asked herself in a low tone, "What the hell am I doing thinking about killing a girl? I can't believe I let my sister get me started with this," she told herself.

It only took her a few minutes to force the thoughts of murder out of her head and get back to her studies that night. She had no idea how she would get away with it anyway. But after she had put up one of her school textbooks on her small bookshelf inside her room, her new book of *Vodou Practices and Mysteries* fell off of the shelf.

Leslie stopped in her tracks. *Ayanna's been in my fucking room!* she told herself immediately. *Because I know I put this book up better than that. And who else would be in here looking for something? Unless . . . Bridget? . . . But Bridget is more thorough than Ayanna. She would have put it back the way she found it. And then Yula?*

Leslie shook her head in disbelief. "No," she told herself, "Yula would say something about it . . . with her scared ass," she concluded.

Just like that, her mind became distracted again.

Now I can't even trust my roommates for my privacy. So she walked over to the door and locked herself in her room. And while she held the book of *Vodou Practices and Mysteries* in her hands, she figured, *Why not flip through it again? And I'll handle whoever was in my room later.*

As her thumb bent back a page, Leslie opened the book to the chapter dealing with visualization.

That's interesting, she told herself. *Is this something I'm supposed to know? Why* this *page?*

She lay out on her bed to read it, and as she read, the simplistic ideas made plain sense to her. *Just concentrate on something, and fill out the picture,* she told herself. But that's when things got . . . spooky . . . to use a word for it. Because the first image that popped into Leslie's mind was the face of Phyllis, her sister's adversary. No matter how hard Leslie tried to change the imagery, she couldn't. Phyllis continued to pop back into her head. Her Popeyes uniform, her name tag, her crooked nose, dark lips, and her foul attitude were all fresh on Leslie's mind. And then Leslie could see a clear image of the girl's battered face in several frames, looking up and sideways. And it scared the hell out of her!

"Shit!" Leslie cursed to herself as she sat up from her visualization in a panic. She looked back at the door to make sure that it was still locked. And it was. So she calmed herself and took a few slow, deep breaths. *Do I really wanna go there?* she asked herself of her vision. But her curiosity wouldn't allow her not to.

She told herself quietly, "Okay. If I really am a priestess . . . and I have it in my blood . . . then I guess I'm about to find out."

She stood up and clicked off her light to have total concentration inside the dark of her room, at close to midnight. She then lay flat on her back on the bed and folded her arms over her chest, zombie style, and closed her eyes to breathe deeply and visualize.

Okay . . . here it goes, she told herself.

Phyllis popped right back into her mental view, as Leslie now expected. She was behind the Popeyes counter again, in full uniform. Leslie began to erase the store counter in her mind, while focusing to put Phyllis out on the street.

Done.

But instead of daytime, Leslie focused to make it night.

Done.

But now there were cars and people everywhere. She needed to have Phyllis there by herself. So she erased the cars and the people.

Done.

But where was the corner bus stop? Phyllis needed to be at the corner, and at the bus stop. She catches the bus home from work. Only . . . there is no bus coming that night.

And then . . . Leslie visualized a round light. It moved up the street, in slow motion toward Phyllis, who stood at the corner. She was right at the edge of the curb. But then she disappeared.

Where did she go? Leslie asked subconsciously. *I lost her!*

Phyllis appeared again, right as the round light reached her at the corner. She looked back . . . and she looked back . . . and she looked back, three times in Leslie's vision, before she flew into the light.

Shit!

Leslie shook herself out of her deep trance and felt her heart thumping against her chest.

"Oh my God!" she whispered to herself. She sat up in her bed and tossed her hands to her temples in the dark of the room. "Oh my God! . . . I am . . . I *am!*"

She struggled to catch her normal breath, and was nearly panting from her visual ride. Then she looked over at the red-lit numbers on her clock as her heart continued to thump. The clock read 12:28.

That was almost forty minutes! she exclaimed. *But it felt like it was only seconds!* And she continued to whisper through her rapid breaths, "Oh my *God!* . . . Oh my *God!* . . ."

≈

Leslie was up bright and early the next morning, and still looking to track down Ayanna. The longer it took, the more she worried about it.

I gotta stop sweating that girl. She's not gonna tell anybody, she tried to convince herself while walking out the door for campus.

"Wait up, Leslie!" Yula hollered down the stairs.

"I'm already out the door, Yula!" Leslie hollered back up to her and continued on her way.

Yula rushed down the stairs and out the door to catch up to Leslie anyway. She asked, "You wanna go to a basketball game at Xavier tonight? Bridget has four tickets for us."

Leslie had another day off from work. "Who are they playing?" she asked.

"SUNO," Yula answered, while struggling to keep up with Leslie's brisk pace.

Leslie told her, "I'll think about it."

"Well, Bridget was going to ask you last night, but I told her that you were up in your room doing your work, so she told me to tell you in the morning."

"Where is Bridget right now?" Leslie asked her.

Yula grinned at the question. "She supposedly went over to tell her friend Eugene that they need to slow things down, but she somehow didn't make it back home last night, right? I mean, why couldn't she just have called him and told him that over the telephone?"

Leslie smiled at it herself. "Because then she wouldn't be able to get her last freak on."

And they both laughed.

Leslie asked Yula again, "And you still haven't seen Ayanna?"

Yula shook her head. She said, "It's like, ever since she had that last freestyle session at the club that we talked about that night, she's been hangin' out more in the streets, try'na hook up a rap contract, I guess."

Leslie nodded and held her tongue.

Yula smiled and added, "And she—" She stopped herself in midsentence.

Leslie looked at her and asked, "She what?" right as they made it to Gentilly Boulevard to cross the street onto Dillard's campus.

"Nothing," Yula answered. "It's not important."

Leslie eyed her and ignored the green light. "What did she say?"

Yula refused to answer her. "Leslie, I don't need to put no bad blood between y'all. I just think that . . . Ayanna takes longer to get over things."

"Get over *what?*" Leslie pressed her. She was hating the fact that she had opened her mouth to Ayanna now.

Yula took a breath and said, "Remember that night when we were playing with that . . . Ouija board, and you told Ayanna that she talks too much. Well . . . I still think she's kind of upset about that. And I think it's petty, myself."

"So, what did she say about it?" Leslie questioned.

Yula didn't like the position that she was in. She said, "Look, Leslie, that's between y'all. I don't need to be in the middle of that."

Leslie nodded and was disappointed with the partial information. She mumbled, "All right," and began to walk across the street without Yula.

Yula caught up with her again and asked, "Is something bothering you today, Leslie?" She was genuinely concerned. Leslie's mother dying recently was yet another blow to her armor. It had to be affecting her somehow.

But Leslie would not allow herself to crack. She answered, "I'm cool. I'm just not the happy-go-lucky type, Yula. That's all. And it helps me to stay prepared for all of the shit that I go through."

Yula nodded her head and was speechless. What more could she say? She wasn't as peachy and cheerful as Bridget could be. So she thought to herself, *Well, at least Leslie didn't tell me to leave her alone. She let me walk with her at least. So I'll just settle for that and keep her company.*

Leslie made it to her classes only to daydream the hours by, while thinking about her recent thoughts and the events that had led her to them. And the day was over much faster than usual.

"Damn, it's five o'clock already," she commented to herself. *And I gotta get this killing shit off my mind! It's not gonna happen. It was only a visualization. I can't make that shit happen for real anyway.*

So when she made it back to the house, she was all for going to the basketball game at Xavier, just to take her mind off things.

Bridget, of course, was pleased to hear it. She was already dressed to go, wearing new black jeans and a gold Xavier sweatshirt.

Leslie looked her over and joked, "What, are you ready to transfer on us?"

"No," Bridget told her. "Eugene bought this for me."

"Is he gonna be at the game?" Yula asked her with a grin.

Leslie smirked and said, "Of course he is. What kind of question is that?" Bridget just smiled it off. But there was still no Ayanna. However, Leslie didn't want to ask about her again. But instead, Bridget brought it up.

She said, "Well, Ayanna didn't want to go, so now we have a ticket to give away at the door."

"Or sell it," Leslie told her. *I could buy a hot dog and pop with it,* she thought. "Well, let me go upstairs and get ready then," she told her housemates.

Leslie freshened up, put on a turquoise wrap blouse with her blue jeans, brushed her hair with sweet-smelling oil, and sprayed a touch of perfume on her wrists to rub into her neck. But by the time she had made it back downstairs in a cheerful mood, happy to be going out for enjoyment for a change, she had a telephone call waiting.

Bridget held up the receiver and said, "It's your sister. But let me clear the line with Ayanna first."

Just hearing that Ayanna was on the phone made Leslie anxious to reach out and grab it to talk to her. But she restrained herself and told Bridget, "Tell her I said hi," instead.

Bridget relayed the message, cleared Ayanna from the line, and handed the phone to Leslie to talk to her sister.

Leslie took the phone and expected more bad news. "Hello," she answered.

Laetitia came right out and gave it to her. "Leslie, Jurron is even moving his new clothes and shit over to this bitch's house now! I swear to God, I'm ready to kill her!"

Leslie walked away from her friends, and they knew the deal already, so they allowed her the extra space for privacy.

God, I'm glad I don't have a sister like that! Bridget praised herself. *I mean, I've always wanted a sister or something, but . . . I wouldn't take Leslie's sister for the world! She's always calling over here about something.*

Leslie asked her sister calmly over the phone, "How do you know that?"

"Because he just bought some new clothes, and now I can't find 'em nowhere in the house!" Laetitia shouted.

Leslie shook her head and thought, *What are you going through his clothes for anyway? You losing your damn mind, girl!*

That's when Laetitia told her big sister, "Leslie . . . if I kill this girl and they find out about it, and I go to jail . . . would you adopt Renée and Anna? Because, I mean . . . they love you, Leslie."

Leslie was speechless for nearly a minute as she rethought the situation. *I think my sister needs some professional help!* she realized. *But I don't have the time to be watching my nieces every day while she works this shit out.* So Leslie made her final conclusion.

She said, "Don't do that." Then she spoke in French. *"Il reviendra."* He will return.

But Laetitia doubted it. She said, "What makes you say that, Leslie? This girl's trying to turn Jurron against me. I mean, he even started talking about how I don't do *this* and how I don't do *that.* And I know that she's behind him sayin' that shit. My li'l habits didn't bother him before."

Leslie said, *"Il faut lui dire que tu l'aimes et que tu vas essayer de changer."* You tell him you love him and you'll do better.

Laetitia responded, "What? That won't work."

Leslie snapped, *"Dis-lui immédiatement!"* You do it—immediately! "Now I have to go," she said in English. "I'll call you back later and we'll finish talking then. But I'm ready to go to a basketball game right now," she told her sister purposefully.

"What game?"

"A game at Xavier."

Laetitia said, "Oh," feeling left out as usual.

Leslie repeated, "We'll talk later. *Tout ira bien."* Everything will be fine.

Laetitia paused and responded sourly, "Yeah, whatever," before she hung up the phone.

Leslie hung up the phone on her end and shook it off. Her sister was killing her.

Bridget asked, "Is everything all right?"

"Of course not," Leslie answered. She added, "But I have my own life to live. So let's go."

However, before they could all make it out of the door, Leslie snapped her fingers. "I forgot. I'll lock the door and meet y'all at the car," she told them as she dashed back up the stairs.

When Leslie reached Bridget's car outside, she carried her loaded-up school bag with her.

Yula looked at Leslie's bag and couldn't believe it. She thought, *Now that's dedication. Some of these basketball games are boring anyway.*

On the other hand, when Bridget spotted Leslie with her school bag, she thought, *Leslie needs to give herself a break. My God!*

Leslie climbed into the car with her own thoughts: *I have to leave this game no later than eight-thirty to make it back to Popeyes on time.*

... Of a First Kill

"The Barn," as Xavier University called its small, wood-accented gymnasium, was jam-packed for the hometown rivalry basketball games, starting with SUNO's Lady Knights against the Gold Nuggets of Xavier, before the men's game would begin. And what would a basketball game featuring two predominantly African-American schools be without more thumping bass music from the local Big Tymers of the Cash Money Millionaires, pushing their latest hit through the pounding speakers that surrounded the basketball floor: *"I'm the number one stun-nah / What, what-what-what/ I'm the number one stun-nah / What, what-what-what . . ."*

So Bridget, Yula, and Leslie walked into the gym to their own theme music, while searching through the stands to find seats.

"Damn! Who dat?" a few of the overzealous guys in the stands questioned as the three ladies passed through.

Bridget overheard the hype and grinned from ear to ear with Yula, while Leslie had more pressing things on her mind.

One spectator in the stands tapped his friend and said, "Yo, dawg, that girl right there in the turquoise, man . . . she 'bout the baddest black girl I ever seen in my life. Am I seein' things out in this bitch, or what, man? Damn! Tell me I'm seein' things."

His friend looked in Leslie's direction and smiled.

He said, "Yeah, I know her, man. That's Leslie *Bo-day*. I went to high school wit 'er."

His boy got wide eyes and everything. He responded, "Yeah? So, I'm sayin', man, what's the scoop on 'er? Holla at a nigga. Holla at me!"

His friend began to laugh and shake his head. "Ain't shit goin' on wit *her*, man, but the books and her family. Unless she changed in college."

"Well, what school she go to?"

"She go da Dillard."

"Well, introduce me to her, man. Introduce a nigga."

His friend refused to. He said, "For true, I'on even know 'er like that, man. She stayed to herself in school. I'd probably have to introduce myself to her for her to even remember me."

Leslie looked around the gym from her seat and was actually pleased with her decision to come. It was pretty lively in there as the girls' game got under way with the tip-off.

Yula whispered to her, "It's plenty of hotties in here, Leslie. You see anything you like? I know *I* do."

Leslie started laughing, exposing her straight white teeth and illustrious glow right as Bridget's man, Eugene Duval, walked into the gym. Leslie looked dead into his eyes and continued to smile. She then leaned into Yula and commented, "Guess who's here."

Spotting them in the stands, with Leslie sitting there looking . . . fabulous like she did, Eugene fucked around and tripped up the steps in their direction.

Yula and Bridget caught his clumsiness and started laughing.

Bridget joked and said, "Oh my God, now he's embarrassing me in here."

Yula said, "That's 'cause light-skinned guys ain't got no real flow, Bridget."

Leslie only smirked at the humor. She read the situation correctly and thought to herself, *You know what . . . I think this boy likes me . . . I mean, I had a hunch about it before, because he's always pressed to say something to me at the house. But that shit right there? . . . Oh, that was just too obvious.*

Bridget had a seat ready for him, next to her.

Eugene sat down and immediately asked them, "I guess y'all saw me trip up the steps, hunh?" to get it all over with.

Yula chuckled and told him, "We couldn't miss it."

Bridget hugged his right arm and teased him. "Awww, I still love you, baby."

Leslie just looked away. She asked herself, *Should I just look at him to make sure I'm right? . . . No, I'm not even gonna go there,* she told herself with discipline. *He don't turn me on no way.*

She heard Eugene ask Bridget snidely, "So, where's your other girl, Miss Rap-a-lot?" referring to Ayanna.

Leslie kept her straight face and thought, *Okay, he doesn't like Ayanna.*

Then he spoke to Yula in a monotone, "Oh, hi, Yula."

Leslie thought, *Okay, he's not sweating Yula. That sounded like he was patting a dog on the head. Good girl, good girl!*

Then he leaned forward in his wooden seat to face Leslie. He said, "And dum . . . Leslie, what brings you out the house on a weekday?"

Leslie smiled for a half of a second. *Yup, he likes me,* she told herself.

Then she answered his question. "Somebody asked me if I wanted to go, and I didn't have anything else to do, so I came. It's that simple."

Eugene responded, "Oh," and was speechless. So Leslie turned away from him again.

But then he asked her, "You didn't have anybody you wanted to bring with you? What did y'all do with the extra ticket?"

Oh my God! Leslie thought before she even looked at him again. All eyes were on her, but she slid a glance at Bridget to see if she was catching on to things. And she wasn't. Bridget was sitting there holding on to Eugene's arm, dedicated to love, with a big, stupid grin on her face.

Leslie thought to herself, *This damn girl is blind as a bat! I wonder if Yula is getting it.* So Leslie slid a glance at Yula, who was beaming crookedly from the intrigue.

Yeah, Yula got it, Leslie concluded just from her twisted smile.

She then decided to answer Eugene's second question. She said, "Why, you got a friend you wanna hook me up with? Another Creole boy who likes it brown?"

Oh my God!.Yula thought to herself. She immediately flung her hands to her face, shocked that Leslie had the audacity to say that out loud and right in Bridget's face, at that. And although Bridget felt uncomfortable about it, all that she could do was laugh it off with her man.

But in his anxiety, Eugene went ahead and added insult to injury.

"Well, you know what they say, 'The blacker the berry . . .'"

Yula took her hands down from her face and dropped her mouth wide open.

You talk about embarrassment, Bridget could not believe that he had said that. Sure, he could think it, but since he was a Creole—who were known for sticking to their own shade when it came to love and marriage—

and Bridget was nearly as dark as Leslie was, Eugene's thoughtless response made Bridget's relationship with him seem comparable to jungle fever from a white man.

Eugene assessed the tension in the air and went to correct his statement. Even a few students in the rows in front of them turned back to give him a spiteful eye. They all understood the superficiality of the Creoles. And none of them liked it. Eugene probably couldn't even use the N-word around them.

So he backed up and said, "I didn't mean it like that, to call you . . . I mean, your skin is nice . . . I just meant, you know, the popular sayin'."

Yula spoke up and said, "Quit while you're ahead, man. Just quit it while you're ahead."

Or quit while he's behind, Leslie thought to herself. *That's just what his ass get. Slick-ass motherfucker! Now Bridget has something to think about it.* And Leslie went back to watching the basketball game as if the slip of tongue had never happened.

Nevertheless, Bridget was more upset with Leslie than she was with Eugene. She sat there and thought, *Okay, I've just about given up on Leslie now. She did that shit on purpose! I guess she really doesn't like Eugene. I mean, I know his love for me is genuine. So what if he likes brown sisters? If he didn't we'd be mad at him for that, too. So Eugene loses either way with some people, just because he was born light!*

The conversation between them all became stale, until Leslie decided that it was time for her to go. She looked down at her watch, and it was close enough to eight-thirty to begin her retreat. The boys' game had started by then, and the Barn had a standing-room-only crowd. So she stood from her seat and began to make her way to the crowded steps to walk out of the stands.

Yula asked her, "Where are you going, Leslie?"

"I got work to do," Leslie answered gruffly.

Me too, Yula thought to herself, prepared to leave with her. *It's hot in here anyway.*

She said, "Wait up, Leslie, I'll go home with you."

Bridget didn't say a word. She was growing tired of coaching Leslie into sociability.

But when Leslie turned to eye Yula, Yula read the obvious irritation on her face and decided to sit her behind back down. She said, "Well, never mind, you can go. I'll just see you at the house."

Leslie nodded to her and went on her way. She thought, *Thank God!*

This girl sweatin' me so bad now that I need a towel. I got shit to do!

As she headed out, Bridget and Eugene both tried to act as if they didn't care. However, they both did. They separately wanted to be a part of her life. Leslie was an intriguing human puzzle for both of them, and they were strongly attracted to her depth.

≈≈≈

All Leslie thought about on her bus ride toward downtown was how disloyal men were, and how ridiculous women were for falling for them so hard. But such was life, and there she was on her way to straighten a girl out for trying to take a man who clearly didn't desire to be kept at home in the first damn place.

Leslie mumbled, "This is all crazy." *But I'm just gon' have to do whatever to be able to live my life in peace,* she insisted.

However, she continued to doubt her visualization. And her doubt was what led her so readily into her plans. She wanted to prove to herself that nothing dramatic would happen that night. It couldn't happen. It was too unreal. Anyone could visualize a scene if they concentrated on it. But that didn't mean that it would actually happen. What if Phyllis was not even at work that night?

So Leslie changed back into her ugly clothing and baseball cap while in between transfers from the buses that she had to catch. She slipped the clothes that she had worn to the basketball game inside her school bag, and then shoved her school bag inside a brown paper bag that she had unfolded. After all, what would a poor, uneducated ghetto girl be doing with a school bag at night?

Leslie had thought it all out, and planned it well. But it was all . . . nonsense, really. She was certain of it! Even her father had told her so. But he had also . . . killed a boy for her . . . and gotten away with it. Or did he really kill that boy Bernard? Maybe Bernard had simply run away from home. Or someone else had killed him. Or maybe . . . anything could have happened to him. But as Leslie rode the second bus toward her destination, her doubts turned into nervousness and fear.

Shit! What the hell am I doing? Am I really ready to do this? she asked herself again. She fought girls in her youth plenty of times for Laetitia, but this time the stakes were drastically higher.

When she looked out of the bus window, it was clearly nighttime, a

dark, dry, and peaceful night, just as she had . . . visualized. Her heart began
to race accordingly, as the bus traveled closer and closer to Popeyes.

Leslie looked down at her watch, which read 9:39 P.M.

Oh, shit! she told herself. *What if she's really there tonight? . . . I'll be right
on time at ten.*

≈≈

Blocks away from where Leslie rode the bus, the employees at Popeyes were
taking their last orders for the night, including Phyllis.

"Can I take your order?" she reluctantly asked a woman with three
children.

Damn! Phyllis was thinking. *I don't feel like doing this shit right now. I
should get somebody else to take her order. She prob'bly gon' order a whole bunch of
chicken and expect to get extras just because we're about to close soon. She look like
the type.*

Sure enough, the woman with three children asked Phyllis, "Can we
just get a bag special?"

Phyllis took a deep breath before she asked the woman, "What is a bag
special?" She had a good idea of what the woman wanted, she just wanted
to hear it from her mouth.

The woman told her with a straight face. "Well, y'all 'bout to close
soon, right? So why don't you just dump a couple boxes of y'all old chicken
in a bag and I'll pay you for it."

Her children began to smile, but they damn sure looked hungry.

Phyllis humored herself and said, "That'll be thirty dollars."

The woman grimaced and said, "Thirty dollars? Not even nem family
boxes cost that much. I said the old chicken. Look, I'll gi' you seven dollas,
but that's all I got."

Phyllis quickly lost her patience with the woman and said, "Somebody
else get her. I'm going back to wash my hands. I'm ready to go." Then she
grinned and added, "I'm having company tonight. And it ain't my baby's
daddy . . . he's somebody else's," she said with a wicked laugh.

"Girl, you need to stop that shit before you get in trouble wit somebody," one of her coworkers warned her.

"Oh, whatever, girl, they all belong to somebody. Ain't no damn stray
dogs out here for real. Them the kind that get you rabies and shit," she joked,
while she left the woman and children standing at the counter unattended.

"You're not gonna take my orda'?" the mother asked Phyllis.

Phyllis ignored her and grimaced at the manager as she went on about her business.

She asked the small brown man of a manager, "What do you want me to do, clock out five minutes early? Because you know how I get when I'm tired. And I'm tired right now."

The manager told her, "Go ahead and get ready, then," as he stepped to the cash register to fill the woman's last order of the night.

The mother explained to him, "Look, sir, my kids and I are hungry, and I know you're not gon' do nothin' with that old chicken but throw it away . . ."

The manager listened to the whole sob story and had a warm heart, so he granted the woman her wish of a "bag special" before they locked the doors for the night and packed things up.

Everyone had a ride home that night but Phyllis. She didn't particularly care to be dropped off at the Florida projects, where she lived at the moment. She wanted to believe that her stay there was only temporary, and when she had moved into a more respectable place, then she would allow someone to give her a ride home. So she walked out to the bus stop by her lonesome, with the manager being the last to see her that night.

He drove out of the miniature parking lot at Popeyes in his little white Toyota and told her, "Be safe, Phyllis."

"Yeah, yeah," she said, and blew him off.

≈≈≈

When Leslie saw Phyllis walking out from Popeyes toward the corner bus stop by herself, her legs became weak. Nevertheless, she felt herself moving in the girl's direction to confront her. And as she continued to view the dark streets that surrounded them, she noticed the lack of people and cars that were out that night.

"Oh shit!" she whispered to herself, moving steadily closer to Phyllis at the bus stop.

Phyllis was enjoying the empty streets for a change. *This is jus' how I like it! Nobody out here to work my nerves tonight. 'Cause ghetto people don't know how to act. I need to hit the damn lotto and move away from all of this shit. Even get me a new gotdamn man when I do it. I mean, I hate to be a home wrecker, but that boy Jurron ain't gon' last for me. I mean, he got a good piece of dick and everything, but he ain't got no fuckin' money for me, so I know that ain't gon' last. I'll prob'bly send his ass back to his li'l fam'ly when I find somethin' better anyway.*

When she turned momentarily, she spotted the crazy girl in the baseball hat who had wasted her time in the store the other day. Phyllis sucked her teeth and turned up her nose to the girl.

What the hell she doin' out here tonight, ho'in' for some money or something? she asked herself. *Crazy-ass girl got the same damn clothes she had on yesterday. And what's up wit da big brown paper bag and shit? She try'na make Erykah Badu's song into a prophecy or something? It's all like that for her crazy ass?* Phyllis continued to spite the girl.

On Leslie's end, when Phyllis turned and spotted her, she shook in her stance, thinking that the vision was over with.

Oh, shit, she saw me! I don't remember that. I knew the shit wasn't gonna work! she told herself frantically. *And there's no light coming down the street. So let me just say what I gotta say for my sister and get out of here.*

However, when Phyllis turned away from her and intentionally walked to the edge of the curb to give herself more space, the one round light appeared down the street from them and began to move forward in their direction.

Oh my GOD! It's happening! It's happening! Leslie screamed to herself.

Phyllis saw the one round light moving up the street toward her. She thought, *Look at this. People can't even fix their damn car lights in the 'hood.* Then she noticed that the streetlamp across from her was beginning to flicker. *Now the motherfuckin' light is 'bout to go out. What the hell else could happen?*

She felt the presence of the crazy girl in the baseball cap nearby her, and instead of recognizing her humanity, and turning to speak to her, or smile, or scorn her, or anything, Phyllis went to further ignore the girl. She went as far as to actually pull the hood of her black jacket over her head and turned her back to Leslie to send her a final message of disdain.

At that point, Leslie's doubts and hesitation evaporated. Because when Phyllis made her final decision of ignorance, the night-light across the street from them blacked out, and she disappeared from view in the dark, just as Leslie had visualized.

Leslie told herself, *Okay, that's it! This bitch deserves to fuckin' die! She's gonna spite me like that in the dark, and don't even know who the fuck I am! Well, I'm the priestess, bitch!* And Leslie launched herself into the girl.

Phyllis thought, *Wait a fuckin' minute,* and felt eerie about her surroundings for just a second. But when she turned her head back to check up on the crazy girl behind her, it was too damned late for her ass!

Leslie shoved her with a moving force, right into the light that had reached them in the street. And Phyllis flew into the round light headfirst from the velocity of Leslie's push, and thumped straight into the hard grille of an old car.

Bloomp!

Phyllis's body ricocheted after the hit, and spun back up into the air, landing at the curb, right at Leslie's feet. Then the streetlamp popped back on, where Leslie could see Phyllis's battered face, looking up and sideways from the curb, just like in her . . . visualization.

The passenger inside the old car shouted, "Shit, man, you hit somethin'!" He had a rolled-up blunt of marijuana in his brown hands.

The driver shook for a second behind the wheel, and forced himself to regain control of the car. Once he did, he was rather unconcerned about it in his state of high.

"Fuck it, man. It was prob'bly a dog or something." Then he got irritated with his friend. "Pass me da fuckin' blunt back, man. Stop being greedy, nigga. I bought that shit."

Back at the curb, poor Leslie became . . . sick to her stomach. *Oh my God! I didn't just do that. I didn't do that!* she told herself. *Something got into me!*

But she did do it, whether something got into her or not. It was pre-medi-tated murder! That's how the American law would see it. They surely wouldn't want to hear some voodoo story. So Leslie got to stepping in a hurry. And as she walked, and walked, and walked, she continued to beg herself to wake up! Only . . . she never did. Because she wasn't dreaming anymore.

When the bus had finally arrived late to take Phyllis home, the nightlight across the street flickered off again. In the dimly lit street, the bus driver failed to see her body lying up against the curb. And since no one got off of the bus at that stop, Phyllis's body was not discovered until early that next morning, when people began to travel to work at the start of a new day.

Illusions . . .

Jurron Chesterfield sat out on the steps of Phyllis's building at the Florida Avenue project, located on the other side of the train tracks from Desire. And the only reason the Florida project was less . . . notorious than Desire was because it was considerably smaller. However, the projects were the projects no matter how one offered to slice the ugly piece of dirt pie.

Jurron was twenty-two years old, and soon to turn twenty-three. He was an average guy, and nothing fancy to look at. He wasn't particularly tall, short, or built in any special way. He was just a young African-American man who was still trying to figure out what exactly it was that he was put on earth to do.

He took out a pack of Camel cigarettes, lit one to smoke, and continued to wait well past eleven o'clock for his new piece of action to arrive home from work that night.

"Come on, girl. How long you gon' make me wait tonight? Damn!" he told himself out loud.

Jurron was not an impatient young man, though. In fact, he had so much patience that the everyday struggle of maintaining a steady job was not an issue for him. A steady *j-o-b* would pretty much come when it came. Then he would move out of the projects and do . . . whatever, whenever. He just wasn't pressed about it. It wasn't in his blood to be pressed. Or not anymore. Because he had learned, after a few efforts to be more urgent about life, that rushing took more out of him, and it usually created situations where he would need to keep rushing. Why run one lap and not two? Why run two laps and not three? And if you run three laps, then you may as well go ahead and complete the whole mile. But Jurron didn't know if he had a mile in him to run every day. So urgency was something he felt more comfortable avoiding.

He continued to wait there patiently at the projects, while smoking a cigarette. Soon he began to nod his head, snap the fingers of his free hand, and tap his feet to the slow music that was on his mind from the popular R&B group Destiny's Child: *"Say my na-a-ame / say my na-a-a-ame . . ."*

After a while longer, Jurron was joined by one of the Florida project tenants who knew him.

"Ay, man, gi'me one nem cigarettes."

Forget about asking! You demanded what you wanted in the ghetto. Because asking wouldn't get you much. So Jurron pulled out his pack of cigarettes and gave one up on demand.

His friend looked at the pack and then at the short, white cigarette in his brown hand.

"Fuck you doin' smokin' *Camels*?" he asked.

Jurron smiled and took out another one for himself, chain-smoking to pass the time.

He said, "They all gon' kill us the same way, man. It don't make no diff'rence."

He lit both of their cigarettes with his lighter and started to smoke again.

His friend from the projects took one puff and asked him, "Who you waitin' on, Phyllis?"

Jurron took a puff and answered, "Yeah."

His friend nodded. Then he said real candidly, "You know she a ho, right?"

Jurron stopped smoking for a second, just long enough to smile and to shake his head.

"Everybody a ho for somebody, man," he responded. He paused and added, "Even ya' momma," with a sly grin.

His friend took a second for the humor to calculate before he laughed.

He said, "You a funny motherfucka, man. You lucky I ain't offended by dat shit."

"That's because it's the truth," Jurron told him.

His friend took another puff and nodded with his eyes squinting from the smoke.

"I guess if you wanna look at it dat way."

"That's how you lookin' at it," Jurron countered.

His friend disagreed with the logic. He argued, "I wa'n't talkin' 'bout nobody's mom, man, I was jus' talkin' 'bout Phyllis. I mean, 'cause she a ho, man. For true."

Jurron looked at him and said, "Phyllis got a son. He just live with his nanna, that's all."

His friend took another second to catch the irony before he laughed out loud to himself.

"Aw'ight, I see ya' point, man. I see it. But you know why her son don't live wit her?" his friend asked him. "'Cause she a ho," he answered for himself.

After another second, they both shrugged things off and went on to the next subject.

"Whatchew think about this new president, man? I mean, they should have a law against a motherfucka's son runnin' for president, and then winnin' nat shit. They even cheated for dat motherfucka to win.

"George Bush Jr.," the Florida project tenant stated.

Jurron smoked his cigarette and didn't flinch. He asked with his free hand up in the air, "Is it gon' change all this out here?" referring to the dim and dispirited environment of the projects. He said, "We got shit like this all over America, man. Which president gon' change that?"

His friend chuckled at it. "You right. It ain't gon' make us no motherfuckin' diff'rence."

Jurron said, "That's why I'on vote. For what? President ain't gon' listen to me."

His friend laughed even harder. "You's a funny motherfucka, man!" He couldn't stop giggling to himself.

Jurron remained calm and said, "It's da truth."

Since he wanted to talk about the truth so much, his friend finally calmed down and asked him, "Don't you got two daughters from that girl with the skin disease over at Desire?"

Jurron nodded and answered, "Yeah."

His friend paused before he asked the obvious.

"You jus' want some diff'rent ass, den, hunh?"

Jurron blew out his smoke and said, "You know how it is. Your dick call out for variations." And he giggled at it.

His friend said, "An' nat ho young, too, ain't she? Is she outta high school even?"

He was referring to Laetitia again.

Jurron stopped laughing. He said, "She dropped out. She got tired of people fuckin' wit 'er about her skin. I told her to ignore dat shit, but she wouldn't listen. Now she jus' . . ."

He stopped. He was giving his project friend more information than he needed. Jurron didn't like the idea of Laetitia being called a ho, either. If anything, she was his ho, because Jurron was the only one who had ever touched her intimately.

His friend added further insult when he asked, "That young ho got some good shit, man? It look like she do." He sounded as if he wanted to try her out himself.

Jurron didn't like the sound of that. He said, "That's enough talk about her, man."

His friend frowned and responded, "Fuck you care? You over here."

Jurron said, "Yeah, man, but she still . . . she still my fuckin' girl." *And she da mother of my kids,* he thought to himself.

His friend grinned, deviously. He asked, "You don't think she fuckin' nobody else, while you ova' here creepin'? I mean, you be stayin' na night at Phyllis crib. I'm surprised you ain't got your own key already."

Jurron was beginning to get irritated. He responded tartly, "Man, I know she ain't fuckin' nobody else. I know my girl." He had had enough of his friend's mouth. He wasn't really his friend anyway, just some guy that Jurron would kick it with for a minute whenever he visited the Florida projects. So he was ready to shut his mouth and get back to minding his own business.

The project tenant picked up on the stale air rising between them when Jurron turned his head from him. He realized that his company was no longer wanted. He was nearly finished with his cigarette anyway. He said, "Well, thanks for the cigarette, man," and was ready to walk off.

Jurron nodded and never turned to face him. "Aw'ight," he responded dryly.

When he was alone again, and still waiting for Phyllis, he began to have a guilty conscience.

He shook his head and spat, "Now this motherfucka got me thinkin' 'bout Tee."

And he *did* think about her. He remembered how fresh and innocent Laetitia was when he first met her in the Seventh Ward, four years ago. She was thirteen then, and he was eighteen. And he related immediately to the struggles that she was having with her skin disorder.

He told her, "My cousin in Milwaukee has vitiligo. Ain't nothin' wrong wit it. People just act stupid about it, that's all. All it is is jus' a diff'rent shade of skin. It's like having a birthmark, really. And a lot of people have birthmarks."

He laughed and told her, "You can't catch nothin' from no birthmark." He said, "But most people just don't know enough about it."

Laetitia felt close to him for that. She felt closer to Jurron than to anyone, including her own family members. Because Jurron was an outsider, who had no reason to be sympathetic. Of course your immediate family would sympathize with you. They have to live with you. But how do you move on and start your own family without an outsider to understand? So Laetitia ran to Jurron every chance she got, and with open arms. And at first, he was just being nice to her, as a platonic friend. It wasn't anything sexual, although he realized that she was pretty. He told her so.

He said in simple and honest words, "You look good, Laetitia. And you can't worry about your skin color all the time. Just think about your nice nose, and pretty lips, and pretty eyes." Then he laughed and added, "And your tight body."

Laetitia did have a tight body. So she laughed at it, and felt good. But everyone realized that about her. You would have to be a blind man not to see the superb development of her curves. And if a blind man were to touch her . . . But that was a problem for those who could see. They were apprehensive about touching her body with theirs. Yet, there were still the neighborhood scavengers who would touch her just for the hell of it in their natural lust. However, Laetitia was nobody's fool. And she realized that Jurron's friendship with her was genuine. He hadn't even come on to her. It wasn't about that. He was just being humane to her situation. Besides, she was a little too young for him. Not that he would never touch a young woman, just not her. Because he respected her. She was a young lady, who Jurron had no intention of defiling.

But then . . . Laetitia came on to him a year later at age fourteen.

He told her, "Umm . . . I don't really . . . ," and he stopped himself, not wanting to hurt her feelings. It had nothing to do with vitiligo, it was just that he didn't want to go there with her. Her innocence and youth were both too . . . hardy for him to disavow. She was his little friend, and he wanted them to remain platonic.

But then she told him, "I know I'm a lot younger than you. But you're the only person that I trust. You understand me. And I mean . . . I just wanted to know what it feels like, Jurron. Please. I won't tell nobody. Honest. I wouldn't do that to you."

And when he looked into her searching, begging, and starving eyes, he was touched by it, and that forced him to have to deal with her proposition. *Aw, man, why me?* he asked himself. He figured he would have been better off had he ignored the girl and felt sorry for her from a distance, instead of getting involved with her. But now he was in trouble. He feared what she would do, or more important, who else she may run to for love, who may not be as . . . humane as he was. So in his humanity, Jurron decided that his own heart would be purer for her to experience than a number of other guys who surrounded her in their bleak neighborhood. And in his mind, he would become her savior. So he took her up on the offer to let her experience the touch of love.

Jurron remembered that first day, where Laetitia lay out on his bed, naked to the world, and staring up at him in all of her innocence. And instead of him just getting it over with, he gently kissed her naked body. He even kissed her private parts, which she felt the most embarrassed about because of her vitiligo. It seemed to discolor her private parts on purpose, as if to cripple her sexuality. But Jurron was not afraid. And when he explored her with his tongue, down there, where it felt . . . the best . . . she cried tears of joy and promised herself that she would love him forever . . . and no matter what.

Jurron entered her with his part, while wearing no protection. He did so mainly to secure the trust in her that he was free of ignorance or deceit about her skin disorder. And when he did, he had never felt a body before that fit his tool so . . . perfectly. It was such a perfect fit, that every move he made inside of her, back, forth, straight, or sideways, all gave him incredible jolts of bliss.

Gotdammit! he panicked to himself. *I done fucked up now!* Because he realized on that first occasion that he would never be able to resist her. And Laetitia held on so desperately for all of his love, and moaned so good when he emptied all his heat inside of her, again, and again, and the next day, and the day after that. Then Jurron had cried from his . . . obvious addiction.

He sat there at the Florida projects in the present, thinking everything through, while still waiting for Phyllis past midnight. Then he finally mumbled to himself, "What the fuck am I doin' over here waitin' for dis . . . for dis *ho*? That girl loves me back at home, man. And we got two daughters now . . ."

He thought about it some more and concluded, "Let me take my ass back t' da crib."

But as he stood up, he saw someone moving toward him in the distance, and he waited just in case it was Phyllis. Until he saw that it wasn't.

I guess she was supposed to play me t'night, so I could realize what I got back at home, he reasoned to himself. *Laetitia would never have me out here waitin' like this. That girl would fuck around and quit her job if they wouldn't let her leave early enough to see me,* he joked to himself with a grin. He then made his way back across the train tracks to his apartment and to his loved ones at Desire filled with rededication and purpose.

"I got a family now," he told himself as he walked. He thought, *I gotta keep remindin' myself of that shit. It ain't just about me no more.*

≈≈≈

Laetitia sat up in the dark of her living room with one lit candle, looking as evil as she could make herself. She was dead serious about using whatever power she wished herself to have to get her man back.

But like her older sister, she didn't really believe that it would work. She was just desperate to try it, or to try anything that she could. So when Jurron slid his key inside of the door and walked in, she felt embarrassed that he had caught her there in the dark with a candle, and she didn't know what to say or do. She was so shocked that he was there that she didn't move to hide anything.

Jurron asked her, "What are you doin'?"

She stared at him for a full minute, and was at a loss for words. Then she thought about her big sister's advice to her earlier that day and went for broke.

She explained, "Jurron, I just wanted you back. I mean, I love you and I'll do better now. I'll be good at whatever you want me to be good at. I promise."

Jurron listened to her and shook his head with a smile. *I can't believe this shit. This girl loves me to death, man!* he told himself as he sat down beside her. He was immediately turned on by her undying commitment to him. So he nudged his hand in between her legs and began to rub her there. Laetitia reciprocated and did the same to him.

She asked him, "You wanna go in the bedroom . . . or you want it right here?"

He tugged at her nightclothes and panties. "Let's do it right here."

When they engaged in their usual activities on the sofa in the dark, with Jurron on the bottom, he continued to peek out at the singular lit candle on the coffee table in front of them. He asked himself, *What the hell was she doin' in here?* even as her steady rhythm upon him brought him to another powerful climax.

"Awww, baby," he moaned to her, caressing her bare hips. "Damn, you still got it!"

Laetitia laughed and bounced her weight upon him. She was overjoyed that she still had him. And Jurron was glad that he had come back home to what was real, and what would always be there for him . . . no matter what.

≈≈

Miles away, inside a plush basement that had an extralarge projection television screen, surround sound, and state-of-the-art stereo equipment, Ayanna Timber sat on a black leather sofa while listening to several instrumental hip-hop tracks to write rhymes to. Her new connected friends, Beaucoup and DJ Whiz Kid, were nodding their heads in the background to the steady thump of the beat.

However, Ayanna was having an affliction of writer's block. She couldn't concentrate on penning her lyrics. She had been writing them for days now, and trying to maintain her focus. But all that she could think of was the cost of ransom she had to pay for trying so hard to push her way into the rap music business as a girl. The problem was, Beaucoup wanted to continue sleeping with her on the sly, and that made Ayanna wonder how sincere he was about helping her out in the first place. Was it only a front just to get her pants and panties off for him? He still hadn't introduced her to the real New Orleans movers and shakers, Master P or the Cash Money Millionaires. So Ayanna could not concentrate on her rhymes anymore.

Coup finally looked over her shoulder and said, "What's up wit ya' flow t'night, hunh? You ain't *got it* right now? You wanna take a break and go out to eat or sump'um?"

Ayanna took a breath and nodded to him. "Yeah, I'm hungry."

He nodded back to her and said, "Aw'ight." Then he looked to his DJ friend. "What can I say, Whiz? She ain't feelin' it t'night, man."

Whiz nodded back to him. He said, "That's normal, man. Every rapper needs their breaks to think sometimes."

Coup said, "Aw'ight, well, we'll see how she feels later on. You still gon' be up?"

Whiz looked and was afraid to turn Coup down. The street generals had influence that way. They made you want to rethink all of your decisions with them, because you never knew when they could help you out of a jam . . . or choose not to, based on what favors you provided to them lately.

So Whiz thought about it and answered, "Yeah, I can stay up." However, he hoped that he wouldn't need to that night. It was already after midnight.

Beaucoup followed Ayanna out the back door of Whiz's basement and walked over to his Navigator to let her in. Before he opened the door with his electronic key ring, he pressed his pelvis up against her behind and began a slow grind against her backside.

He said, "You just wanna chill t'night instead?"

Ayanna rolled her eyes at the question, out of his view. She forced herself to tell him, "Nah, man, I'm ready to go back home." Yet she failed to push him away from her.

He grinned and asked, "You sure you don't want no more of this t'night?" while still forcing his pelvis into her behind.

"Yeah, I'm sure," she responded in a monotone.

"But I thought you said you were hungry."

"Yeah, I'm hungry to go da fuck back home t'night," Ayanna finally snapped at him.

Coup noticed her sour mood and backed away from her. "Look here, 'Yana . . . like I told you before, if you really wanna get in nis rap game, you gotta be able to stay up late, like er'rybody else do. You can't be no early bird. Go back in nere and ask Whiz, hunh. He'll tell you."

Ayanna said, "Yeah, but I still have school to go to."

Coup looked at her and frowned. He said, "Aw, girl, don't start talkin' nat school shit now. You ain't been talkin' about it wit me. So what dat mean? You'on want dis no more, t' get put on this music game. Because it's all a game, jus' like er'rything else out here. And you gotta know how da play it."

Ayanna sighed, realizing that she had gone along with Beaucoup's game for a couple of weeks of bullshit, just so he could get her on her knees for his doggie style, while amusing himself with her rhyme flow.

"Aw'ight, come on, den, girl. I'll take you back home," he told her, as he unlocked the doors with a press of his key ring.

Ayanna hopped into the high-seated SUV and was satisfied with her final decision. She decided that it was time to leave Beaucoup alone and get back to her schoolwork. She figured she would try her rhymes out somewhere else in the near future, with someone who really cared.

Beaucoup looked over and asked her, "Where you want me to drop you off t'night?"

She looked at him and said, "At school again. Gentilly Boulevard."

He looked her in the eyes and said, "It's damn near one o'clock out hea' now. Ain't nobody up at that damn school. But you still don't want me to drive you home, hunh?"

Ayanna looked out of the passenger side window and tried to ignore him.

He said, "Ay," and smacked her leg through the baggy jeans that she wore. "I'm talkin' to you ova' here. Ma-fuckas don't ignore me when I'm talkin'. Ya heard me?"

Ayanna looked at him and remained speechless.

Coup shook his head and went to spite her. "Yeah, you fuckin' college girls are all la same. You ain't got no heart for dis street game. And that's what rap music is, basically. It ain't nothin' but another street hustle. And if you can't stick it out wit *me,* what makes you think you gon' be able to roll wit dem *true game* ma-fuckas. 'Cause see, this rap game shit ain't really my game. I'm jus' fuckin' wit it right now to try and help you out."

He stared into Ayanna's face and awaited her response.

But Ayanna was fed up with his damn street-life philosophies! That boy didn't know every-fucking-thing! If he did, he would no longer be on the streets.

So Ayanna got smart with him and asked, "Are you finished yet?"

Coup took a second to think over the slight before he chuckled at it to humor himself.

"Now see, if you was a guy, I'd have to smack you in your fuckin' mouth for dat smart shit. But since you a girl, I figure I might jus' drop you off at one of these projects, and pay one of these real N'awlins bitches out hea' to take a bite out ya' ass."

He smiled at the idea and said, "You from Houston, right, wit dem Fifth Ward niggas? Mister, Mister Scarface an' nem. Well, you betta represent out dis motherfucka, girl, talkin' shit t' me like dat."

He actually drove her through some of the torturous project areas of New Orleans. But it was nothing alien from what Ayanna had seen before in southwest Houston. And she told him so.

"These girls out here don't scare me. They go to the grave like everybody else."

Beaucoup looked into her face and laughed. He said, "Oh yeah?" and pulled the SUV over to park in the middle of a dark, ramshackled street. Ayanna could talk the street, but she had not actually been in a fight with a girl since early high school days. So in a hot minute, her heart began to betray her mouth as it beat rapidly.

Beaucoup pushed one foot out the door and turned back to Ayanna before he stepped out.

He said, "Are you sure you're ready to get it on out hea'?" He was calling her bluff.

Ayanna took another breath and said, "Look, I jus' wanna go da fuck back home."

Coup looked into her scared face and started laughing again. He knew the deal. She was a college girl trying to play the streets. So he climbed back into his Navigator with her.

"Yeah, I thought you ain't had no motherfuckin' heart for dis," he told her, as he started to drive her back toward Dillard's campus on Gentilly Boulevard. Coup rarely shut his mouth when he was on a roll, so he kept talking to her during the ride.

"Let this be a lesson to you, 'Yana. You ain't got shit for dese streets out hea'. So don't even fuckin' fake it no more. Jus' stay ya' li'l ass in college and get ya' education. And that's the same thing I told my li'l sista."

Then he stared into Ayanna's face again before he nodded to her.

He said, "But you got some good pussy doe from the back, I'll gi' you dat. Maybe you'd even be able da turn a motherfucka out, if you stopped dressin' like a fuckin' tomboy. That shit ain't cool. I mean . . . you can flow witcha rhymes and all . . . but you a fuckin' *girl*! Recognize dat shit! You'on see Foxy, Lil' Kim, and Eve out here dressin' like no ma-fuckin' guys. That shit ain't no turn-on for niggas. And who you think you sellin' to when you try'na rap? You see dat girls at dat club wa'n't inna dat shit. Guys is into it. And they want a rough bitch that they can fantasize about in some sex clothes."

He said, "Like that bitch Amillion, that roll with Roc-a-fella; Jay-Z an' nem." He shook his head with a smile and added, "I'd fuck da shit outta dat girl. I mean, nat's the kind of rap bitches that niggas wanna see. Ya *heard*?"

Ayanna finally spoke up and said, "She can't even fuckin' rap, wit her mouse-ass voice."

Coup grinned at it and said, "Well, I'd tell you dis . . . she can put her pussy on my mustache anytime she want. Anytime she want!"

That's when Ayanna asked him, "So . . . you were never gonna put me down in the rap game in the first place. Unless I changed my image or something?"

Beaucoup just looked at her and smiled. He said, "Like I told you . . .

that rap shit ain't my fuckin' game. I'm a real hustler. I ain't selling no motherfuckin' fantasies t' niggas talkin' nat rap shit. I mean, I listen to da shit. But
all lay talkin' 'bout is the shit that I'm doin' onna streets. So I jus' wanted to
see how far you wanted to go wit dat shit. That's all. I wanted to see what
you had in you. That's interestin' to me. How far will a ma-fucka' go t' get
what they say they want in life?"

Ayanna sat there and was appalled. On her way out of his Navigator at
Gentilly Boulevard, Coup told her, "And if you see that girl I asked you
about before on campus, Leslie *Bo-day*, you tell her that *Bo-coup* said t' holla
at 'im."

He said, "And that pretty nigga that roll wit me sometimes, Pierre, who
was at the club wit me dat night, that's her brother."

Ayanna didn't even care about the inside information that he was giving
her about her housemate at the moment. She was too ticked off at being
played by him. So she cursed his ass while she walked down the street
toward the house.

"Fuckin' punk-ass motherfucka!" she spat into the air. Ayanna's feelings
were hurt. She was dead serious about rap music, and Beaucoup seemed to
know everyone there was to know in New Orleans to set her up with
something major. But his so-called help was only an illusion. He had been
playing her for a fool the whole time.

She cursed him all the way home, with tears of anger leaking from her
eyes. Not only had she been played for her dreams but she had also allowed
him to ram himself into her, like the dog that he was. But what did that
make *her*?

"Mother*fucker*!" She continued to curse the air in her frustration. Her
housemate was the last thing on her mind when she arrived at home.

Ayanna walked in the door and lay out on the sofa without pulling the
bed out, or bothering to take her clothes off. She mumbled quietly to herself in the dark, "Fuck it, I'll get over it. I'll get over it," she repeated, as she
wiped the tear stains from her face with a hard rub of her palms.

"You'll get over what?" a voice asked her from the dark.

Ayanna took a quick breath and hollered, "Shit!" right before Leslie
walked out from the kitchen in her nightclothes, an extra-long Mickey
Mouse shirt that stopped above her knees.

Ayanna asked her, "What are you doin' in the dark like that? You try'na
make me have a heart attack or something?"

Leslie stopped and stared at her. "I couldn't sleep."

"But that don't mean you have to be in the dark," Ayanna told her.

"Yeah, but I'm still tired, so I don't want the light in my eyes," Leslie countered.

Ayanna nodded to her and didn't know what else to say. She hadn't been around Leslie for a while, ever since she told her that . . . secret.

Ayanna remembered what it was and became spooked again. *What does she want from me?* she asked herself. All of a sudden, the hurt that she felt from Beaucoup became ancient history. It was now Leslie who she was worried about.

Leslie took a seat beside her on the sofa and asked, "So, what were you crying about?"

Ayanna looked at her with her eyes just beginning to focus in the dark. She asked, "How did you know I was crying?"

"I could see you. And I could hear you. It sounded like you were crying," Leslie answered.

Ayanna asked her, "You can see me . . . in the dark?" She was thinking about voodoo powers.

Leslie answered, "I was already in the dark, so my eyes were used to it."

"So how come you didn't say something to me when I first walked in?"

Leslie cut the bullshit questions and asked her, "What are you getting at?"

Ayanna immediately backed down from it. She said, "I mean, walking around in the dark is just . . . weird, Leslie. That's all."

Leslie ignored her response and went back to her interrogation. She had been anxious to talk to Ayanna alone again for weeks. She asked her again, "So what were you crying about? What do you have to get over?"

Shit, she heard everything I said in here! Ayanna exclaimed to herself.

"You can hear everything in the dark, Ayanna," Leslie responded to her.

Ayanna became even more spooked. "How do you know what I was thinking?" she asked. She leaned away from Leslie on the sofa.

Leslie told her, "Look, girl . . . if you wanna act afraid of me, then I'll give you something to be afraid of. Now stop acting like Yula and answer my damn question. What were you crying about?"

Ayanna took another breath and went to explain the situation. Not that she wanted to, she just felt like she had no choice in the dark, with Leslie threatening her. What if she did have powers?

Ayanna answered, "I met this guy at the club a few weeks ago, and I thought he was gon' hook me up with some connections in rap music down here, but . . . he jus' played me."

"He played you how?" Leslie asked her.

Ayanna looked at her and wanted to keep her business to herself, just like Leslie would. But then Leslie read her mind again. It was easy to do. Ayanna had always been obvious. She was an open book to Leslie, where Leslie was more like hieroglyphics to her and to everyone else.

So Leslie told her in a low tone, "You know something private about me now. So it's only fair that I know something private about you."

And when Ayanna looked into her hard, probing eyes, she knew that the only way out was to tell Leslie what she wanted.

"All he wanted to do was get me up in bed with my ass out, just to see how far I would go to get a hookup."

Leslie looked at her and was silent for a minute. Then she stood up to leave.

But before she left, she told Ayanna as she stood at the staircase in the dark, "Don't even worry about it. Everybody gets what they got comin' to them. You got yours for being stupid, and eventually . . . he'll get his for being a fuckin' snake in the grass. Because the gardener has a shovel for his ass."

And when she walked back up the stairs, she did so without having to warn Ayanna again to remain quiet about their secret. Because Ayanna knew in her gut . . . that Leslie was not to be . . . fucked with.

. . . of American Stardom

Professor Marcus Sullivan viewed the raw footage from Kaiyah Jefferson, one of the two African-American students at Tulane University who were participants in his study of human sociology on camera. It was part of the new wave of human evaluation in America. Everyone was doing it! Even the major American television networks were chasing the real human stories. In fact, "Professor Sell"—as his students liked to call Marcus because of his rapid speech, similar to a movie pitchman—was a Hollywood reject in his mid-forties, who had returned to his home state of Louisiana to teach at Tulane only until he could find an ingenious way to take another shot at moviemaking. Many of his students realized as much. So they were eager to take him up on his zany ideas of studying humans, while he was actually collecting film story material on the sly.

Marcus watched the young African Americans that Kaiyah had captured on video, as he rubbed his eyes to stay awake in a dark campus projection room after hours. He was also trying his best to unravel his prejudice. Was an African-American story important enough to study? . . . Not much in the business of Hollywood, but in sociology, Marcus had to force himself to agree that it was.

Yet . . . the African Americans whom Kaiyah had so eagerly filmed on camera for the project were so . . . so . . . stereotypical, with their baggy clothes, street-gang bandannas, wild hairstyles, slang speech patterns, and their apparent desire to be . . . show-offs. Every last one of them seemed to want to entertain with jokes, self-promotion, rapping skills, or play a footage-wasting game of peekaboo, while jumping in and out of the damn camera lens!

Marcus shook his head and tried to stomach it all. "Jesus Christ, this isn't a rap video, for crying out loud! It's a sociological documentary!" he yelled at the screen as he forced himself to continue viewing Kaiyah's footage. That would be fair, at least. He could say that he had watched every minute of it, and that there was just not much there to tell an original story that was not . . . typical African American.

Then Kaiyah's camera zoomed in on a close-up. "That's Leslie Beaudet. She's from New Orleans, and she tells us what time it is down here. Go ahead, Leslie, say something for the camera."

Marcus focused in unison with the lens as he sat up in his chair.

"Wow," he told himself. "She has just . . . flawless skin. And those eyes . . . Wow!"

An African-American subject finally had his full attention without him cringing.

"Leslie *Bo-day*," Professor Sullivan repeated from the recorded narration.

Then she spoke into the lens: "What do you want me to say?"

"Say anything," someone told her. "Tell us something extra about N'awlins. Talk about that voodoo shit down here. Speak in French, L. Do *anything*, girl. Anything!"

But she remained calm as the camera locked in on her. Then she turned from it and declined to speak. "Mmmpt mmm."

And that was it. She had nothing more to say.

Marcus repeated, "Wow!" a third time. And he rewound the tape.

"What do you want me to say?"

He rewound it again.

"What do you want me to say?"

He then rewound the footage back to Leslie's opening statement: "Y'all all in here tellin' y'all business. You don't even know what she's gonna do with this stuff . . ." Then she asked her friends, "A documentary for who?" while the camera zoomed in on her exotic dark face.

After taking the footage all in, Marcus nodded his head and was convinced. "Now, *she's* a story. Those eyes don't lie. And I'm willing to bet that Leslie has plenty to uncover. We just have to get her to want to tell us."

So he rewound the footage once more, going all the way back to the beginning of "the chocolate crew." He took notes this time in the dark, and he became anxious to see Kaiyah Jefferson in class the next day, so that he could pull her aside and tell her that she had captured an interesting subject.

"Leslie *Bo-day*," he repeated to himself with a satisfied nod. "She's the one."

≈

Understandably, Kaiyah Jefferson was excited about the news before she had even heard all of her professor's comments on her footage.

She nodded to him in their discussion of "the chocolate crew" and said, "I really liked them. They'll be as excited about this as I am. Especially Bridget. She was pushing real hard for it, but I couldn't make her any promises, you know."

Professor Sullivan smiled and let his student ramble in her excitement before he calmed her down and told her exactly what he thought.

"Well, I'm actually pleased that you didn't promise Bridget anything, because I'm not interested in her. Bridget obviously has her own agenda here. I've watched plenty of the running-for-office type. And they all want to control the camera for their personal *edited* story lines."

He said, "We don't need that. We want to film honest social behavior and not politics. So Bridget Chancellor is out."

Kaiyah shut her mouth and listened for the catch. *Please don't tell me he wants to do Ayanna,* she thought. *She's so . . . ghetto! We don't need that either,* she pondered. *My people surely don't need her story right now.*

However, Professor Sullivan tossed out that idea as well.

"And ah . . . Ayanna Timber," he uttered, while looking down at his notes, "she's too stereotypical of the hard-core rap culture. I mean, is she really in college, or what?"

Kaiyah even chuckled at that. She was relieved that he wasn't interested in Ayanna.

He went on and said, "And Yula Frederick? There's no story there. She barely even looked at the camera. But Leslie," he said with a climactic pause, "Leslie *Bo-day* is your winner. So I need you to get back in touch with her, and see if you can get her to talk."

Kaiyah looked at him skeptically. She said, "May I ask you why you want to do her? Bridget told me that she doesn't . . . open up to people much. We can see that in the footage."

Professor Sullivan got excited and countered, "Yes, but she was not afraid of the camera, she just needed to know why she would want to reveal herself, and that tells me that she really wants to. You just have to make her certain that her story's important."

He said, "She's basically asking us, 'Do you really want my story?' And she's not gonna give it to us unless she knows that it's going to mean something to her."

Kaiyah put two and two together and responded, "I thought you said that we're not offering anyone money."

Marcus shook his head and was slightly irritated that Kaiyah was not getting him.

He said, "No, she doesn't want money, per se. She wanted your sincerity, and your sincerity means more to her than money."

He explained, "Leslie is very dignified. And a lot of Americans are not right now. Most of us will do anything for the camera. But Leslie won't. And she wants us to get that."

He asked, "And what's this about the voodoo and the French? Can you go back and see what that's about? And she's from New Orleans? That means we can go more in depth with her story by getting her family members involved. I bet some of them are a lot less cautious around the camera. In fact, I'm willing to bet they are!"

Professor Sullivan finished his comments and looked all giddy about it, but Kaiyah was not.

Here we go again, she mused. *Another white man is trying to tell me what he thinks I don't know about my people. That character analysis stuff has gone to this white man's head! And if I know anything, this girl Leslie and her family need money, like Bridget says they do; if we're not going to offer her anything to record her life on camera, then she's not gonna do it.*

Kaiyah grinned as she concluded to herself, *She's gonna have dignity all right, dignity not to do this for free. So this man is gonna have me wasting my time with this!*

Nevertheless . . . she was still game to try it. And why not? She was an American opportunist just as Professor Sullivan was.

≈≈

Bloomp!

Phyllis's battered body spun up in the air again in Leslie's dreams as she awoke at four o'clock in the morning.

Shit! she snapped to herself. *I can't get it off my mind now. I actually . . . killed somebody . . . But she deserved it! She deserved it!* Leslie tried to convince herself in the dark silence of her room. She mumbled, "I'll buy a paper in the morning to see if it really happened."

So for the next two days, she searched through the various crime, obituary, and local sections of the *Times-Picayune* for any news on a girl named Phyllis of the Ninth Ward, who had been struck and killed in a hit-and-run car incident.

And Leslie found . . . nothing in the newspapers that would validate her fears.

≋

Kaiyah Jefferson of Tulane met up with her new friend Bridget Chancellor on Dillard's campus for lunch, with her handheld camera in tow and all of the details of the filming on her mind. And Bridget was jumping for joy about their meeting.

"Oh my God! I can't believe this! I'm just so-o-o excited right now. So he really liked us?" she asked of Kaiyah's instructor. Then she quickly added, "But what about Leslie? What did he say about her? He didn't want her in it, right?" Bridget assumed. "I mean, because she wasn't really participating with anything. And maybe it's for the best to leave her out, because she would just get in the way."

Bridget was talking a mile a minute, and she was still upset with Leslie about her sleight of tongue with Eugene at the Xavier basketball game. Poor Eugene spent the rest of that night trying to explain himself to Bridget and Yula, during and after the game.

However, Kaiyah had to wipe away Bridget's snide face of glee, even though she didn't want to. She liked Bridget's political agenda. Kaiyah would rather show a positive face of African America than anything else. Nevertheless . . . an assignment was an assignment, and it was surely better than not having one at all.

So Kaiyah sucked up her own disappointment and went to give Bridget the news. She hoped that Bridget would agree to help her out, so she went about explaining things . . . carefully.

"Well, how much do you really know about Leslie?" she asked.

Bridget studied Kaiyah's face before she answered her.

"Ah . . . to tell you the truth, Leslie only lets you know bits and pieces about herself. And at this point, I couldn't even begin with her. It just seems like the closer I try to get to her, the more complicated she becomes. So I'm ready to just leave her alone."

Kaiyah nodded to her. "How did you all become friends?"

Bridget began to lose her patience with it.

"I mean, are we still trying to work with her on this? Is that what your teacher said?"

She was hoping that he hadn't said that, because Leslie had overrun her bill of affection, and Bridget was just about ready to cut her losses on the girl and move on.

Kaiyah noticed as much, and became even more careful with her words. She said, "Well, I'm just trying to get more details on the hardest person for us to film, because you're obviously the easiest," she told her.

Who could ever turn down a perfectly timed compliment?

Bridget attempted to hold back her smile and couldn't. She said, "Well, since you put it that way," and beamed across the small white lunch table. She said, "I had a psychology class in my freshman year with Leslie. And we got to talking one day, and she was really smart. So, I introduced her to Yula, who I had nursing classes with, and then Yula knew Ayanna from her sociology class, and then we all ended up going places together, and we all just liked each other."

She thought about it a second and added, "Or at least we thought we did. Because I'm beginning to wonder about that myself now."

Kaiyah grinned and said, "A lot of college friends grow apart." And she had a strong hunch about how the girls all came together, but she asked the question anyway.

"Whose idea was it to live together?"

Bridget grinned again and confirmed her friend's assumptions. "That would be my idea."

"And how did Leslie respond to it?"

Bridget thought about it. She answered, "She didn't say it, but I would assume that she was very pleased about it, because she immediately started cooking us these slamming Creole and Cajun dinners. And she had said that she could cook and that she worked at a restaurant and everything, but I had no idea she could cook like that."

"And what about the French and voodoo stuff?"

Bridget looked and smiled. "Well, she does speak fluent French because her family is Haitian, but I don't know about that voodoo stuff. That's just stuff that Ayanna was always interested in."

"So Ayanna's been asking her about that a lot?" Kaiyah questioned. She was just about ready to pop the big question on Bridget.

Bridget answered, "Yeah, but Yula didn't want to know anything about that, that's for sure. When we had a Ouija board out, Leslie didn't really know how to work that, and we all just ended up talking all night. So I really don't know if Leslie knows about that. But I doubt it."

Kaiyah was on a roll. This Leslie girl was getting more interesting by the minute. And she figured that she had warmed Bridget up enough to record her responses on camera now.

"So, would you be willing to start off the documentary by talking about how you met Leslie and the rest of them?" Kaiyah asked her. "And I'll just ask you the same questions over again."

Kaiyah hated to deceive Bridget that way; however, she wanted to be successful with her assignment, even if she had to withhold the truth about her real subject.

Bridget eagerly obliged with spunk. "Okay."

So Kaiyah set her up for it while she adjusted her camera. "Okay, so what I want you to do is state who you're, why you came to Dillard, what you're studying, and then you go right into how you met your friends, and starting with Leslie."

Bridget jingled with anxiety and prepared herself for the camera.

"Okay . . . three, two, one," Kaiyah counted down from behind the lens as several Dillard students began to watch from inside the cafeteria.

Bridget looked into the camera with a wide smile and braids, and said, "Hi, my name is Bridget Chancellor, and I'm a sophomore nursing student here at Dillard University in New Orleans . . ." She spoke with perfect posture, poise, and diction, while feeling like an American star.

≈

Leslie was called to the telephone at Hot Jake's restaurant, while back at work that evening.

She took the receiver in hand and answered, "Hello."

"Leslie, guess what happened?" her sister, Laetitia, asked her in hyper and low tones.

Leslie took a breath and ran her eyes quickly through the kitchen to see who might be watching her. Then she walked into a more secluded area.

"*Quoi?*" she asked her sister in French.

Laetitia shocked Leslie when she answered her back in French, *"La fille que je n'aime pas a été tuée par un accident de voiture."* The girl I don't like was killed by a car. She had been practicing her response in French for hours, just for Leslie.

Leslie asked her, *"Comment le sais-tu?"* How do you know?

Laetitia went back to English and answered, "Everybody's talking about it."

Leslie took another breath with her fears finally confirmed. She had killed someone. For real!

She asked, *"C'est dans le journal?"* It's in the newspaper?

"You know I don't read no newspapers like that," Laetitia responded. "But everybody is talking about it around here. And they . . . *ont trouvé le corps dans la rue où elle travaille."* Found her body on the street where she works.

Laetitia was surprised herself at how the French came back to her when she felt she needed it. But in reality, all that she needed was a reason to try harder. And murder was definitely a reason.

So Laetitia asked her big sister while still in her excitement, *"Tu ne crois toujours pas en le pouvoir de notre famille? Je l'ai demandé."* You still don't believe in our family power? I've been asking for this.

Leslie tried her best to cool the fire. *"Rien qu'une coïncidence. Tu ne sais même pas ce que tu dis."* It's only a coincidence. You don't know what you're saying.

However, Laetitia was adamant. She said, "I *do* know what I'm sayin'. And . . . *elle a reçu la monnaie de sa pièce."* She got what she deserves.

Leslie stood frozen while her sister continued: "And then Jurron came back home, and I told him what you told me to. And . . . *nous avons bien fait l'amour"*—we made very good love—she commented with a giggle.

Leslie remained silent. She told herself, *I have to speak to Daddy about this in person again.*

She told her sister, *"Merveilleux.* Wonderful. Now I have to get back to work."

But Laetitia wasn't finished with her yet. She said, "I mean, Leslie, it was like you knew that it would be all right and that Jurron would come back to me. I mean . . . *comment tu l'as su?"* How did you know? "I'll tell you how. *Nous avons le pouvoir,* that's how!" We have power!

"Look, I have to go," Leslie snapped at her sister hastily.

"Okay, but as long as you know," Laetitia responded to her. "I'm not gonna stand for anybody trying to ruin my family. I'm not. Because they all I got, Leslie. They all I got."

When Leslie hung up the telephone, she could barely move.

Shit! she stressed to herself. *This girl is crazy! And she doesn't even know anything . . . or does she?*

With Leslie standing there meditating inside the secluded kitchen area, Jake suddenly snapped her out of it and told her to follow him into his small private office.

What now? Leslie asked herself as she followed him. She began to panic, wondering if Jake somehow knew something. So when she walked in behind him, she was hesitant, with apprehension.

Jake sat down in his black leather chair behind his tiny wooden desk, with a safe box at his back, and he told Leslie to shut the door behind her.

Leslie looked at him and lingered there at the door before she moved.

Jake smiled at her and asked her, "You don't want everyone out there to know about your *raise,* do you?"

With that, Leslie was able to relax again as she shut the door behind her.

Jake nodded and said, "I realize that with you being the older sister, and basically . . . ah . . . the most responsible of Jean's children, that a lot is going to fall on your shoulders now that your mother's passed. So I've decided to give you a three-dollar-an-hour raise to help out.

"How does that sound to you?" he asked her as he grinned.

Leslie nodded and forced herself to grin back at him. It wasn't that she was not pleased with the raise, she was just boggled down by the other issues on her mind at the moment.

She said, "It sounds good to me," and began to smile at the irony of it all. A murder didn't seem so . . . *bad* anymore. She began to feel that she could get away with it . . . just as her father had done before her. It was redemption. Karma. The way of the world.

Payback
Is a Bitch!

Well, Ayanna, it's February, and that means Black History Month—the shortest month of the year—where we get to learn about all of the accomplishments of our people until next year. And in New Orleans, of course, February means that Mardi Gras is coming, where all those rich white folks come down here to act like fools out in the middle of the streets.

"Did you know that they didn't even used to let black people into those silly parades?" Yula asked Ayanna across the dining room table, where they were both doing their schoolwork.

However, Ayanna was barely paying attention to Yula. She wasn't paying attention to her schoolwork either. She was daydreaming with her books open, while wishing for another life.

She opened her mouth only for sarcasm. "Yeah, I know. 'I have a dreeeam, I have a dreeeam, I have a dreeeam' . . ."

Yula laughed at Ayanna's Martin Luther King Jr. speech, which was made famous on the historical March on Washington during the American sixties, when blacks, Jews, women, and other excluded Americans fought for equality and human rights.

Yula stopped laughing and said, "That's not funny, though."

"So why did you laugh, then?" Ayanna asked her.

Yula paused and shrugged her shoulders.

"I don't know. I mean . . . it just seems like we're always laughing about something."

"*We* who?" Ayanna asked her. She wanted to make sure that her assumption was right.

Yula answered, "Black people," and confirmed it.

Ayanna said, "So what? White people laugh, too."

"Yeah, but they don't laugh all of the time like we do. I mean, it just seems like we're always clownin' each other. You know what I mean?"

Ayanna sighed. She didn't feel like hearing it. The conversations never changed anything. Black people would continue to be black, and laughter was their way of life, no matter what the circumstances were. You were even ostracized for taking things too seriously when you didn't laugh. So Ayanna stated, "Who really cares, Yula? Who? I mean, life goes on."

Yula frowned and studied Ayanna's posture at the table. She was slumped over and drained of her usual, hyper energy. She had always had a smart mouth, but her snappy attitude had been more boastful than depressed. Now she seemed more depressed, which was unusual for her.

"What's wrong with *you*?" Yula asked her.

"Nothin'," Ayanna snapped at her. "I'm just try'na do my fuckin' work! So can you shut up a minute?"

Yula was not offended by it. On the contrary, she was amused. She had rarely had an opportunity to get under Ayanna's skin, and she saw the moment and seized it.

"Ayanna, are you upset because your li'l rap connections didn't work out the way you expected them to? I mean, because everybody can't be no rap star," Yula told her friend.

"Well, I'm not 'everybody,'" Ayanna countered.

Yula just grinned at her. She teased, "Everybody wants to be a star. I hear so many people walking around campus talkin' 'bout, 'Oh I'm just doin' this until I can get my acting, singing, dancing, and modeling career together,' as if we all can be performers and make millions of dollars. And that's just unrealistic, Ayanna."

"Maybe for *you*," Ayanna retorted, eyeing Yula's size.

Yula was still not offended. She said, "It looks like somebody just got their li'l feelings hurt out in the real world. Well, just take a number and stand in line with the rest of us, Ayanna, because I got smacked in the face by reality too."

"Whatever," Ayanna huffed at her. She tried to focus on her work again, right as Bridget walked in with her friend Kaiyah from Tulane. She had her handheld camera with her.

Bridget grinned in their direction and hummed, "I have good news, guys."

Ayanna grinned back at her and said, "That's 'girls.'"

"No, it's 'ladies,'" Yula corrected her.

"Anyway," Bridget told them. "We were chosen for the documentary!" she added with glee.

Ayanna smiled and looked over at Yula. "See that?" she asked.

"That don't mean you gon' be no star, Ayanna."

"Watch me."

Bridget cut in on their ongoing argument and asked them, "So, are you guys in on this, or what?"

Yula looked and asked, "All of us? I mean, Leslie's not here."

That's when Kaiyah unraveled her pitch. She said, "Well, since we all know that Leslie's going to be the hardest to interview for the camera, I came up with the idea to let you all talk about her first, and then we'll introduce her after she warms up to the idea."

Yula nodded and said, "Oh, that's smart."

However, Ayanna was unmoved by the girl's . . . cleverness, as well as a bit skeptical about her plans. "And what if she don't 'warm up' to it?" Ayanna asked her.

Kaiyah said, "Well, that'll be up to you all. I mean, surely no one can force her to do it, but if you guys are all friends in here, then . . ."

Her point was well taken. What influence did they all have on Leslie . . . if any?

Bridget said, "Look, I've been thinking about this all day. And this may be the best thing for Leslie to finally break her out of her shell. I mean, it could be good for her."

This girl has definitely forgotten who we're fuckin' wit! Ayanna thought to herself with a look at Bridget and her camera-holding friend.

She said, "I don't know about this idea, man. I mean, what do you want us to say about her?"

"Just say how you all met her," Kaiyah answered simply enough.

Ayanna looked at her a minute longer to figure things out for herself.

"So . . . if this documentary is about all of us, then why are you so concerned about Leslie?"

"Yeah," Yula seconded her.

Kaiyah went on to explain things. "Well, we'll get a chance to do each of you, but to save camera time, I just figured that we'd start off with the hardest."

"Yeah. It makes sense," Bridget agreed with Kaiyah.

Meanwhile, Kaiyah was hoping and praying that Professor Sullivan would acquiesce after her ingenious work at directing the action, and agree that all of "the chocolate crew" were important in how they related to each other. And if not . . . she would just have some explaining to do. But later, after she had successfully completed her assignment.

However, Ayanna wouldn't budge on it. She figured that she had the most to lose if Leslie didn't like what was going on. She didn't want to chance any . . . voodoo madness in Leslie's response.

So Ayanna advised them all, "If you really want to get Leslie involved in this, then I think you should just ask her first. Because she's very busy, and I don't think she would like how you're jus' . . . plannin' this on her."

Kaiyah went for broke and joked to Ayanna, "Yeah, because we wouldn't want her using any voodoo on us, right?"

Yula laughed nervously, followed by Bridget, as Kaiyah chuckled at her joke herself. But Ayanna's heart skipped a beat, and she remained serious.

"That shit's not funny," she told them.

Kaiyah couldn't stop herself. She was a skeptic, and every phenomenon had to be proven to her. So she responded, "I mean, come on. There's no such thing as voodoo. People are just going to believe in what they want. It's just like with magic. There's always a trick to it. You just have to find it out."

Ayanna said, "Yeah, well, you find that shit out on your own," and stood up from the table to leave them.

Bridget said, "She was only joking, Ayanna. What's wrong with you?"

Ayanna thought about the voodoo book that she had found in Leslie's room, and she felt a sudden urge to hide it away to protect Leslie. She was choosing to be on her side. Because if voodoo was indeed real, and Leslie was a young priestess, then Ayanna didn't want to be on the wrong side, like Bridget would be. And Ayanna told her so.

She said, "Bridget, is this your idea? Because if it is, then you betta rethink this shit. Because if she gets pissed off . . . I mean, we still have to live with her."

Ayanna figured that she was only being logical about it.

Yula looked, thought about it, and agreed with Ayanna again.

"She's right, Bridget. Leslie even cooks our food in here."

Kaiyah began to laugh. Maybe Professor Sullivan was onto something after all with choosing Leslie. These girls seemed scared of her. So Kaiyah thought to herself, *I need to mix things up again.*

She turned to Bridget and asked, "Well, you don't believe in this voodoo stuff, do you, Bridget?"

There was a pregnant pause inside the room. Bridget was stuck in between the bridge. On one side was loyalty to her friends, and on the other was a chance to do something special, a chance to move forward, to explore, and to be brave in life. It was a chance to create a little . . . drama. Americans had grown to love drama. So had Bridget. So she walked across the bridge to be delivered into her fate.

"No . . . I don't believe in it. I mean . . . Leslie's just quiet, that's all. And people always think strange things about introverts," she told everyone.

Ayanna stared her down and said, "Okay. That's on you," and she gathered her things to head out the door. She was going to finish her studying back on campus.

Yula looked around in the aftermath and took a deep breath. She said, "Well, I guess I'll get back to my homework now." She didn't know what else to say. But she was thinking, *I sure hope Bridget knows what the hell she's doing. I mean, is she still pissed at Leslie about that Eugene shit at the basketball game? Because if she is, then she needs to get over it. Because this is wrong!*

≈

When Bridget walked Kaiyah back out of the house, she immediately began to have second thoughts about things. She asked her, "Why did you . . . set Ayanna off like that? Now she's not gonna want to be involved in it."

Kaiyah shook her head in her determination and countered, "No, the real question is, why is she so obviously afraid of Leslie? I mean, I think she knows something."

"Knows what?" Bridget asked her, a bit irritated. Maybe it wasn't such a great idea after all. Kaiyah seemed to be rather insensitive.

She said, "Well, people get cold feet all the time with camera work. So I've just learned how to instigate things to get their emotions going." She sounded as if she was a professional director.

However, Bridget felt less certain about their plans now.

She said, "Well, now we have two people to get involved again."

Kaiyah thought fast and responded with a grin, "Maybe we can offer her a freestyle rap session on camera or something. You think Ayanna would go for that? I know she loves to rap."

It finally hit Bridget. Her friend Kaiyah was out to use whatever ploy that she could to get what she wanted on camera.

So she asked her hypothetically, "And what if Ayanna doesn't want to freestyle on camera? Then what?"

Kaiyah shrugged her shoulders and maintained her arrogant grin. "Well, I guess we'll just have to come up with something else to get her back in." *And if she doesn't cooperate with us . . . well, Leslie's the real catch here anyway,* Kaiyah thought to herself. *I'll just get to her on my own.*

Get what you want at all costs was the name of her game. But by that time, Bridget had seen the light of day, and she had figured her friend from Tulane out.

She thinks she's better than us because she attends Tulane while we're over at . . . little old Dillard. Yeah, I know her type from Ann Arbor, Bridget pondered. *She thinks that we'll do anything just to get on her stupid documentary! And I actually fell for that . . . shit! Well, not anymore. Watch this.*

Bridget nodded and smiled to her. She said, "Well, I'll do all that I can to make sure that everything works out just right for the documentary, because I really, really want to do this."

Kaiyah smiled right back at her. "Cool. So we'll stay in touch then. And in the meantime . . . see if you can just tweak Leslie's interest on it. I mean, don't tell her everything outright. You just . . . you know, find a way to make it happen."

Yeah, like you're trying to do with me, Bridget thought.

She smiled and said, "Okay, I'll do that," as she walked Kaiyah over to her car. And when she drove off down the street, Bridget frowned and told herself, *I will never return her phone calls again. And if she ever catches up with me . . . I'll just tell her that I'm too busy doing easy homework to talk right now. And I'll see how she likes that!*

Bridget walked back into the house to face Yula at the dining room table. She confessed, "You know what, Yula, I believe I have some apologizing to do. Because that girl Kaiyah was only out for herself. She doesn't really care about us."

Yula looked at Bridget and smiled from ear to ear. She was proud of her. The rich girl was finally using her damn brains! So Yula let her in on a little secret.

She said, "You know what, I thought the same thing right after that girl started making jokes about voodoo. I mean, I laughed and all, which was wrong . . . but that girl shouldn't have said that. She doesn't even know Leslie. She was just stereotyping her because she's private about her life and her parents are from Haiti. That girl was just try'na get a rise out of us."

≈

Leslie felt good that night, while on her way home from work with leftover food from the kitchen. She had killed someone, and she got a raise. And her little sister had her man and family back in order, or as much order as they could muster for the time being. So Leslie walked home that night with an unusual bounce in her stride.

At the same time, her housemate Ayanna was headed back to campus, and they spotted each other on Gentilly Boulevard.

With everything that had gone on that night with the girl from Tulane, Ayanna froze for a minute at Leslie's sight, and that made Leslie suspicious of her.

"What's the problem?" Leslie asked her immediately. She was suspicious of everyone after committing a murder.

Ayanna was even slow with her words. "Ahh . . ." She wasn't sure what she wanted to say.

That made Leslie paranoid. And when she got paranoid, she became more forceful about her assumptions.

"What the fuck you do, girl?" *Do I have to kill two people in two nights?* she asked herself, while jumping to conclusions.

That sent Ayanna into an unexpected panic. *This girl is fuckin' serious!* she thought, while reading Leslie's dangerous eyes. They didn't look friendly at the moment. And then the words just tumbled out of Ayanna's mouth. "I told them not to do it. I swear to God! I told them not to do it!"

Leslie was perturbed by it. "You told *who* not to do *what*?"

Ayanna blurted out, "Bridget an'nem. They were in there talking about tapin' your life on video, and then that girl Kaiyah started making jokes about . . . you know . . ." Ayanna was uncertain if she even wanted to say the word. But it was too late by then. Leslie still had her penetrating eyes on her.

"No, I don't know," she snapped. "She started making jokes about what?" she asked Ayanna pointedly.

Ayanna took a breath and answered. "Voodoo." But before Leslie could respond to it, Ayanna backed up and swore up and down, "But I didn't say anything about that, Leslie. Honest! The girl just up and said it all out the blue. So I'm thinkin' that Bridget must have told her about it.

"And then I started thinkin' about that book you got up in your room. And I was wondering if Bridget might have seen it too, because I didn't tell anybody. I swear to God I didn't, Leslie!" she continued to confess.

"And I'm sorry that I went into your room like that, but I was jus' . . . I was jus'—"

"Shut up," Leslie finally told her with a raised hand to stop Ayanna's fear-induced gibberish.

Ayanna calmed down and shut her mouth in a hurry.

Leslie told her, "I'll handle it in my own way. But I don't want you coming back home tonight, because I don't want them thinking that you told me anything. So you find your little friend or whatever to spend the night with, and after I'm finished doing what I need to do, you can come home tomorrow morning."

"What are you gonna do?" Ayanna nearly whispered to her.

Leslie scared the girl stiff and said, "None of your damn business! Just keep everything to yourself. You hear me?"

Oh, shit, this girl is serious! Ayanna repeated to herself. There was nothing in Leslie's eyes or tone of voice that said otherwise. So Ayanna wasn't taking any chances with it.

She said, "Aw'ight, man, but I'm jus' sayin', L, don't go—"

Leslie cut her off and said, "I'm not. Okay? Now go your own way . . . and I'll handle it."

Ayanna went to obey her. But before she could take too many steps in the opposite direction, Leslie called out her name to give her a final warning.

"Ayanna?" Leslie waited for their eye contact again. When she had it, she warned, "Don't *make* me have to *hurt* you! You hear me? So when I tell you to keep this to yourself . . . I *mean* it."

Ayanna nodded her head and believed with all of her heart that Leslie was crazy enough to tell the truth!

≈≈

Okay, is this how it's gonna be? Where I can't have no fuckin' peace in my life, no matter where I turn? Because if it is, then no one else is gonna have any peace either, Leslie told herself as she marched toward the house.

She didn't know exactly what she would do as of yet, but she knew that she would do *something*.

I'll just act like nothing happened, and I let Bridget play her own cards, she pondered. *Bridget always tells on herself anyway. So all I have to do is wait for it. And then I'll decide what to do. I'll just let it come naturally.*

I didn't do anything to have her in my business like this any-fucking-way! she thought. *And like my little sister said . . . I don't really want to be evil or nothin' . . . but people are just fucking asking me for it!*

Leslie calmed herself as she approached the patio steps to the house. She walked up the three wooden steps and took a few deep breaths at the door before she opened it with her key. As soon as she walked in, she put on a smile and offered up her bag of food from Hot Jake's.

"I got leftovers tonight. So who wants to fight for the nuke? I've already eaten."

Yula grinned from the table and joked, "Well, I'm on a diet now."

"Yeah, right," Leslie joked back to her.

Yula laughed, knowing better. "Diet" was a dirty word in her dictionary.

Bridget sat there at the table and smiled herself, as they were both doing homework.

Leslie frowned and asked them, "Are y'all cramming for a test or something?" It was well after eleven o'clock at night, and they were not even dressed in their nightclothes yet.

Bridget said, "No, we were just up talking, mostly." Then she added, "And we were waiting for you."

Leslie eyed her and said, "Waiting for me for what? What's going on now?"

Yula heard Leslie's words and knew some of her struggles, so she immediately shook her head. Leslie could never get a damn break!

Bridget came out with it up front. "Leslie, we just wanted to apologize to you, because we wanted to be in this Tulane documentary. And we knew that you weren't into it, but they wanted all of us, especially you, and your background."

Yula caught on to the word "we" that Bridget was using, and she spoke up to clarify things.

"Well, I didn't know about the documentary thing like Bridget did. I just laughed when the girl made a joke about . . . voodoo," Yula admitted.

Then she jumped to Leslie for mercy and forgiveness.

"But I mean, I didn't really laugh because it was . . . funny or anything, it was just like . . . a nervous laugh, because the girl just came out of nowhere with it."

Bridget explained it more evenly. "She caught all of us off guard with that, and it became real obvious to me that she didn't really care about us, or our bond as friends, because she was just trying to get us on camera. And Ayanna pretty much stood up for you and told her."

Leslie paused and kept her cool, playing out her role of ignorance.

She asked Bridget, "But isn't she your friend?"

Bridget said, "Obviously not. That's why I'm not gonna return her phone calls again."

Leslie eyed them both and asked, "So where is Ayanna now?"

Yula shrugged and said, "She broke out when that girl Kaiyah was still here."

Leslie probed them for more information. "But why would Ayanna leave?"

Yula and Bridget both looked at each other instead of answering.

Bridget said, "Well, to tell you the truth, Ayanna really kind of . . . freaked out when Kaiyah started talking about voodoo." She said, "That girl is pressed about that stuff. I think she's more involved in it than anybody. She's scaring herself with that."

Leslie said, "I told y'all I don't know anything about it. And that girl Kaiyah got that from the tape. Ayanna was running her mouth about it as usual. Y'all don't remember she asked me that? She told me to say something in French, too."

Yula looked at Leslie and was amazed. She said, "You got a good damn memory, Leslie, because I don't remember anything we said when that girl was here the last time."

Leslie told her, "That's why you should never run your mouth too much, because you never know who might be listening."

Bridget cut in and said, "Well, that's what happened. So after Ayanna left, we just wanted to wait up for you guys so that we could all apologize to each other."

Leslie smiled at that. She asked, "What did *I* do?"

Yula curved her eyes back over to Bridget and awaited the drama.

Bridget took a breath and answered, "Well, I've been really thinking about how you treated Eugene at the basketball game the other night, and . . . I just really thought that it was uncalled for."

Yula nodded her head to help Bridget out on it. She said, "And that poor boy apologized to us all night long for it." *But I think he has a thing for Leslie,* she kept to herself. *I can jus' see it in his eyes the way he looks at her. But Leslie is pretty. I gotta give that to her.*

Leslie sized up the situation and decided to back down. "Okay, I'll apologize to him." Then she added, "You want me to say it over the phone?"

Yula looked at Leslie in alarm. She thought, *Uht oh. Don't do that, Bridget! Don't do that!*

But Bridget was the trusting fool.

"Okay, well, we'll just call to him up tomorrow then," she agreed.

Leslie told her, "Why not just get it over with and call him right now? I'm sure he's probably still up."

Yula bounced her head back to Bridget, while observing the tennis match of the minds. And Yula was certain that Leslie was ready to wipe Bridget's slow-minded ass right off the court!

Damn, this girl can be stupid! she thought to herself of Bridget. But Yula was powerless to get in the way. Leslie's serve of the ball was moving far too fast for Yula to stop it without burning her own hand off in the process.

However, Bridget hesitated, giving Yula hope that she would change her mind. But then Bridget nodded and went along with it. "All right, then, let's just get it over with."

Before Yula could even grimace at the bad move on Bridget's part, Leslie's glance in her direction was so lightning quick and subtle that Yula wasn't even sure if it had actually happened. But she felt it, and she knew instinctively to stay out of it.

So Bridget walked over to the telephone on the kitchen wall, and she went to dial the seven numbers to Eugene's dorm room.

When she got him on the line she asked, "Oh, so you're up?"

Eugene answered rather hesitantly, "Umm, yeah, I'm up."

Bridget paused, having second thoughts again.

I knew I shouldn't have called him tonight! Something told me not to call. But Leslie . . . she made me do it! she tried to convince herself.

Meanwhile, Eugene stammered over the line, "Umm . . . let me call you right back."

Bridget didn't want to ask him why while standing there in front of Leslie and Yula, so what choice did she have?

She thought fast and responded, "Okay, I'll hold on," as she walked away from her friends and toward the kitchen.

"Where are you going, Bridget?" Leslie asked her. "I thought you wanted me to apologize."

Bridget held up her index finger to hold Leslie off. "Wait one minute," she told her. Then she spoke back into the receiver where both of her friends could hear, "Oh, okay, well, call me right back then." And she hung up.

Yula assumed the situation and was mortified.

She thought, *Damn, I know for a fact now. I'm not fuckin' wit Leslie! Ayanna was right! It sounds like Bridget caught her man cheatin'. Or Leslie caught him, I should say. I know how the down low works with guys. They always tell you that I'll-call-you-back shit. But I told you them damn light-skinned guys ain't no good! No way in the world he could have just one girl. Or not while he's still in college. Bridget was probably always sharing him!*

Leslie forced herself not to smile, while thinking vengeful thoughts.

That's what she gets, for wantin' to fuck with my business all the time. Now I'm gonna fuck with hers!

"Was he busy?" she asked Bridget.

Bridget smiled and nodded it off. "He was just getting out of the shower."

Wrong game. Even Yula knew it when she looked away from them.

Leslie asked, "At close to midnight, he's getting out of the shower? He was getting himself dirty pretty late, hunh?" she questioned with a grin.

Yula had to hold in her own laugh.

Bridget snapped, "What are you trying to say, Leslie?" It became clear to her by then that Leslie was out to do more than apologize. She was obviously trying to teach Bridget a lesson.

Leslie shrugged her shoulders and responded, "You tell me. I mean, does he need to be apologized to, or should we just let him run around on his leash and forgive him?"

Yula's mouth dropped wide open at the table. She quickly moved to hide it with both hands.

Oh my God! Leslie is the beast! she told herself.

Bridget got Leslie's point, and she walked out of the room and toward the stairs without another word.

Yula watched the whole fiasco. *What's gonna happen now?* she asked herself. *I think Leslie may have gone overboard this time. Bridget's father still got us covered on this house. But can she legally kick Leslie out if she's still paying her share of the rent? Or maybe Bridget won't want to give her any breaks anymore.*

In the middle of Yula's musings, Leslie looked over at her and said, "Now we'll see how Bridget takes it since I have to go apologize to her ass."

Yula looked up at her and was in awe. *Wow!* she thought to herself. *She knew she went overboard. She did it on purpose!*

And when Leslie walked off to follow after Bridget up the stairs, Yula continued to think, *Damn! This girl Leslie is like . . . a damn calculator. She adds, subtracts, divides, multiplies, and she does equations. I mean, this girl is jus' . . . deep!*

The Price
of Love

I *don't think I like this girl anymore,* Bridget thought to herself as she slammed the door to her room. She paused there inside her room and mumbled, "I don't even think I really know her." She began to wonder if maybe her father back home in Michigan was right; many poor people would always be poor unless they uplift themselves.

Her father had told her during her freshman year at Dillard, "Baby, I know you mean well when you talk about your desire to give back to the community, but the reality is, a lot of poor people have been poor for so long that they don't know how to be helped anymore. And you can only help those who you can."

Bridget thought about that conversation a year ago with her father, and about the stubbornness of her friends to see progress, and she found herself moving closer to her father's conservative views. There would always be people who were less fortunate, and there would be nothing that she could do about it.

But why would Eugene answer the darn telephone if he knew that he had company over like that anyway? Bridget mused. His stupidity had nothing to do with Leslie's foul attitude. Or maybe . . . Leslie had it right with her cynical behavior, and Bridget was the one who needed a reality check. So she was confused. Which way was up?

A light knock on the door broke Bridget from her conflictions. "Yes," she answered.

"Can I come in? It's Leslie."

Bridget paused and asked herself, *For what, to bite my hand again?*

Nevertheless, she remained confident in reconciliation. So she moved to open her door.

Leslie met eyes with her and apologized before she walked in. "I'm sorry, Bridget. I guess I . . . I mean . . . I'm just so used to people doing me wrong, that I forget who my real friends are sometimes. But I'm not in the right all of the time either. I mean . . . I just have to admit that."

Bridget listened to her, and it made sense, so she nodded. "I know how you feel," she said. "I thought that I was friends with Kaiyah, but . . . she was just trying to use me to get to you."

Leslie frowned at her and asked, "But why? Why is she so interested in me?"

Bridget dropped her head and had her own facing up to do. A poverty-stricken girl named Leslie Beaudet was more . . . interesting than her. So Bridget looked into Leslie's eyes and confessed it.

"I mean, like I said before, Leslie, you have a lot of . . . character, I guess. And you know, a lot of people just want to know what makes you tick."

Leslie looked into empty space while inside Bridget's room and shook her head. "I don't get it," she commented out loud. "I just want to be left alone. I just wanna . . . be able to do what I need to do." *But people are always bothering me!* she reflected to herself.

Bridget asked her, "But would you want to be left alone with no one?"

Leslie had never even thought of that. She looked bewildered by the question.

"'No one,' meaning what?"

Bridget shrugged her shoulders and thought about Eugene again. She answered, "I mean . . . someone to share life with. And not like . . . with your family members."

Leslie dropped her eyes. To love someone seemed so . . . costly to her that she couldn't imagine being able to afford it. Her mother loved her father and lost him. Her father loved her mother and lost her. Leslie loved her brother and he had . . . failed her. And to save her sister and her nieces from their broken hearts, Leslie had to kill someone. So who could she imagine loving without a price to pay?

Leslie shook the thought from her head and said, "I don't have time to think about that."

Bridget just stared at her, and felt sorry for her.

Leslie read the pity in her eyes and looked away.

"Well, I just wanted to apologize to you, that's all," she stated, and turned to walk back out.

Bridget didn't know how to respond, she just wanted Leslie to stay longer. She wanted to finally crack her shell. And maybe love was what Leslie needed most.

"Have you ever loved anybody, Leslie? I mean, outside of your family?" Bridget forced herself to ask before Leslie could reach the door to leave.

Leslie took a deep breath without turning to face her. "No," she answered. Then she turned and asked Bridget, "Are you satisfied now? You have something else that I don't have."

"I didn't mean it like that," Bridget told her. "Why are you always on the defensive? I was just asking—"

Leslie walked away from her and out of the room before Bridget could finish her sentence.

"You can't keep running away from people and hiding behind your fears, Leslie. Everybody needs to love!" Bridget shouted into the hallway after her housemate.

Yula even heard her from downstairs. She looked up from her schoolwork and shook her head.

"Bad move, Bridget. Bad move," she mumbled to herself.

Then she heard the door to Leslie's room slam shut.

Bloomp!

Yula shook her head again and smiled.

"Oh, drama," she told herself with a chuckle.

≈

"Fuck that girl know about love?" Leslie spat to herself inside her room. *She doesn't love anybody. She just rents people, like us in this house. That's what all rich people do. They don't know what love is about unless they've been poor. Then we'd see how much they love somebody!*

But as Leslie pounced on her neatly made bed, she became unraveled by the thought of love anyway. She had tried it once, back in her early high school days. Twice even. And it was not really love, but sex, and with someone she thought was a good guy. Since it was no good the first time, she tried it with him again, but to no avail. Then he must have bumped his head or something, because he began to act as if he owned her.

"Where are you going, Leslie?

"Where were you when I called you last night?

"Oh, don't act like you don't know me today."

So Leslie was forced to tell the boy, "Look, don't get yourself hurt. So just leave me alone."

But he didn't believe her. Until . . . a group of New Orleans hard rocks showed up at their academic school and McDonough 35 to beat down some punks, and he became a victim that day. But was it through Leslie's warning, or just a coincidence? . . . He believed it was Leslie, so he left her alone from that day on.

Then there was another guy. Courtney Taylor. Leslie had heard stories about him. The rumor was that he had molested people, but no one wanted to confirm it. They only whispered about the things that he had done, as if he were a bogeyman who could torture them through the night without anyone knowing. And Leslie's serene attractiveness caught his eye one day.

"Damn, who dat! Li'l momma right dere prob'bly got da sweet chocolate."

The hard rock types were always harassing the girls after school at McDonough 35. It meant more to them to break down a smart girl. It proved that their game was tight, and not just with easy girls from the local schools.

So Courtney stuck his tongue out at Leslie, and wiggled it around inside of his mouth, looking sinister. Leslie understood that warning Courtney wouldn't work. So she brought a razor blade with her to school. And when he approached her, she allowed him to get close, close enough to cut.

All that Courtney remembered were her eyes. Her eyes were locked on his when she told him, "Don't you ever bother me again."

He didn't even feel the razor blade slice through his jacket and cut the skin on the left side of his torso until she had walked away. Then he hid the blood from his friends. He discarded the soiled jacket, while holding a new respect for the girl in secret . . . and for the rest of his life. So he made sure to remember her name . . . *Leslie Bo-day*. Because he realized that day that Leslie would go there to survive, where most of the girls had only . . . talked about it.

But no, Leslie had never known love outside her family. So when she stretched out across her bed in her room that night, with her eyes to the ceiling to meditate on her lack of intimacy, she became seduced by new visions.

A young and eager man caressed her dark breasts in his hands, with his thumbs, stroking her nipples ever so lightly. His wet tongue circled them, before he sucked them hard. It seemed so real that Leslie moved her arms and hands to caress his head into her bosom and hold him there, as his tongue began to slide down the crease of her stomach. And then . . . he filled her with himself and stretched out her walls. And it felt . . . *good!* So good! Then she looked into his face, as if opening her eyes in the dark, and . . .

"Shit!" Leslie snapped to herself, shaking from her trance. She raised her hands to her temples, and shook her head inside her palms.

"I can't believe this," she mumbled. "Why? Why him?"

Outside her room, she heard the telephone ringing.

Yula answered it downstairs, and walked to the stairway to yell, "Bridget, it's for you!"

Leslie heard Yula's call, and she could feel her seducer on the telephone, lusting for the complexity of her intoxicating brownness . . . and no longer the simplicity of Bridget's virgin drink.

Bridget answered the phone with an attitude. "So . . . how come you had to call me back?"

Eugene was defensive in his answer. "I was finishing something up. What are you talking about?"

"Finishing up what?" Bridget asked him.

"A homework assignment."

"What kind of homework?"

"Calculus."

He was an engineering major. But Bridget refused to believe him. She said, "Well, how come you just didn't tell me that when I called?"

Eugene paused to calm himself and to reevaluate the conversation.

He asked, "So, you were calling me to accuse me of something?"

Bridget froze. There was dead silence over the phone. Then she thought of . . . Leslie.

Inside Leslie's room, Leslie thought of Eugene, the seducer in her new vision, and she listened in on the silence of Bridget in the next room.

Over the phone line, Eugene began to think of Leslie again, wondering if she was there in her room. And suddenly, Bridget could sense the tension of the lust that surrounded her. It was a queasy feeling in her gut. But she was in denial of it.

"Well, what did you call me for?" Eugene began to press her.

Bridget was ready to say anything in her moment of confusion. She said, "You know what . . . I've been thinking that we need to give each other a break anyway."

Eugene frowned on the other line. *Here we go with that shit again,* he told himself.

He asked, "Bridget, why do you keep saying that when you know you don't mean it?"

She answered, "Because I know that you don't care about us as much as I do. And if you're not going to care, then maybe we need to start seeing other people or whatever."

Eugene asked her, "Is that what you want me to do?"

No, Bridget thought to herself immediately. But her mouth was not sure. She said, "I don't know anymore."

Eugene paused. He asked, "Is that what you called me to say earlier?" He was playing at something, as if he knew that there was more to her late phone call that evening. But Bridget refused to tell him, because she could feel it, too. It all added up. Everyone had a curiosity for Leslie, including Eugene, and Bridget was growing tired of it. The last thing she could stand was Eugene being interested in her. But it was only a hypothesis, a wild guess, until she could prove it. However, she felt it stirring. So she had to ask him about it anyway.

"Do you find Leslie attractive?"

Eugene paused again . . . and then he smiled, and was glad that Bridget could not see him through the telephone.

"Why would you ask me that?"

Bridget answered, "I don't know. It's just . . . how you looked at her at the basketball game."

"What do you mean, how I looked at her?"

"I mean, this whole . . . 'blacker the berry, the sweeter the juice' thing."

Eugene stopped smiling. He said, "Aw, here we go with that again. I thought we went through that already."

"Well, just answer the question."

It was the moment of truth.

Eugene paused and thought about it. *Don't go for it!* he told himself. *It's a trap!*

"Why, you don't think she's attractive?" he asked Bridget instead of answering.

Bridget answered, "I think she's very attractive."

Don't go for it! Eugene repeated to himself.

"Well, that's what you think," he responded to Bridget.

"And you don't think the same?"

Eugene stopped her interrogation and asked, "Is this what you were calling me for?" faking his irritation.

Bridget went for the gusto on him. "Actually, she wanted to talk to you."
And Eugene stopped breathing.

He said, "What?"

"I said she wanted to talk to you," Bridget repeated.

"About what?"

"She wanted to apologize."

"Apologize for what?"

"About what happened at the basketball game."

"What about it?"

Eugene was blown away at the thought of talking to Leslie. Nothing else could compute at the moment.

Bridget paused herself before she asked him, "Do you want to talk to her?"

Eugene thought to himself, *I can't believe this is happening! Is this a setup, or what? I just gotta stay cool!*

He finally asked, "What is this all about?"

Bridget became teed off with the whole game of it. She marched out of her room with the cordless phone in hand and right up to Leslie's locked door and knocked on it.

Leslie took a deep breath inside her room before she answered, "Yes?"

"It's Bridget, Leslie. Do you still want to apologize to Eugene?"

Yula heard Bridget asking from downstairs. It was after midnight, and she was still studying. But when she heard Bridget knocking on Leslie's door to ask her to apologize to a boy who had the hots for Leslie, Yula figured that Bridget had lost her mind!

"Is she crazy?" Yula mumbled to herself. *She must not want that boy no more.*

But Leslie stopped the games. "No," she answered through her door. "I don't have anything to say to him. You can tell him whatever you want yourself."

Bridget felt slightly relieved. But Eugene felt crushed.

"I guess that's the end of that idea," he joked over the line to save face. But inside he thought to himself, *This girl just keeps getting chances to dis me . . . Well, fuck her too then!*

He asked, "So, Bridget, you're not serious about this seeing other people thing, are you?"

Bridget smiled, feeling a lot more confident as she walked back inside her room.

She answered, "No. I just get confused sometimes."

Yula concluded things from downstairs with a shrug of her shoulders. *Well, I guess that's the end of that. Leslie just don't like his yellow ass.*

However, up in her room, Leslie began thinking about reading up on her book again . . . and on the powers of . . . sexuality.

≈≈≈

Jean-Pierre sat glumly in front of his daughter at the Open Arms Homeless Shelter in the early afternoon. Leslie had skipped class that day to come and seek words of wisdom from him, and to see how he was coming along in their family loss.

Jean shook his head and told Leslie, "Life is . . . a challenge to us all, my child. *Impossible de prédire.* It is unpredictable. So we can only . . . do what it tells us to do. *Il faut que nous obéissions parce que nous n'avons pas le choix.*" And we obey because we must.

Leslie asked him, *"Mais si la vie te dictait de faire du mal?"* But what if life tells you to do wrong?

Her father looked at her with barren eyes and responded, *"Qu'est-ce qui est juste ou faux, nous allons tous mourir de toute façon?"* What is right or wrong when we all die anyway?

Leslie's eyes averted to the chest pocket of her father's light blue shirt, where she could imagine the imprint of her mother's soul on his heart from the doll that he had made in her likeness.

She said, *"Ça coûte cher, l'amour?"* The price of love is heavy?

Jean nodded to his daughter and answered, *"Oui . . . comme l'air que nous respirons."* Yes . . . and so is the air we breathe.

So it really doesn't make a difference then, Leslie told herself. *It's all just a part of life, no matter who we love . . . or who loves us.*

≈≈≈

Who you loved made a hell of a difference to Jurron Chesterfield, as he sat alone for a minute in his living room at the Desire projects. All that he could think about was the candle that Laetitia sat in front of in the dark that night, the same night that Phyllis had died. Although there was no one being sought after or charged for her death, Jurron was suspicious that someone had killed her. Someone who didn't want them together.

He thought about the newfound self-esteem that Laetitia seemed to have around the house lately, and how she began to remember her French, and speak it fluently now to their daughters. Laetitia seemed to have grown up in the span of a week. And it was all . . . unexplainable to Jurron.

He took out a cigarette, lit it, and sucked in his first toke. He blew out the smoke and mumbled, "This is some voodoo shit," as just a figure of speech. Black Americans used the word often, to explain the unexplainable. Particularly in situations that involved love. But that didn't mean they actually believed in it, no more than Christians wanted to damn God whenever they jammed a toe.

So when Jurron alluded, "That damn girl done got desperate to keep me," he did it in jest. And on one hand he was flattered by the idea, but on the other . . . *Now what if this girl try da kill me one day?* he pondered. But he continued to laugh it all off as ridiculous.

"Nah. Get da fuck outta hea'. She ain't got no fuckin' voodoo. I'on care if her peoples are from Haiti. I'on believe in that shit." Then he smiled and said, "She got some voodoo pussy though, I'll give her that. She got some bomb-ass pussy!"

So why did his heart betray his consciousness when he heard Laetitia's keys dangling at the door with the sound of his daughters?

Jurron panicked from the sofa and spat, "Shit!" He didn't know if he wanted to keep his cigarette lit or not, because Laetitia had begun telling him that the smoke was bad for their children. So before they could all make it in the house, Jurron jumped up to toss the cigarette into the sink of dirty dishes to snuff it out and destroy it inside of the garbage disposal.

Laetitia entered the house and sniffed the smoke immediately. She looked in Jurron's direction, and into his guilt-ridden face. She said, "Jurron, I told you about smokin' in the house. And all you have to do is go outside with it."

Jurron looked her over, and with all of the courage that he could muster, he told himself that nothing had changed, and that he was still the man of the house. So he could do as he pleased!

He said, "Look, y'all wa'n't even *in* here. So I jus' figured I'd catch me a quick smoke. Don't sweat me about that shit, girl. You see I put it out."

He had no idea how Laetitia would respond to him with her newfound confidence, but just for good measure, he added, "And whassup wit dese dirty dishes in here? You waitin' for a maid?"

Laetitia looked back at Jurron and thought about telling his ass to wash them himself. He had been home longer than she had been that day. But then she thought about what her big sister, Leslie, had told her, to tell Jurron that she loved him anyway and that she would do better.

So she nodded her head and said, "I'll wash 'em."

She headed straight to the sink after taking off her jacket.

Jurron stepped aside and out of her way as his daughters rushed to his legs. "Dad-deee. Dad-deee."

He picked them both up in his arms and kissed them.

Laetitia smiled at him from the sink, while getting her hands and arms dirty in the water.

She said, "And *I* love you, too . . . Daddy."

Jurron grinned and chuckled at it as he nervously thought to himself, *Yeah, this girl is crazy! She prob'bly would kill me if I tried to leave her. This girl love me t' death!*

≈≈≈

Leslie looked out of the window on her bus ride to North Carrolton Avenue on the west side of New Orleans. She was headed over to Xavier University before going to work. She figured she had to, because she could not concentrate lately without thinking about . . . Eugene. The boy had been calling her in his lust. So she was going to answer his call, before it drove her insane with wonder.

Bridget had given all of her housemates enough information on Eugene to make Leslie's search for him an easy task. And although she had never cared to hear about him, she remembered things. So she arrived at Xavier's student-friendly campus and traveled straight to the Living and Learning Center dorm, where Eugene opted to live among his fellow students instead of commuting from his New Orleans home.

Leslie ignored the curious stares from students who had never noticed her on campus before. And she imagined that there was no guarantee that she would find Eugene on her first attempt. Nevertheless, she was bold enough to have him paged at his dorm if she needed to. Because she had not traveled there to leave fruitlessly.

However, she found that there was no need to go to such drastic measures to find him.

Oh, my God! she told herself. *How easy can this be?*

Eugene Duval was in clear sight of her as soon as she had reached his dorm. He was wearing a bright gold sweatshirt on the warm and sunny day, while talking to his friends on the campus benches. So how could he be missed?

Nor did Eugene miss the sight of Leslie, even in her dull gray sweatshirt and faded blue jeans, which was rather mundane for college girls on the sunnier days, where they could wear their more eye-popping skirts and wraps. But Eugene was keen to Leslie's dark beauty, which stood out to him in any clothes.

Leslie met his eyes from a distance, and she looked away to continue walking as if she hadn't seen him there at all, and as if she was not there to see him.

When Eugene spotted her, his words got stuck in his mouth. "Aw, man—"

With the backs of his friends facing Leslie's view, they had no idea what had stopped Eugene's words. By the time they turned their heads to look, she had made it out of sight and turned the corner of the building.

What the hell is she doin' up here? And why is she walking behind the dorm? Eugene asked himself in disarray.

"Who you lookin' for, man?" one of his friends asked him.

Eugene paid him no mind. He figured he had no time to waste.

He said, "Ah . . . I'll be right back," and hustled on his way after Leslie behind the building.

His friends looked at one another and asked themselves, "Where da hell is he goin'?"

One of them shrugged in response. "I'on know, man. That boy be on missions sometimes."

They shared a laugh at Eugene's eccentricities and his unexplainable spurts of independence.

Eugene hustled his way around the rear of the building, and asked himself, *Who is she here to see? And how come she walking around the back? Is she on the down low?*

He was still confused by it all, and he wondered if he actually witnessed a mirage.

"Am I losin' my mind out here?" he joked to himself as he rounded the corner. But when he spotted Leslie sitting on the steps of the emergency exit, he stopped and was embarrassed that he had followed her.

Leslie read his embarrassment and smiled at him.

He said, "Ah . . . what are *you* doing here?" What else could he say?

Leslie stared into his eyes and said, "Come here."

Eugene had to hold his jaws tight to stop his mouth from falling open.

Is this really happening? he asked himself. But he was already moving forward toward her, a puppet on a lustful string.

When he arrived at her feet, Leslie asked him, "Tell me what you want."

Eugene found himself hesitating on everything.

He responded, "Hunh?"

Stupid! Leslie thought of him. *Why is he in my dreams? I still don't get it. Does he want me that bad? Make him say it, then!*

So she repeated her demand to him, "Tell me what you want from me."

Eugene backed down from her forwardness.

"What? What are you talking about?" he asked her.

Leslie stood up and said, "Look, I don't have a lot of time for this. I have to go back to work. So you better ask for what you want while you got your chance."

When she stood up, she brushed his body with hers, and it sent rapid sensations up to Eugene's brain that rocketed back down to his penis. The girl even smelled good. Not that she wouldn't, but it all added to his nostalgia in an explosive second of delight. So he could only imagine how her full package would feel to him.

She was right there, and close enough to kiss. Eugene could even feel himself leaning toward her pert lips. But Leslie leaned away from him, as rhythmically as the head of a cobra.

"No. Not here," she told him. She met his lust-filled eyes that were filled with the dream of her . . . and she finally understood. There was something to be gained from his passion. There was something to be felt and experienced. Because Leslie was still a woman . . . and sexual. Eugene was a man, her opposite in every way, and he too was sexual. And their polarity was unbelievably attractive.

"Tell me where to meet you after work . . . after eleven," she told him.

Eugene could feel his heartbeat as he answered her.

"I don't know where. I mean, what about Bridget? She could—"

Leslie cut him off and answered, "She won't. Bridget is very . . . secure. You can tell her anything, and she'll still love you. She has that much love to give."

I realize that now, Leslie mused to herself. *She's rich with it. But I'm not!*

"How do you know that?" Eugene asked her. He doubted it.

Leslie said, "I live with her. So I know."

Eugene decided to trust her instincts. He had no choice. He knew that he had to have her. He needed Leslie as much as he needed food. He was starving without her. The call of her womb was that strong for him.

He opened his mouth and said, "I can meet you at Hotel La Salle on Rampart Street." It was the first place that came to mind. North Rampart Street was an easy meeting place, right above the French Quarter downtown. And no one would pay two college students any mind there.

Leslie knew the place as well. So she nodded to him.

"I can be there before midnight."

And they both . . . stood there for a moment in silence, while feeling each other out.

Does she really want to do this? Eugene asked himself.

Is this really supposed to happen? Leslie asked of herself.

Yet, they both agreed that it would.

"Okay, so . . . I'll set up the room . . . and you just call me when you get there," Eugene told her.

Leslie nodded to him.

"Okay." Then she added, "And you'll get your wish."

Eugene nodded back to her and said, "All right then. I'll see you later on."

And when they separated from each other, Eugene could feel the tightness in his crotch, while Leslie could feel the looseness in hers.

≈≈≈

Eugene called Bridget later that afternoon to make sure that his rendezvous with Leslie would be safe for that evening.

"You sure you don't want me to come over and make everything up to you tonight?" he teased Bridget.

"I don't need that kind of a makeup," Bridget responded to him. "And why does everything have to be so physical between us?"

Eugene joked and said, "What do you want, a metaphorical relationship now, where we just talk about things?"

Bridget ignored the question and countered, "Smart-ass."

When they hung up, Eugene pondered his addictions to himself. *Every guy wants it, man. It's not just me!* he convinced himself. *And ain't nothin' wrong with it. Sex is natural.*

Eugene had always been headstrong about what he wanted and how he felt about things. And he never asked to be born into a Creole family. He would have rather he had just been black. It would have made his life a lot simpler. So all of his life he struggled to be included in the dominant culture of African-American brown people, despite the more-than-subtle hints from family and friends to maintain his Creole roots. But what roots were they—pride in a dead culture that claimed French and Spanish but spoke neither? Nor would they be recognized as a lost party of France or Spain. It was a cultural delusion, based mostly on skin color. Yet the Creoles had found a way to separate themselves from other Americans of the African diaspora. And when Eugene had studied all of the facts of the shaky separation, he felt cheated . . . and phony.

"Why are we supposed to be so different?" he had asked his Creole friends in high school at the prestigious all-boys Catholic school of Saint Augustine's. And why was it so natural for the Creole girls at the sister school of St. Mary's to expect him to approach, date, and one day marry one of them?

His friends responded, "Why not? They look good."

"So do a lot of other girls," Eugene had argued with them. But they could never quite see what his point was. His parents figured that his stage of denial would soon fade away. Even his younger brother and sister found it peculiar that Eugene would refuse to date his own type. And in their youth, they considered it embarrassing for their older brother to maintain a . . . craving for *darkies*. What the hell was wrong with Eugene? How come he just didn't . . . get with the program like the majority of the Creoles?

However, Eugene argued, "All of us don't separate like that." And he was right. So he figured that he would be one to buck the system of the light-skinned caste, and marry dark. Nevertheless, he could never quite fit in with the browner boys. They knew that he was Creole. It was obvious to them. So they expected Eugene to act like the rest of his type—cool but uncool, black but not black, down with the people, and then not down at all.

Eugene concluded that the shit was all confusing. Who the hell were the Creoles? Every black person that he knew of in New Orleans could trace their history to European, Native American, and African heritage, and many to French and Spanish. But yet, they never ran around claiming a separate culture to themselves. So it just didn't make any sense to Eugene to limit himself in that way. Which led him to date several dignified brown girls like Bridget Chancellor, who had more wealth and social esteem than his own family.

Then Eugene met Bridget's housemate Leslie Beaudet, who was as real as it could get; Haitian, with fluent French, and a real cook, with the most exotic dark hair and skin that he had ever witnessed in his life! And somehow, someway, Eugene felt that if he could possess her, he could return to the source of blackness, and start over again, reborn through her purity, if such a thing even existed in America. Leslie was heavily Native American herself, and she could have been included in the other minority caste of so-called black Indians, from her mother's side. So how many hypocrisies of culture had America created?

≈≈≈

Eugene secured their room at the Hotel La Salle, only to begin having doubts.

"What if she don't even come?" he asked himself jokingly. *She never liked me before,* he reflected. *So why would she change her mind now?*

He shook his head while watching cable television inside the room, and he spoke to himself out loud again. "This is just weird, man. I don't know why I even went for this. She's not gonna show up."

Then he thought something terrible. *What if she turns around and tells Bridget about this whole thing to prove to her that I'm a player? And what if Bridget asked her to do it?*

He suddenly panicked and jumped from the bed.

"What the hell am I doing? I can't believe I fell for this!"

When he looked at the clock, it was eleven-thirty already.

"Will they let me get my money back?" he asked himself. "Shit!"

But he still hesitated to leave. He had to play it all out, even if it was a setup. He just had to have his chance, a chance with Leslie.

The telephone rang and caught him off guard.

"Oh, shit!" He jumped again, before he calmed down to answer it. "Hello."

His heart beat with full desire as he prayed for his wish to come true.

"I'm on my way up," Leslie told him.

Eugene took a breath and answered, "Okay. I'm here." And when he hung up the phone, he just stood there in shock for a moment.

"This is crazy! I'm actually gon' get her, Bridget's fuckin' roommate," he told himself.

He shook his head again and repeated, "This is crazy!"

But when Leslie knocked on the door, he surely went to answer it.

"Hi," she said to him when the door swung open.

Eugene's pants were already suffocating his tool. "Hi," he said back to her.

Leslie walked into the room with her things as Eugene closed and locked the door. After she had placed her things down into a neat pile on the dresser, she walked over to the bed and sat on it.

Eugene thought to himself, *Now how exactly do we start this?*

Leslie answered his question by repeating her earlier demand to him a third time.

"So, tell me what you want."

Eugene looked and was no longer hesitant with her.

He said, "You know what I want?"

She responded, "Not exactly. You just wanna kiss me?"

He looked at her quizzically and answered, "Naw." *And I hope she didn't come here thinking that,* he snapped to himself.

She said, "Well, express yourself to me then."

Eugene looked at her tempting dark figure on the bed and grew tired of the words. He wanted to see her buck-naked brownness *yesterday.* So he joined her there on the bed and went after her lips again. Leslie allowed it this time, and she kissed him back, as he lay her out across the bed.

No sooner than her back hit the burgundy quilt, Eugene's hands reached under her sweatshirt and up to her bra.

He's moving fast! she exclaimed to herself. *He really is desperate for me.*

Eugene went after her breasts with his tongue, just like in her visions, and she caressed his head into her bosom. Then his tongue slid down her stomach and tickled her at her belly button. That's when Leslie lost herself, with her eyes wandering about the off-white painted ceiling, while Eugene tugged and pulled to unravel her clothing until she lay naked. Then he joined her in nakedness, vanilla skin against dark chocolate brown. But before Eugene could enter her, Leslie stopped him, placing both of her hands between her legs.

"You got something to use?"

Eugene climbed up to get his protection, while Leslie anticipated what she knew would be good. She had imagined it already.

"Oui, merci, mon chéri!" she moaned in French. Yes, thank you, my sweetheart!

Eugene had to compose himself before he blasted off too early. *I can't believe this! I can't believe this! I can't believe this!* he repeated to himself with every push into Leslie's dark body.

She grabbed his behind with both hands and pulled him in farther, deeper, closer, where she could feel him more.

"You like it?" Eugene asked her in his concentrated panting.

"*Oui. Oui. Je l'aime bien. C'est même mieux que dans mes rêves!*" It's better than in my dream!

Eugene rowed himself with her faster and faster until he practically bounced in bliss and bit his lips to release himself and make their opposing bodies become one.

"*Oooooh, Eugeeeene,*" Leslie squealed as she grabbed hold of him.

Eugene moaned back to her upon the release of his joy, "*Lez-leee . . . Lez-leeee . . .*"

Leslie searched for his lips with her fingers in the dark of the room. When she found them, she pulled them down into a kiss, in French, with her tongue extending into his mouth.

She told him, "*Je sais maintenant pourquoi c'était toi. Parce que tu es le meilleur.*" I know now why it was you. Because you are the best.

However, Eugene understood none of her French. So he told himself, *Maybe she can even teach me the language.* And he kissed her back.

Possession

But when it was over, and Leslie had indulged in the pleasure principle, she felt vulnerable for allowing herself to be moved that way.

Now what? she asked. She didn't want to become another fool for so-called love. So she pulled away from Eugene's arms to cover up her nakedness in the sheets.

"What are you doing?" he asked her. He had gotten comfortable with her there in his arms.

"Il fait froid ici," she told him in French. It's cold in here.

Eugene looked into her eyes and was puzzled by it.

"You know I don't speak French."

Leslie eyed him and asked, "Why not, you're a Creole, aren't you?"

Eugene smirked and grunted, "Hmmph. It's just a name."

"You're not proud of it?" she asked him.

"Not particularly," he admitted to her. "I mean . . . what's there to be proud of?"

Good question. Did skin color equal pride alone?

Leslie furthered the intrigue when she asked him, "Are you proud of me?"

Eugene looked at her and was baffled. Of course he was proud of her. He was proud of having her. But was he proud of her, Leslie as herself? The truth was, he hardly knew the girl. He only knew that he was drawn to her in the most mysterious way. Then again . . . lust was not mysterious at all, it was consistent with humanity. Yet, who could be proud of lust?

"Are you gonna answer my question, or do you want me to leave you alone?" Leslie pressed him.

Eugene was stalled in his thoughts for a moment. He took in Leslie's dark brown face, her body, and her long black hair before he responded to her.

"I mean . . . you're beautiful. You really are." And he meant it, too.

Leslie grinned at his compliment and asked him, "Would you take me home to your parents?"

Shock curled the edges of Eugene's face before he could fake his cool. Once he realized that Leslie had baited him into the obvious, he shook his head and looked away from her, ashamed of his family history.

He said, "It's real complicated, man. I don't understand most of it myself. I mean, I've spent all my life trying to understand it."

Leslie studied the flush of his light brown body, and how easily it showed the various colors in his veins, where her dark brown tone was virtually impenetrable.

She asked him curiously, "Would you take Bridget home to your parents?" She knew that he hadn't. Leslie was from New Orleans, and she knew the Creoles, just as her father had known the snobbish mulattoes of Haiti.

Eugene figured that Bridget would indeed be the lesser of the two evils. She was a richly cultured woman, where Leslie was . . .

But no words could quite explain her. What was she? Who was she? Eugene had never known a girl from the street who was so educated and proudly bilingual. But he did know that Leslie was from the street. He felt it in her. And it was the enchantment of her rawness that had drawn him to her. Eugene had always wanted to experience a connection to the street. Yet he realized that he could never take that reality home with him. He was not strong enough to fight for it.

Leslie turned her eyes from him when she read his weakness. Then she turned them back to him . . . and plotted.

"Are you going back to Bridget?" she asked. She felt, for a moment, as if she had stolen something. However . . . she didn't plan to return it. Bridget owned enough already. Leslie felt that it was her turn to own something.

Eugene pondered her question, and thought to himself too hastily, *Of course I'm going back.* Then he caught himself and asked, *But what does she want from me now?* in regard to Leslie.

Leslie took a breath and accepted their fate, or at least from Eugene's view.

She sighed and said, "I guess you have to, right? I mean . . . she's still your girl." Then she hooked him and added, "So . . . what am I to you now?"

Shit! Eugene cursed to himself. *This was a dumb idea! What the hell was I thinking?*

Leslie shook her head and appeared to be letting him off easy. She climbed out of the bed and said, "Don't worry about it. I'm not gonna mess y'all up." And she headed for the bathroom.

When she made it inside and shut the door, Eugene was able to breathe again.

He mumbled to himself, "Thank God! Thank God!"

But then the bathroom door swung back open.

Eugene averted his eyes in the direction of the bathroom and heard the shower water running.

Leslie appeared in the doorway and told him, "I'm taking a shower."

Eugene nodded his head and said, "Okay."

What do you want me to do? he asked of himself.

Leslie answered him with her own question, "You comin'?" She made sure to slip back into the bathroom and shut the door before he could respond. It would be his call, and a classic setup.

The girl was cunning. So Eugene smiled and shook his head. He mumbled, "Aw, naw, fuck that. That's obvious. She must think I'm a fool."

Yet . . . the shower water sounded so . . . inviting to him. He could just imagine Leslie's brown body of curves under splashing, soapy water from behind a shower curtain.

He shook his head again and told himself, "Naw, don't do it, man." However, his tool ignored the plea of his conscience.

What if she's down to blow me? he thought to himself. And he began to vibrate with desire.

"Shit!" he cursed himself. He wanted to remain glued to the bed instead of succumbing to Leslie inside the shower. His heart rate increased as he continued to curse his insidious lust, right up to the point where he sprang from the bed and told himself, "Fuck it! I might as well get it over with. I've already gone this far."

When he entered the bathroom and stepped into the shower to join her, Leslie smiled at him.

"Hi," she told him. She had never been so giddy.

It was too late for Eugene to turn back the pages of his fate. He looked at her smooth dark skin covered with slick white bubbles from the cleansing soap, and he prayed to heaven.

My God! What did I do to deserve this?

Leslie read his desire and reached out her soapy hands to caress his tool with a slow stroke of her fingers around his tip.

"Ooooh," Eugene moaned to her. His entire body seemed to fold into her hands as he bent over and shook at his knees and at his shoulders.

"What do you want me to do with it?" she asked him.

Eugene could hear his heartbeat above the shower water that pounded against his naked body: *Boomp-boomp . . . boomp-boomp . . . boomp-boomp . . . boomp-boomp . . .*

"I want you ta . . . ta suck it," he nearly whispered to her.

Leslie could hear her own heartbeat as she slowly descended to her knees and allowed the shower water to wash the soap away from Eugene's private parts: *Boomp-boomp . . . boomp-boomp . . . boomp-boomp . . . boomp-boomp . . .*

She inhaled another breath before she tasted him.

"Oh . . . oh," Eugene moaned, while grabbing for the crown of her head.

This motherfucker! Leslie thought to herself as she pleased him. She didn't have great memories of pleasing guys. But all that Eugene could think about was heaven . . . heaven . . . heaven, until Leslie stopped.

Eugene looked down at her and begged for her to continue.

"Don't, don't stop. Naw."

However, Leslie broke from his hold and rose to her feet with conviction. And when she stood there with him face-to-face again, she demanded that he return her favor.

"Do me."

Eugene looked into her eyes with desperation, and in them he saw the stare of no mercy.

He opened his mouth to plead with her anyway. Besides, he had never tasted a girl before.

"Come on, come on," he begged, with his hands upon Leslie's shoulders, attempting to push her back to her knees. He was bouncing on his toes with the anticipation of a climax, but Leslie held her ground with him and stood strong.

"You do me first and then I'll finish with you," she told him.

And those eyes of hers wouldn't let up. They just wouldn't. So Eugene crashed to his knees in the shower water and sunk his head between Leslie's legs.

"Ouiiiii," Leslie moaned in French. "*Bon chien. Lèche-la-moi.*" Good dog. Lick it up.

And their hearts beat in unison while Leslie grabbed for the crown of his head: *Boomp-boomp / boomp-boomp . . . boomp-boomp / boomp-boomp . . .*

"Tu seras mon esclave," you will be my slave, Leslie told him. *"J'ai toujours été l' esclave pour tout le monde. Maintenant je devrais en avoir un."* I have been a slave for everyone else. Now I shall have one.

Then Leslie heard only her heartbeat, as she overruled him: *Boomp-boomp . . . boomp-boomp . . . boomp-boomp . . . boomp-boomp . . .*

Eugene understood nothing of what she said, he only knew that he wanted to serve her as quickly as possible, so that she could get back to serving him. And when Leslie had been satisfied by his tongue, she slid back to her knees with wicked intentions in mind.

He's gonna dedicate himself to me. Right now! she told herself as she began to finish his pleasure.

"Oh, Lez-lee. Oh, Lez-lee," Eugene moaned.

She stopped and asked him, "Am I doing it right?"

"Yeah."

She pleased him and stopped again.

"Do you want this?"

"Yesss. Oh, yesss," he told her.

"Do you care about me?"

Boomp-boomp . . . boomp-boomp . . . boomp-boomp . . . boomp-boomp . . .

"Yeah!" Eugene responded in the affirmative, afraid that she would stop if he didn't.

Leslie controlled his every move with the tickle of her tongue, and she began to slowly rake his chest and abdomen with the points of her fingernails.

"I want to please you so badly, baby," she told him.

"Unh hunh," he moaned back to her. Eugene could feel her nails slowly digging into his skin, but he was helpless to stop her. He was almost there. Climax. So he couldn't stop her. And Leslie knew it. So she waited until she felt him about to reach his lustful goal, and then she stopped abruptly, and looked up into his squinting eyes of bliss to ask him her most important question: "Do you think you could love me, Eugene?"

"Hunh?" he grunted to her. *Not now! Why you gotta ask me that now?* he questioned. His body began to shake uncontrollably. He needed her to finish the job. Pronto! She *had* to finish. It was torture to go that far and not finish. Torture! And Leslie realized as much.

"I said, do you think you could ever love me?" she repeated.

She touched him with her tongue just enough to make him squeal.

"*Yesss!*" he confessed to her.

So Leslie forced herself to finish him.

"OH, YES! OH, YES! LEZ-LEEEE! OH, GOD! OH, LEZ-LEEEEE!"

"You love me?" she asked him again, in the heat of his pleasure.

"*YEAH! YEEEEAAAAHH!*"

When he released himself to her, Leslie's nails raked his skin with more intensity. However, Eugene was so . . . exhausted from the experience that he failed to notice his own pain . . . until he had been marked by his lust.

≈

When they had satisfied each other and climbed out of the shower, the sting of Eugene's chest and abdomen finally became apparent to him.

"Ahhh, shit!" he whined, cringing from the sharp pain. He looked down and saw the multiple fingernail scars that ran down his chest and into his pubic hair, and he was appalled.

"Fuck! Look at my fuckin' chest!" he shouted at Leslie.

Leslie studied the obvious and held back her laugh.

"Oh my God," she told him, faking concern. She looked into his eyes with bewilderment and said, "I'm sorry. I didn't mean to do that."

Eugene asked, "You're sorry?" indignantly. *This fuckin' bitch!* he incensed to himself. *She fucked my whole chest up, and all she has to say is she's sorry! This girl is fuckin' crazy!*

Leslie read his disdain and went to grab a towel to dry off and leave him in the bathroom.

"Where are you going?" he asked her.

She looked into his face with her eyes filled with sorrow. "I didn't mean to make you mad at me. So I'm just gonna leave now."

Eugene piped, "Leave for what? It's done now."

Leslie looked at him and dropped her head toward the tile floor of the bathroom.

"I didn't mean to do it," she repeated. "I just . . ." And she allowed him to fill in the blanks.

Eugene shook off his anger and pitied her. And in her moment of weakness, he saw an opportunity to become her savior, so he took it.

"Come here," he told her.

Leslie stepped over to him slowly, with her white towel still wrapped around her.

Eugene pulled her into him and grimaced. "Ahh," he whined again as Leslie's towel met the fresh scars on his chest. He said, "I mean, you did it now. Just don't do that shit again. My skin can't take that shit."

Leslie nodded her head to him obediently. "I'm sorry," she repeated.

Eugene continued to shake it off. He was gratified that she had pleased him so well. He said, "I told you, don't worry about it. I needed a break from Bridget anyway." He smiled and added, "Now I *have* to stay away from her for a while. Thanks to you," he joked.

Leslie shook her head and grinned.

She said, "But I didn't mean to do that. Honestly. It just . . . happened."

≈≈≈

The realization of power can definitely be corrupting. Leslie was beginning to taste its grip upon her conscience. What else could she . . . manipulate? And it was not as if she wanted to use her will without reason, but as she said, things just . . . happened, particularly to those who failed to believe that a product of American poverty could *have* any power. Like Kaiyah Jefferson, the privileged and confident student from Tulane.

Kaiyah decided to take her assignment into her own hands, and to force her subject to cooperate. She refused to be denied as she searched Dillard's campus with her camera in tow to track Leslie down. She was determined to secure the poor girl's tragic story, and without any help from Bridget, who had begun to screen her calls.

However, Leslie spotted Kaiyah in the distance, standing outside the cafeteria at lunch hour. So she froze, and thought to herself, *See, this is what I'm talking about! Why is this girl sweatin' me like this?*

Leslie slid into a campus building to plot out her response. She had grown tired of avoiding things. The ghetto yoga had worn off. She thought of active retaliation now. Code red! She nodded her head and thought up a plan. *I got something just for her ass . . . Courtney Taylor.*

She turned to search for a pay phone, and spotted one down the hall from her.

"Perfect," she mumbled to herself.

She went to use the phone and dialed an old phone number out of memory.

"Hello," a hard and raspy voice answered.

Leslie responded in the language of the streets, "Ay, dis Lez."

"Ay, girl, whassup?" her contact responded.

"Nuntin', man, jus' schoolin', dat's all. But I'm try'na find my brother right about now. I heard he been buyin' from C.T. now."

There was a slight pause over the phone.

Her contact doubted her. "Naw, get outta hea'. Pierre? That's for true? He couldn't stomach the streets when he was younger."

Leslie said, "He ain't young no more either. So you got the number? I wanna call him and see."

"Who, Pierre's? I don't have his number. I ain't see him—"

Leslie cut him off and snapped, "Why would I be callin' you for his number? You think I don't have it? I don't want my brother to lie to me anyway. It ain't like he gon' tell me something like that. So I wanna hear it from the other side."

It all made sense, so her contact acquiesced. "Okay. His pager number is . . ."

Leslie memorized the number and made the page immmediately, leaving the pay phone's return number with a 911 code. She waited by the phone for the return call.

"Are you using the phone?" a fellow student asked her.

"Yes, I am," Leslie told her.

The girl nodded and walked away. However, a second student never bothered to ask. She walked over and was full ready to pick up the receiver with her change in hand.

Leslie warded her off and said, "I'm using this phone right now."

The girl looked at her and grimaced.

"Look, I need to make a quick phone call," she insisted.

Leslie repeated herself with more authority, "I said, I'm using it."

"It don't look like you're usin' it."

Leslie warned her, "Girl, if you don't get out of my motherfuckin' *face . . .*"

The phone rang right on time before things got physical.

Leslie answered, "Hello."

Her angry friend walked away in a huff to find another pay phone to use.

"Who dis?" Courtney Taylor asked over the phone line. There was no need for being cordial. Whoever paged him already knew what time it was, unless they had a wrong number.

Leslie responded to him in French, *"C'est la fille qui s'appelle Beaudet."*

It's that girl named Beaudet.

Courtney immediately thawed out his cold tone, and grinned. He didn't understand her French, but he did realize who he was talking to. He subconsciously rubbed the left side of his torso where the Haitian girl had cut him years ago. But since then, they had become cordial, and Courtney had nothing but respect for Leslie. His scar was their little secret. No one else even knew about it.

He said, "Whassup? Whatchew doin' pagin' me? I thought you was in college now."

Leslie said, "I am. And they got plenty of snitch programs up in here."

Courtney frowned and said, "Snitch programs? What you mean by dat?"

Leslie looked up the hallway to make sure she had enough privacy to map out her plans. When the hallway was clear, she explained, "They have federal agents on certain college campuses on the low, and they've been asking students if they would like to be paid college tuition to help in a drug eradication program. And they have undercover agents on campus too."

She said, "And I'm calling you on this because I did some snoopin' around, just to see what they were talking about, because I heard that they marked off areas around New Orleans, including the Seventh Ward, as testing grounds. So I was just calling you up to be on the lookout for any college students who might start hanging around out there out of the blue. You know, just people who are not supposed to be there."

Courtney curled up his face and said, "Damn, that's goin' on?"

"Yeah, they're getting serious around here," Leslie told him. "But I mean, we grew up in the Seventh Ward. And I just know how it is out there in the streets. I mean, everybody don't get a chance to go to college. And I just think it's unfair, myself."

She said, "I mean, it's just obvious that America would rather lock everybody up instead of giving us more money for education and health care and shit. And now they're up in here trying to use money to make us snitch on each other. And I just think it's a damn shame."

Courtney nodded his head as he took in Leslie's every word.

She lookin' out for a nigga, he told himself. *She lookin' out!* It wasn't as if she had not done it before. Leslie understood the code of the street from early on. They played by different rules. Why should the outside world judge them when they never had to live on their terms? So when Courtney and his gang had a rivalry with a group from the Ninth Ward, Leslie remained silent about a shoot-out that she had witnessed when the police came around and questioned the neighbors. And it wasn't as if she was *loyal* to the Seventh Ward over the Ninth. That would have been trivial. She had friends and family members who lived in the Ninth Ward, and her sister had moved there with Jurron and their daughters. Leslie just viewed the street life in the same way that the American military viewed international warfare. War was always going to happen. And there were no rules to it. Not really. The strong would dominate the weak, who would need to survive with broken spirits and egos, until the weak had found a way to win. And there was nothing that the police could do to stop it, just as the United Nations was powerless to stop the constant warring between Jews and Muslims in Israel. War was life!

So Courtney thanked Leslie for her understanding.

"Good lookin' out, Lez. I appreciate that."

"Don't worry about it. Just keep it to yourself," she told him. "Because some people got big mouths, and I don't want this to come back to me and what I'm trying to do up here in school."

Courtney frowned and said, "Now Lez, you know I don't even go out like dat. My business is my business. I've always been that way . . . and so have you," he reflected to her.

Leslie said, "I'm just trying to keep everything straight. So I had to lie to your boy to get your pager number. I told him that Pierre was buyin' from you."

Courtney started to laugh. He said, "That boy ain't try'na be around me like that. I mean, y'all like night and day, Lez." He joked and said, "Maybe you should have been the older brother."

Leslie chuckled and said, "Tell me about it."

Courtney told her, "I'll handle that. I'll tell my boy sump'in. I mean, he don't know how we know each other."

Leslie searched the hallway for privacy again before she warned him. She said, "But I'm gon' tell you, some of these agents that they're using got game. It ain't like they're sending amateurs out there. So if push comes to shove with these people . . . then you might just have to do what you need to do. You feel me?"

Courtney took in her serious tone and thought it over. He nodded with the phone receiver in hand and said, "Aw'ight. I'll keep my eyes open, then."

Leslie hung up the phone and took a deep breath. She mumbled, "Now let me go see what this girl wants from me," as she headed back outside toward the campus lawn.

Kaiyah Jefferson nearly walked right into her. Was it another coincidence?

"Oh, God, hi," she responded to Leslie. "You're just the person I was looking for."

Leslie looked at her with skepticism. "Looking for me for what?" she asked. She eyed Kaiyah's camera at her left side.

Kaiyah explained, "Well, I know that you're not volunteering to tell your story on camera, but I just wanted to talk to you about it first."

Leslie said, "Well, I have classes to attend right now," to brush her off. She asked sarcastically, "What happened to *your* classes?"

"I have a break in my schedule," Kaiyah answered her. She added, "But you know what, this is so important for us that I would miss a whole day of classes to do it."

Leslie studied her words. "Important for *us*?" She waited for Kaiyah to explain herself.

Kaiyah said, "Look, I shouldn't be telling you this, but you're the only African American who would be included in this college project. And without you, we won't have any representation. And that wouldn't be right, because the majority of the city of New Orleans is black. So you have to do it."

I don't have to do anything! Leslie thought to herself.

But she responded with a question. "Why you choose *me*?"

"Because you're smarter than everyone else," Kaiyah answered her. Then she whispered, "I mean, between me and you, everyone else was making fools of themselves for the camera. And you were the only one who had any self-respect about what was going on. So I wanted you to be the one to represent us, even if you didn't want to. I mean, it would just make all of us proud to have a student who . . ."

Kaiyah made sure to release her words with the right tact.

She said, "I mean, you're bilingual, intelligent, driven . . . and obviously you're beautiful. And you're about taking care of business. And that's why I want *you*."

Leslie sighed and looked away for a moment to gather her thoughts. The girl was making a damn good case to do it. Leslie was even tempted by her. Kaiyah had gained her respect in her methods. However, Leslie responded with a shake of her head.

She said, "Do you realize how white people look at us when we're poor? They don't look at us as human anymore. We become . . . Frankensteins or something. Then they act as if something's special about us being smart, and knowing what's going on in the world. As if we're not supposed to have brains and feelings anymore. And you're just supposed to take whatever the hell they give you."

Kaiyah jumped right in and said, "That's why they need to hear it from you, Leslie. We need for you to tell them. And you're the only person who can get it right. Or the only person who *I've* met. Everyone else gets too emotional about it. But I mean, you're just . . . real calm and logical."

Leslie looked at her and said, "I'm not that calm. And I don't come from calm places."

Kaiyah didn't quite know how to read that response. Was it a warning, or was she simply telling the truth?

"Well, I need you to at least think about it," Kaiyah pressed her.

Leslie shook her head again and said, "There's nothing to think about. I'm not gon' change how white people think about us." She looked Kaiyah over and added, "Or how *we* think about us." *Because you don't know shit about me,* Leslie thought of the situation. *You don't know that my family had money and lived in a nice, big house before my father lost his job. You don't know that my mother died of AIDS. You don't know that my brother sat and watched me while I was violated. You don't know that my father . . . killed somebody for me. And you don't know that I killed somebody for my sister and my nieces. And all of that shit needs to die with me!*

She figured that revealing all of her misfortunes and the murders that had been committed would only lead to finger-pointing judgments about her and her family without any resolutions. Americans loved to judge. Everything was white or black, left or right, rich or poor, masculine or feminine, and right or wrong with them, while the more thoughtful Americans were hounded by taunts of being indecisive and liberal, as though there were no complicated realities or explanations of humanity that deserved more time and understanding to work out. How could Americans so easily judge what had been going on with humans for thousands of years anyway, the same America who had legalized slavery, abortion, and the death penalty? Were they not all complicated issues? How did Americans explain those three predicaments?

So Leslie figured she had it right. There were no rewards for making hard choices in America. The Maker had to judge them. And Leslie left it up to the Maker.

She said, "If they really want to understand what's going on, then all they need to do is take it to the people on the streets. I don't need to explain it. I got other shit to do."

She said, "And if I tell you where to go, don't put my name out there. Because I don't want people coming back to me and riding my back about the shit. You hear me?" she asked of Kaiyah.

Kaiyah looked into Leslie's face and thought, *Oh my God! Professor Sullivan was right. She wants us to prove that we're really interested in changing things.*

There was a hint in Leslie eyes that begged for understanding. Kaiyah could see that in her. So she agreed to Leslie's proposal. "Okay, if I do that . . . you know, get the background information on camera about where you come from, would you be willing to talk to me after that?"

Leslie studied the girl for a moment. *This girl is really pressed,* she told herself.

She asked, "You're gonna go out there with a camera?"

"Yeah, why not?" Kaiyah asked her. She was down for whatever.

That made Leslie curious. *I wonder what would happen if . . .* She shook her head and thought better of the idea. She said, "You know what, I don't think that's a good idea."

But Kaiyah was adamant. She thought it was a great idea! She would prove that she was worthy of Leslie's story by going into the heart of indiscriminate poverty.

"No, I'll do it," Kaiyah insisted. "I'm not afraid of it."

And I'm not afraid of you! she added to herself.

Kaiyah's defiance was her undoing. She still refused to believe in the laws of the jungle, as if she could walk into an open cage with a wild lion and live to brag about it.

Leslie read the defiance in the girl and scorned her for it. Kaiyah viewed the ghetto as if it was some obscure amusement park. And Leslie considered that to be disrespectful, as disrespectful as white Americans could be of the daily atrocities that took place in the 'hood.

Leslie spat to herself, *This bitch thinks it's a damn game! Okay then. We'll see if somebody's playing with her ass.*

So she nodded her head and agreed to it. "Okay, then. If you can do that . . . then I'll think about it. But like I said, don't use my name. Because I don't need people calling me up about it."

≈≈≈

Leslie felt guilty that night while at work at Hot Jake's. This girl Kaiyah was about to put herself in a dangerous situation, and she didn't know any better. However, Leslie could not call off her plans. She refused to. How would she even explain it if she tried? Would she tell Courtney to just ignore the girl with the camera, and tell him that she was harmless? Would she confess to him that she had made up the whole story about federal agents and snitches to try and save the girl? Or would she tell Courtney to keep his cool and avoid all contact with her?

Leslie thought about it, while reflecting again on the shortcomings of her mother, the tragedy of her father, the cowardice of her brother, and the dependency of her little sister to sacrifice anything for love, and she decided that it would be Kaiyah's fate if something . . . tragic would happen to her. Life was meant to be lived. And just as Leslie and her family had suffered so much in their choices . . . so shall others suffer with the choices that they make.

So Leslie came to her conclusion. *Live and let die,* she philosophized, while inside the kitchen. There could be no second-guessing. Kaiyah had chosen her own fate. And Leslie thought no more about it. However, she did think about herself and Eugene that night. She wanted to see him again. And she saw no reason not to.

Why should I continue to deny myself any pleasure in life? she questioned. *Everybody else goes for what they want. And it's obvious that he wanted me. So I want him back now.*

But first she wanted to make sure that her second rendezvous with Eugene would be available.

She took a break from work to call home and shoot the breeze with Bridget.

"Hello," Yula answered at the house.

"Hey, Yula. It's Leslie. How's things going?"

"Couldn't be much better, girl!" Yula answered with pep. "I got two A's in my first two exams."

Leslie grinned and was proud of her. "And how does that feel?" she asked Yula.

"It feels good. Damn good! I mean, I studied hard for these tests."

However, Leslie had to cut her short to get back to the purpose of her phone call.

"Um, where's Bridget right now? Is she around?"

"Yeah, she's here." Yula added in a whisper, "She's kind of upset with me, though, because she got a B and C on the same two exams that I got A's on. She won't admit it though. I mean, you know how Bridget is. She lets her pride get in the way.

"But don't tell her I said anything to you about it though," Yula commented. "I don't want to add oxygen to the fire. So let's keep it in the house," she joked.

Leslie chuckled and said, "Girl, you know me. Let me talk to her."

Yula went to call Bridget to the phone.

"Who is it?" Bridget asked from the top of the stairs.

"Well, it ain't you-know-who. It's Leslie!" Yula hollered up to her.

Bridget thought, *What does she want?* with distaste. She wasn't in the greatest of moods that night.

Yula asked, "Are you gonna pick up the phone, or what?" *Petty ass!* she thought to herself. Bridget was taking the whole competitive envy thing too far.

Bridget sighed and answered, "I'll get it," before she went to retrieve the cordless telephone.

When she answered the line, Yula was signing off with Leslie.

"All right, then, Leslie. And don't work too hard over there. Because if anybody deserves a break, it's you."

Tell me about it, Leslie thought, while remaining silent. She realized that Bridget was on the line, and she was cautious not to give anything away.

It wasn't until Yula hung up the phone that Leslie began to converse with any intent.

She told Bridget, "I've been thinking about you."

Bridget was surprised to hear it.

"Oh, yeah." She was curious. "And what did you think?"

Leslie said, "I was just thinking about . . . you know, having somebody. And I think you're right. I do need that feeling. It just adds more . . . meaning to life, I guess."

Bridget sighed and mumbled, "Yeah, well, sometimes it doesn't seem like it's worth it."

"How do you mean?" Leslie asked her.

Bridget calmed herself and thought about whether she wanted to reveal anything to Leslie. After reviewing her thoughts on it, she decided that she would. Leslie seemed to be opening up by even making the phone call. Bridget felt that she was finally cracking the girl's shell, piece by piece. That was what she had always wanted from Leslie, her confidence in friendship.

So Bridget confided her recent thoughts about her own love life. She said, "I think Eugene is cheating on me. I don't think he's as serious about me as I am about him."

Leslie took in the information carefully, and went to work her intuition.

She responded with excellent tact, "Let me ask you a personal question, if I may." She waited for Bridget's response in the affirmative.

Bridget paused, still curious, before she agreed to allow it. "Okay. Go ahead."

Leslie asked her, "Have you ever met his parents? I mean, he is a Creole, right? And you're a 'chocolate crew' girl."

"So . . . what are you trying to say?" Bridget asked her, slightly on the defensive.

"Answer my question first. Have you ever met his parents?"

Bridget began to shake her head. *She is constantly going out of her way to offend me for some reason,* she thought.

"Why, Leslie? Why is that important to you?" Bridget finally snapped at her.

Leslie responded calmly, "Well, if you're going to feel all attached to him like you do, then I just would have figured that you would have met his parents by now. And if not, then maybe you need to reconsider your relationship with him."

"Well, he hasn't met my parents yet either," Bridget reasoned.

"Do your parents live in New Orleans?" Leslie asked her on cue.

"I mean, where is this going, Leslie?" Bridget questioned her in a huff.

"*You* brought it up," Leslie reminded her. "I was just calling to tell you that you were right, and then you started talking about Eugene. So do you want the truth from me, or not? Because, see, I grew up in New Orleans, and I know how it is here with them people. And you can have all the money that you want, they're still gonna look at you as a darkie. That's just how they've been trained to think."

That's why I never liked that boy, Leslie kept to herself. It would have been too revealing for Bridget to hear.

Bridget was floored! That damned Leslie just had too much ammunition for her.

She responded, "Can we please change the subject now?"

Leslie answered, "Actually, I have to get back to work now. I just wanted to call and tell you that you were right, because I was just thinking about what you said the other night."

"Okay," Bridget told her. She was more than ready to get off the phone with the girl. And as soon as she hung up the line with Leslie, she thought about calling Eugene with a bone to pick about the family that she had never met. But first, she had to brainstorm how she would bring it up. Leslie had caught her off guard with the family idea. Bridget was still trying to negotiate the personal relationship with Eugene, not a cultural and historical one. After all, they were both African Americans. Or were they? So Bridget was made to feel *less than,* because of the shade of her skin again, and this time not by white people. However, even the white kids in Ann

Arbor had to respect her, because her daddy made more than most of their daddies, and in an academic field.

But Leslie beat Bridget to the phone call to Eugene. She didn't need to think about what she wanted to say. She only thought about what she wanted to do. Leslie had grown tired of thinking about reasons not to indulge herself in some of the pleasures of life. And she would think no more. She wanted to feel, like everyone else was doing.

"Hello," Eugene answered.

Perfect! Leslie thought.

She came right out and asked him, "Can I meet you same place, same time tonight?"

Eugene sat up in his desk chair, where he struggled to finish his work. Leslie had already been on his mind that day.

He joked to her, "You won't scratch me up this time?"

"I promise," she told him.

Eugene grinned hard, and was a giddy boy with a new toy out of the box. "Aw'ight, we can do that. But I'm just warning you in advance about your nails. So don't make me have to bring some leather gloves tonight."

Leslie laughed out loud and said, "Bring them, then." Then she went to butter him up. "I just want to see you again. Is that okay? I mean . . . but I don't want to be there if I'm not wanted."

Eugene responded too hastily. "Oh, you're wanted. You just have to know how to act."

Leslie stopped smiling. *I have to know how to act?* she repeated to herself. She didn't like the sound of that comment from him. *Guys always think they can dictate shit. I hate that!*

Yet she responded, "Okay."

On Eugene's end, he took a deep breath and was glad that he had gotten away with his chauvinism. *I better watch what I say to this girl. I don't really know her that well yet,* he thought.

"Okay then," he told her. "I'll see you later on tonight."

A minute after he had hung up the phone with Leslie, Bridget called him.

"Hello," he answered calmly again.

"It's Bridget."

"Oh, hi, girl. What's up?" He wanted to sound excited with her to camouflage his guilt, but his happy tone only made Bridget pressed to get to the bottom of things with him. She didn't want to change her mind and go soft on him.

"I need to see you tonight," she informed him.

Eugene paused. "Why?" he asked her cautiously.

He was already thinking of excuses that he would use not to see her.

Bridget said, "I have an important question to ask you, and I want us to look each other in the eye when I ask."

"When you ask me what?" Whatever it was, she could do it over the phone.

"I'm on my way over there right now," she told him.

Eugene panicked, thinking about his chest and abdomen, just in case they got into something.

He said, "No you're not. I got studying to do tonight. I got a test tomorrow."

"That never stopped you from seeing me before," she reminded him.

Oh my God! I don't need this shit right now, he fumed to himself.

"Well, I won't be here when you get here," he responded boldly to her.

"Why, you have somewhere to go?" Bridget asked him. It was already after nine.

Eugene answered her cunningly, "If you wanna force me to go to study hall to finish my work tonight, then so be it. Because I don't have time for the petty arguments tonight."

"Petty arguments?" she repeated. "Is that what you think we have?"

"A lot of them. Yeah."

Bridget finally broke down and let the cat out of the bag.

"Well, let me ask you this, then. If I wanted to meet your parents for dinner to see how serious you are about us, would you do it? Because you haven't done it so far."

Eugene snapped, "What do my parents have to do with anything?"

"What do your parents have to do with anything?" Bridget repeated to him. "I can't believe you're even asking me that. Do you ever think about me meeting them one day? Has that thought even crossed your mind?"

Eugene suddenly thought about the family questions that Leslie had asked him. So he probed Bridget for more information about it.

"Why are you asking me about this all of a sudden? You never asked me about it before."

Bridget said, "To tell you the truth, Leslie brought it up to me. She says she knows how Creole people are down here. And I just wanted to get to the bottom of things before I get my feelings hurt."

Eugene thought fast and responded, "Aw, man, that girl *hates* me, Bridget. She'll say anything. You can't tell that by now? She just doesn't like me. I can't believe that you're calling me up about that."

He poured it on thick, too. He said, "See, that's what I mean when I say 'petty arguments.' That girl has you all hyped-up for nothin'. And you know she don't like me."

Bridget calmed down and thought about it. But she was still pressed about the issue of meeting his parents. So she reasoned with him.

"Okay. You're probably right, she doesn't like you. But still, when are you going to introduce me to your parents?"

Eugene sighed and said, "Look, we'll have to talk about this another day. You messin' up my concentration with this. Can we just talk about it another day? Please, Bridget."

"Don't patronize me," she snapped at him in response. "And we *will* talk about it before we do *anything* else." She was so teed off that she hung up the phone on him.

Eugene held the phone away from his eardrum and just shook his head.

He asked himself, "What the hell is this girl doing?" in reference to Leslie causing trouble.

I mean, is she purposely trying to break us up? . . . Maybe she is, he thought. Then he thought again about the scars that Leslie had raked down his chest.

Shit! he concluded to himself. *This girl is crazy!*

Yet . . . he didn't pass up the opportunity to tell her so to her face that night at the hotel.

≈≈≈

As soon as Leslie walked into the hotel room, Eugene asked her at the door, "What the hell are you doing talking to Bridget about my family?"

Leslie looked him over and sized him up.

"I mean, she talks about you twenty-four seven. She always brings you up. And then she started telling me how good you were in bed and whatnot. And I didn't want to hear that, because now I could agree with her. So instead of smiling or something and giving us away, I started a little catfight so that she could still think that I didn't like you. Unless you want me to say nice things about you now. Then she'll really start thinking that something is up, because I never really talked about guys like that with her. And she knows that."

Leslie calmed herself and let him take it all in. Then she bluffed him at the door.

"Well, if you don't want my company now, then I'll just go on back home," she told him.

Eugene looked her over and shook his head with a smirk. He said, "Sometimes, I listen to what you say, and you make it seem as if nobody ever wanted you."

Leslie searched his eyes for pity. She said, "Sometimes I feel like I'm not wanted. Or at least not by the people who I want to be with." She looked down to the floor again.

Eugene took her hint and said, "Come here." When Leslie reached him, he added, "I want you. We're just in a complicated situation here. I mean, you understand that, right?"

Leslie nodded her head into his shoulder. "I understand it. And I was just trying to protect us."

"Aw'ight, I get it," he told her. Then he smiled and added, "You're kind of smart."

Leslie looked him in his face and smiled back. "Kind of?" she asked him sarcastically.

Eugene laughed it off. "No, you *are* smart," he corrected himself.

But Leslie didn't want him to think too much about her smarts, she might have scared him off that way. So like a smart woman would, she decided to massage his ego.

"Like I said, I just want to be able to see you," she repeated to him. "I mean . . . you kind of got me hooked now."

Eugene laughed out loud again and said, "Kind of?"

Leslie chuckled at it herself. "No . . . I *am* hooked."

They read the passion in each other's eyes and kissed . . . before they made it to the bed again. Eugene forgot all about interrogating her on those scars that she had given him with her fingernails. However, Leslie was not as careless as he was about her words and actions.

So she told him, "And try not to bring up my name to Bridget about anything, because you might end up telling on yourself. So just keep acting like we hate each other."

The Full Moon

K aiyah Jefferson took a final deep breath to calm herself before she
climbed out of her car on the north side of Claiborne Avenue. She
had her handheld camera ready to film the hard reality of New
Orleans's impoverished streets, guerrilla style.

"Well, here I go," she told herself. She actually felt as if she was docu-
menting important footage that would one day contribute to the correction
of the disparities of race and poverty in America. She found it unbelievable
that the new millennium had started, with America's forty-third president
in office, and yet there were still numerous urban American streets with
potholes, loose trash, broken sidewalks, and entire blocks of boarded-up
housing, where unattended brown children played out in the streets, while
the adults wandered about in search of . . . the existence of anything worth
living for, and a validation of their purpose in life.

Sure, Kaiyah had seen it all before. Many Americans had at least driven
through the shambles of the cities and seen it with their bare eyes. But to
film it in live action made it surreal and touchable. The camera was able to
bring the aimlessness of poverty into greater focus. Kaiyah had never been
that close to it before. Her parents had been able to move up and out to
greener pastures without her ever having to experience the climb. But she
was now among the carnage, and found herself able to relate to the feelings of cynicism that Leslie Beaudet had expressed about effecting real
change there. There was just too much to do. Entire generations would
need correcting. A damn time machine would be needed to extract the

roots of the misery before it had spread to the minds and souls of the great-grandchildren like it had.

My God! Kaiyah thought to herself, as the lens of her camera zeroed in on the fast-aging neighbors, who had not yet bothered to pay her any mind. However, the children quickly caught on to her. They were very much attracted to cameras. Video cameras were the new communication source of the technological world, even for those who lived in adverse poverty.

"Are you makin' a movie?" a curious boy asked her. He was excited to see her there. She looked important. More children followed his lead.

"Can we be in it?" a little girl asked next.

Then they all asked.

"Oooh, oooh, can I be in it? I can act. For real!"

Kaiyah began to laugh out loud as the children all bombarded her in the midst of her work.

She said, "I'm not filming a movie. I'm just getting footage of your neighborhood."

"Excuse me, did you say you were filmin' a movie?" a grown-up finally asked her. She was a still-hopeful mother in her early thirties.

She said, "I have a fifteen-year-old daughter who loves to act. Do you have a part in your movie that you could use her in? I could go get her for you in a few minutes. I have to go to the store first to buy some diapers and baby formula. I have a newborn at the house that my daughter's watching right now."

Kaiyah began to shake her head and shut things off. She stopped her recording.

She repeated, "I'm not doing a movie. I'm just filming the everyday happenings of the area."

She thought to herself, *My God, these people don't have a clue. I can't possibly film a movie with this small camera. I guess I must look like a director or something, since it's obvious that I'm not from around here.*

Kaiyah couldn't help but to feel herself placed firmly above their condition. She was only visiting, but they were all there to stay.

"What, you mean like a documentary or something?" the mother asked her of her camera work.

More grown-ups began to gather.

Kaiyah nodded her head and said, "Yeah, like a documentary." But she would never tell them that it was about poverty unless they assumed as much on their own. Kaiyah wasn't sure if they would be ashamed of it or irritated by it.

"Well, you need to interview anybody?" an older man in his forties asked her. "I'll do an interview with you," he offered.

"Mmm, hmm, I'll talk too," another woman spoke up.

Kaiyah couldn't believe her ears. And it wasn't as if they were all willing to talk, but there was enough of them willing to talk to disavow Leslie's attitude about it. Or maybe it was Kaiyah's tall, lean, and wholesome college-girl look that had turned them on. She looked like someone who they could trust with their stories. And that's what Kaiyah told herself. She was trustworthy. So she grew more confident about her work there as she walked through the area with less apprehension. Although there were still those who shied away from the camera and refused to cooperate, Kaiyah began to feel more secure with what she was doing . . . until . . . her lens accidentally caught a drug transaction. A shaky older man passed his rumpled money to a stern-looking young man for the trade of a transparent capsule carrying an addictive substance of human escapism called crack.

Kaiyah went to shut off her camera in a panic. But then she got bold and reasoned to herself, *This is a part of their reality. This is what goes on here. Some people are addicted to drugs, and others are taking advantage of that.*

So she decided to leave the camera on instead of heeding a film cut.

Someone shouted, "Ay yo, what the fuck is *she* doin'?! Who da girl wit da camera?!"

Kaiyah was suddenly shocked into submission. In a snap, she was surrounded all at once by an army of the young, territorial men who lived in the neighborhood. She had obviously walked right into their protected drug turf. And suddenly the hopeful mothers, children, and older men of the community seemed to have evaporated into thin air.

Oh, shit! Kaiyah panicked to herself. *This is the part that Leslie was talking about!*

Hoodlums, young and old, seemed to jump from front porches, round the corners, hop out of parked cars, and leak out from everywhere to find out what she was doing there with the camera in broad daylight. And they damn sure were not approaching her to cooperate for some documentary. So Kaiyah immediately apologized to them.

"I'm sorry. I didn't mean to walk through here. I—I didn't know," she stammered.

"You didn't know what?" someone asked her harshly.

Kaiyah couldn't even concentrate on anyone's face. As far as she was concerned, they were all ready to kill her.

"I, I, I didn't know . . ." she continued to stutter as her heart rate increased. She was smart enough not to say what she didn't know, because she realized that speaking of drug territory would immediately sound convicting of why she was there in the first place. Of course she knew where she was. How could she not know, and still be there? Only people who knew even came there. There was no such thing as a bystander in drug territory. Especially one with a video camera.

Someone shouted, "She po-po, man. They probably sent her out hea'."

"Well, take the fuckin' camera from her!" someone else decided.

Kaiyah became defensive of her property.

She said, "I'll let you take the tape, but you're not taking my camera."

"Bitch, I'll take your fuckin' life out here!"

"What she doin' out here wit a camera anyway, hunh?"

"I told you, she fuckin' five-oh, man."

"No I am *not*," Kaiyah argued. Her life depended on it.

Someone snatched the camera from her hand before she could move to protect it from them.

"Give it back!" she shouted insanely. "I am not the police. I'm a college student, and I was just shooting footage of the neighborhood," she explained to them. "Now I've obviously made a mistake by walking through here. So I'll give you the tape, but I want my camera back," she whined to them.

That was all that Courtney Taylor needed to hear as he listened in and watched from the background, with one of his trusted friends beside him.

That's the college game right there, he told himself with a nod. *She one of them special agents.*

Someone else yelled out his exact thoughts on it. "Aw, that's game, man. That bitch probably made extra copies of the tapes already."

Kaiyah argued, "How would I be able to do that? I'm standing right here in front of you," she snapped at none of them in particular.

"Well, what else you got in that camera bag, hunh?"

"Yeah, check to see if dat bitch wearing a wire, too?"

Before Kaiyah could back out of harm's way, someone slugged her with a punch to her right ear.

"*Ahh!*" she yelped and stumbled forward.

Another punch landed to her left cheekbone and knocked her from her feet.

"Fuck that bitch up!" someone yelled as rapid punches and kicks poured in on Kaiyah's helpless body on the ground.

"They don't send no bitches out here to fuck wit us! Fuck dat shit!"

Courtney Taylor tapped his friend on the arm as they continued to ob-
serve the wild scene from the background. "Come on, man. Let's use that broken ride? We gon' need to dump that shit after this. I know what this shit is."

His friend nodded and followed right behind him. "Aw'ight."

And as quickly as the beat-down on Kaiyah had begun . . . it was over.

"Are you all right?" someone asked her as she lay there covering herself
on the ground.

She looked up and cried, "Oh my Goddd! Oh my Goddd!" However,
the pain that she felt was not as bad as she thought it would be.

The older man helped her back to her feet and said, "Let me walk you
to your car." As he walked with her, he began to chastise her. "Now, I don't
know what you think you were doin' back there, but that was the wrong
side of the street to be on," he told her.

He said, "Now I don't know if you da po-leese or what, but you better
get on outta hea' befo' anything else happen ta ya."

That's when Kaiyah began to notice the final faces of the neighborhood. The young women of the neighborhood began to appear. And they
were there to pity her, while they stood on their high porches as nothing
more than passive observers.

"That's a shame," the young women commented, shaking their heads in
unison. "They shouldn't even have done that to her. She wasn't hurtin'
nobody."

All the while, Kaiyah walked slowly past them with her throbbing pains
and bruises. She thought, *How come no one is calling the police? What is wrong
with these people? I just got beat up in broad daylight, and all they can say is, "It's
a damn shame"?*

So when she climbed into the driver's seat of her car and started her
engine, she told herself that she hated those people. How could they so easily allow that to happen to her?

Kaiyah drove off with shaky nerves, and was unsure if she should turn
left or right at the first corner. And she decided to turn right, another bad
move.

Courtney Taylor waited for her in the passenger side of an unmarked
car with his friend at the wheel. They had separated from the pack of thugs
on their own private mission. Courtney had not even told his friend all of
the details.

"Yo, he' she come, man. So I'm gon' pop her and you just roll out,
aw'ight?" he ordered. Courtney held a nickel-plated gun on his lap that was
hidden below the dashboard.

His friend looked at him from the driver's seat with his window fully down and asked, "You sure you wanna do this shit, man? I mean, they already whipped her ass," he added with a chuckle.

But all that Courtney could think about was Leslie Beaudet's eyes when she had cut him years ago. And her recent words replayed in his ears: ". . . if push comes to shove with these people . . . then you might just have to do what you need to do. You feel me?"

Courtney nodded to himself in sync with Leslie's last words to him. *Yeah, I feel you.* He was pressed to prove that he would take it there, to the point of no return, because he knew that Leslie would. And since she had challenged him that way, he wanted to take her up on it.

So as soon as the college girl had reached their car in hers, Courtney told his friend at the wheel, "Aw'ight, lean back." He took aim with the gun before his friend could question his motives a second time. And he fired three steady shots into the driver's-side window of his mark.

Pop! Pop! Pop!

"Drive!" he yelled to his friend as soon as the shots had broken the college girl's window and struck her. His driver took off and sped down the street, making rapid turns as Courtney slid down low inside the passenger seat.

As soon as Kaiyah had been hit, her body jerked away from the wheel, causing her car to crash into the parked cars to her right. And as the blood began to flow from her head and neck, where she had been shot, there was no chance of her survival.

≈

When the news of Kaiyah Jefferson's death hit the local section of the *Times-Picayune* in New Orleans the next morning, Leslie paged Courtney from another pay phone as soon as she had a break in her classes. Courtney called her right back.

Leslie answered his call and said, "So, I guess you had to do what you had to do, then."

It was no big deal anymore. Leslie had prepared herself for it. Kaiyah must have done something to deserve it, and she had reckoned with her own judgment. Because the ghetto was not some visitor's safari to be toyed with.

However, Courtney had read the newspaper article that morning himself, and some of the facts within the article failed to add up. Not that they were supposed to, with a federal agent cover-up. But the overflow of support that the girl received was unusual for the secrecy that he figured would surround the death of a real agent. The article even reported on the college girl's assignments with her camera. So Courtney began to suspect that maybe she was just a college girl, a college girl who Leslie had a beef with. So he asked Leslie for the truth.

"You know what, was that girl really a fed like you said she was, or was she just some fuckin' college girl?" *who you didn't like,* he bothered not to add.

Leslie paused . . . what was done was done.

She answered, "What difference does it make now? You made your decision."

And Courtney was . . . astonished.

He thought to himself, *This girl is evil! She set me up for that shit. And she probably set the girl up to come around wit her camera like that. Because that shit was crazy!*

Leslie headed off an argument from Courtney when she told him, "Just remember that the *judge* pulled the trigger, and not the *jury.*" Then she hung up the phone on him.

When the line went dead, Courtney Taylor realized that there was nothing he could do about it. He couldn't bring the girl back and undo his mistake. But now he would need to hide from and dodge his own judgment. As for Leslie . . . she would meet her judge too. Courtney was sure of it. However, he realized that he would not be the one to do it. Leslie had just proven that she was a queen to his pawn, and he didn't have enough moves on the board to play her with . . . and expect to win.

There were times in life when a young man's pride was forced to take a backseat to his instincts. So Courtney mumbled to himself, "Yeah . . . let me just leave this girl the fuck alone."

≈

When the rest of "the chocolate crew" heard the news about Kaiyah Jefferson's tragic death, they began to discuss it at the house, with Ayanna Timber trapped in a serious dilemma.

Leslie did that shit! she panicked to herself. *Leslie did it!*

However, she wouldn't dare to tell anyone. She still had to live with the girl, while having no proof of anything. She only had hearsay and threats, that may not stand up to scrutiny.

"I mean, what was she doing over *there,* of all places?" Bridget questioned of Kaiyah's death. The location where she had been killed in the Seventh Ward was not known for friendly sightseeing.

"Ain't that where Leslie's from?" Yula asked.

Ayanna's eyes grew wide as Bridget and Yula looked to her for the answer.

She lied to them in her response. "I mean, I don't really know." All that she could think about was Leslie's words to her on Dillard's campus weeks ago: ". . . all my life, it seemed like, whenever someone did something bad to me, something real bad would happen to them. Like, I had my own war angel watching over me."

Yula frowned at Ayanna's ignorance, as she became more certain of her facts. She said, "Leslie did live in the Seventh Ward."

Ayanna went to confuse them on purpose. "I thought it was the Ninth," she said.

Yula said, "No, her *sister* lives out in the Ninth."

Ayanna snapped, "Well, why are you asking *me,* then, if you know so much, Yula?"

"Because I know you know," Yula snapped back at her.

Bridget cut them off and said, "Why are you two arguing about this? I mean, what difference does it make?"

It makes a lot of difference, Ayanna thought to herself. *Your dumb ass just don't know shit!*

Yula asked, "Well, where is Leslie now? Does she work tonight?"

"Hmmph, probably," Bridget grunted. "Her behind is always working." Then she added tartly, "And she needs to get a love life."

Ayanna and Yula looked at each other.

Yula warned, "Bridget, you know what, you better be careful of what you wish for." *Because your Creole man got the hots for Leslie.*

Ayanna looked at Bridget and agreed with Yula. "Exactly."

But Bridget was tired of playing the nice-girl role to befriend Leslie. She responded, "Whatever. I mean, Leslie just gets to say whatever she wants around here, so it's time for me to start saying whatever *I* want."

Ayanna smirked and thought, *Yeah, right. As long as Leslie ain't here, you'll say that shit.*

Yula burst out laughing, knowing Bridget better.

She said, "Bridget, you know good and well that you don't wanna tussle with Leslie. So you might as well just keep your tough-girl role to yourself in here."

≈≈≈

Leslie took a breath and concentrated at the bus stop. Her sister, Laetitia, had been in good spirits of late, and she had asked if Leslie could watch her girls again on her day off from work, so that she and Jurron could go out to the movies and dinner. And Leslie agreed to it. But the catch was, she wanted to see Jurron there with them. He had been missing in action for far too many evenings.

However, those damned bus rides through the 'hood were more than Leslie could stand! So she readied herself for another killing if she would have to.

I mean . . . fuck it! she told herself. *I am who I am. I'm the redeemer. And if anybody fucks with me from now on . . . they're just gonna get hurt.*

She boarded the bus that afternoon with the possibility of harming someone on her mind. And as if her fate was written in stone, there were no front seats available in the crowded bus that day. So Leslie slowly made her way to the back, where the fools usually were.

"Hey, man, stop fucking with my braids before I kick your ass in here," an irritated boy warned his antagonizer.

"Oooh, he callin' you out, man. He callin' you out," someone instigated. It was the same old shit!

Here we go again, Leslie told herself. *When do they ever stop this shit?*

She found an aisle seat near the back door and sat down to mind her own business.

"Aw, dat nigga need to get a fuckin' baldy wit his nappy-ass head. I'm just try'na help him out by pickin' his pees," the antagonizer responded.

"Ha ha ha ha!" the instigators laughed.

The braided victim of the slander shook his head and got up for his stop that was approaching. But he couldn't leave without a comeback line. His peer group respect depended upon it. It was just the way of the 'hood. The battle of wits meant everything for the immaturity of youth.

So he responded, "Look, man, when you gon' go to da dentist and get your teeth fixed? Don't they hurt your mouth? Damn! They look like you eat bricks for dinner."

But no one laughed too hard at the victim's joke. The stale silence told Leslie that the boy's antagonizer held more social dominance. It wasn't as if his joke was funnier. However, the bullies were always given the benefit of the doubt. They had earned it with their intimidation factor.

To confirm Leslie's hunch, the antagonizer jumped up and pushed his victim in the back of the head before he had reached his stop. The boy stumbled forward and fell right into Leslie, bending her neck painfully sideways.

"Shit!" Leslie hollered.

"Sorry 'bout dat," the victimized boy apologized to her.

Leslie looked right past him and to the boy who had shoved him. The mean-spirited boy looked at Leslie as if he could care less about her. So she sized him up and began to visualize him.

The same older woman who had calmed Leslie down the last time she had encountered a confrontation on the bus stared into her face again as Leslie focused to block everyone out. And as she continued to visualize another kill, the woman studied her intense concentration and eyed the two boys simultaneously.

When the bus stopped at the approaching corner, the victimized boy went to jump off at the back doors. His antagonizer followed him and attempted to get in one last shove. And it all happened in a flash. The first boy flew from the bus with the second push, and his antagonizer's untied shoelace was accidentally caught in the closing doors as the bus began to move forward.

"Ay, my fuckin' shoe is caught! Open the back door back up!" the boy hollered up front to the bus driver.

In his embarrassment and impatience, he went to push the doors to force them open. But the doors opened on their own before he could meet them with his hands. With his forward velocity, the boy flew cleanly out of the doorway, with his shoelace still caught inside the edge of the door. So his body swung cartoonishly alongside the moving bus before he finally fell out of his shoe, falling headfirst into the massive rolling wheels of the bus.

"AHHH!"

"Oh, my God! STOP DA BUS! STOP DA BUS!" the high-school-age girls yelled.

But it was too late for their terrified screams to save the boy as the bus, filled with New Orleans's passengers, crushed him under the wheel.

When Leslie broke from her trance, she met the curious eyes of the older woman who sat a few seats in front of her. The woman was convinced that Leslie was more than an average bus rider, just as she had suspected the last time they had crossed paths.

The bus driver stopped the bus. Everyone climbed off to wince and cringe at the crushed upper body of the unfortunate boy. But Leslie jumped off and got to stepping in search of a cab, as the older woman continued to watch her. Was the tragic event another coincidence . . . ?

She is one of us, the woman thought of Leslie with conviction. *And she is strong. Very strong!*

As Leslie headed on her way, she could feel the woman watching her. But she was not apologizing for her actions. What would be . . . was *meant* to be.

≈

Leslie arrived at the Desire projects in a taxi and was swollen with confidence. She had always felt above the tentacles of poverty, but now she had a clear reason to feel that way.

I will kill every last one of these motherfuckers if I have to. They don't care about me . . . and I don't care about them, she thought to herself of the 'hood. *I should have never been put with these people in the first place!*

However, she did care about her sister and her two nieces, enough to protect them at all costs.

Jurron felt Leslie's concern for her family as soon as he met eyes with her.

"Is everybody all right over here?" she asked as she walked into their apartment and eyed him.

"Lez-lee," her nieces yelled. They ran and jumped aboard her legs to welcome her back.

"*Bonjour, ma petite nièce.*"

"*Bonjour.*"

"*Bon-jour,*" her nieces responded in French.

So did Laetitia. "*Bonjour, ma chère sœur.*" Hello, my sweetheart sister.

She stepped up to give Leslie a loving hug.

Jurron nodded and answered Leslie's lingering question, "Yeah, we doin' aw'ight."

"Are you?" she asked him through her sister's hug.

Jurron thought to himself, *Tee's whole fuckin' family is sweatin' me, man. I mean, why da hell is she lookin' at me like that? I'm doin' all I can out here.*

Leslie answered his question without him even verbalizing it. She read his defensive posture.

She said, "Some of us can stand to do a lot better out here. And I'm tired of holding my tongue about it." She had been waiting to catch Jurron for a long time coming.

But Laetitia interjected in French, respecting her place as the woman of her household, *"J'ai tout mis en ordre maintenant, Leslie."* I have everything in order now. *"Il a du respect pour moi maintenant."* He has respect for me now. *"Et il fera mieux."* And he will do better. *"Je vais m'en occuper."* I will make sure of it.

Leslie looked at her sister with pride, liking the new strength that she showed. So she smiled. *"Tu sais que je t'aime, fille,"* she told her. *"C'est pour ça que je suis ici."* You know I love you, girl. That's why I'm here.

"Oui, je sais," Laetitia responded, smiling back to her big sister. Yes, I know. *"Et je t'aime."* And I love you.

Jurron stood there and was more puzzled by it than ever. *This is crazy,* he thought. *I don't like all this shit at all. Laetitia usually didn't talk all this French. But, I mean . . . it* is *a part of her family, though,* he reasoned. *But I'm sayin' . . . where does that leave me?*

As soon they left the house to go out, Jurron made sure to ask Laetitia what she had said to her sister in French that had calmed her down like it did.

Laetitia smiled and answered, "I just told her to respect my household, and that we would do better, you know. Everybody can't get a college education like her. It takes some people longer to get on track sometimes." *And we're gonna get on track now,* she held to herself. Laetitia had thought up some recent plans about it.

Jurron was satisfied enough with her answer to smile a little bit and feel more secure.

This girl is all right, he told himself. *I mean . . . shit gets a li'l weird every once in a while, but . . . Laetitia's all right. She really got my back.*

≈

Leslie read to her nieces in French again before putting them to bed. From the back window of their room, she looked up and spotted the full moon beaming down on her in radiant light blue. And she felt at peace with herself through all of the drama that had stirred up in her life of late. Then she looked down and thought of her nieces as they slept in their small beds.

What kind of life would they be able to afford? What kind of struggles would they go through? And who would try to harm them as Leslie, Laetitia, and Pierre had been harmed in their young lives in poverty? And there was nothing cute about it. No popular rap song could ever make it all good. Never! The ghetto had been treacherous to them, as well as to their parents, and there was no way that any of them could sugarcoat their collective pains with a glaze of frosted icing. Their real pains would crack through the layers of sweetness and bleed through . . . like the shine of the full moon through the project window.

So Leslie decided to use any power that she could to protect the next generation of her lineage. She put her hands on the forehead of Renée, the oldest, and closed her eyes to say a silent prayer.

To the one God who hears all things, hear me now. I will offer up my life, for you to invest all of the powers in me, to protect all who I love, and this child, from this day forward, from any unlivable harm that shall befall her or those who she shall choose to love.

When she had finished with Renée, she placed her hand on Anna's forehead, and repeated her prayer: *To the one God who hears all things . . .*

Meanwhile, plenty of others prayed for protection, solutions, and answers as well, and from any source in which they could believe. So back at the house near Dillard University's campus, Bridget had talked Yula and Ayanna into using the Ouija board to ask it questions about Leslie.

Yula commented from the table where they sat, "If this thing didn't work the last time we tried it, what makes you think it's gonna work now?"

Bridget answered, "Like Ayanna said, I didn't know what I was doing the last time. But now I do. You have to call a source to use, an ancestor who's close to the person that you want to know about, like . . . Leslie's mother."

Ayanna was already hesitant about the whole thing, but she was still curious. However, when the usually light-headed Bridget got too deep for her, she changed her mind.

"Wait a minute. You're gonna call Leslie's mother from the grave to ask her about her? You gotta be outta your damn mind!"

All of a sudden, Yula became the brave one. "Why not?" she asked. "I mean, that's how it's supposed to be done if we really wanna find out the answers to what's going on."

"Look, we just ask Leslie, then," Ayanna reasoned. Although, she didn't want to be the one to do it. Maybe Yula would volunteer to do so, since she had grown so confident of late with her new study habits, dedication, and better grades.

However, from miles away, Leslie could feel something stirring as she sat and watched videos on her sister's large color television set.

I wonder what my roommates are up to, she thought to herself. *I haven't spoken to them all day. And I know they heard the news about that girl Kaiyah by now. And Ayanna knows that . . .*

Leslie wasted no more time. She went to grab the telephone to call them.

When the phone rang at the house, it scared them all.

"Shit!" Bridget panicked as she tried to concentrate on the board.

Ayanna remained still, as she took a breath to calm her racing heart.

And Yula nervously laughed out loud at it. It was spooky timing.

"Get the phone, Yula," Ayanna challenged her.

Bridget looked to Yula herself. "I mean, you are closer to it," she commented.

Yula conceded, "Aw'ight, aw'ight, I'll get the damn phone," and climbed up from her chair.

"Hello," she answered.

"What are y'all doing?" Leslie asked her, straight to the point.

Yula took a quick breath, and was surprised by it. She looked to her two other roommates, who were sitting at the table with the Ouija board out, while attempting to gather information on Leslie through supernatural forces. And Yula froze in her words.

That made Leslie suspicious of them. So on a whim, she asked Yula, "Y'all not playing with that Ouija board again, are you?" Leslie was halfway smiling when she said it.

But Yula's eyes popped open over the phone as Ayanna and Bridget watched her. *Oh my God!* Yula thought to herself. *This girl is really . . . she's really . . .*

She was so surprised by the question that she couldn't get all of her thoughts together.

I knew that was her. I knew it! Ayanna panicked, reading Yula's expression on the phone.

And Bridget was clueless. "Okay, so who is it?" she asked Yula.

Leslie continued into Yula's ear, feeling that she was onto something, "You know that thing don't work for people who don't believe in it. And y'all don't believe in witchcraft or nothing . . . do you, Yula?" she questioned her.

Yula was still speechless. So Leslie took charge and finished her off with another assumption.

"Whose idea was it anyway, Bridget's?" she asked. "Now, I know you don't want to follow her, Yula. I mean, think about it. Bridget tries way too hard to be a leader, but the reality is, she's not. Even if she tries to pay for it. So just go ahead and put that stupid game away."

When Yula hung up the phone from her dictated conversation from Leslie, she looked over at Bridget and shook her head.

"I don't think we want to play that thing tonight," she commented.

"Why? What did she say?" Bridget snapped defiantly. She had had enough time to realize that it was Leslie on the phone.

Ayanna stood up from the table and began to walk away from it as soon as Yula said the words. Ayanna thought to herself, *If Bridget wants to play that brave shit tonight without knowing who she's fuckin' with, then she's gon' play that shit by her damn self.*

After Ayanna and Yula denied Bridget her position of leadership, Bridget pouted to herself while she sat alone at the table with her Ouija board. *Well, if they want to listen to Leslie so much, then maybe they should all move into another house with her.*

JUSTICE

Life III

Mardi Gras

In the early spring in New Orleans, thousands of tourists annually bombard the French Quarter for the Mardi Gras (Fat Tuesday) celebration to commemorate the Christian ritual of the forty-day fast before the death and resurrection of Jesus Christ, Easter. The Mardi Gras had become one of the most grandiose ritual celebrations of the New World, second to the carnival celebration of Rio de Janeiro, Brazil, and arguably equivalent to the carnivals of Port of Spain, Trinidad, and Salvador, Bahia. However, only the Mardi Gras of New Orleans had been able to enforce a restrictive level of purity to its European roots by limiting the participation of African descendants and the ingenious Native Americans who had grown to share in the excitement of the ritual. After all, the carnival celebrations had been brought to the New World by wealthy Europeans to use as an annual release for their own lower-class citizens, and not for the colored outsiders who seemed to dominate the events with their own cultural ideas.

The carnival events were used symbolically to make the lower classes feel as if they had parity with the upper classes, if only for one week out of the year. So during the celebrations, the wealthy classes of Europeans would allow themselves to mingle with, be ridiculed and defaced by, the lower classes in an exuberant show of satire, parody, entertainment, and sheer buffoonery.

Each new year, since his first in New Orleans from Haiti more than twenty years ago, Jean-Pierre Beaudet would watch the elaborate floats, colorful costumes, unlimited alcohol, and public displays of lewd sexuality that went on up and down the jam-packed streets of the French Quarter during Mardi Gras, and he realized then, as he did now, that it was all a wonderful display of . . . nonsense to protect the status quo. Then things would return to their normal hierarchies once the celebration was over on Ash Wednesday.

How wonda-ful would Mardi Gras be if I killed a dozen or so of these pat-tron-izing white people today? Jean thought to himself spitefully. Behind his belt that morning, he had carried along his five-inch blade that had been sharpened with the most fatal precision.

"What you thinkin 'bout, Gene? I know somethin' on your mind. You ain't said much of nothin' all day," the older man Freddie said to him. He was hobbling along with a dark brown wooden cane as Jean walked slowly beside him.

A whole group of the guys from the Open Arms Homeless Shelter had made it out to the Mardi Gras celebration as they did every year. The other men were there to enjoy whatever moments they had left to celebrate in life, but Jean had other thoughts on his mind.

"These people have no i-dea how much poverty there is around the world. And yet they make a mockery of us with their wealth each year," Jean snapped.

He said, "How much of this wealth could have been well spent to build bet-ta homes and to pro-vide me-di-cines and food for not only the poor peoples around the world but for the poor right here in New Or-leans?"

The younger man Ray was with them that day as well.

He chuckled at Jean's spiteful words and said, "Shid, these whiteys would rather throw money to dogs than to give it t' us. That's just the way they are, Jean. Ain't shit we can do to change it."

Jean nodded and said, "May-be not." *But there are some things we can do to get their at-tention,* he thought privately to himself.

These people have un-leashed AIDS, poverty, despair, and evil all around the world. And then they celebrate in our faces, as if they've done na-thing to harm us, Jean thought. *And they took my Anna!* he added to his thoughts of pain as he clutched his chest where his heart lay under his shirt.

"Oh, excuse me. I'm sorry," a young drunken white woman said after bumping into Jean on the sidewalk. She was loosely dressed and wearing no bra. She wore several beaded necklaces around her neck, the symbol of participation in Mardi Gras.

"You don't have to be sorry, li'l momma," Ray responded eagerly to the woman. He eyed the colorful beads around her neck and said, "This is Mardi Gras. Come gimme some sugar."

The young woman opened up to him in a flush of rosy cheeks and hugged Ray right there on the public street among the heavy crowds. Ray pressed his pelvis fully into hers and moved in rhythmic circles before they jovially separated from each other.

When it was over, Ray exclaimed, "I *luh* dis Mardi Gras shit, boy! It's the only time of year where I get to squeeze a rich white girl's ass and titties without goin' na jail for it."

"Or gettin' your damn self hanged," Freddie added to him with a knowing chuckle.

Jean failed to see the humor in it. He said, "I read in some true his-tory books that du-ring the days of A-meri-can slavery, the masters would often allow their slaves a day of free-dom. And on that day they would allow the slaves to con-sume so much wine that the slaves would neva' think of run-ning away to have real free-dom."

Freddie nodded his head against the stability of his cane and mumbled, "Mmm, hmm. That there is for true, Gene. And they still doin' that right now. 'Cause that's all we do durin' all of these holidays is take a day off to get crunked up, as these kids out here call it now."

Ray grinned at them and kept his thoughts to himself. *If you two motherfuckas know so much, then how come y'all both in a homeless shelter with the rest of us? Shit, Clarence got it right! But I ain't gon' say shit out loud about it, 'cause Clarence got intestine and bladder problems right now and couldn't come wit us. And I bet it got somethin' to do wit fuckin' with Gene like he do. I know it! So I ain't got a gotdamned thing to say to Gene's ass.*

Ray watched Jean with intent for the rest of their outing at the Mardi Gras to make sure he never offended the Haitian man like Clarence would often do.

Pierre, Jean's son and firstborn, watched his father as well, with a view from the crowd, where he traveled with Beaucoup and a few of his street soldiers.

"Ain't dat ya' pop ova' dere, Pierre?" one of the street soldiers asked him with a smirk. They never liked Pierre's pretty-boy ass to begin with. And they were all being tolerant of Beaucoup's liking of the boy.

Pierre nodded his head and mumbled, "Yeah."

"Ain't you gon' go speak to 'im?" someone else asked.

Beaucoup began to laugh at their instigation. "He don't have to talk to his pop if he don't want to. They both grown-ass men." And with that, Coup silenced everyone. Until he spoke again.

"These white people go crazy as shit out here, man," he commented with a chuckle. They all watched as bead-wearing white women lifted their shirts to reveal their pale breasts to the men who cheered them from the balconies above.

"Didn't you fuck a white girl out here last year, Coup?" one of his soldiers asked him.

Coup began to laugh out loud again. "Yeah, but I ain't fuck 'er out here on the street wit dese other crazy motherfuckas. I took her ass to a hotel."

He grinned and said, "The bitch had gotten robbed out here, right. And she told me that she couldn't find her friends. So I said, 'I gi' you some money if you take a li'l trip wit me an' shit.' And she was like, 'Take a trip where?' And I said, 'To a li'l hotel out hea'.'"

His soldiers began to laugh, knowing good and well where the story was going. Pierre grinned and chuckled at it himself as Beaucoup continued with his story.

"She said, 'Well, I've never done anything like this before.' I said, 'Me neither. I've never had a white girl before,' lyin' my ass off, right," he told them with a laugh. "And then she asked me if I had any protection. And I said, 'Hell, yeah!' 'cause I ain't know who dat bitch was fuckin' wit like dat out hea', man. I mean, she looked good, but fuck dat shit. If she gon' fuck me, she'll prob'bly fuck another motherfucka wit game.

"So, we gets to this hotel room, right. And before I can bang this white girl and get my shit off wit 'er, she start suckin' my rock. And I'm like, 'Damn!' And she sucked that ma-fucka so good, that when I came, I thought I wa'n't gon' have no more cum left in my system. I mean, she sucked all lat shit outta me."

His soldiers broke out laughing as they pushed their way through the crowded streets of Mardi Gras, while begging for anyone to question their authority. New Orleans was their city; those other people were only visiting.

Beaucoup concluded his story and said, "Shid. So I was thinkin' maybe I should give this white girl a code number for the next time she came down here. And I gay' dat bitch a hunnet and sent her on her way."

Before Pierre could take in the conclusion of Coup's story, his sister Laetitia was all up in his face with his nieces and their father, Jurron, standing nearby.

"Bonjour, Pierre," Laetitia greeted her brother playfully.

"Bonjour."

"Bonjour," her daughters joined in.

Pierre was stuck somewhere between joy and embarrassment. He was joyful to see his sister and her family out there having a good time like everyone else, but he was embarrassed because Beaucoup had been riding him so hard about allowing his sister to continue living in the projects.

So Pierre immediately asked his sister in French, *"T'as besoin d' argent?"* You need any money?

She looked at him as if it was obvious. *"Tout le temps."* All of the time.

Pierre didn't expect for her to answer him in French. He expected a simple "Yes," in English. Although Laetitia knew French, she had spoken it less than any of them.

After she answered in the affirmative, Pierre looked to Jurron.

"Whassup, man?" he asked him civilly.

Jurron nodded and responded to him with a hint of guilt, "We doin' all right."

Are you really? Pierre questioned to himself. He turned to the side and pulled out at least $300 to give to his sister. He looked to Jurron and nodded back to him.

Protect this shit out here, he thought to himself, hoping that Jurron would get the message.

He did. So Jurron returned the nod.

"Good lookin' out," he commented to the younger, taller man.

"Okay, den. I'll see y'all around," Pierre told them.

Laetitia responded with a smile before her brother could walk away from them, *"Oui, merci. Ne sois pas un étranger. Parce que nous t'aimous."* Don't you be a stranger anymore. Because we love you.

Pierre looked back at his baby sister and was frozen in his stance for a minute. He hadn't witnessed Laetitia that . . . confident with herself or with her French in a long while. She was even wearing less makeup to hide her skin blotches that day.

Pierre mumbled, *"Je vous aime aussi,"* I love you all too, in amazement before he walked off to join Beaucoup and the street soldiers, who all waited for him.

Beaucoup had watched the whole thing go down.

He got excited and said, "That's how you sposed to treat your sisters, nigga. You remember that shit." He gave Pierre a masculine hug of respect in front of his crew.

But the soldiers still didn't like Pierre. They all thought to themselves, *Fuck this toy-ass nigga! He ain't worth shit! He gotta be told how da treat his own family. Fuck kind of shit is that?*

As their crew shoved their way through the crowd, Courtney Taylor eyed Pierre from a distance with his own crew in tow, while wearing a green feathered mask.

Fuck outta here! That nigga hangin' out wit Beaucoup an' nem now? Courtney pondered. *I wonder if Leslie know that. Knowing her . . . she prob'bly do. Don't much of shit get past that girl. So she could have had me set up again if I tried something wit her.*

"Ay, C.T., look at this white boy right here. You think he got a knot on 'im?" one of Courtney's friends asked him, breaking him away from his private thoughts. They all wore colorful masks and beads to blend into the crowds.

Courtney studied the drunken young man through his eyeholes and read his body language. The mark looked drunk enough, but maybe he was too drunk for comfort.

Courtney shook his head and said, "Naw, man, he might be undercover out here. That shit look like an act. And he ain't got no friends wit 'em. Naw, man, fuck dat!"

Not everyone was out there at the Mardi Gras celebration to just enjoy themselves. Courtney and his crew had used the event as an annual payday. They would study the crowd and pick out victims for robbery. On a couple of fortunate years, they had collected nearly $2,000 between them from the unsuspecting tourists who walked the streets of New Orleans with their guards down. And although Courtney was still in hiding from the recent murder in his neighborhood, only the cursed found themselves arrested during Mardi Gras among all of the crazy crowds, feathered masks, debauchery, and accepted intoxication. Courtney figured that Mardi Gras would be one of the safest places to hide in New Orleans.

"Ay, yo, you see him right there," Courtney told his crew, eyeing a white man with his wallet out. He didn't even have to finish his sentence.

"Oh, we got him," his friends commented.

"Drop it off at the spot and change y'all shit up," Courtney reminded them.

"We know the deal," they told him.

Two of the masked marauders swooped through the crowd to make their move, while a third masked friend studied ahead to see if anyone was watching them before giving the attack signal.

When the coast was clear, he gave the signal by singing a hit song from the New Orleans rapper Juvenile, as loudly as he could to draw attention to himself and away from his partners in crime.

"I got dat fire!"

One of the two masked marauders then picked the man's wallet from his back pocket as the other cleared a path to run.

The man looked behind him and patted his pocket for his wallet before he panicked and realized what had happened to him.

"Hey! . . . Hey, stop those guys! Hey! Police!"

But by the time the words had spit forth from his mouth, the thieves had already made it around the corner. They were moving through the street among thousands. And only in American movies did uncoordinated white men take off after culprits in a crowd with expectations of being successful.

But in real life, the victimized white man tossed up his hands and cursed, "Fuck me!" Because there was no way in hell that he would catch those guys through the crowd of Mardi Gras.

As the boys hustled down the street and through the crowd, Leslie Beaudet looked up the street from where they were running and spotted a bewildered white man in search of a prayer to retrieve his stolen wallet.

Leslie grinned and thought, *That's just what his ass get. I hate when these white people come down here for Mardi Gras and act a damn fool just because they can. And then the only way that we can get in their float parades is if we're in the damn marching band in high school. And we make up the majority of the population in this city. That shit don't make no damn sense! So it serves his ass right. I hope a lot of these white people get robbed down here today.*

"What are you thinking about, Leslie? You've been quiet all day," Yula asked her. All four of "the chocolate crew" were there at the Mardi Gras that day for their second year while attending Dillard together. However, Leslie had been experiencing the madness of the celebration for years. The only time that she found much enjoyment in it was when the black Indians of New Orleans—her mother's sect—would perform in their costumes and floats. But, of course, they were never a part of the main "white people's parade," nor were the African-American Zulu organization who marched early in the morning and before the afternoon crowd would come out.

Leslie joked to Yula in her response. "Yula, you make it sound as if I'm like Ayanna or something with my mouth always running."

Ayanna smirked at the slight in her name, but secretly she was growing tired of being afraid of Leslie. She had been thinking about moving out of the house to find a saner place to live, or transferring from Dillard altogether to attend her local Houston HBCU (Historically Black College or University) at Southwest Texas State University. Or . . . she could stand up to Leslie and fight for her self-respect.

And they still had not gotten to the bottom of Leslie's mysteries. They had not yet found a way of pinning her down on anything.

With that thought on Bridget's mind, of unraveling the mystery of

Leslie, a wooden voodoo doll caught her eye from the window of one of the many commercial stores that they passed while strolling through the crowded street of the French Quarter.

"Wait a minute," she told her friends as she stopped to have a closer look. She walked into the store alone, before Yula followed her in.

Fuck this shit, man! Ayanna spat to herself. She remained outside the store, and was alone again with Leslie. *I can't just let her control me like this. I'm not some fuckin' puppet!*

So she began to walk in the store herself, knowing that Leslie watched her.

"Go 'head in there with them, Ayanna," Leslie teased her. "I'll just wait for you outside."

Is that another threat? Or is she try'na tell me what to do now? Ayanna asked herself, second-guessing. Leslie was driving the girl mad. And in her nervousness, Ayanna accidentally stumbled into the door on her way in.

"Shit!" she cursed to herself. She looked back at Leslie to make sure she was making the right decision.

Leslie asked her, "What are you looking at me for? I didn't do that. You see any dolls in my hand?" she asked Ayanna with her open palms out. "Bridget wants the doll, not me."

Ayanna finally broke down and asked her, "Leslie, what is up with you, man? I mean . . . why you doin' this to me?"

Leslie studied the seriousness on Ayanna's face before she answered her.

She said, "That's the same question that I ask God every day. And you know what . . . he never gives me an answer. So it's time for me to find my own answers."

And she walked away into the crowd.

Yula walked out a minute later and asked Ayanna, "What happened to Leslie?"

Ayanna was still watching the crowd that Leslie had disappeared into. She shook her head and answered, "I can't tell you. I don't know what the hell happened to that girl. But whatever it was . . . it must have been some terrible shit."

Yula looked into Ayanna's face and asked her, "What are you talking about?" She was not in on the secret understanding that Ayanna and Leslie had.

Ayanna shook her head again. "I don't even know myself," she answered before she went ahead and walked inside the store to join Bridget.

Yula stood there outside the entrance and looked into the crowd, attempting to spot Leslie in the thick of it. When she failed, she began to understand Ayanna's confusion on the matter. So Yula mumbled to herself, "I pray for you, Leslie. Whatever it is . . . I pray for you."

≈

Leslie walked aimlessly through the crowded streets of Mardi Gras, with a million thoughts on her mind.

Nobody understands the shit that I go through. Nobody! Am I just supposed to sit here and take this shit? For what? I'm not that kind of person. God should know. He made me. So whatever I end up doing . . . it's all on him. He should have never put me in this situation. I didn't ask to be black and fuckin' poor. I didn't ASK for this shit. Who wants to be spit on like this every day?

In the middle of her angry musings, a store item caught her eye from a window as well. It was a red Mardi Gras mask with bluish peacock feathers that flowed to the side, with reddish orange feathers that extended down to the shoulder.

Leslie stopped and stared at it for a second. Then she went inside and picked one up to buy.

"This is a very pretty mask," the white woman clerk told her. She smiled as she took Leslie's money.

Leslie asked her, "How many times have you said that today?" and caught the white woman off guard with it.

She answered, "Ah . . . not that much, I don't think."

"So you don't even remember, then?" Leslie questioned her.

The white woman continued to smile and was embarrassed. Everyone else had been especially nice to her that day. However, they had been mostly white customers, and happy tourists. But those damned local blacks were always peculiar. They never seemed to be satisfied with anything.

So the woman rolled her eyes as she rang up the price. She handed the young black woman a brown paper bag to carry her mask in, and she was glad to see her leave out the store.

"The hell was her problem?" she mumbled to herself as the young black woman left.

Once she was back on the street, Leslie looked down at her watch. It was time to make her important phone call.

She found a pay phone and dialed the seven numbers.

"Hotel La Salle," the receptionist answered.

"May I have Eugene Duval?" Leslie asked her.

"Hold on while I connect you."

"Thank you."

"Hello," Eugene answered in his room. Leslie's phone call was a little late, and he had become antsy, more unsettled than he already felt about seeing her there that night. Nevertheless, he couldn't tell Leslie no. Or not yet. But he was surely thinking about it. Their rendezvous was becoming one-sided. Leslie was getting all that she wanted out of it, but Eugene began to think that he didn't want it anymore. And the Hotel La Salle was running up his new credit card. Eugene was ready to air some of his concerns with Leslie as soon as he heard her voice over the phone.

She said, "I'm sorry I'm a little late. But as you can imagine, it's pretty hectic out here."

Eugene told her immediately, "Look, man, it was kind of rough getting this room in here during Mardi Gras. I mean, they jacked the prices up by a hundred dollars this week." He was just about to tell her that it would be their last time there for a while, but he stopped himself short to hear Leslie's response to his complaints.

"Well, I'm on my way," she told him with no empathy allowed.

Eugene frowned with the phone in hand and said, "Right now? I mean, I'm trying to go out there, too. I haven't been out there yet."

Leslie snapped, "It's all the same damn thing, Eugene. You're not a tourist. You live here like I do. They're not doing anything new this year."

Eugene said, "Yeah, but I still wanna go down there, though," as if he would miss something.

Leslie told him, "You can go after I leave then. Because Bridget's starting to get . . . cranky now anyway. I think you might have to give her some tonight. So, you know, you come down here with her, and then go back to the house and do the makeup thing. But after *me,* though, at the hotel. Because, I mean . . . it seems like I can't do without you now."

Eugene couldn't believe his damn ears. He grinned to himself over the phone and thought, *I can't believe this damn girl. She's crazy! But . . . I like that, though. She's just different.*

Leslie added, "And I promise not to touch you with my nails. I've been good with that lately, haven't I?"

Eugene laughed and answered, "Yeah, you have." He changed his mind about taking a new hard-line stance with her. He asked her, "Well . . . how long will it take you to get here?"

Leslie smiled and answered, "Twenty minutes. I'm leaving right now."

"Aw'ight. Cool."

As soon as Leslie left the pay phone to head on her way through the crowds and out of the French Quarter, she spotted her father in the distance talking to Laetitia and her young family.

"Shit. I don't need to see them right now," she told herself. She snuck off in an alternate direction to avoid her loved ones while pushing her way through the crowd. *They could all learn something from me about how to control the situation anyway,* she mused.

The situation she referred to was love, or whatever humans wanted to call the attachments they had between needful men and women.

≈

Leslie arched her back and rode her full naked weight into Eugene's pleasure point with hers.

"Oh, Eugene. It just gets better every time," she panted to him in English.

But it didn't feel that way anymore for Eugene. He had become too cerebral about their sex, and his feelings of guilt had begun to override his lust. So he went through the motions as Leslie began to ignore him. Isn't that what guys did to their women? They didn't care half of the time whether the woman had been satisfied or not, as long as they got *their* satisfaction. Leslie had heard enough complaints from women, young and old, to validate the point. So she could care less if Eugene was no longer feeling her. He was going to do what she wanted him to do, or suffer the consequences.

During their break, Eugene tried to gather up the strength that he needed to finally deny her.

He said, "You know what? This is really slimy of both of us," as they lay next to each other on their backs.

Leslie shocked him when she responded, "I know." Then she added, "But so are a lot of other things that go on in this world. So who are we to judge?"

Eugene thought about her logic and countered it. "But I'm sayin' . . . that don't mean that we have to go there. I mean . . . we all make our own decisions on things."

Leslie asked him, "And what decisions did *we* make?"

Eugene backed up and said, "That don't mean we can't change our minds, though. I mean . . . we can all stand to ask for forgiveness some-times."

Leslie frowned at him and said, "Ask *who* for forgiveness?"

Eugene looked at her and answered, "God," as if she should know better.

Leslie responded, "Whose God? Is he the God of all of us, white, black, yellow, and brown? And how come God is not a she? Wouldn't *she* be more forgiving than a he? It makes sense to me. Maybe we all got it wrong. And that's why she doesn't forgive much. Because we don't ask the right way."

Eugene was utterly confused. He sat up and asked Leslie, "What are you talking about? God *does* forgive us. What do you think Mardi Gras is all about? I mean, we celebrate the forgiveness that God has for us."

"By acting like fools out in the middle of the street?" she questioned. "That seems very hypocritical to me. And when will God let black people celebrate freedom from poverty, along with all the rest of the poor people in the world?"

Eugene looked away for a minute and thought, *Damn! This girl is . . . I can't even say it.*

Leslie said, "I don't wanna talk about this anymore, Eugene. I hate talk-ing about this kind of stuff. I mean . . . it just makes you feel so . . . helpless. And mad. You know what I mean?"

Eugene searched Leslie's dark eyes and tried to find something left in her soul that held on to hope and optimism. And although he didn't want to say it, he thought to himself, *No. I don't know what you mean. Because I never feel helpless. I mean . . . tomorrow is always another day.*

Leslie nodded her head in sync with his thoughts. She could read them through the pity in his eyes as he stared at her.

She said, "I used to think like that, too. For most of my life I thought that things would change. So I just kept working hard, and hoping that everything would be all right. But you know what? It just seems like every time I think I've turned that corner . . . things only get worse."

Eugene held his tongue and understood her despair. He relaxed back into the pillow and allowed Leslie to cuddle with him there. But as he began to get to know her better, he found that he liked her less and less. She seemed to have too much pain locked up inside of her, and he damn sure didn't want to share it. So even as he hugged Leslie against the soft cushion of the hotel pillows, he began to reminisce on the happier times that he had had with Bridget.

≈

Eugene felt exhilarated at how . . . refreshing it was to be with Bridget Chancellor again after being underneath the mental weight and exhaustion of Leslie Beaudet. And as the excitement of Mardi Gras continued with the flambeaux torches that lit up the night, Eugene was a puppy with a returned ball in his paws as he bobbed along with Bridget inside of the still lively French Quarter.

In his excitement, he squeezed Bridget's hand and asked her, "Do you believe that God forgives us?"

Bridget looked into Eugene's eyes and responded, "Where did *that* come from? Why, you have a guilty conscience about something?" she asked him. All was not so quickly forgiven with her. She still had a bone to pick with the boy for leaving her confused and lonely for weeks.

Eugene took a breath and said, "Man, it's just . . . I've just learned a lot lately. That's all I can say right now. But answer the question, though," he pressed her.

Bridget said, "Answer *my* question." She was fed up with playing the nice girl role, and if she had learned anything from being around Leslie, it was that more . . . hostility was needed sometimes to gain respect from those who take you for granted.

However, Eugene had been around Leslie now for weeks himself, and he just wanted his old Bridget back, the happy-go-lucky Bridget.

So he paused for a minute and said, "Look, Bridget, I know I haven't been treating you right lately, man. I know it. But I'm trying to do better now. And I just want us ta . . . t' go back to how we had it before."

"And how was that?" Bridget asked him. "With you not taking things as seriously as I do?"

Eugene faced her and held both of her hands in his, as the crowds continued to bump into them.

He said, "Then maybe I'll take things more seriously now," with all honesty in his eyes. "I mean . . . I just realize what I have now. And I mean . . . I love you, Bridget."

Eugene had no idea that he would say that to Bridget that night, but the timing felt right, and it just came out of his mouth at that moment. Was it desperation?

However, Bridget chose to hold back her elation at the moment and made sure to go for the jugular . . . like Leslie would do. So she kept a straight face and asked him, "You love me enough to introduce me to your parents?"

Eugene looked straight into her eyes and found the courage he needed to say, "Yes." And he meant it.

After that, Bridget told herself, *Now, Leslie! Take THAT!* And she melted into Eugene's arms and kissed his lips.

"Awww, isn't that nice? Love is in the air," an older white woman said to them with a Polaroid camera around her neck. "Would you guys like to take a picture?" She pointed the lens of the camera at them before they could give her the okay. And when they smiled at her, she snapped their picture.

Eugene immediately dug into his pockets and asked, "How much is that?"

The camera woman waved his money off. "Oh, no, no, no," she told them. "I'm not charging anyone. I'm just out here doing this for love," and she handed them the fast-developing picture.

They all looked at it together, before the camera woman repeated herself: "Awww, love is in the air."

At the same moment, the hard-pressed eyes of Jean-Pierre Beaudet watched the young couple with envy. He remembered falling in love with his Anna many years ago inside of the same French Quarter. And Jean could not convince himself to leave that night until he had shed blood in her honor with his knife. Because in his eyes, white people were guilty of destroying his love for life. And for destroying Anna's love.

They were all guilty by association, just as blacks were all guilty of being second-class American citizens. White people had to prove that they did not passively accept the conditions of racism, just as blacks had to prove that they were educated and dignified enough to rise above the ignorance of their stereotypes. Jean felt that white people had to prove their humanity by going out of their way to make things better for the poor people in their wake, who lived no better than those in the shacks of Third World countries. And how could blacks prove much of anything while living in such adverse conditions? Wasn't America the First World, and one of the wealthiest nations on earth? Then prove it by taking care of its own poverty, and correcting the ugly history of racism! Jean felt that there needed to be a national agreement to finally lift the veil of acceptance of the inequalities in America, and then let their example of healing establish a model to correct the inhumane conditions of all peoples in every nation . . . regardless of their race or class.

And if white people declined to prove that they were just, then many of them deserved to die. Or at least that's what Jean-Pierre had thought to himself. They had hell to pay, and not just in America, but all around the world. They had not shown much sympathy or support for his beloved Haitians and their known struggles with unstable government, poverty, or their fight with the epidemic of AIDS either. So Jean was ready to lay down his life to repay his ancestors and his wife in white blood.

Yet . . . he could not bring himself to do it. Because he understood white people. They were the last warriors of the earth, and the most savage of fighters. Not only would they slay him for his minute bloodshed against them but they would then take the war to his children, to his grandchildren, and to their children, as they had already done to the colored people of the world. So in the eleventh hour before battle, Jean thought about his youngest daughter, Laetitia, and how she had surprised him that day with her French. He thought about how she smiled so vividly that day with his granddaughters . . . and with their father with them. And Jean realized that there was still hope left, with which to overcome their struggles. Hope and an iron willpower not only to survive, but to succeed in the face of desperation, was the only way to defeat white people. In a word, it was resilience that was needed. Laetitia's resilience had shown her father the way.

Jean wandered about in the French Quarter that night until he arrived at the scene of the crime that had happened more than a decade ago, where he had lost his job as a noted cook at Le Château restaurant on Chartres Street. And he suddenly heard the voice of his late wife, Anna, speak to him: *"Ne laisse pas tomber tes rêves. Nous allons réussir ensemble."* Don't you give up your dream. We will make it together.

Then she added to him in English, "Laetitia needs your help now. They all do. Pierre and Leslie. So bring our family back together," she whispered in his ear. "I'm all right, Jean. I'm all right in heaven."

Jean broke down and cried right there on the street, as he watched the customers who flowed in and out of Le Château for their exquisite meals, where they dined in dimly lit elegance.

And he responded to his wife out loud, "Yes, An-na. I know. I know. And I love you so much. I love you!"

But as the busy tourists of the Mardi Gras celebration took in the man's tears and his mumbled words to himself, they viewed him as just another homeless black man who had lost his last wits. They cared less about his past. Black Americans were always crying about something. Either that or they were raising hell out in the American streets with their petty crime. That's just how they were, a sad group of people who needed to learn how to move on and prepare themselves for better days. Because wallowing in their unfortunate past would not help them. White folks had pasts too.

A Reckoning . . .

Even after the festive mood of the Mardi Gras celebration, Tulane University professor Marcus Sullivan remained dumbfounded by the shocking murder of his African-American student Kaiyah Jefferson. He was still trying to comprehend things, while sitting in his home theater in Algiers, across the Mississippi River from the New Orleans French Quarter.

"What in the hell is wrong with these people?" he asked himself out loud. "Why would this group of . . . thugs go out of their way to shoot and kill an innocent college student just for being in their neighborhood, for God's sake? I just can't understand that."

What he did understand is that the dean of sociology at Tulane had canned his great idea of filming college students as sociology cases. He was also forced to place Marcus on probation. Nevertheless, Professor Sullivan failed to reveal all of the details to university officials, or to New Orleans investigators, on exactly why his student was there filming the impoverished, drug-infested area of the Seventh Ward in the first place.

Marcus was still trying to piece the complete puzzle together himself. So he had made copies of Kaiyah Jefferson's footage before he handed the tapes over to Tulane University officials in cooperation with the New Orleans police. As he watched Kaiyah's video footage of "the chocolate crew" for the twentieth time within the privacy of his home, he looked specifically for something in Leslie Beaudet's dark eyes that would tell him more about her.

What am I missing here? he asked himself. His instincts told him that the recent events might have something to do with her. He could just feel it. Or was that feeling more related to his prejudice of dark skin? Dark skin was fine when it made jokes and acted a fool for the camera, but not when it stared at you with . . . a hint of contempt. Maybe Leslie's eyes brought out the fear of Professor Sullivan's own demons. How did he really feel about black people?

"Y'all all in here tellin' y'all business," Leslie told the camera again. "You don't even know what she's gonna do with this stuff." Then she questioned, "A documentary for *who?*"

Professor Sullivan scrambled for his remote to freeze the video on Leslie's eyes at that exact moment. He looked into them once more, peering straight ahead at the camera, and he shuddered.

"Jesus Christ!" he spat to himself. "How dare you? How *dare* you?" he repeated. "She doesn't want to be judged. But judged for what? What have you done, Leslie?" he asked the screen, as if expecting a response. "What are you being judged *for?*" *For being black?* he pondered to himself. But how complicated was that? He didn't know how being black felt any more than he knew how women felt in their frequent contempt of men. And Leslie was black and a woman, a double complication.

That's when he began to feel guilty about his lack of understanding.

I naively sent my student right into the belly of the beast, he thought to himself. *I have no idea what I'm dealing with here. She just looked . . . interesting,* he reflected of Leslie. *Now I know that she's much more than I had bargained for. I can't seem to pin her down.*

He allowed the tape to roll forward.

"Say anything," the loudmouthed rapper girl named Ayanna told Leslie again. "Tell us something extra about N'awlins. Talk about that voodoo shit down here. Speak in French, L. Do *anything,* girl. Anything!"

Professor Sullivan pressed pause on his remote again.

"Voodoo," he expressed to himself. "Could that be serious?"

He had continually ignored it before. It had failed to compute with him, because he didn't want to believe in it. His mind had shut the information out as illogical. He figured that the rapper girl was just running her mouth. But now . . . he had no choice but to investigate it further.

He nodded his head and told himself, "I'll just have to take a visit into town and buy a few books on . . . voodoo tomorrow and find out what the hell it's all about."

≋

Leslie listened to her sister, Laetitia, over the telephone, as she told her all about how nice their brother, Pierre, had been to her, Jurron, and the girls when they had spotted him at the Mardi Gras celebration a few days ago.

"And he gave you three hundred dollars?" Leslie asked her. "Who was he with?"

"Some guys. I don't know," Laetitia answered halfheartedly.

Laetitia never pays any attention to details, Leslie thought to herself. *So why would I think it would be different now just because she's speaking French again?*

"So when are y'all gonna start trying to find a better place to live?" Leslie pressed her.

Laetitia paused for a minute. She had to prepare herself to explain things to her big sister.

She said, "Leslie, you know what? I'm tired of people telling me where I should live, and how I should spend my money, and how I should be doin' better for myself. Because the fact is, I'm not even eighteen years old yet. So I'm doing all right for myself. And I have some plans to move. Yes. But three hundred dollars ain't gon' help us do that."

It'll buy another television set, though, won't it? Leslie mused to herself. But instead of sharing her cynicism with her sister, she asked her, "Would you still be doing 'all right' for yourself if you had lost Jurron to that girl you were sweating so much?"

Leslie couldn't help it. Laetitia's tart attitude had instigated her to go there.

Laetitia paused again after hearing Leslie's question. She thought to herself, *Why would she bring that up?* as if her big sister knew something.

So she responded in French, as her heart began to pound from associated guilt to murder, *"Qui . . . cette fille qui a été tuée?"* Who . . . that girl who was killed?

Leslie watched the abused telephone cord again, while she stood inside of the kitchen. The telephone cord remained stretched out of shape, dangling to the floor, twisted and deranged, and twirling without reason . . . like her life. So she decided to walk away from it, stretching the dirty white cord into the dining room.

"Yeah," she answered her sister.

Before Laetitia could respond again, Leslie heard her roommates approaching the front door, while engaged in some passionate conversation. So she cut the discussion with her sister short.

"Let me call you back from work. I have to go now."

"Oh . . . okay," Laetitia responded with further hesitation. Leslie was leaving her hanging and curious.

As soon as Leslie hung up the phone in the kitchen, Yula and Bridget stormed into the house engaged in a heated argument.

"Bridget, I'm just being honest about it!" Yula exclaimed. "I mean, slavery was evil and all of that, but even if we do get reparations for it now, there are so many people who are so . . . messed up by everything that they would just go out and waste the money. And you *know* it! So what we need first is education and . . . and skills," she argued.

Bridget countered, "Yeah, but that shouldn't be a substitute for what they owe us. Some people can't afford to learn any skills."

Yula frowned and said, "Well, like you already said, Bridget, your great-grandparents were sharecroppers with no money, but your father still got an education, and he worked himself into having money. And that's what we all have to do. We can't keep making all these excuses for everything."

She said, "Because I'll admit it, if it wasn't for Leslie, I wouldn't be doing what I need to do. But Leslie set me straight."

Before Bridget could open her mouth to slander her, Leslie walked out and surprised them with a sheepish smile.

"Thanks, Yula. I knew I was good for something," she joked.

Yula grinned and said, "Oh, shit. What's up, Lez? I didn't know you were here. You don't have to work today?"

"I'm on my way out the door right now," Leslie told her.

That's when Bridget decided to increase the bite of her argument.

She said, "And what about when he says that blacks who are children of recent immigrants shouldn't deserve any money. How would that be fair to Leslie? Her father's Haitian."

Yula thought fast and said, "Well, you can give up your share to her, Bridget, because your family surely don't need the money."

Leslie finally asked them, "What are y'all talking about?"

"This white man wrote that reparations is racist and a bad idea for black people. And I'm not saying that we don't deserve it, like he says, but we do have to prepare ourselves for it," Yula answered.

They waited for Leslie's response. Bridget and Yula were both certain that Leslie would have one. And she did.

Leslie opened her mouth and said, "It *is* racist. Everything America *does* is racist. When they hire you for a job, it's racist. When they fire you, it's racist. When they deny you a loan, it's racist. When they give you a loan, it's racist. And when they lock you up, it's racist. Even when they let you go, it's racist. You know why? Because America always wants to know if you're black or if you're white. And that's racist, a preference or a prejudice for a particular race. And they damn sure have one on everything that they do!

"And if you want to ask me if I think they'll give us reparations?" Leslie questioned herself. "No. Why? Because they're racist, and we're not the right color to get it."

Bridget and Yula were both . . . silenced!

Bridget thought to herself, *Damn!* She had finally gotten it! Leslie Beaudet was . . . unbelievable. Everyone else seemed mortal compared to her. So . . . who the hell was she?

Before Leslie left them for work, she turned to Bridget and said, "I heard you, too."

Bitch! she kept to herself.

She walked out the front door and continued to curse Bridget for her sly remark about recent immigrant parents.

"That bitch is getting on my last nerve!" Leslie told herself as she walked to work. "I swear, if I had some place else to live right now, I would . . ." And she stopped herself from voicing it.

≈≈

Jake brought the telephone to Leslie at the restaurant that night with a call from her father. But Leslie refused to receive it.

She whispered, "Tell him I'll call him back. I'm just real tired right now." And she held her ground by not taking the phone from him. So Jake was forced to do her bidding.

"Hey, ah, Gene . . . she just stepped into the ladies' room a minute. I'll have her call you back in a few."

"Make sure she does," Jean told him.

When Jake hung up the phone, he asked Leslie, "What's going on? Is everything all right with you?"

Leslie repeated, "I'm just tired."

Jake studied her face. Her energy did look low that day. She lacked her usual vibrancy.

He asked her, "You need a few days off? I mean, I know this has been hard on you lately."

Leslie thought about it. Jake was being a real angel to her. So she nodded to him and agreed to it.

"I'll be back," she commented, as she began to undo her apron.

"Oh, I know you will," Jake responded with a grin. "I just don't like seeing you like this. But what do you want me to tell your father?"

"I'll call him when I get home," Leslie lied. She didn't want to talk to her father. She didn't want to talk to anyone in her family at the moment, except for . . . Pierre. Maybe Pierre would show her some good fortune and lay enough money on her so she could afford a nice place of her own, *tomorrow,* because her patience had run thin on saving and planning. How long did she have to continue to wait to live? And she didn't want to stay in the dormitories or around campus anymore. She thought about finding a nice place near Lake Pontchartrain, where she could walk along the water near SUNO's campus and take in the fresh, clean air, while fantasizing about another life.

Not even her studies held her interest anymore. Although she hadn't shared the information with anyone, Leslie's grades had not been much higher than C's that semester. Dillard University was no longer the glue that held together her sanity. There was nothing left but . . . the sweet lust of Eugene, Bridget's man, who had recently found his way back home to her.

I should have never told him to make her happy that night, Leslie thought to herself, as she headed back to the house. *Now she's all fucking happy again, and working my nerves.*

When Leslie walked past a pay phone on Gentilly Boulevard, she was suddenly struck by her new craving for love.

I'm gon' call that boy right now, she told herself. And she did.

"Hello," Eugene answered the phone at his dorm. He was just about to head out the door and go hang with the boys of Xavier. Sometimes hanging was necessary to let your troubles loosen and sag low, so that you could drop them to the ground and get back to work. The male gender was particularly adept at that, dropping the daily baggage. But some of them took the hanging too comfortably, and they ended up sagging so low that they could no longer pull themselves back into busy organization. However, Eugene was not that type, and he realized when it was time to get back to work. But then again . . . Leslie Beaudet had tempted him to stray off course, and to stay there.

"I need to see you tonight," she told him. No conversation was needed.

She had grown desperate for him. And she had no idea how to use tact with the new feelings of love that she had never experienced before.

Eugene shook his head with the phone in hand and told her, "I can't do it. I—"

Leslie cut him off and said, "I'll pay for the room tonight."

What was the use in saving for the future if a hundred dollars was needed to save your life for today? Leslie felt as if she would die if she didn't see that boy. Those crazy feelings for him had just snuck up and grabbed her. She didn't even comprehend it. Her desire for Eugene was no longer logical. It had become her water, her bread, her sugar, her everything. And with that, she connected to her sister's logic. Live for today, and love for today, because tomorrow is a motherfucker. And the crazy love connected Leslie to her mother, and to Bridget, and to every other woman who had craved a man. What was there left to live for, if you had no one to share the shit of life with, while trying to figure out a way to somehow make it feel . . . better . . . together.

Nevertheless, Eugene wanted no more of her.

"You know what? I've been thinking about this, and we can't do this no more," he told her.

"Tell me to my face, then," Leslie challenged him.

Eugene froze and stood in silence.

This goddamn girl is try'na to drive me crazy! he told himself.

He said, "I got a lot of things to do tonight."

"So does everybody else," she responded on beat.

Eugene could see where that argument was going: nowhere fast. *This girl is gonna have something to say for every excuse that I make,* he mused. So he realized that he was not getting off of the phone with her without at least telling her that he would meet her there at the hotel, whether he meant it or not.

"Aw'ight, I'll see you there later on, then," he told her hastily.

"I'll be there in an hour," she responded.

Eugene grimaced and said, "What?"

"I got off from work early tonight."

"Why?"

She paused. "I didn't feel too good."

Oh, shit! Eugene thought immediately. *What is she trying to pull now?*

"What *kind* of sickness? I mean, if you're sick, then why you wanna see me?" he asked. What if it was contagious? He didn't want it.

"I'm not sick," Leslie assured him with her tone.

"You just said you didn't feel good at work. So what does that mean?"

"I'll talk to you about it when I see you," she told him.

Eugene slipped and told her out loud, "I'm not really feelin' this no more, man."

Leslie ignored it and said, "I'll see you in an hour," before she hung up the phone on him.

"Hello . . . ," Eugene said into the phone. Once he accepted the fact that she had hung up on him, he cursed, "Shit! I'm not gonna see this girl tonight. Who the hell she think she is? She don't have me on no fuckin' strings!"

Eugene thought about the scratches that she had inflicted on his abdomen on their first meeting. Fortunately, they were not as bad as he first thought they were, and they had healed quickly.

He nodded to himself and concluded, "She did that shit to me on purpose. Fuck that girl! I'm not seein' her no more." And he left out of his dorm room to meet up with his friends.

Meanwhile, Leslie traveled downtown to an automatic teller machine to withdraw $100 from her account. She had been the only sibling in her family to have a bank account, and the only one who had finished high school to enroll in college. And for what, just to feel as miserable and as hopeless as she felt now? Poverty, not only of economics but of the human spirit, was a living quicksand. The more Leslie struggled to find peace and a safe haven to breathe, the more the swamp tugged at her knees, working hard to bend her fully over and take her under.

"You can work all you wanna work, but if you ain't *meant* to be rich, you ain't gon' *be* rich. You don't know that by now?" her mother was asking her from her deathbed again.

Leslie nodded her head with her crisp twenty-dollar bills in hand and thought, *You're right, Mom. It doesn't make a difference. So are you happy now? You've finally broken me down!*

"Are you happy now?" Leslie repeated out loud. *So I'm just gonna do whatever I need to do out here to survive,* she thought as she walked away with her money. And she meant it.

≈≈≈

Eugene's friends at Xavier were discussing the intangible and impenetrable nature of women that night, of all things.

"And why do they always think you're neglecting them when you got shit to do? We don't sweat them when they go out wit their girlfriends."

"I know, man."

"Unless we want some ass that night," one of the four friends joked.

They laughed.

"Yeah, that's different. But if they give up a quickie before they go out, then it's cool."

Eugene didn't have much to add that night. Leslie Beaudet had invaded his consciousness, and he couldn't seem to block her out as the time ticked closer to the hour in which she gave him to meet her at the hotel.

"What are you thinking about, Eugene? You know Bridget be sweatin' you too, man. I've been around y'all. I know."

They laughed again. However, the mention of Bridget's name served to give Eugene the courage that he needed that night to handle his business with Leslie.

Dig it, he thought to himself. *What if she tries to tell Bridget about us if I don't show up tonight? I need to handle her shit, and let her know that it's not gon' work!*

"Eugene? Where's your head at, man?" his friends asked him.

Eugene snapped to attention and informed them, "I got something to do right quick."

His friends knew the deal. *Here he goes again,* they thought to themselves, as Eugene hurried off.

"It must be that Creole shit or something, man," one of his friends joked out loud. "That boy *keeps* shit on his mind!"

However, when it became a half hour later than the meeting time, Leslie began to plot while sitting in the hotel room alone.

What am I gonna do to him if he doesn't come? she asked herself. She had not yet considered herself a priestess in an everyday context. She only used it when the mood suited her. Nor did she follow the countless recipes of enchantment from the books that she had read. Leslie used more of her intellect, if anything. She was a natural priestess, changing the laws and practices as she saw fit. After all, there had been no one there to . . . initiate her. So her father was right, loose power was indeed a menace to be feared. And Leslie was loose with power in New Orleans. What pity would she have for Eugene Duval?

What pity do they have for us? she asked herself of men.

She watched the BET (Black Entertainment Television) cable channel, which was full of videos of hard-core black men who chased less-than-black women. Or at least while up on the video screens.

"Them niggas love themselves some French vanilla," Leslie told herself. "Where the hell is the chocolate?"

Everything seemed to irritate her now. It wasn't as if she had never tasted the color codes of the world before, she was just growing . . . sick of it! And her sickness made her vow to hurt Eugene if he failed to show that night.

"Okay," she told herself, "if he plays me, I'm gon' fuck up him and Bridget."

She stood from the bed a minute later and cursed herself, "Fuck was I thinkin' when I told him to go back out with her? That was just plain stupid! Shit!"

But Eugene was not to disappoint. He was just running late. However, he was irritated himself that night. He was pressed to keep a noncompromising edge for what he deemed a final discussion with Leslie. He even spoke to the receptionist with edge.

"I'm here to see Leslie Beaudet. You have her room number?"

"Ah . . . ," the receptionist responded as she looked it up, "she's in room eight thirteen." It was against hotel policy to give out a room number, but the Creole receptionist did it anyway. She recognized Eugene as one of their own, and his attractiveness had swayed her judgment.

"Thank you," he said, with no thought about her.

He walked over to the elevator with edge. But then he became hesitant.

"Damn," he mumbled to himself, "why she gotta be in room . . . *thirteen* and shit?"

He tried to laugh off his superstitions before he arrived at her room, because he knew that there could be no give with Leslie. She was a tigress, and tigresses needed to be dealt with as fiercely as they dealt.

Leslie bounced up from the hotel bed and grinned as soon as she heard the knock on the door. But by the time she opened it, she was all business. But so was Eugene.

He walked right in and told her, "We're not doing anything tonight. So I don't know what kind of ideas you have, but you might as well kill 'em."

Leslie looked at him and told herself, *That's the wrong word to use up in here with me, boy.*

She asked him, "Do you think you can love two women at the same time?"

Eugene calmed down and studied her mood. She seemed . . . at peace with him still, as if they were having a simple walk in the park.

He asked her, "Why? You want me to love you and Bridget. That's crazy."

"Is it?" she asked him. "You fucked me and Bridget."

Leslie was being rather blunt, so Eugene let his own words fly, as ridiculous as they may have sounded to a woman.

"Fuckin' is different. And girls always get the two confused."

Leslie paused . . . and she momentarily looked away from him.

He's not coming back to me, she thought to herself. *I just lost him. So now what should I do? Should I keep him anyway?*

She nodded her head and said, "All right, then. I understand. So we go our separate ways."

Eugene waited to see her eyes to make sure she meant it. Once he saw them, he responded, "Yeah. That's what we need to do."

Leslie nodded a second time and said, "Okay . . . can I have a last hug?"

Eugene immediately thought about his abdomen and rejected Leslie's plea.

"Naw, that's all right. I don't want you puttin' no scars on my neck or on my back this time."

Leslie said, "I'm not," as she moved closer to him.

Eugene backed away toward the window.

Leslie said, "All I'm asking you for is a hug. You can't give me that? I mean, it's that simple."

"No it's not," Eugene told her. "And I don't wanna hug you. I told you, there's nothin' going on tonight. I don't even wanna touch you."

Leslie didn't like the sound of that. Eugene was pouring on the hot sauce a little too strongly for himself.

She repeated, "You don't wanna touch me? Why? Am I a disease now? Fuck are you talkin' about, you don't wanna touch me? All I'm asking for is a damn hug."

Leslie had never felt that vulnerable. It was different when people were bothering her. She could do something about it. She could make them fear her and leave her the hell alone. However . . . she couldn't make someone love her, no more than they could make her love them.

Once she realized that, she went soft again.

"Okay, let's just get this over with. I'll keep my hands to myself, and down at my side, and all I want you to do is wrap your arms around me. Okay? Can you do that for me, just this last time?"

Eugene felt the idea was ludicrous. "For what?" he asked her.

The boy just didn't get it. Leslie needed a hug to feel human, that's all. She wanted him to validate that they were both warm-blooded organisms.

But how was he supposed to know that her possession was over? So Eugene continued to be as cold as a reptile in the snow. He was only trying to protect himself. He didn't know what Leslie really needed.

He spat, "Hell no! I'm not hugging you."

Leslie opened her arms and offered herself to him anyway, a sacrificial lamb, just to feel his warmth again.

Incensed by it, Eugene went to push her away. "Stop it!" he expressed to her. "And if you think I'm afraid of Bridget finding out about it, I'll fuck around and tell her myself. I don't care anymore," he boasted. "Because you're not gonna have me like this."

As he extended his arms to push her away, Leslie grabbed them and locked her hands around his forearms. The soft shit was over.

Leslie became vengeful at hearing Eugene's boast.

She told him point-blank, "Don't do that."

"Why? Because Bridget owns the house that you all live in?" Eugene concluded. "I know what time it is. Now get off of me."

Leslie let him go, but with a warning. "I don't wanna have to hurt you," she told him. "Don't do that," she repeated firmly. She took him seriously, which was a most dangerous predicament.

But her warning made Eugene more confident in his rejection of her.

"Girl, you crazy. I should have never gotten involved with you. So I learned a lesson from all of this," he told her.

Leslie warned, "You gon' learn another lesson if you don't hug me. Now all I'm asking is for us to squash this negative energy. That's all I'm sayin'. We can't end it like this. So we squash it, and then we can go our own li'l ways without bothering each other anymore."

"I'm gon' go my own li'l way regardless," Eugene continued to boast.

In a flash of her mind's eye, Leslie saw Eugene fly toward the window in a desperate struggle with her. And as he tried to free himself from her rage, they both crashed through the window, falling eight stories down to their deaths.

Leslie shook her head and told herself, *No!* to deny the spontaneous vision. She would not let her life end that way, not over some damn . . . Creole boy! So she took a deep breath and told him, "Just leave, then. Get away from here. And I'll pray for you."

Eugene looked at her fierce dark eyes and told himself, *Let me get the hell outta here. This girl is insane!* He left immediately, while watching his back. He looked up the hallways as he waited for the elevator. He prayed that the elevator would take him to the ground level safely. And when he hit the streets of

New Orleans, he walked as closely to the buildings on the sidewalk as possible, as if an errant car would strike and kill him at any moment from the street.

Fuck! he cursed himself as he walked. *What the hell is wrong with me? What did I just do? This girl got me scared as shit! Damn, I should have never fucked with her!*

Back up in the hotel room, Leslie held back her tears. *I am not gonna cry for some fuckin' boy!* she spat to herself. *I am not gon' cry for that shit.* But the tears rolled from her eyes anyway, not because of Eugene alone, but because of the accumulated pain that she continued to hold back. And she thought again of her big brother, calling out his name in her tears, *"Pi-erre . . . Pi-erre!"* Then she echoed the words of her father when she had told him the terrible news of her violation in her youth, *"J'ai mal partout."* I ache all over.

... of Sheer Madness ...

Pierre Beaudet watched the downtown New Orleans streets from the passenger side of Beaucoup's Navigator, and spotted a paranoid Creole boy hustling up the sidewalks.

Fuck is his problem? Pierre wondered. *Nigga look like he saw a ghost out here.*

For a second, they met eyes and zoomed in on each other, where Pierre was able to take in the stranger's entire face, while the stranger took in his. Their eyes locked in and froze on each other, as if they were both on pause from a video screen.

Pierre shook it off and thought, *Hmm, that was weird. It felt like I was right up next to him.*

A second later Pierre's pager went off. He looked down at the number and noticed the code that he had given to his sister Leslie. But . . . she had rarely used it. She barely even called him. Pierre was cool with that in light of the guilt that he had been holding for his sister. Nevertheless, he knew that he would have to face up to their unspoken situation one day. It was inevitable. So he got out his new cell phone and called her back, while still in the presence of Beaucoup.

"Who dat?" Coup asked him right on cue.

"It's my sister," Pierre answered him flatly, while making his phone call.

He was surprised when a hotel receptionist answered the phone.

"Hotel La Salle."

Pierre looked up on instinct and read the sign that was right outside his passenger-side window. The Hotel La Salle was right there next to them.

"Yo, stop the car for a minute!" Pierre demanded of Coup.

Coup looked at him as if he had lost his mind. *Fuck is he talkin' to like dat?*

"Do you have a Leslie Beaudet staying there?" Pierre asked the receptionist over his phone.

She answered with hesitation, "Ah . . . may I ask who's calling?" She became skeptical and nervous. *Didn't someone else just go up to her room?* she asked herself. She had already broken hotel policy by giving out the room number instead of calling upstairs earlier. It was just that . . . the boy looked so good. But she was more alert this time, and she couldn't see whoever was on the phone.

"Tell her it's Pierre," the man told her.

"Thank you," she said. She dialed Leslie's room while holding Pierre on the other line.

"Hello," Leslie answered. She was shocked that she was receiving a return call so quickly. Pierre had not been one to count on in the past.

The receptionist informed her, "You have a Pierre on the line. Is it okay to send his call through, or would you like me to tell him that you're out?" the receptionist asked. All that she could think of was drama breaking out at their hotel, and she wanted to save everyone from it.

However, Leslie told her, "Yes. Put him through," with an inadvertent sniff of her nose.

Shit! she cursed herself. She didn't want everyone to know that she had been crying.

The receptionist caught on to it. "Are you okay?" she asked.

"Yeah, I'm okay. Just put . . . him through."

Leslie was just about to say "my brother," but she changed her mind. The receptionist didn't need to know all of that. Leslie just wanted to set the woman's mind at ease, because she could tell that she was being cautious for her. Leslie even thanked her for it.

"Thank you for caring," she responded. "But I'm okay. Put him through."

Inside the Navigator, right outside of the hotel building, Beaucoup changed his mind about reprimanding Pierre for his tone of voice with him. He became curious. Pierre had said the key name that Coup liked to hear from him . . . Leslie. Coup held a crush for the girl. The longer he befriended Pierre, the more he thought about his gorgeous, ghetto-fabulous little sister. Or at least that's how Beaucoup thought about her. Leslie was a respectable star, and she didn't even know it yet. But he would let her know it if he ever got close to her in some way.

He asked Pierre, "What's goin' on? Is your sister all right?"

He pulled the Navigator over to the curb.

"I don't know yet," Pierre told him. He waited patiently for the receptionist to put him through. And as soon as he came on the line, Leslie could hear all of his urgency.

"What's going on?" he asked her. Then he told his sister in French, *"Je suis en bas, devant l'hôtel."* I'm right outside the hotel.

"Vraiment?" Leslie asked him. Really? *"Je suis dans la chambre huit cent treize."* I'm in room eight thirteen.

No more conversation was needed between them. Leslie needed to see her big brother, and Pierre understood that.

"J'arrive immédiatement," he told her in more French. I'm coming up at once.

Beaucoup didn't need to know everything. But he caught on to the secrecy and smiled. *Now these motherfuckas try'na get secretive on me wit dis French shit,* he thought to himself. *I wish I knew another fuckin' language, though.*

Pierre opened the passenger-side door and told him, "I'll be right back, man."

"Aw'ight, den. I'll wait up for you," Beaucoup assured him.

Pierre hurried into the hotel and caught the elevator up to the eighth floor to see his sister. He shook his head while on his way up and told himself, "Leslie's always been working hard, man. And . . ." *She still don't seem to be gettin' anywhere wit it,* he thought. Her patience seemed to last forever, while the future moved in slow motion. It didn't seem fair to Pierre. And he had himself to blame for some of Leslie's despair. In fact, Pierre had always wondered how much their secret had pained his sister. So by the time he reached her room, he figured it was only right to throw himself at her mercy. Whatever she needed, he would give to her. And whatever she needed him to do . . . he would do. Because he owed her, and he was tired of running away from his debt. It was time to pay up.

When Leslie heard his knock on the door, she took a deep breath before she answered it. She wondered if she should allow her brother to see her tears. She had cried most of them into her pillow and flipped it over to hide the evidence. But she decided that she would not hide her tears from her brother. Not anymore.

What am I still hiding shit for anyway? It won't make a damn difference! she snapped to herself. So when she opened the door to find her brother, Pierre, standing there, she went for her needed hug and just grabbed him into it.

Pierre was surprised by it. He hadn't actually hugged his sister in . . . years. He couldn't even remember the last time he had hugged her. He could only remember hugging their mother. Even that had been years ago.

Leslie mumbled into her brother's shoulder as she continued to hold on to him at the door.

"I'm tired, man. I'm just so fuckin' tired . . . of all this shit."

Pierre understood exactly what she meant. He had just been thinking about that himself. How many marathons could Leslie run without rest? He took a deep breath of his own, grieving for his sister. Then he . . . squeezed her uncontrollably.

"I know, man. You always been working, Leslie. You always been workin'."

He was sorry for her for everything. He just couldn't seem to get the words out. So he continued to squeeze Leslie in his arms instead, as if the pressure of his arms would send the message of love and understanding to her brain.

And it did. But at the same time it hurt. So she told him, "Pierre . . . I can't breathe."

Pierre loosened his grip around her and felt embarrassed by it.

"My bad, man. I jus' . . . I feel you, Lez. I know what you've been goin' through." Then he looked into her eyes, and told her, "I'm sorry, Lez. I'm sorry." And his eyes couldn't take it anymore, so he looked away again.

In a second, Leslie smiled and felt bubbly inside. She began to nod her head against her brother's shoulder while shaking him as she stood there in their embrace.

"I still love you, Pierre. It wasn't your fault." Fresh tears ran down her face again. She added, "It's just . . . a messed-up world we live in. And it was nobody there to help us . . . and nobody there to help Daddy . . . and nobody there to love Mommy . . . and Tee."

Pierre hadn't cried in years either. For what? He was a man. Or at least he had the gender, size, and age of a man. But he rarely felt . . . manly. He had felt boyish for most of his life, and was in need of someone to save him from all of his nightmares, and from his . . . father.

"Pi-erre must learn to be a mahn, Anna. You are tea-ching him not to be a mahn!" he could still hear his father exclaiming to his mother.

"He has time. You don't need to rush him," Anna defended.

Only for Jean to yell, "He has no time! This world will not wait for him to grow up, An-na! You do not unda-stand this world. He will either live to be a mahn, or he will learn to live on his knees in this world. That's the way it is. And he has no choice!"

So whenever Pierre felt his father's spiteful eyes on him, he had felt ashamed, and he was sorry to be Jean's son.

"Maybe I shouldn't have been born, then?" Pierre had often mumbled alone to himself. "I didn't ask to be no man. I'm only a kid."

And as the kid stood there in the hotel room doorway, wrapped in his sister's arms as her tears of pain emptied into his chest and into his heart, Pierre cried to himself in silence, where no one would hear him. Who had ever heard him cry anyway? He was a ghost, a young and unskilled black male in America.

≈≈

Once Pierre and Leslie had cried themselves out and forgiven each other in an attempt to heal, Pierre asked his sister the obvious question, "So . . . what are you doin' up in here?"

He didn't want to get into her business, but he had to ask her the question. She had called him there, didn't she?

Leslie had no more to conceal. She answered her brother in a naked response with no further pretensions. "I was supposed to meet some li'l . . . boy in here . . . and he wasn't feeling me no more. So he left."

Damn! Did Pierre want to hear all of that from his little sister? *Hell, no!* But he had asked her for it.

Before he could grin away his embarrassment from the hotel bed where they sat together, Leslie laid more naked information on him.

"The fucked-up thing about it is that he's my roommate's man," she told him.

Pierre took a pause to regroup as Leslie continued: "And we were fuckin' wit each other, or whatever, and then this motherfucka gon' come up here and tell me that he don't wanna touch me no more, like I'm some fuckin' disease now. And his ass wanted me first."

Suddenly, Pierre's ears began to ring the bell of his conscience. He thought to himself, *Damn, she sounds just like Mom in here. That's how mean Mom talked . . . right before she died.*

"So, he just left you, hunh?" he asked his sister rhetorically. He wanted to break up Leslie's blunt candor in the hope that she would tone it down. But Leslie was on a roll.

She said, "And how 'bout the motherfucka's a Creole. Of all fuckin' people, right. I don't know how I allowed myself to get involved with him."

Pierre froze. The image of the stranger he saw scaling the walls of the buildings a minute before Leslie had paged him popped into his head.

That was him? Pierre thought to himself. He just felt it. *But why was he so fuckin' scared like that?* Pierre chuckled a bit, attempting to camouflage his intrigue about the matter. Then he asked his sister, "So, what did you tell his ass before he left? I can tell you were mad."

Leslie looked into her big brother's face and said, "He had the nerve to tell me that if I thought he was bullshittin' about not wanting to be with me anymore, that he would tell my roommate about us himself, like a damn asshole. So I told him, 'Don't do that shit.' You know, we can go our separate ways without all of that, because I still have to live there.

"And that asshole got all big and bad about it like he's just try'na hurt me on purpose," she explained. "And for what, just because I wanted him like he wanted me and he couldn't handle it?" She narrowed her eyes into slits and said, "I swear, y'all guys are a motherfuckin' trip."

Then she paused a beat for her conclusion.

"So I told his ass that I would pray for him. Because if he really does that shit . . ."

And she left it at that.

Pierre nodded his head and felt his sister's vengeance. *He ain't gon' tell her,* he told himself in silence. *I'll make sure of that. I'm tired of people fuckin' with you too.*

He opened his mouth and said, "That nigga in the wrong just like you. So how is he gon' jus' go drop dime like that?"

"Because it won't affect his ass like it will me," Leslie answered. "All he's losin' is a silly-ass girlfriend. She'll fuck around and forgive him anyway. But I'm losing my fuckin' place to live."

Pierre had heard enough! He wanted to react spontaneously for a change and before he would lose the nerve. So he stood up and said, "I got a run to make right quick, Lez. But when I come back, we gon' talk about this. Aw'ight? You still gon' be here?"

Leslie nodded to him. "Yeah, I'll be here. I might as well order a movie or something. Ain't shit on TV."

Pierre grinned and agreed with her. "Yeah, you right about that. Nothin' for us to watch." He asked her, "So, this guy go to Dillard with y'all?"

Leslie stopped and studied her brother's demeanor for a minute, as he stood there ready to leave for some unknown destination.

Is he asking me what I think he's asking me? . . . No, it's still Pierre, she told herself. *He don't have the heart to do nothin' like that.*

So she answered, "No, he goes to Xavier. I mean, I wouldn't be that much of a fool to fuck with a guy who lived on the same campus as us."

Pierre laughed it off and said, "Aw'ight, den. So, I'll see you later on." He wanted to surprise his sister with the news of a beat-down. He figured that the Creole boy had asked for one. And Beaucoup was waiting right outside as backup for whatever.

But before her brother could leave her, Leslie asked him, "Laetitia said you were with a bunch of guys down at the Mardi Gras. Who you hangin' out with now?"

Leslie was still curious about that. Pierre had been speaking with more . . . backbone lately, and he had money to boot. In fact, he dug into his pockets and peeled off $300 for her, just as he had done with their baby sister.

He smiled as he handed Leslie the money. "I'll tell you about it when I get back," he told her.

Leslie took the money . . . and she left him alone about it.

Who am I to judge? she told herself. *I'll just wait for him to get back to me, then. It'll come out sooner or later. It'll all come out.*

≈≈

"So, whassup wit 'er?" Beaucoup asked Pierre as soon as he hopped back into the vehide.

Pierre told him solemnly, "Looks like we gotta handle some shit tonight, man. Some ma-fucka from Xavier try'na play her."

Beaucoup studied Pierre's mug to see how serious he was. "From Xavier? What, he got her pregnant or something?" he asked, while holding down his breath. Coup wouldn't mind getting Leslie pregnant his damn self, if just to prove that he had gone all the way with her.

Pierre told him, "Naw, he jus' try'na take her for a fool. But if we hurry up and drive over there, we can prob'bly catch him before he gets back. He jus' left down here. I actually saw him walking away earlier."

"So, you know 'em?" Beaucoup asked. He wanted as much information as possible. And it was not that he really cared about the situation, he just saw it as an opportunity to get closer to Leslie in an informed way.

Pierre answered, "Naw, I don't really know 'em, I just know what he look like."

"Well, don't she need a ride back home?" Coup asked him.

"Naw, she aw'ight. It was just a coincidence that we were down here at the same time she was paging me."

Coup nodded his head and finally drove the Navigator from the curb.

He picked up his cell phone and asked Pierre one last question, "What's his name?"

Pierre answered, "I don't know his name either. But she said he's one of them Creoles."

Coup frowned after hearing that. He said, "She fuck wit them like dat?" He surely didn't want to hear that. Beaucoup wanted Leslie to be down for the 'hood, and not crossing over to the bourgeoisie, with their bullshit color codes.

Pierre told him, "Obviously it was a mistake, man. So now this ma-fucka den hurt her all up, and he try'na act like ain't shit gon' happen to him."

Beaucoup cracked a devious smile. He said, "That's all I needed to hear," before he went ahead and made his phone call. "Yo, it's Coup. Where y'all at? . . . Well, yo, I need y'all to meet me over at Xavier. I'm on my way over there now. We got a problem to handle ova' dere. So soldier up."

Pierre looked over at Beaucoup and held his nerves at bay. He didn't need any soldiers for one little Creole boy. He just wanted to let the guy know that Leslie was protected. But Beaucoup's soldiers were another thing altogether. They inflicted pain on people.

Beaucoup then ordered Pierre to call his sister back and get the boy's name and dorm.

Pierre thought fast and said, "Actually, I was just try'na handle this without her knowing. She don't even think I know who he is. Because if she knew we was gon' do something about it, she prob'bly wouldn't want me to do it."

Beaucoup looked him over and nodded his head again. "So, you ready to let this ma-fucka get away wit it, den. I mean, how we gon' go up there and not even know his name?"

Pierre said, "We'll find 'em," as if he was ultraconfident about it.

Beaucoup finally shook his head. He said "Yeah, whatever, man. You 'bout t' waste my motherfuckin' time." Nevertheless, he went ahead and put the pedal down for Xavier's campus anyway, just to see where Pierre's heart lay.

Pierre became apprehensive about the whole thing. He was getting more than he expected.

I should have never said shit to him about this, he began to think to himself. *I should have handled this on my own.* But he still wasn't sure if he could. To make matters worse, when they arrived at Xavier, a dark carload of Beaucoup's soldiers had beaten them there.

Coup rolled down the window to them and hollered, "Damn! How y'all get over before we did?"

"Yo, we was already in the area when you called us," they told him. "So, whassup?"

Beaucoup looked back inside the Navigator at Pierre. "It's your show now, man. Tell 'em what you want."

Pierre said, "We should wait over near the bus stop off of North Carrollton. Because I know he didn't walk all the way here from downtown."

Beaucoup nodded and told his soldiers, "Yeah, we 'bout t' snatch up a punk ova' hea' and teach 'em a lesson. It's a family affair. Ya heard me?"

"Yeah, aw'ight. Just let us know who we lookin' for. We got the duck tape," they responded with sinister scowls.

Pierre panicked in his silence. *Duck tape? Aw, dese motherfuckers are crazy! We don't need all that for this one nigga. What the fuck are they talkin' about?*

Beaucoup looked back inside the Navigator at Pierre and grinned. He could read the panic written all over that boy's face. *This motherfucker wastin' all of our time out here,* he thought to himself. But he waited across from North Carrollton Avenue on Xavier's campus anyway.

≋

On the bus ride back to school, Eugene had finally calmed his nerves.

I don't know what that shit was. I guess I just had the jitters from that girl, he told himself. *But now I don't even wanna go back over to their house, to tell you the truth. Bridget is just gonna have to come see me from now on, unless that girl decide to move out on her own or something. Because I have no idea how Bridget would act if I told her that I was fuckin' her roommate.*

That shit was stupid for me to even say that, he admitted to himself. And when he hopped off of the bus on North Carrollton Avenue to head back to campus at Xavier, he felt safe at home again. Little did he know that he was not safe.

Beaucoup spotted him first and joked to Pierre in the passenger seat.

"Here come a Creole boy right now, man. This nigga so bright, he out hea' shinin' in the dark."

Pierre looked and said, "That's him," before he could catch himself and think about it.

Coup spat, "Get da fuck outta here! That's him right there?"

He seriously doubted it. It just seemed too damned easy for him.

Pierre hesitated for a second. It was no doubt that they had found the mark. Pierre just wasn't sure about what they planned to do to him once they . . . apprehended him, or snatched him up.

"If that's him, then let me fuckin' know, man," Coup snapped at him.

Pierre took a deep breath and thought again about what he owed his sister. *I gotta stop being a fuckin' pussy all the time!* he yelled in his thoughts. *I jus' gotta be a man about it, if for once in my life!* So he nodded to Coup in the Navigator and confirmed it.

"Yeah, man, that's him."

Beaucoup signaled his soldiers with a hand whistle from his mouth. *WHEEESSSTT, WHEEESSSTT.*

"Yo, that's him right there."

His soldiers eased out of their dark car so as not to alarm the boy. Then, as if a starter's gun had gone off for a footrace, they quickly ran up and grabbed him while trying to force him back to their car.

"What the hell!" Eugene shouted before a fist met his mouth. Another fist met his head, followed by another, and another, until there was no more struggle. When he had been silenced, they dragged his ass over to the dark car, with not a brave soul there to save him.

Pierre's heart raced inside of his chest. *Oh, shit! They did the shit!* he told himself.

Beaucoup said, "Yo, let's take his ass to that spot near the water. And wrap his mouth up good. I don't wanna hear shit from 'em."

Pierre sat there thinking, *Aw, dese motherfuckers are crazy! What the hell they plan on doin' to 'em?*

Beaucoup looked over to him right on cue and smiled. He said, "You can kick his ass good when we get 'em out here, Pete. We found this spot where nobody come."

"And then we just drop 'em off there, hunh?" Pierre suggested to him.

Coup looked at him and said, "Naw. Then we shoot his ass and throw him in the water. Maybe we'll shoot 'em in both his arms and legs so he can't swim. That would be some funny shit, wouldn't it, Pete?"

Pierre laughed nervously. He could feel knots of fear curling up in his stomach. Coup couldn't have been serious about that. No way in the world! You didn't just kill people like that. What kind of humans just . . . killed people?

Pierre said, "You trippin', man. You trippin'," and tried to joke it off.

That only made Beaucoup and his soldiers seem . . . diabolical, when Coup responded, "Whatchew think this is, man? We ain't playin' out here. This ma-fucka fucked witcha sister, right? Well, we gon' find out."

"Yeah, but we ain't gotta kill 'em to do that, though," Pierre insisted.

"*I* would," Coup told him.

Was he bullshitting, or was he serious?

Pierre waited in confused silence until they arrived at their destination, a dark patch of out-of-use land near the Mississippi River.

"Put that ma-fucka on his knees," Coup told his soldiers, as they dragged Eugene's body out of the car. They had the duct tape secured around his head and mouth where he could breathe through his nose but not talk. They also taped his hands together behind his back.

"Now ask this ma-fucka what you wanna know, Pete," Coup told Pierre.

They were all standing there outside of their cars and in the dim moonlight that shone over the Mississippi.

Eugene looked into Pierre's eyes and felt the lingering stare that he had witnessed briefly from him earlier that night. Pierre looked into Eugene's eyes and felt the same stare, as if it was a prelude to their fate.

Pierre took a breath and asked him, "You know my sister, man? Leslie?"

"Nod your head, before we shoot you in it, nigga," one of Coup's soldiers barked at Eugene with a gun in his hand.

Eugene nodded his head as he whimpered with fresh tears running out of his eyes. *I should have never touched that damn girl!* he thought to himself of Leslie. *I should have never touched her. Look what shit she got me in now,* he told himself as he continued to whimper with his mouth and hands taped.

Coup smiled and shook his head at the boy. "You should have stayed with your own kind, Frankie. But you done fucked up, now. You done went to the dark side of the force. So we 'bout to be like . . . Darth Vader and the emperor out this motherfucka."

His soldiers all chuckled at it. But Pierre didn't think it was funny. It was sick! He just wanted to set the boy straight, not torture him.

Coup ordered, "Yo, give Pete one of them guns."

His soldiers looked at him with apprehension. What the hell was Coup talking about? That boy Pierre wasn't about to use any gun. He looked as petrified as the Creole boy.

Nevertheless, Coup was their general, so they obeyed his orders and gave Pierre a gun to use.

"Now show me what you wanna do, Pete," Coup challenged him. "You wanna take this motherfucka out? Show me what you wanna do."

The soldiers watched and despised Pete as much as they did the crying Creole boy who stood there before them on his knees, whimpering with duct tape around his mouth and hands.

"Shut the fuck up, man!" one of the soldiers finally spat to the boy. "Go ahead and shoot his ass, Pete. I'm tired of hearing his ass cryin'."

"Yeah, Pete, go ahead and pop that ma-fucka," another said.

"Show us what you got, Pete," said another.

"Yeah, show and prove, nigga," said the last.

They all egged him on like a merry-go-round, but Pierre stood frozen with the gun locked in his hand. He looked the Creole in his eyes again, as the boy shook his head, begging for his life. And . . . Pierre couldn't take it from him. He wasn't going to kill a boy where a smack in the face would do. What was the use in wasting a life? Pierre was no killer. So no trigger was pulled. And no hammer was ignited. Or at least not from Pierre.

However, one of Coup's soldiers became so incensed by the two pussies in front of them—one on his knees, and another standing with a loaded gun in his hand that he was afraid to use—that the soldier decided to show Coup what his value was.

BOP! BOP!

"Shit!" one of the other soldiers exclaimed as Eugene's body hit the ground from the gunshot wounds.

Pierre shook in his stance and dropped his own gun to the ground. Momentarily, the soldier with the hot trigger finger aimed his gun at Pierre, before he came to his senses. Pierre was Beaucoup's plaything, a protected toy-ass nigga.

Beaucoup sized up the situation and said, "Damn. What happened to the dude? Anybody out here know?"

His soldiers let out a collective, "Naw."

Coup looked to Pierre, who was still in shock.

They shot his ass! They shot him! I can't believe that! he stood there and repeated to himself.

Coup asked him, "What about you, Pete? You know what happened to him?"

Pierre shook his head slowly. "Naw."

Coup responded, "Good. Let's get da fuck outta hea', 'den. And dump that body somewhere," he told his soldiers.

"Come on, Pete, let's roll. They'll take care of it from here."

Pierre scampered over to the Navigator as if it was freezing cold outside and he was caught without any clothes on.

That's when Coup chuckled to himself and thought, *Yeah, this nigga ain't no killa'. He a punk! It's time to get rid of his ass . . . after I fuck his li'l sister, though.*

... and
Cold-blooded
Murder ...

oup looked over in the passenger side of his Navigator at Pierre and told him, "Yo, I ain't have no idea that nigga was gon' shoot your boy like that, man. But what the fuck was I gon' do after he killed 'em? I couldn't bring the motherfucka back to life. Ya heard me?"

Pierre was sitting there as they returned to the city, while still trying to figure everything out. What the hell would he tell his sister now? And what kind of trouble would she be in? After all, she did threaten the boy. Did anyone else know that she was dealing with him on the sly? What about the people at the hotel? Would they recognize the story and piece it all together?

Pierre's mind was racing in a hundred directions at once.

"Yo, you hear me talkin' to you?" Coup asked him.

"Hunh?" Pierre mumbled. He didn't have enough room left in his brain to hear what Coup was talking about on top of everything else that he was thinking.

Coup told him, "Look, man, don't sweat dat shit. I mean, if you keep your mouth shut, and everybody else keep their mouths shut, then we just brush this shit off like ain't nothin' happened. You think your sister'll say something?" he asked.

Pierre did know that answer. There was no question about it.

He shook his head and said, "Naw. She ain't even like that."

Coup nodded and said, "Good. That's my kind of girl, then, a girl who know what time it is. You don't get no rewards for turning in criminals and shit out here. Or not in the motherfuckin' 'hood, unless you kill some white people. I mean, it's fucked up, man, but niggas were worth more as slaves than we are free. Even them Creole niggas ain't worth shit. They just think they better. But once white folks find out they got black blood in nem, they don't give a fuck about them either. So don't even sweat that shit, man."

Coup didn't think much else about it. He turned on his booming stereo system and started nodding his head to the deafening bass lines, thumping drum kicks, and popping snares of hip-hop music.

"And it don't stop / and it won't stop / I rule the block / wit niggas on the clock . . ."

≈

Pierre never did make it back to Leslie at the hotel that night. She even sat up after midnight watching movies while awaiting her brother's return.

Shit, I don't know why I expected him to keep his word to me, she finally told herself. *He's still the same damn Pussy Pete. Ain't nothing changed with that boy but the season!*

Leslie fell asleep that night at the hotel, and she awoke before six, feeling a sense of doom. Something had happened. She could feel it. But instead of paging Pierre a second time to find out what had happened to him, she decided to wait and test her brother's loyalty to her with a little more . . . patience. So she made her way back to her college house that morning expecting anything.

She bumped into Ayanna, who was on her way out as Leslie made her way in. With Ayanna's usual tardiness to class, she was the last person that Leslie expected to bump into that morning.

"Hi, Ayanna," she spoke to her.

"Hi," Ayanna spoke back, keeping things short.

"What, you can't even talk to me anymore?" Leslie asked her, noticing her haste.

Ayanna searched her eyes to see what she meant by it.

"About what?" she finally asked. "I mean . . . do you really wanna talk to me?"

Ayanna had a point. What was there left to talk about between them? Leslie had nearly scared the girl into a coma.

"Well, how's school coming along this semester?" Leslie asked her.

Ayanna searched her eyes again. *Does she even care?* she asked herself. Yet, she was hesitant to move on from Leslie without being properly . . . dismissed.

Leslie granted her a dismissal. "Well, go on to school, then, since you're in such a damn hurry this morning."

Ayanna was eager to ask Leslie again what she had done to deserve her spite, but she decided to walk away toward Dillard's campus instead. What was the use? Leslie seemed unreachable.

I don't know what the hell this girl's problem is. So let me just stay away from her and keep my thoughts to myself, Ayanna told herself as she walked off toward campus.

Leslie entered the house expecting her next confrontation to be with Bridget, who was sure to be on her way out to school with Yula that morning.

I wonder if that boy came back here last night, Leslie thought to herself of Eugene as she ascended the stairs.

But when Bridget strolled out of her room with her door wide open, it was obvious that she hadn't had any company that night.

"Hi, Leslie," she spoke.

Leslie responded with a dry "Hi."

Yula heard them while walking out of her own room that morning and grimaced.

"What's up with the sour mood with everybody lately?" she asked. "We used to be like a family up in here. Now people are barely speaking to each other. I mean, what's up with that?"

Bridget and Leslie looked blankly at each other and were both speechless.

Bridget thought to herself, *Yula, you're just all happy because you got a couple A's in class.* She even smirked at the idea. Then she grinned and said, "You're right. We have been acting . . . bitchy towards each other lately."

She turned to Leslie and asked, "What do *you* think, Leslie?"

I think you're all happy now because you got your little man back, Leslie thought. But instead of twirling in the mud and creating more dirt between them, Leslie responded with a nod.

"I've had a lot on my mind lately. So I guess I have been a little . . . bitchy." She added, "But it hasn't been all my fault, either."

Bridget nodded back to her. "I was wrong for instigating," she admitted.

Leslie countered and said, "And I was wrong for stirring things up with you."

Yula smiled and said, "Good. Now can we all get along up in here? God!"

They all chuckled for the first light moment between them in . . . several weeks.

Yula added to the camaraderie by inviting everyone to meet for lunch at the school cafeteria.

Leslie was hesitant at first. But then she thought, *Why not? We're still all roommates in here . . . at least for now.* So she agreed to it.

"All right, we'll meet like one o'clock, then. And I'll make sure I tell Ayanna about it when I see her on campus."

Yula was all excited about it. "Well, all right," she said. "We haven't all met up on campus to do something like this in a while. What, you stayed over your sister's house again last night, Leslie?" Yula asked openly. She realized that Leslie had not come home that night.

"I don't stay over my sister's house all of the time," Leslie responded. And that's all she planned to say about it.

Yula got the message and moved on. "Okay, well, we'll see you at lunch, then."

"One o'clock," Leslie reiterated.

"One o'clock," Bridget repeated.

Yula laughed and chimed in, "One o'clock it *is,* then. And make sure you tell Ayanna to bring her ass there on time."

Leslie grinned as her housemates made their way down the stairs and out the house. She walked toward her room in the back and mumbled, "How I would die to have things that simple in my life again." She didn't feel the energy to even go to class that day.

She crawled into her made bed and pondered the last two months of her life. *So . . . how much control do we really have in this life?* she questioned again. *Would it all be the same if I just kept doing what I've been doing, just trying to ignore everything? I mean . . . my mother would have still died of AIDS. My father would still live in a homeless shelter, feeling depressed and ashamed about it. Pierre would still be a punk. And my damn sister would have lost her mind when that little man of hers would have decided not to come back home to her desperate ass!*

But how much have I changed by . . . claiming the priesthood? I mean . . . I really don't even know what the hell I'm doing, honestly. It seems like I'm just killing people. Is that what Vodou is about . . . ?

She shook her head, knowing better. No religion was about murder. Yet murder happened, and sometimes faithful people prayed for it, for vengeance . . . and redemption . . . and even for . . . mercy. Murder made things equal, starting back from zero.

"My father was right not to tell me shit," Leslie mumbled out loud. *But*

I was always that way, she countered in her thoughts. *I never let anybody fuck with me or my family. I mean . . . maybe it was just meant for me to kill people, and I just hadn't done it yet. Maybe that's what I'm here for.*

Then she shook her head to fight off the insanity of her thoughts. She even stood up from her bed to deny it. "That's crazy!" she spat to herself as she paced the room in a panic. "I wasn't fuckin' born to be no killer."

She looked up to the ceiling with her palms out in mercy and pleaded, "But why do you keep letting people fuck wit me? Is it my fault? What did I do? What did I *do?*"

She calmed herself from the helpless energy that she felt and stared up at the ceiling as if there would be some kind of an answer, the voice of God speaking to her from a burning bush, like Moses in the Bible. But when there was no response, Leslie took a deep breath and told herself in defeat, "Let me go on back to school." *Because it's obvious that I'm nothing more than a . . . plaything for God. I'm just a fuckin' . . . voodoo doll. That's all I am.*

≈≈

While on Dillard's campus that late morning, Ayanna Timber took a step toward Gentilly Boulevard and trembled at her sight.

Oh, shit! she thought to herself, as she quickly ducked back into the administration building. She had actually begun to gather information that morning on a transfer from school to her local Houston HBCU at Southwest Texas State, just in case the rift between herself and Leslie failed to clear up. So she was already on guard that morning. And after spotting the two-toned, black-and-tan Navigator owned by her nemesis, Beaucoup, that was pulling up right behind Leslie, her antagonist—who were both locals of New Orleans—it served to make Ayanna's timing for a transfer seem all the more prophetic.

Does she know that I know him? Ayanna asked herself. She was certain that Leslie and Beaucoup knew each other by the way that he talked to her about the French-speaking N'awlins girl. But Ayanna had never been upfront with either of them about her connection to them.

Did they know it all the time? Ayanna asked herself, as she watched them through the small window at the door. *Is that why she's been bitching with me, because she knows that I've been holding back information from her?* Ayanna snapped. *But that's my fuckin' business, though! I don't have to tell her everything! She don't tell us everything about her!*

She continued to watch them through the small window at the door, as her heart raced with all types of apprehension and conclusions.

Inside the plush Navigator, Beaucoup could hardly contain his sinister smile as he eased up on the one person he had driven alone to Dillard's campus to see that morning. He rolled down his passenger-side window and shouted, "Ay, Leslie! Let me holla at you for a minute!"

Leslie looked to her left to see who was calling her, but she didn't stop walking.

Beaucoup asked her, "Whassup?" His vehicle continued to ease slowly around Dillard's campus next to Leslie on the sidewalk.

Leslie focused on his face and immediately asked herself, *Now what the hell does he want?*

She said, "I'm late for class already. You caught me at the wrong time," and she continued walking forward.

I don't fuck with guys like you anyway, she told herself. *You have nothing to talk to me about.*

Sure, Leslie knew Beaucoup. She knew that he was a snake of a hustler, who tried to rationalize his street venom as normal. Leslie had graduated from high school with girls who had fallen for the hypnosis of his serpentine tongue before getting bit.

Why would he ever think that I would have a conversation with him? Leslie wondered. It would have been out of character for both of them. Beaucoup knew damn well that Leslie wasn't having it! They all knew in the Seventh Ward. Leslie Beaudet was all about her schoolwork and her family. And that was it.

But now Coup had a Joker card up his sleeve and he used it. He said, "I got some good news for you, though. That situation you needed handled last night . . . we took care of it for you."

Then he waited to see what her response would be.

And Leslie was . . . stunned!

Motherfucker! she cursed herself. *This is what I'm talking about!* Then she calmed down and thought with ice water in her veins. *He just chose himself, and he don't even know it! And my brother . . . he just chose himself, too, because I can no longer protect that boy. He's just a damned fool!*

So he's been hanging out with Beaucoup now, she concluded. *And he let this motherfucka put a damn price tag on my head.* She wanted to just ignore it all and keep walking, but Beaucoup was already on her campus, invading her private space. So the chess game began.

Leslie headed straight for the passenger side of Beaucoup's Navigator to climb in and talk to him in private. "Let's ride off campus," she told him as soon as she made it in. She reclined her seat all the way back to a lying position.

Beaucoup smiled at the obvious.

He asked her, "What, you don't wanna be seen on campus wit me?"

Leslie ignored his rhetorical question and went to the heart of the issue. "What situation are you talking about?"

"Hunh?" Beaucoup grunted. It wasn't as if he was an amateur at playing the game. You didn't just volunteer pertinent information unless it was beneficial.

But Leslie snapped, "Look, you came up here to deal with me about something, right? So what are you talking about?"

Beaucoup looked away for a minute. He had to regroup. He hadn't planned on Leslie being so . . . assertive with him.

He asked her, "How your life goin' right now, Leslie?" He looked back into her eyes and asked, "Could you use some things? I don't know . . . some good company . . . some nicer clothes . . . protection. Whatchew need? I'm here for you."

Leslie thought to herself, *You got to be kidding me! Am I dreaming this shit? I don't want any of his fucking favors!*

She responded, "I still don't know what we're talking about. I didn't ask you for anything."

Coup countered, "But see . . . I gave it to you anyway, because I'm lookin' out for you and your family like that."

"You gave *what* to me?" Leslie asked him specifically. She would deal with the rest of his information later, and on a step-by-step basis. You had to walk carefully in the presence of a snake.

Aw, she try'na make this harder than it needs to be, Coup told himself. He was tiring quickly of the cat-and-mouse game.

He said, "I think you know what I'm talkin' about. So let's stop bullshittin' each other, before I jus' stop right here and tell the whole fuckin' campus."

"Tell the whole campus *what?*" Leslie insisted from him in her innocence.

Beaucoup stopped his hard-line talk and started laughing.

She's bluffing me, he thought to himself. *This damn girl is bluffing me! But I like that. That just make me wanna fuck her more. I'm really gonna enjoy this shit. Then I'ma get rid of her punk-ass brother. Leslie got what I really wanted all this time anyway.*

So he told her more. He said, "Here's the scenario: like I told your

brother, Pierre, last night, if everybody act like they don't know nothin' . . ."
He held up his hands away from the steering wheel for a second to make his
point as they exited Dillard's campus.

He said, "You feelin' me on that?"

Leslie stared into his eyes from her reclined seat and asked him, "What
did you do?"

"*I* didn't do shit," Beaucoup told her. "I don't have to do shit. My hands
are clean. And if you play your cards right, then so are yours."

Leslie asked him, "How are *my* hands dirty?"

Beaucoup gathered his thoughts to slither out the perfect . . . explanation for her.

He said, "Well . . . sometimes . . . you talk to people who can't get the
job done on what they've been asked to do, so they get somebody else to do
it. And what I'm sayin' is that . . . you always have to go back to the source
of the job. But I don't know nothin' about the source if you act right."

"The source of what?" Leslie asked him calmly.

*If this asshole thinks that I'm gonna sit here and incriminate myself, then he
must take me for a fool!* she mused. *He obviously doesn't know who he's fuckin'
with! I was born for this kind of shit. Ain't no sense in me even denying it anymore.*

Beaucoup shook his head at her response and began to chuckle.

She ain't givin' me a fuckin' inch in here, boy!

He joked, "Whatchew wearing a wire on you or something?"

"Are *you?*" Leslie asked him back. "You came out here lookin' for me.
And I still don't know what you're talking about. So, if you wanna stop the
bullshit so much, then stop it."

This girl got a lot of fuckin' heart up in here! Beacoup told himself. He was
impressed.

He thought, *She ain't shit like her brother. She on na real!* So Coup nodded
his head and asked her, "How close were you with that boy? You still got
feelings for him?"

Before Leslie could answer him, Coup commented, "I know, I know,
what boy, right?"

Leslie showed him nothing. But her eyes told him everything. She was
deeper than he expected.

He answered, "That Creole boy you were fuckin' wit. Do you still have
feelings for him?"

Leslie asked him, "Should I?" and left it at that.

Beaucoup answered, "It won't make no difference now."

They killed him, Leslie thought to herself. *Or did I kill him? Or did he kill himself by talking shit to me like he did?*

She nodded her head, and finally gave up some ground to Coup.

"So now what?" she asked him.

Coup paused for a minute. He wanted to be thanked for his services. And he wanted Leslie to do so with the services of her naked body.

"Like I said earlier," he repeated, "anything you need, and I'm here for you . . . But um . . . sometimes . . . when things may not be goin' right for me . . ."

Leslie stopped him short and asked, "So, in other words, you wanna fuck me? Is that what you're trying to say? I mean, let's be real about it. And how much are you willing to pay? You gon' pay my whole tuition for school? That would free up my hands plenty."

Coup countered and said, "That's all good, but right now, I'm sayin' . . . you like on a IOU for what went down last night."

Leslie asked him, "Is that right?"

Coup looked at her and said, "Yeah. Somebody gotta pay for dat shit. That's how life is. Life ain't for free. It ain't neva' been for free. So, I'on know why niggas keep thinkin' that way. Ain't no such thing as no free food out hea'. Somebody had to pull that shit out da ground, cut up the meat, bake da bread, smash the grapes for the wine, and all lat other shit. Ya heard me?"

Leslie paused and remained silent. The boy wasn't a general for nothing! So she said, "I agree. There's prices to be paid for everything. But I'm looking at straight math with no interest. So how do we settle this?"

Coup looked at her again and couldn't believe it. He had to repeat it just to make sure. "Straight math and no interest, hunh?" he asked her with a chuckle. He said, "Are you sure you a *girl* talkin' like dat? Your brother don't even talk like dat."

Leslie told him, "I'm not my brother. And he's not me. We're just . . . related."

Coup didn't like the sound of that. It didn't sound like . . . girly shit. What was she trying to say? Was she the opposite of Pierre? And if Pierre was a pussy . . . then what was she?

Is she sayin' she's like me? Coup asked himself. That question put him on guard with her.

He said, "We'll figure out a way to resolve it. I mean, I ain't in no hurry about it."

"Why you come up here today, then," she asked him, "instead of tomorrow, or the next day?"

Coup grinned and chuckled again.

He thought to himself, *She sharp. I gotta give it to her. She don't leave no room for error.*

He answered, "I just wanted to see you t'day."

Okay, Leslie thought to herself. *Be a girl now. We finally got down to his business, now it's time for me to handle my business.*

She took a deep breath and looked away while she spoke.

She said, "Guys have always been a disappointment to me. They say they want one thing, so you give them what they want, and then they change their minds and say they want something else." She looked into Coup's eyes and said, "I mean, keep it real. That's all I'm asking. If you just wanna fuck me, then let me know. And then pay me for it. Because life ain't free, right? Well . . . neither is my body."

Coup took in her words and said, "So . . . that's how you've been feelin' lately?"

Leslie told him, "Yeah. And if you wanna roll wit it like that, then we can agree on something. But if I find out that some people like to talk about private situations, then I'll cut the shit loose in a heartbeat. Because all you got in this world is your respect sometimes. And I can't have people talking shit where I lose my respect. That's why I don't deal with everybody like that. But obviously . . . sometimes we all make mistakes."

Coup nodded and said, "Yeah, I feel you on that. So if I jus' . . . let that shit slide from last night . . . then we'll just start from here?"

Leslie shrugged her shoulders and said, "It's up to you. I mean . . . like you said, I could use some things. But I still need to have my privacy. So you can't be driving up on my campus and shit." She stared at him to solidify her point.

He said, "Aw'ight. I can live wit dat. But um . . . I don't really know about this straight math shit. Do you really wanna do it that way? I mean, we gon' put a dollar amount on everything we do? That may not be fair to you. I mean, think about it. What if you need something when I don't? How we gon' handle it?"

Leslie paused to study the situation. Then she came up with a solution.

She said, "This how we'll do it, then. What are you doin' later on tonight?"

Coup studied her face and answered, "Nothin' that I can't change." He wanted to see where she would go with it.

Leslie suggested, "Well, like you said, I'm in debt right now. So to prove that you're gonna get what it's worth . . . let's just hook up tonight. And afterwards . . . we'll just go from there."

Beaucoup tried his hardest to hold back his grin and he succeeded at it. But he failed at holding down his hard-on, and Leslie figured as much. So she reached out her left hand and massaged his crotch under the wheel.

"Yo, don't do that shit while I'm drivin'," Coup snapped at her, turning on his militancy.

Leslie smiled at him, because she had already felt him. She knew that he was interested.

"So, are you gonna give me a pager number or something to call you?" she asked him.

Beaucoup was confused and skeptical at her whole change of attitude.

Is this bitch trying to get wicked on me? he questioned himself. *Is she a whore on the low? I guess I do need to find that shit out tonight.*

He said, "Wait a minute . . . I'm just peepin' how you jus' flipped up your whole script. So you really don't care about that boy, then."

Leslie raised her seat back to the erect position and asked him, "Are you ready to let me back out?" They had driven far enough away from Dillard's campus where she was no longer concerned about who would spot her with him.

Coup said, "You gon' answer my question first?"

Leslie looked at him and answered, "You said it won't matter anymore, right? Well, let me ask you this, how would you rate yourself in comparison to him? Are you gonna go out like he did?"

Beaucoup read her logic and broke into laughter. He said, "Fuck no! That nigga was a punk. You shouldn't have been fuckin' wit dat boy in the first place."

Leslie cut him off and said, "All right, then. Stop acting all sensitive about my shit. I can handle it. Life goes on. So . . . do you want me to call you tonight, or what?"

Coup nodded his head with no more hesitation and agreed to give her a number to call.

After she had written down the number and was ready to climb out of his ride, he asked her, "Like . . . what time are you talkin' 'bout hookin' up?"

"Whatever time is convenient for you," she told him. And she waited.

Coup thought about his schedule and said, "Call me sometime around nine, then."

Leslie nodded and opened the door at the curb, as he pulled over to let her out.

She turned and asked him sarcastically through the window as she stood out on the curb, "So . . . how long will it take for my brother to find out that I'm fucking you for money now?"

Coup smirked for a second before he shook it off. "I ain't gon' do that to you. You laid down how you want it . . . and I gotta respect that."

Leslie responded, "That's all I'm asking from you?"

Coup joked and said, "Yeah, 'cause I wouldn't want you gettin' me taken care of next."

Leslie shook his sarcasm off as well. She said, "People only get what they got coming to them. So if you live right by you . . ."

Coup disagreed with her, though. He said, "That's bullshit. People get what they can make happen for 'em. Or what they can't stop." *And ain't shit gon' happen to me. I can assure you of that,* he thought to himself defiantly.

Leslie paused and thought about his logic for herself. She said, "You're right. Only the strong survive." And then she wondered who was stronger between them.

So she told herself as she walked off, *I guess I'll find out tonight.*

≈≈≈

Leslie hustled to the nearest pay phone to page her brother as soon as Beaucoup's Navigator was out of sight. She had the full intention of cursing Pierre the hell out!

"If you wanna act fuckin' brave now, then do it on your own," she snapped to herself as she paged her brother and waited. She checked her watch and read that it was a quarter after twelve, and she had not yet spoken to Ayanna about their meeting for lunch at one. Leslie still planned on making her lunch date. She planned on doing everything as normal, and then she'd handle her new situation later on that night. But first things first, and that was giving her brother an earful for his continued cowardice!

When Pierre received Leslie's page, while cleaning up his makeshift one-bedroom apartment, he looked at the numbers and thought about erasing them.

He shook his head and mumbled, "Fuck am I gon' do?" He had been thinking that thought for the majority of the day. He had asked himself that same question all night long. What was he going to do with his life?

"I've been fuckin' up forever," he told himself. *Now I done fucked up wit Leslie again.*

It took him a few more minutes before he finally decided to come clean with his sister.

"Fuck it," he told himself, "I deserve whatever I get now."

But by the time he had called her back at the pay phone, Leslie was on her way back to school to make her lunch date on time. "I'll catch up to his ass sooner or later," she told herself as she walked briskly toward Gentilly Boulevard for campus.

Back on Dillard's campus, Yula bumped into Ayanna before Leslie did.

"Hey, Ayanna, did Leslie tell you about us meetin' up for lunch in the cafeteria at one o'clock today?" She wanted to get all of the information out at once.

Ayanna took a breath and asked, "For what?"

Yula frowned at her. "What do you mean, 'For what?'? So we can all sit down and eat lunch together. We haven't had a good face-to-face sit-down since this semester started. And most of the time, it's been either you missing or Leslie missing."

"That's ironic, ain't it?" Ayanna asked her.

Yula grimaced and tried to read her meaning.

"What are you trying to say? You don't get along with Leslie no more?"

"Earth to Yula," Ayanna answered tartly. She began to walk away.

"So you're not gonna meet up with us, then?" Yula pressed her.

Ayanna failed to respond. What difference did it make? She wanted to get the hell away from all of them. She even thought about going back to the house to pack up her things while they had their little lunch together.

I don't need this shit in my life, she thought to herself. *I can go back home to Houston and try to put myself down with somebody for a rap contract. Destiny's Child is blowing up now from home. Maybe I can talk to some of their people. And in the meantime, I can just stay with my grandmom and keep going to school down there.*

She had it all mapped out. She didn't even feel like finishing out the semester at Dillard. Her grades there were not up to par anyway.

"What's up with all these flyers today?" she asked herself as she noticed the yellow flyers all over campus, posted on trees, poles, and littered on the campus sidewalks.

She picked one of them up and read it: *POETRY SLAM and OPEN MIKE, featuring ISIS, the WAR GODDESS, at THE STAGE.*

That's tonight, she thought to herself. "Hmm . . . I think I might go to that. I ain't got shit else to do." So she folded up the flyer and shoved it into her backpack.

Meanwhile, Bridget was on campus trying to reach Eugene for the fourth time that day from her cell phone. She hadn't heard anything from him the night before, either. And she was done with leaving him messages. So when his answering machine came on again, she hung up on it.

"Here we go again," she told herself, breathing heavily. "Why can't guys just do what they say they're gonna do?" She slipped her phone back into her bag to head to the cafeteria for her lunch meeting with her housemates.

I don't even feel like doing this now, she pondered. *I know my mind's not gonna be into it.*

But she showed up anyway to join Yula and Leslie.

"So, Ayanna's late as usual," she commented as she sat down at their chosen table.

Yula said, "I don't think Ayanna's comin'. I talked to her, and she acted like she didn't want to." Yula looked at Leslie but didn't speak her mind at the moment.

"I didn't get a chance to catch up with her," Leslie admitted. "I got sidetracked."

Bridget looked at Leslie and couldn't help herself. She went right for the jugular, like Leslie would do. She said, "Leslie, we never got a chance to talk to you about it, because you've really been on the run lately, but what did you think about that girl Kaiyah Jefferson being killed from Tulane a week ago?

"I mean, I didn't know her all that well, but I even thought about going to her funeral if it had been here," Bridget added.

Leslie nodded, with a tuna sandwich in hand. Yula listened with her sandwich in hand as well.

Leslie answered, "I read about it. And I was wondering why she was even over there."

"Ain't that your old neighborhood, though?" Yula asked her. She hoped that it didn't sound like an interrogation, but they had all been waiting to ask Leslie a few questions about it.

Leslie nodded and said, "Yeah. You think she was trying to dig up something on me?"

She wanted to see how much they suspected.

Bridget answered, "Well, she was asking *us* about you. Maybe she went around there and did the same thing."

"And they didn't like it?" Yula put in.

Leslie responded, "But nobody would kill somebody just for asking questions. Not even in the 'hood."

"It depends on what questions they're asking," Ayanna walked up from behind and stated.

Leslie didn't flinch. *So is this it?* she asked herself. *My roommates are gonna turn me in?*

Yula asked Ayanna, "I thought you weren't coming."

"Well, I changed my mind," Ayanna told her. She took a seat with them at the table for four.

Leslie grinned and said, "Well, here we go. We're all sitting down together again."

"We could have all stayed together at the Mardi Gras if you didn't break out," Ayanna commented to Leslie.

Leslie looked at her briefly and read the newfound courage in Ayanna's eyes. *Okay. So she wants to fight me now,* Leslie thought. *We'll see what she got, then.*

"Yeah, Leslie, where did you go that day?" Yula asked her next.

Leslie thought of Bridget and held in her smile.

She answered, "I had something to take care of. But everybody had a good time that night," she added for Bridget's sake.

That only made Bridget think about Eugene again, wondering where he had disappeared to, and why he had not called her back yet.

"Seems like you always got something to take care of," Ayanna alluded to Leslie.

Fuck her! I'm not gon' be scared of her, Ayanna was thinking. *So if I'm gon' die, she jus' gon' have to kill me then. Because I'm tired of this shit, and I'm not running away from her. There are people back home in Houston who are gonna give me static, too. So I might as well stand my ground right here.*

Leslie looked across the table at Ayanna and said, "Yeah, well, some of us have much less to live for."

Ayanna's heart jumped into her throat, but she forced herself to respond anyway, while her entire body shivered in terror. "I got something to live for. And when it's time for me to die, then I'll just die," she huffed at Leslie.

Leslie could feel the attention of the room beginning to focus in their direction. She could also see her hands around Ayanna's neck, while she choked the life out of her! Yet . . . she remained calm at the table.

She told herself, *It's my fault. I should have never played with the girl. Now she's gonna force me to hurt her.*

Bridget spoke up and asked Ayanna, "What are you talking about dying for?"

Ayanna looked at her with spite and snapped, "Because people *die,* Bridget. You so fuckin' stupid!"

Yula jumped in and said, "See, this is what I'm talking about. We can't even have a conversation between us without arguing anymore."

I have to get the hell away from here, Leslie told herself in the middle of the commotion. She even stood up from the table without realizing it.

"Where are you goin', Leslie?" Yula asked her. "You haven't even finished your food yet."

Leslie shook her head and gathered her things to leave.

"I don't have time for this right now," she told them. She gave Ayanna a lingering stare to make sure she knew to keep her mouth shut before she left.

We're gonna have our fight, girl. Just not right now, Leslie told her with her eyes.

Ayanna went mum as Leslie left them all at the table.

Something is up with this girl, Yula told herself as she watched Leslie walk through the cafeteria exit. *She seems to affect everybody in crazy ways.*

Yula continued to think about Leslie after she had left them . . . as did Ayanna, while Bridget only thought about Eugene, and how happier she was when she was with him, as opposed to being with her used-to-be-close friends.

I can see why normal women can't wait to get married, Bridget thought to herself. *Because anything beats this shit. They are so damned . . . trifling in here! I swear!*

... Is Coming ...

Jean-Pierre Beaudet called his old friend at his restaurant, while looking for his daughter.

"Jake, I have not spoken to my daughter Les-lie in days now. Where is she?"

Jake grimaced in confusion. He said, "I gave her a few days off. She was a little worn out, Gene, so I told her to get some rest. But she said she would call you."

"Have you spoken to her?"

"Not since she left here last night."

Jean didn't like the feeling he had in his gut. *Some-thing is wrong,* he told himself.

He told Jake, "I'll call her at home again."

Jake hung up and stared into empty space in his kitchen. He mumbled, "I don't think that girl ever get no rest. I would disappear if I was her too." Then he added, "But I just hope she come back to work when she's done."

Jean called Leslie at her college house and got no answer. He left no message on their answering machine either. He needed to talk to his daughter right now. So he called his daughter Laetitia to see if she knew where Leslie was.

"Hello," Jurron answered.

"Is my daughter there?" Jean asked him. He had no patience for being cordial.

Jurron frowned and thought, *I hate how this motherfucker talks to me.*

He answered, "She's not here right now."

"Is she with Les-lie?"

Jurron frowned again. *How da hell should I know?* he thought. *She didn't tell me where she was goin'. She's been acting real secretive lately, talkin' all this French shit now.*

He answered, "Not that I know of."

Jean was ready to hang up on him already. *What good is this young mahn?* Jean asked himself of his granddaughters' father. But when he heard Renée and Anna playing in the background, he wanted to speak to them . . . in French.

"Let me speak to my lit-tle girls," he told Jurron.

Jurron thought, *Here he goes with that shit again. Like I'm not even their father.* But he called his daughters to the phone anyway.

"Renée and Anna, come here. Your grandpa wanna talk to you on the phone."

His daughters bounced over to the telephone to talk to their grandfather. Jurron listened as they spoke beginners' French. He sat there piecing together some of the words.

He thought to himself, *Fuck, if they all gon' talk that French shit around here, then I might as well learn some of this shit.*

≈

Just a few miles away in a very private New Orleans home, Laetitia looked around at the peculiar objects of an American voodoo priestess. There were jars of murky liquids, sculptured figurines, combs, dolls, beads, dried-out plants, pipes, playing cards, and all other forms of ancient and mystical objects. In fact, the entire room that they sat in looked ancient.

"Did you bring me what I need?" the priestess asked Laetitia.

Laetitia nodded and placed her bag of items on the old wooden table where the two of them sat and faced each other.

"Not on the table," the old woman scolded her.

Laetitia quickly moved her bag of things back to the dusty hardwood floor.

"Push the bag to me on the floor," the woman told her.

Laetitia did as she was told. The priestess kept her steady eyes on the girl and studied her spotty face of brown skin mixed with pale white blotches from vitiligo.

"You are an outsider," the priestess told her. "You were born an outsider. Embrace it."

Laetitia nodded to her and was prepared to learn all that she could to become a priestess herself.

The old woman dug into Laetitia's bag without looking and pulled out an old hair comb. She felt the comb in her hand, still without looking, and told her eager visitor, "You come from wealthy roots . . . but the earth has become sour."

Laetitia cracked a smile and remembered when the *Bo-days* lived on *Tramay* Street in a grand white house. But then she became solemn, when she remembered moving into the poorer section of the Seventh Ward, and the mean-spirited neighbors who teased her there daily.

"You have known years of internal pain," the priestess told her. She could read it in Laetitia's eyes, and in the way that her hands moved nervously about the table.

The old woman reached out to calm her young visitor by caressing her hands in hers.

She said, "Your pain will become your wisdom . . . You are to use that pain. Rediscover it . . . and share it with me," she told Laetitia as she gently massaged her hands.

Laetitia searched her eyes to make sure.

"Now, my child," the priestess odered her with a squeeze, "you cannot fear your pain. Pain is an everyday occurrence. It is like food and water. Share it with me."

Laetitia took a breath and remembered.

She said, "People were always . . . teasing me about my skin. And they acted like . . . like I wasn't supposed to feel nothin' from it. But it hurt me."

Tears dropped freely from Laetitia's eyes as easy as water drops from a broken faucet.

"And I kept askin' myself, *Why me?*" she said. "And then . . . like you said, I was an outsider, because my father was Haitian. And he wanted us to speak French. But . . ."

"You didn't want to," the priestess finished for her.

"I didn't want them . . . to keep teasing me about everything. I mean, I jus' wanted . . ."

"To fit in," the priestess finished for her again. "And that is how we lose our power, my child. Because to be normal is to be nothing and no one. But to stand out . . . we must have courage, the courage to embrace our uniqueness."

Laetitia nodded to her.

"Do you know the French *now?*" the old woman asked her.

Laetitia answered the question honestly for the first time in her life, because she realized that her lies would not work with this woman.

"I always knew it. I jus' . . ."

The priestess shook Laetitia's hands at the table and snapped, "You denied yourself your family treasures to *fit in.* Didn't you?"

Laetitia bit her lip in shame as she sat in silence. Fresh tears continued to roll from her face.

The old woman said, "We continue to deny ourselves all of our power, to fit in to foolishness, helplessness, and pity. And we make ourselves the sheep to be eaten by the hungry wolves. Do you understand me?" she asked as she squeezed Laetitia's hands even tighter.

Laetitia nodded her head in agreement with the old woman and did not complain.

"You learn to embrace the pain, and treasure all of your wealth, and you will rule over the sheep."

Laetitia told her, "I know. I understand now. I do."

The priestess studied her eyes to see if she told the truth. "Do you?" she asked her.

Laetitia nodded.

The old woman dug into the bag again with her right hand, and pulled out a recent Polaroid picture of Laetitia, Jurron, and their two daughters at the Mardi Gras celebration. She held the picture up to her face and said, "I see. Your spirits have been uplifted lately. And you no longer hide yourself."

Laetitia answered, "No," and it was the truth. She had begun her maturation.

"Do you love him?" the old woman asked of Jurron. She smiled before Laetitia could respond, because the answer was obvious. Women rarely smiled so widely for men who they did not love. The woman *was* love . . . and love was her strongest enemy.

"Of course you do," the priestess answered for herself. "But are you afraid of losing him?"

Laetitia took a breath . . . and answered, "Not anymore."

The priestess began to laugh out loud at the table.

"Now, you see the power of accepting the pain, my child. Loss is life, and life must accept the loss, or be controlled by it."

But there was much more information inside of the bag. The priestess could feel it. So she became impatient, as she dug inside with her right hand again. She was discarding Laetitia's new branches for a picture of her old roots.

"Yes," the priestess responded with a nod when she had found them. She looked into the dark eyes and determined stance of Jean-Pierre Beaudet of Haiti, and at the exotic beauty of Anna-Marie Cooke of New Orleans, and at the soft, innocent face of Pierre Beaudet, and then she . . . stopped . . . at the eyes . . . of the sister.

The old woman commented, "Your roots run deep into the earth. Tell me about them. Starting with your father."

So Laetitia began to tell the old woman, one by one, about her family members—their strengths, their weaknesses, and so forth—until they had reached her older sister, Leslie.

By that time the priestess had pulled another picture from the bag. It was one of Laetitia and Leslie in a jovial embrace in their earlier teen years.

"Lez-lee," the priestess repeated out loud after she had heard the name. *I thought I knew you,* she told herself. *You're my young friend from the bus. And how strong you are. Now I shall hear about it. And it is meant for me to hear. Your sister brought it to me. And you love your sister. So it was meant to be.*

"And how was *she*?" the priestess had been eager to ask.

Laetitia smiled, as though a great secret was to be revealed between them. And it was. Only . . . Laetitia failed to realize it.

She said, "Leslie was always the smartest. She got the best grades. She spoke the most French. And she could speak it fast, too."

"And how did she get along with your mother?" the priestess asked her. "Did she love your mother as much as you and Pierre loved her?"

Laetitia's hesitation and the confusion in her eyes told the story before she could even voice it.

"Umm . . . Leslie was more of a . . . daddy's girl. I mean . . . she seemed to get along with Daddy more."

"And you and Pierre?" the old woman asked. "How did you get along with your father?"

The twist on Laetitia's face told the story again.

"I mean, we were young back den," she tried to explain.

The priestess cut her off and said, "But so was Leslie."

"Yeah, but Leslie . . . she . . . she never *seemed* young," Laetitia responded. "She, like, knew stuff before everybody else did. And, you know—"

The priestess cut off her rambling and asked her, "And how did Leslie respond to those who teased you?"

Laetitia began to smile even wider than the first time. And her smile turned into a chuckle.

She answered, "Leslie would . . . fuck them up." And she felt embarrassed by her candor. She said, "Excuse me. I didn't mean to say that."

"Yes you did," the old woman corrected her. "You speak your mind, and your mind will never lie."

Laetitia nodded to her and went on with her story. "Sometimes, like, the girls would try to lie about it or whatever, and I was always scared to tell, because they would always say that they would get me later if I told her. But like, Leslie would just . . . know. And she would say to me in French, *'Qui a dit ça?'* Which one said it? And they wouldn't know what she was talking about, right. And then she would just jump on the right one, every time, and whip their ass!"

Laetitia even got animated with it. Her whole body told the story as she got more excited.

She said, "And I felt sorry for some of these girls, because Leslie was like . . . I mean, when she gets mad . . . it's like . . . a demon or something jumps in her."

The priestess leaned back her head and laughed out loud.

So the War Goddess has come, she told herself. *There have been many impostors . . . but now she is here!*

"So Leslie has always protected you?" the priestess asked Laetitia rhetorically. "And not Pierre."

Laetitia stopped smiling. She said, "Pierre hated when we moved the most. And I remember he ran away a lot to our cousin's house, on my mother's family."

"And how was *his* relationship with Leslie?" the old woman asked.

Laetitia hesitated again. Then she grinned. She said, "It may sound crazy or whatever, but I always thought that it would have been better for all of us if Leslie was the boy. Or, you know, like . . . if Pierre was more like Leslie.

"And I mean, I think even our father would feel that way," she added.

"So Pierre didn't have it in him?" the priestess asked her.

Laetitia shook her head and answered, "Unt unh. And Daddy would always ride him about it."

But one question intrigued the priestess about Laetitia. It continued to pop into her head.

Why now? she asked herself. *Why do you want to embrace the apprenticeship now, my child? What has happened in your life to finally push you to it?*

So she continued to flip through the pictures, coming back to the most recent Polaroid of Laetitia and her new family.

"And what has uplifted your spirits at home lately . . . after the passing of your mother?"

Laetitia did not seem to mourn long, which was unusual, in light of how much she longed for her mother's kindness. However, the question seemed to startle her. She became nervous again.

She answered, "I don't know if I can tell you," with a conscience of guilt.

The priestess looked into her young visitor's eyes and said, "Of course you can. This is my sanctuary. How can you become my apprentice without trust?"

Shit! Laetitia cursed herself. The truth would be revealed. And the truth was, a voodoo spell had worked recently for her. So she wanted to learn all of its power now, and make her family wealthy again through its use.

Slowly she confessed, "I had . . . a problem that needed to be handled recently."

The priestess followed the natural logic of Laetitia's life, and immediately asked her, "And did you tell Leslie about it?" Leslie had handled her problems, their brother's cowardice, their mother's weakness, and their father's pride all by herself. So the question became an easy one.

However, Laetitia grimaced at the question. She was not yet done with her confession.

She answered, "Yeah, I told her, but . . ." And her mind suddenly froze as she remembered the question from the last phone call that she had had with her big sister. Leslie had asked her, "Would you still be doing 'all right' for yourself if you had lost Jurron to that girl you were sweating so much?"

Laetitia then remembered her own words to Leslie after the big news: "I mean, Leslie, it was like you knew that it would be all right and that Jurron would come back home to me. I mean . . . *comment l'as-tu su?*" How did you know? "I'll tell you how. *Nous avons le pouvoir.*" We have power! "That's how!"

And her mind rapidly scrolled back to the conversation she had had with Leslie at her apartment the same week as Phyllis's death.

Leslie had asked, "What did you find out?"

And Laetitia told her, "I got her phone number. I know where she works. And she lives right over in the Florida projects."

Leslie asked her, "What she look like?"

And Laetitia told her, "You know, typical light skinned, fat ass . . . you know what guys like."

Then Leslie asked her, "So, what do you want to do to this girl?"

And Laetitia smiled when she answered, "Umm . . . maybe I can work up some of our voodoo stuff on her."

But she don't believe in it, Laetitia told herself as she sat at the table in a sudden panic.

However, all of her recollections and the confusion on her face had sealed the clues to the truth. She told herself, *I left that note with all of Phyllis's information right on the coffee table where Leslie slept that night . . . Oh my God! . . . She . . .*

When Laetitia realized what she was telling herself, she stared right into the eyes of the priestess and revealed everything in her bewilderment.

"Umm . . . can I come back another time?" she asked the old woman. She wanted to call Leslie immediately and ask her some detailed questions that were on her mind.

The priestess grinned at her. She grinned at Laetitia's ignorance and began to laugh.

"Are you sure you have what it takes to become an apprentice?" she asked her young visitor. "Because if you did . . . then maybe someone else would have had more faith in you."

Laetitia tried to ignore the old woman as she gathered her things to leave in a hurry. And as she scampered out the door, while still hearing the mocking laughter of the old woman, all that she could think about was how Leslie had always been able to deceive her whenever she needed to.

The priestess continued to laugh with delight after the young girl had left her.

"Leslie will be famous," she told herself out loud. "Yes, she will. And they will call out her name for generations."

≈≈

Leslie walked into a no-frills hotel holding two brown paper bags of her clothing and her accessories. She was dressed homely again, with her hair up in a bun under another dark baseball hat. She swaggered over to the receptionist at the front counter in an exaggerated ghetto mode. It took the receptionist as little as two seconds to size her up as a drug-addicted trick turner who worked the streets at night. But money was money. And if the girl had any . . . then she could rent a room there.

"Umm . . . y'all got any rooms up in here?" Leslie asked the clerk.

"Yes, we do have rooms," the civil black woman responded.

Leslie leaned into the counter. "But I'm talkin' 'bout, umm . . . a room for me to *stay* in."

The receptionist took a deep breath. *Now, this ain't none of my business, but some of the people who stay here are some of the most ignorant customers I've ever come across in my life.*

She told Leslie, "Well, as long as you know that the rooms are not free, then I'll see what I can do for you."

Leslie put down her bags and pulled out a pocket full of crumpled-up bills.

"Well, how long can I stay for two hunnet?"

The receptionist counted out the money first, before she answered, "Four nights."

Leslie looked at her with a dazed stare and said, "I'll take it, den. But which room, 'cause I don't like no first floors. Gimme one on 'na third floor."

The receptionist went on about her business and tried to find an available room on the third floor without further indignity with the young woman.

"Room three twenty-two," she told her, as she prepared the plastic key card.

"Thank you," Leslie responded as she swaggered toward the stairs to reach her room.

The receptionist quickly turned her head to help the next customer.

Let me go on back to my business, she told herself.

Leslie went up to her room in a state of driven confusion. She knew she had to get away from her campus house before the heat kicked in and her roommates were able to piece together more of her puzzle. But she had no idea what she planned to do now.

She sat down on the hotel bed and did . . . nothing. What was there to do?

My life is ruined now, she mused. "All because of dumb-ass Pierre!" she snapped out loud. *But I put myself in that position by calling him and telling him what happened last night,* she argued to herself. *But I didn't know his dumb ass was gonna go out and have somebody killed. I didn't ask him to do that shit. Or did I?*

She was even confused about her thoughts. What had she asked for?

I mean . . . maybe it was just meant to happen, she concluded. *And it seems like . . . I can't stop it now. It's just taking control of me. Whatever it is that's inside of me.*

On instinct, she clicked on the television, just in time to catch a New Orleans news report.

"The body of a young man was found today, floating under a wharf in the Mississippi River. Investigators say that the man had died of two gunshot wounds to the head, and that he had been wrapped, execution style, with duct tape around his mouth, and that his hands had been taped together behind his back."

Leslie quickly turned the television back off before they could interview the officers at the scene. She thought again about calling her brother, Pierre, to curse his ass out! At least *she* would have handled things more cleverly. But then she stopped and calmed herself to think about it.

Wait a minute. If he was killed execution style, then maybe they'll think it was drug related. Hmm. That might not be that bad, she admitted to herself.

Then she thought deeper about it. *But how will my roommates look at it?* she questioned. *But they don't know that Eugene and I had something going. I mean, Yula knew that he might have liked me, but that's all she knew.*

In a minute, Leslie found herself trying to figure out a way to return her life to normal and get past the recent murders.

"But Ayanna!" she stood up and spat in a rush of panic. *What will that bitch think? And what will she say to them?*

"Damn!" Leslie cursed herself as she paced the room.

She thought the unthinkable. *What if I make a doll of her? Would that shit work? I've never even tried it yet . . .*

"But I don't need no damn dolls," she told herself out loud. *All I have to do is think about it. And if she opens her fucking mouth . . .* "Then I'll just have her ass killed, too. I'll do it my-fuckin'-self," she promised.

She calmed herself again, only to explode in a mental rage of blasphemy.

You just remember, I didn't ask for this. I didn't ask for none of this! You made me this way. You should have never put me in the situation, God! Whose God are you anyway? Not my God! My God is about justice for all people. So I'm taking it, on whoever the hell threatens mine!

Now you deal with that! And you do what you're gonna do.

When she calmed herself again, she dug into her bag and pulled out the new mask that she had bought during the Mardi Gras celebration. She held it gently in her hands and marveled at how pretty it was indeed; a radiant red mask of power, with slanted golden eyes of mystique, and the beautiful, bluish yellow peacock feathers, with long orange and red feathers that cascaded downward toward the earth.

Leslie stepped in front of the long mirror above the cheap dresser in her hotel room, and she tried on the mask for the first time. It fit her perfectly.

She told herself, "Now we'll see who's the baddest, *Bo-coup.* Meet the young *priestess.*"

You want a project bitch for real? she asked as she stood in front of the long mirror with her mask on. She finished her thoughts out loud: "Well, now you'll get your chance."

≈≈

Professor Sullivan flipped through the various texts that he had bought on voodoo and Vodou in his office back home in Algiers. He viewed the table of contents to scan the subjects and depth of the books that he would read. He wanted to get a basic idea of what he was dealing with, and time was of the essence. He still had his regular school assignments to address. So he read first for an overview of the misunderstood, dark religion, before he would dig into the details.

The basic inclination of the Vodou religion was based in ancestor worship. The family lines were the most intimate source of belief and power, passing down certain traits of strengths, weaknesses, and eccentric personalities. Those ancestors who were known for certain traits of strength were called on in times of need. Certain ancient personalities were also deified into minor gods of honor and worship.

Professor Sullivan stopped his reading and thought it over a minute.

This is very similar to most religions. In a way, all religions are ancestor worship. Moses of the Jews, Jesus of the Christians, Muhammad of the Muslims, Buddha of the Buddhists, and so forth.

However, he thought, *this religion seems to be a lot more personal. They're just as inclined to honor their grandmothers and grandfathers, as they are the higher deities and Bondye, the Supreme One, who they consider too high for interpretation.*

Therefore, the religion of Vodou seemed more accessible to the common people, as opposed to the hierarchies of the major Western religions, who claimed to know the will of God.

Professor Sullivan went on to read about the various male and female deities, who reminded him of Roman, Greek, and Egyptian mythology. And he became further convinced that the religion of Vodou was equally as logical or illogical as many Western society beliefs that were studied at the university level. He then read of the living priests and priestesses who were called on for their mystic connection to the spirits and for biddings from the ancestors, usually for a fee.

The professor began to smile. "There will always be a class of society to carve out a profit where a profit is to be made off the delusions and short-comings of the masses," he told himself.

As he flipped through the pages that discussed the various possessions, visions, spells, sacrifices, and rituals that were used by the priests and priest-esses, he began to wonder more about Leslie Beaudet's ancestry. The books even came with various illustrations.

And she's Haitian, he told himself of Leslie. *Haiti is a phenomenally poor country with a predominant African ancestry.* He imagined that community priests and priestesses would amass a great deal of power in poverty, much like the intelligent or gifted classes of most societies. Because the priests and priestesses were deemed special. They seemed to control the roots, or at least to channel them.

"So, what Haitian blood and power do you have running through your veins, Leslie?" Professor Sullivan asked himself in jest. However, she was becoming more interesting to him.

And as he began to chuckle in mockery, one of the illustrated books slid from his desk and dropped to the floor, creasing a page.

Marcus Sullivan was then forced back to seriousness. He picked up the fallen book and viewed the page that had been creased: the glaring, illumi-nated eyes of a woman stared back up at him from the opened text.

Ounsi Kanzo, the spiritual initiate of will that moves and transforms earth, is what he read to himself. The *Ounsi Kanzo* held a flaming pot, or calabash, representing a trial by fire . . . or war. And the text read that her inner sub-stance was fire, radiating from the passion of her eyes. Through her eyes, she saw the world as it was, with its good and evil, and its love and hate, and its gentleness and violence all in one, and without pretension or hypocrisy.

Professor Sullivan read on to find that the *Ounsi Kanzo* initiates of the Vodou society had been known for their violence. They were the war class, with a history of runaway slaves, who had made fast alliances with the Native American tribes who reflected their fire for freedom and justice.

Professor Sullivan stopped reading again and thought about the cultural history of New Orleans, and its exotic blend of French, Spanish, African, and Native American blood, and the people who reflected New Orleans in the new millennium. It had largely become a place to ignore poverty, much like Haiti and Rio de Janeiro, Brazil.

And as the professor thought about Leslie's outside place in all of the racial overtones of New Orleans, he realized that her dark skin excluded her from the class of light-skinned Creoles, as well as from the wealth and social position of American whites, who had all locked Leslie and her family into the volatile desperation of the ghetto, a prime situation for Vodou. And then he felt guilty.

"Jesus Christ!" he told himself as he pondered her situation. "What else does she have to turn to?"

He wasn't sure if he was right about who Leslie was and what she may have done, but he was sure about one thing. He told himself, "It's only natural for her to become defensive. Anyone would in her position." Then he paused with his conclusion: "And then we take up arms. It's natural. Humans have always killed to defend themselves . . . And we always will."

. . . Right Now!

Yula shook her head at the house and fumed, "I can't figure Leslie out for nothin'. That girl is just . . . I don't know."

However, Bridget was tired of the mystery surrounding her eccentric roommate. *I'm ready for her to move out, period, to make it easier on all of us, since she wants her privacy so much. I'm ready for everyone to move out, to tell you the truth,* she told herself. *Then I can get my own place somewhere . . . I wonder if Eugene would move in with me . . . But what would my father say?*

Bridget grinned to herself and thought, *An apartment would be cheaper for him anyway. And they don't always pay me their rent on time in here.*

"What are you thinking about?" Yula asked her.

Bridget shook her head and answered, "Nothing."

Yula smiled and assumed, "Eugene. That boy's back on your mind again. I can't blame you, though. Dedication is a hard thing to find from a guy."

Bridget smiled and said, "You got that right, girl. That's the truth."

KNOCK! KNOCK! KNOCK! KNOCK!

Yula looked to the front door and winced. "Damn! Is that the *police* or something? Why can't they ring the doorbell?" she asked as she marched to answer the hard knocks at the door. Yula was ready to give whoever it was an evil stare-down until she looked through the peephole. Two investigating white men were standing in the doorway in dull suits.

"Oh shit, Bridget, it *is* the police," Yula whispered back into the house.

"Is Bridget Chancellor in?" they asked through the door.

Bridget immediately thought of her innocence. *I didn't do anything. What could they want from me?* She walked right up to the door past Yula to answer it.

"I'm Bridget Chancellor," she told the two officers who stood inside of the doorway.

Yula stood back and thought, *Better you than me.* Not that she had done anything to warrant guilt, she had just learned that police officers knocking on your front door was not usually a positive thing to have.

They asked Bridget, "May we ask you a few questions?"

"Sure," Bridget told them. She opened the door wide and let them in.

The first officer did the talking, while the second officer wrote down notes in his notepad. They both inspected the house and Yula, while Yula watched and listened. She peeked at her watch to read what time it was. It was after five o'clock already, and fast approaching six.

"Have you watched the news anytime today?" the first officer asked Bridget.

Bridget grimaced and answered, "No. Why?"

The officer nodded before he looked to his partner. His partner gave him a blank stare. It was his call. The first officer then looked back to Bridget with a pause. He asked her, "What is your relationship with Eugene Duval? You left several messages on his answering machine, starting at—"

"Seven twenty-six P.M. last night," his partner filled in for him with his notes in hand.

"Are you his girlfriend?" the first officer asked.

Yula was all up in their faces trying to figure out what was going on. At first, Bridget was embarrassed that they were sharing her business. But then she thought about Eugene and panicked.

"Well, what . . . what happened? What did he do?"

"That's what we're trying to find out," the second officer answered.

"We need you to be totally honest with us, Bridget. Okay?" the first officer asked her.

Bridget stood there with her mouth open.

"O-kay," she finally told them.

"Was Eugene involved with any drugs that you know of?"

Bridget froze in shock! She couldn't even comprehend an answer.

Yula's eyes widened as she rushed out a statement in defense of Eugene's character. "He's not even that kind of a person," she told them. "-He's just . . ." *A pretty boy,* she kept to herself.

The officers turned to her. "So what kind of person was he?" the second officer asked.

The first officer frowned at his partner's bad use of tense.

Bridget caught on to it and said, "Wait a minute? What kind of person *was* he? What are you saying? Did he . . ." She was unable to finish her statement before her voice trailed off in horror.

The first officer shot a look to his partner to allow him to do the rest of the talking while he placed a soft hand on Bridget's shoulder.

"Oh my God!" Yula exclaimed as she watched and calculated. "Oh my God!"

Shit! the first officer snapped. *Now we'll get nothing but a bunch of hysterics out of them.*

"What *happened* to him?" Bridget demanded from the officers. "What *happened?*"

Tears swelled up in her eyes before they confirmed anything. So Yula rushed to her side.

The first officer took a deep breath and told her, "Someone out there didn't quite like Eugene as much as you do."

His choice of words made Bridget think of Leslie. Leslie seemed to almost hate Eugene for some reason. But why would she have anything to do with murdering him just because they didn't get along? *That's crazy!* Bridget told herself. *But how did he die?*

"What did they do to him?" she asked the officers, expecting the worst. Yet, she prayed for a miracle. Maybe he had only been injured. Maybe she was having a bad dream. Everyone asks themselves if they're dreaming in times of turmoil. And everyone prays to God to change their fate. But sometimes . . . there is no happy ending.

The first officer looked to his partner to give the bad news. He was better at that than speaking with any deal of tact. So the second officer opened his mouth with his notepad closed and said, "Eugene Duval was found dead this morning, floating near the docks on the Mississippi River."

Yula squeezed Bridget tight as the officer continued: "He had been shot twice at close range in the head, tied with duct tape around his mouth, and his hands had been tied behind his back . . . execution style."

Bridget never screamed and yelled with the hysterics that they all expected. She just cried into her hands and took it all in with one question.

She looked up from her hands and asked them all, "Why?"

"That's what we're here trying to find out, ma'am," the first officer assured her.

Dinng, donng!

Yula looked toward the door again. *What now?* she thought to herself before she walked to answer it. When she looked through the peephole, there were two more plainclothes officers there. One officer was a middle-aged black man, and the other was a young white man.

Yula let them in and said, "Join the terrible party," as she swallowed hard from the news.

The black officer stepped inside with his young partner, and they immediately looked toward the other team.

"Hey ya, Gil. We got this thing here covered," the first officer from the first team told the black officer.

"You have *what* covered?" the black officer asked him for clarity.

In the confusion, Bridget felt an urge to slip away from it all where she could clear her head. She fled to the stairs and then up to her room, where she shut the door and locked it. Once she had her privacy, her cries became more animated and open.

"Whyyy?" she cried to herself. *"Whyyy?"*

Back downstairs, the four police officers conversed amongst themselves, while Yula eavesdropped on their chatter.

"The Duval murder. We're already *here* on that," the first white officer told the second team.

The black officer from the second team frowned at him. He said, "We're not here on that. We're here on the Kaiyah Jefferson murder, the student from Tulane who was shot and killed in the Seventh Ward a week ago."

The first officer looked at Yula and asked, "What does that have to do with them?"

Yula looked back to the black officer and felt guilty. Kaiyah Jefferson had been there to the house with her camera. Twice!

The black officer answered, "We've been going through hours of camera footage that the young woman shot that were seized from the university, and it's taken us a while to question all of the students she filmed. This was one of the last on our list."

The first team looked at each other before the first officer commented, "Well, isn't *that* a coincidence?" He asked Yula, "Are you familiar with the Jefferson girl? What kind of character was *she?*" he asked Yula snidely.

Yula swallowed another gulp of air. *Shit! This is getting too deep for me,* she told herself.

She said, "I didn't really know her that well. She was . . ." *Bridget's friend,* she kept to herself.

The black officer took out a list of names as his young partner stood by and observed.

"I have a Bridget Chancellor . . ."

"She just went up to her room," the second officer from the first team responded. "I'll go up and get her."

"Ayanna Timber," the black officer continued.

Yula answered, "She's not here right now."

"Yula Frederick . . ."

"That's me," Yula answered meekly. Her heart began to pound with apprehension. She got so nervous that her chest began to hurt.

Oh my God! she continued to tell herself.

"And Leslie Beaudet," the black officer finished from his list.

Yula stopped for just a second to grimace. "She's not here either," she commented.

"Why did you make that *face* about her?" the black officer's young white partner asked her. It was the first thing he had asked.

All eyes were suddenly on Yula. Even the second officer from the first team listened in for her answer as he descended the stairs with Bridget.

Yula thought about it and said, "No reason. She's just . . ." And she shut her mouth again.

Let me stay out of this, she warned herself. *If Leslie did something, then let them catch her on their own. I don't need to be involved in that. We don't have any proof of anything anyway.*

"So where *is* Leslie?" the black officer asked her.

Bridget had had enough about her! Enough of thinking about her! Enough of dealing with her! And enough of even hearing her damn name!

She snapped, "Why does everybody always ask about Leslie? She obviously doesn't want to be bothered! And I am tired of her! People are dying out here and all you wanna know about is Leslie, Leslie, fucking Leslie!"

Everyone in the room looked around at one another and was stunned by the outburst.

Sounds like we've like hit ourselves a sour note there, the first white officer mused.

"Well, we're still gonna need to ask her some questions," the black officer stated.

"Well, fine!" Bridget spat at him. "She works on Gentilly Boulevard at Hot Jake's fucking restaurant, in the kitchen!"

The officer's young partner stepped up to reprimand her for her tone and language.

"You just calm yourself down. We're only doing our jobs here," he told her. The black officer held him back.

"She's fine, she's fine," he told his young partner. "Let's just give her some room. There's a lot happening here."

With that, Bridget slid into a fit of uncontrollable tears for her loss of Eugene. And Yula said . . . nothing at all. It was Bridget's move. And Yula couldn't blame her. Things had definitely gotten out of hand.

≈≈≈

After the police had left Hot Jake's restaurant that night, Jake was agitated himself.

What the hell *is going on?* he asked as beads of sweat formed on his forehead. He locked himself into his office to call Jean at the homeless shelter.

"Yeah, can I have Gene *Bo-day,* please? It's an emergency," he told the man who answered the phone inside of the recreation room.

"Yeah, hold on a minute. *Hey, Gene!* Telephone!"

Jake waited anxiously for Jean to pick up the other line.

"Yes, this is *Jahn,*" Jean answered, correcting his name for the millionth time.

Jake rushed out and asked him, "Have you spoken to your daughter yet? This is Jake. I'm at the restaurant, and some police officers jus' came by here asking me all kinds of questions about her. Laetitia called over here looking for Leslie earlier, and Pierre called for her. Now what the hell is going *on,* Gene?" Leslie was the last person that Jake would have suspected of bringing trouble to his front door. But she had, and he wanted to know what it was about.

Jean paused for a minute in his thoughts. He had had a feeling about his daughter in her unexplainable absence. He asked, "What kind of questions did they ask?" He was curious, and in need of vital pieces of information to shape his mental puzzle.

Jake answered, "They were asking all kinds of questions about her work schedule here, and what kind of a person she was, what she did on the job, what kind of family she comes from, and the motherfuckers were takin' *notes.* And that shit jus' made me nervous, man."

Sweat of anxiety poured freely down Jake's round face as he spoke.

"Did they say what they were in-vestigating?" Jean asked him calmly.

"I don't know, but it didn't seem like nothin' small. I could tell by how many questions they asked me. If it was something small, they would have jus' asked me a few questions."

That was all that Jean needed to hear. He nodded his head with the phone in hand and said, "I'll see what I kin find out."

"You do that," Jake told him. When he hung up the phone, he wiped the sweat from his face with both of his meaty hands.

On Jean's end, he hung up the phone and pulled out some loose change to call Laetitia with.

"Hello," she answered hastily. She was anxious to find Leslie as well.

Jean asked her in French, *"Qu'est-ce Leslie a fait ces derniers temps?"* What has Leslie been up to?

"Oh, Daddy," Laetitia responded, startled by him. She hesitated and forgot her French again in her nervousness. "Umm . . . I don't know," she responded in English.

Jean said, "I'll call you later on," and hung up the phone in a flash.

"Hello? Papa?" Laetitia spoke into the phone, confused.

Jurron watched her from the couch and thought to himself, *What the hell is going on around here?* Laetitia had been acting . . . jittery ever since she walked back in from her errand. However, Jurron kept his thoughts to himself for the moment while he continued to entertain his daughters with a disappearing quarter in his hands as they tried to guess which one it was hidden in.

Jean hung up the phone and hastily walked out of the homeless shelter and into the streets of New Orleans in search of his daughter. With a grim face he whispered to himself, *"Ó, Leslie, ne me dis pas que tu a pris les affaires en mains vis-à-vis de ce que tu imagines tu connais à propos du Vaudou."* Oh, Leslie, please do not tell me you have taken things into your own hands with what you imagine you know of Vodou. *"S'il te plaît!"* Please!

~~~

Pierre's cell phone began to vibrate on the bed at his makeshift apartment, where he had remained all day. It broke him out of his stupor. He had remained in a daze since the murder the night before. He continued to think about what he could do, and hadn't done, and should do, and shouldn't have done for his tortured sister Leslie. He expected to hear from her soon. But the phone number on his cell phone was from Beaucoup and his soldiers.

Pierre shook his head and mumbled, "I'm not calling them. If they wanna talk to me, they'll just have to find me." And he was glad that he hadn't revealed his new place to anyone.

Miles away inside of his Navigator, Beaucoup awaited Pierre's return phone call while sitting with one of his most trusted soldiers.

"You think he gon' call back?" the soldier asked him with a doubtful grin.

Coup grinned back at him. "Naw, fuck 'em. That nigga bitchin' now."

His soldier asked him, "Did you know Will was gon' shoot dat nigga like dat last night?"

Coup thought about it. He answered, "Naw, but he showed where his heart at. That boy a real soldier," he responded with satisfaction.

"And guess who I'm hookin' up with t'night after all this shit?" Coup asked.

"Who?"

He grinned from ear to ear and answered, "Pierre's li'l sista, Leslie."

His soldier got excited and asked, "For true?"

Coup asked him, "Nigga, do I lie?"

There was a slight pause before they broke into laughter.

"How'd you do that?" his soldier asked him.

"I jus' rolled up and kicked it to her on na IOU tip."

His soldier's eyes grew wide. He said, "You told her what happened?"

Beaucoup calmed himself, identifying his soldier's concern with witnesses. He said, "She cool, man. She know what time it is. I mean, she kicked it back to me, like, 'Whassup f' t'night?'"

The soldier looked at him and said, "Aw, you bullshittin', man. You bullshittin'."

Coup shook his head. "No I'm not." He looked into his soldier's eyes. "But yo, this hea' . . . is jus' between me and you, man. Ya heard me? 'Cause I'm gon' get rid a dat nigga after dis."

The soldier grimaced and asked, "Pierre? I thought he was ya' boy."

Beaucoup smirked and said, "Now how I'm gon' look after I fuck his sista? I can't hang wit his punk ass after that. He might start gettin' i-deas." He smiled deviously. "I might jus' let y'all take his ass on a long ride somewhere."

The trusted soldier smiled, but he also thought to himself, *Damn! Coup don't give a fuck about nobody. Nobody but his own family. Or at least he say he do. I even wonder about that sometimes.*

Beaucoup quickly snapped him out of it.

"Yo, stop thinkin' so hard, nigga. Thinkin' too hard get niggas in trouble. Ya heard me?"

The soldier nodded at Coup's warning. A street general couldn't let anything slide. Ever!

Coup laughed things off and said, "Shit, that girl might not even call me t'night. But stay around for a minute in case she do. I gave her your number."

The soldier looked at Coup with the question *Why you keep giving people my number?* But he knew better than to ask it. Coup was just sinister that way. He was forever covering his own ass.

≈≈

As the clock slowly ticked past nine, with everyone in search of her, Leslie meditated inside of her hotel room on how everything would go that night. She remembered the whispers back in high school that Beaucoup liked his girls on top, or from behind. They also gossiped that he had often gotten high to heighten his sensations. And his soldiers were always somewhere nearby.

So Leslie input her information and visualized the scene in her mind. When she was satisfied with the results, she took a breath, gathered her things inside of a brown paper bag, and made her phone call.

When Beaucoup heard the cell phone ring inside the Navigator, he asked his soldier to remain silent. "She told me to keep it on the low, so don't say shit. And let me borrow this phone until I'm done wit her."

The soldier allowed it without a word. What else could he do? It was a general's order.

"Hello," Coup answered the phone.

Leslie was straight to the point. "So where do we meet?"

Coup smiled at his soldier in the passenger seat and gave Leslie the name and address of the hotel where they would meet that night.

"What name will it be under?" she asked him.

"Ah . . . Butch James," Coup answered with a chuckle.

Then she warned him again, "And like I said before, if there's people around who like to talk . . . then I'm walkin'."

"Naw, this jus' between me and you," Coup told her while smiling to his soldier again.

Leslie didn't believe him, but it didn't matter. She realized their fate already. There was no way out. She had to do what she had to do to become who she would become.

She said, "All right, then. I'm getting ready now. Be there before ten."

Beaucoup hesitated. He never liked anyone giving him orders. But he smiled it off anyway. Leslie was different. She understood things. And Beaucoup liked her that way.

"Aw'ight, den," he told her. "I'ma go get da room now."

When he hung up the phone, Coup looked at his soldier and said, "I want you to go over there with me and stand outside on the corna like a bum or something, and watch her come in."

His soldier laughed and said, "Aw'ight." And they went to order the hotel room.

Leslie left her hideout room wearing the same ragged sweat clothes and baseball hat that she had walked in wearing. She carried a brown paper bag with her. She walked outside and to the bus stop to wait for the bus, while still exaggerating a ghettocentric swagger. She even gave a few onlookers a pair of rolled eyes until they looked away and stopped themselves from judging her.

She paid her fare and rode the bus to a stop that was two blocks away from Beaucoup's hotel. She then slipped into an alleyway to change her clothes. She hurried to pull off her dingy sweats, revealing black lingerie and hosiery. She let her hair out and pulled out her mask from Mardi Gras to cover her face. Then she folded up the sweat clothes and baseball hat to slide into the brown paper bag to hide. And when she walked out of the alleyway, she had transformed herself into a convincing hooker, with a small black purse at her side. The cars began to slow down accordingly to entice her. Leslie teased and ignored them in route to her destination.

Beaucoup's soldier eyed the mask-wearing hooker from the corner where he idly stood, and he turned up his nose to her. *She probably ugly as hell, that's why she got that mask on,* he assumed to himself. *I wouldn't fuck wit no hooker wit no mask on.* So he looked away from her while watching the streets for buses and taxis that may drop off Leslie, the college girl.

From behind her mask, Leslie sized up Beaucoup's lookout standing on the corner immediately. She slipped inside the hotel doors as soon as he had turned his head.

She moved swiftly to the front counter and whispered to the young Latina receptionist, "What room is Butch James in? I'm trying to be real discreet. Okay? I'on wanna make no scene in this nice hotel."

The receptionist got her point and went to send the woman on her way as quickly as possible.

"Room nine eleven," she whispered back. She tried hard not to stare when the scantily dressed woman in the colorful mask walked over to the elevators. And when it was over, the young receptionist shook her head and told herself, *It's none of my business what people do.*

Leslie rode the elevator up to the ninth floor and took a breath before she walked out.

Well, here goes my life, she told herself as she walked toward the room.

Beaucoup was already inhaling some potent marijuana smoke inside the room. When he heard the tap on the door, he reached for his pistol on the nightstand and neatly pushed it in between the mattress and box springs of the bed.

I don't trust no bitch to play wit me. If she comin' up in here, then she gon' get what I plan to give to her, he insisted as he walked toward the door and fondled himself. But when he looked through the peephole he became confused.

Who da fuck is that? he thought to himself of the woman in the Mardi Gras mask.

Leslie lifted her mask just enough to smile at him.

"Oh, shit! I thought you had the wrong-ass door for a minute," Coup told her as he unlocked the door to let her in.

Leslie walked in and placed her right finger to her lips. "Shhsh, don't tell nobody about this," she told him. "But I like to do a little fantasy acting. It just makes things more . . . interesting."

Beaucoup couldn't believe it! The girl was a real character. So he lost all of his reservations about her and started laughing out loud while the marijuana smoke invaded his lungs and his brain.

"Aww, shit! You like t' fantasize, hunh? Oh, we gon' have a good time in here then. I got a few fantasies for you to do," he told her.

Leslie dropped her small purse to the floor on the same side of the bed that Beaucoup had stuffed his gun under the mattress.

Meanwhile, Ayanna Timber sat in her seat at the jam-packed performing arts auditorium on Dillard's campus, listening to the various spoken-word poets that night before the headliner took the stage: Isis, the so-called War Goddess.

There was an extra loud applause from the crowd when she was introduced, which made Ayanna wonder what she had been missing.

Well, who is this chick? And how come I've never heard of her? she asked herself.

The brown-skinned, Afro-topped sister called Isis stepped on stage wearing a bright gold outfit as eye-popping as an Egyptian queen and just smiled at everyone as they continued to clap for her.

"Oh, thank you, thank you. You all are just too kind. Who paid you to do this?" she joked. "No, it's just really good to feel this kind of love rising up in the room, sister to sister, brother to brother, brother to sister, and sister to brother. Y'all know what I mean? That's love, the kind of love that we need up in here, y'all. Y'all feelin' me on that?

"I *said,* are y'all *feelin'* me on that?" she asked the crowd more intently for a louder response.

"YEAH!" the enthusiastic college students yelled to her.

She said, "Well, this is how we're gonna do this first poem. I say my part, then I point the microphone to y'all, and y'all say, 'We *feel* you!' Y'all got that?"

"Yeah!" they yelled up to the stage again.

She stopped and said, "Now y'all done messed that up already. Y'all supposed to say, 'We *feel* you,'" she reminded them. And everyone laughed.

Ayanna smiled herself, digging the sister's natural charisma and great stage presence. Isis was a true headliner. She understood how to move the crowd.

She grinned and said, "Okay, here we go," as she prepared herself for her first piece.

"I'm so tired of brothers braggin' about the ghetto," she said, and held the microphone out for the crowd to respond:

"We *feel* you!"

She grabbed her crotch onstage and added, "'Can I get a bitch? Can I get a ho?' . . . Nigga, hell no!" and held the microphone out to the crowd again.

They laughed and responded, "We *feel* you!"

"They want young sisters who get down for whatever but never up for the cause . . ."

"We *feel* you!"

". . . while fantasizing on bright blue eyes and straight blond hair . . ."

"We *feel* you!"

". . . but, um, not me, 'cause I see perfectly and refuse to go there . . ."

"We *feel* you!"

". . . is it because I'm too black, pushed to the back, and square . . ."

"We *feel* you!"

". . . or maybe, child, I just never found time to care about Barbie dolls who never bothered to represent *me* . . ."

"We *feel* you!"

". . . and where's *my* Kenny . . ."

"We *feel* you!"

". . . a *brown* one, with hair like *mine* that's *kinky* and *black,* and have him drive around my crib and pick me up in his lonnng Cadillac, with those plush, soft leather seats that recline waaaay back . . ."

The crowd continued to laugh and nod their heads as they responded, "We *feel* you!"

Ayanna smiled, enjoying herself in the crowd. *I like this. She's mad cool!*

At the same time, Leslie Beaudet was mad clever, while back at the hotel room with Beaucoup as they began to undress.

"So, how you want me to do you, baby? I got some real nice twists and twirls if you want it on top," she teased him in her hooker lingo.

Beaucoup started to laugh, feeling as if he was filming his own movie. Only chicks in those old seventies films said cool shit like that. So he decided to play his own pimp role in their mini movie.

"Well, put it on me, baby. Drive me crazy up in here. Let me see how much scratch you gon' make out on the streets for me, li'l momma," he told her in his own pimp lingo.

Leslie heard his words loud and clear as Coup slid on his oversized condom.

Okay, so he's really getting into this shit, she told herself. *And I'm gon' have his foul ass right where I want him.*

She took a peek at his monstrous tool and thought, *Damn! That shit looks like it's gon' hurt . . . But then I'm gon' hurt his ass . . . and he won't even feel it.*

When she finished undressing, she put the mask back on with her naked body and long, black hair. Then she asked him, "You want me to keep the lights on, baby, or turn nem off? 'Cause they hurtin' my eyes. We need to light a candle or something in here."

Beaucoup studied her curvaceous, dark brown body and couldn't believe that he was about to dig into her. *Damn, I can't believe this shit! I'm 'bout t' fuck 'er,* he told himself, while holding in his smile. A general could never appear too pleased with things outwardly. Too much expression tended to make people assume things.

He said, "Yeah, you can turn the lights off. But we don't need no fuckin' candles. You can jus' keep the shades open on the window, and let the light from outside shine up in here." He grinned and added, "Then I can check out the silhouette of your body while you fuck me. . . . And take that mask off too. I wanna see your face in here."

"Your wish is my command, baby," Leslie told him. She did everything that he had asked of her. And while she climbed on board his boat to set her plan in motion, Coup's soldier became impatient while standing outside on the corner. He was still waiting for a college girl to show.

"Man, this damn girl ain't showin' up f' dat nigga. She fuckin' wit 'em," he mumbled to himself spitefully. *I knew that shit didn't sound right. Why would she wanna fuck him? She ain't on no street game like that. She in college,* the soldier reasoned. However, he knew that Coup would order him to wait out there longer anyway. So he did.

As Leslie eased her way onto Beaucoup's tool with a wince, her father walked through the streets of New Orleans's Seventh Ward for the first time in years, in search of answers to life that would help him understand more, and hopefully track down his daughter before it was too late.

He walked through the broken, dirty streets of urban New Orleans, where they used high front steps and porches just to remain above the trash and mud level. And he realized that poverty itself was evil.

I re-member the same in Haiti as a child, he told himself. *And wherever there is hun-ger and des-pair . . . there will be death and murder.* Jean then remembered the black American boy, turned evil, whom he had cut into pieces with his machete knife for violating his daughter.

How evil was that? And how evil would Leslie be, now that she was a grown woman, who had never learned to accept the ghetto blues as passively as her mother, sister, and brother had? What would Leslie do, a child who had been robbed of peace and of human sunshine. What would she do when it became her turn to judge? And what would she do with *her* knife?

While Jean walked through the dark, merciless streets of "N'awlins" and asked himself the vital questions about his oldest daughter, Ayanna Timber sat up straight at Dillard University's auditorium to hear the poet Isis ask her own questions in an awakening poem:

"Whatever happened to the *Cornbread, Earl & Me* in our soul food? / I can't taste it now / not like I used to taste it / not like I wanna taste it / not like my momma tasted it / and my nieces and nephews never had a taste / . . . of revolution, y'all.

"Whatever happened to . . ." Isis stopped and yelled into the microphone dramatically, *"'They shot Cornnn-breaddd! They shot Cornnn-breaddd!'*

"But too many of us have never seen the movie," she added calmly, "and too many of us have forgotten how to revolt / not to just steal shit / For the Rodney Kings of the world / *No Justice, no peace!* / So let me take my piece / Well, how long will your stolen piece last? / As long as the white man's who stole America? / So what does that make you / thief number two? / I want what you owe me without stealing."

The crowd responded, *"Woe!"* and clapped their hands, while nodding in agreement.

She asked them, "Whatever happened to the red, the black, and the green? / Y'all don't know / Well, let me tell you / it's been replaced by the greenbacks, the white ice, and the platinum . . . Baby / bling-bling / do your thing / and make sure that your bitches and hoes got no clothes on / and no Common Sense / 'cause he never went platinum / he's only doing gold and hasn't crossed over to the new form of currency yet / Or will he? / We'll see / Nas did it / Nastradomously."

Ayanna smiled and mumbled, "Oh, that's low. She don't like Nas." *Nas is still conscious with his shit,* she mused. *He's just trying to compete for radio time. The radio stations don't play shit positive. I noticed that.*

Isis continued and asked: "Whatever happened to the 'hood that cared a lot / that shared a lot / the 'hood that said, 'This all we got, so let's make the best of it' / and when people got shot / we knew the criminals and turned them in / or not / ourselves?"

With that, Ayanna's heart began to race as she immediately thought of Leslie. *Did she kill that damn girl from Tulane?* Ayanna asked herself. *And if she did . . . would I turn her in? Or would she fuckin' kill me?*

The issue had still not been resolved. And Ayanna could no longer focus on the poetry as she slipped into her own thoughts and questions. *What am I supposed to be doing with my life?* she asked herself. It had not been the first time that she had asked herself that question. But the question was becoming more urgent, and beginning to take up a larger chip of space on her mind.

I can't jus' let her scare me into a fuckin' corner like . . . a mouse or something. I gotta fight her if I have to. I mean, shit, at least I fought for something, Ayanna reasoned. She concluded, *I would be fighting for my peace of mind . . . just like she's fightin' for hers.*

Ayanna felt . . . justified in her conclusion. A fight with Leslie was inevitable for her.

We jus' gon' have to get it on, then. Leslie's jus' gon' have to show me what she got!

But did Ayanna really want to witness the fire of Leslie's war? Could she handle it . . . ?

Just then, the poetic War Goddess named Isis seemed to instigate the fight on Ayanna's mind with the poem that her name was derived from.

She said, "Now, I'm giving y'all a fair warning," from up onstage. She said, "The brothers don't really like this poem. Especially the ones who know that they're doin' sisters wrong. They get all hot and flustered when they hear it. But here it goes anyway. It's called . . . *War!*"

The word hit Ayanna's ears and registered in her brain at the same time that she thought of war with Leslie, and she found herself able to pay attention again as the poet Isis prepared herself for her closing poem. She said sternly with the microphone in hand, "In what book / in what land / in what time / was it said . . . that / women would never shed blood . . . for freedom?"

As Isis spoke to the crowd at Dillard's auditorium, Leslie Beaudet rode Beaucoup into a pleasurable frenzy in his hotel room, while she chanted to him in her seductive French: *"Je vais te tuer comme le serpent que tu es."* I will kill you like the snake that you are. *"Tu ne mérites pas de respirer."* You don't deserve to breathe. *"Je vais te couper parfaitement."* I will cut you perfectly. *"Et je n'aurai pas assez de pitié pour te laisser crier."* And I will not allow you enough mercy to scream.

However, Beaucoup could not translate the language. And Leslie felt far too good for him to care as she rode him. It all sounded *great* to him. He had no idea what she had planned.

"Oh, shit!" he moaned to her uncontrollably. "Oooh, shit!"

I can't believe this bitch feel this good! he thought to himself. *Gotdamn! I'm dyin' and goin' to heaven in this bitch!*

How ironic were Beaucoup's thoughts at that moment. Although . . . heaven was a major question mark for him.

On Leslie's end, the sex hurt more than it pleased her. And she preferred it that way. The pain served to remind her of what she was there for.

≈

Isis, the War Goddess, continued with her poem to the students on Dillard's campus simultaneously with Leslie's ride.

She spoke with the fire in her own eyes. "Don't you realize that blood is shed from every mother / from every daughter / and to every child / born to this earth? / Life alone is revolutionary for a woman," she shouted to them.

While in the hotel room, Leslie felt Beaucoup just about to reach his climax, before she leaned over to the side of the bed for her purse.

"What are you doin'?" he complained, grabbing her back. "Don't do that right now."

But Leslie had already retrieved what she had leaned for, and she slid it into the sheets below his notice.

"I'm sorry," she lied to him. "You like it like this, baby?" she asked with a twist of her hips.

"Oooh, yeah," Beaucoup moaned and shut his eyes. "Ooh, shit yeah!"

Back at Dillard's auditorium, Isis stated, "We bleed constantly / for life / The woman was born for strife / and we accept the knife that wounds us daily / from our loved ones / as well as from our enemies.

"But lo and behold," she said, "if we were to use our knives / razor sharp from the pain of betrayal / then God help / the man / woman / and child / who may land on that fateful blade . . ."

"Ooooh, shit!" Beaucoup moaned in the hotel room when his climax took ahold of him. And how vulnerable was even the strongest man at the point of climax?

Isis said, "You betta pray / that you are fortunate enough / to die . . ."

Leslie seized the moment with her hidden blade in her right hand, and brought it down across Beaucoup's windpipe in one stroke that severed it before he could even blink.

Isis continued: ". . . from the haste of a man / rather than the slow / poking / blade / of a woman . . ."

As the blood began to squirt from Beaucoup's neck, he reached out with both hands and grabbed at Leslie's shoulders, while grabbing for her neck. But she had visualized his defense and was ready for him. So she brought her blade down into his right arm, causing him to release his hold upon her. She did the same to his left arm, as Isis continued with her poetry:

"The bitch stabbed me . . ."

Beaucoup thought those same words, but he could not speak them. He could only lean up in his last, desperate breaths to try and head butt or bite Leslie before he died, only to meet her strong left hand on his forehead, and feel her cold blade stab him one last time in his heart, before she pushed his head back into the soft, white pillow that had been stained with his fresh crimson blood.

And the War Goddess finished her poem as Beaucoup faded away from the living:

"The bitch shot me . . . / The bitch poisoned me . . . / the bitch burned me alive . . . / like / a pregnant mother / squeezing the fragile skull / of her infant child / between her legs / as he struggles to fight his way out from her womb / for a breath of life / that he finds denied him / as his mother snuffs out his air / with the entanglement / of her umbilical cord."

When Isis went silent, at the same moment as Beaucoup's life, the crowd moaned in unison, "Oh, shit!" as they all cringed.

And Leslie sat there at the hotel and watched the blood as it continued to leak from the lifeless body of her enemy . . . before she climbed off of him and walked into the bathroom . . . to wash off her bloodied blade . . . and her bloodied body . . . under warm shower water.

Leslie . . .

After her shower, Leslie retrieved her evidence from the room, including the cell phone that Beaucoup had carried with him. She slipped out of the fire exit of the hotel and made her way back to the alley to find her brown paper bag. Once she found it, she quickly pulled on her homely sweat clothes and baseball hat. She then tossed away the battery of the cell phone before she smashed the receiver beyond repair. She discarded the rest of the evidence in separate trash bins in the alley, including her Mardi Gras mask, before she calmly walked back to the bus stop to await a bus.

At his same corner, Beaucoup's trusted soldier was still waiting for Leslie to arrive.

"Shit!" he cursed himself for the seventh time. "This nigga's wastin' my whole night, out hea' waitin' f' dis girl." Then he thought to himself, *Maybe she was already in there waitin' for 'em or somethin', and that nigga jus' didn't tell me.*

So he walked to use a pay phone to call Coup on the cell phone that he had borrowed from him. But of course, his call was not received.

"Shit!" he cursed again. "Now what he do to my phone? Now if I leave here, he gon' get all mad about the shit, but in the meantime, I can't even fuckin' call 'im."

The soldier shook his head in defiance. "See, that's why I hate this motherfucker sometimes, man. I hate 'em!" Nevertheless, he continued to wait, because it was a general's orders.

≈≈≈

Back on Dillard's campus, Ayanna Timber nodded her head and was satisfied with the poetry performances she had experienced that evening, particularly those from Isis.

"That was phat. I was feelin' that shit. I'ma write me some deep poems like that," she told herself as she left.

She walked home that night, energized, and was accosted by two plainclothes police officers before she could reach the front door.

"Ayanna Timber?" the black officer asked her.

Ayanna looked and questioned him with her eyes. *Who are you?*

The officer read the question in her eyes and answered it. "I'm Detective Gilbert Hines, and this is my partner, Brian Willard."

The younger, white officer nodded to her and remained silent.

Ayanna asked them, "Yeah, and? What do you want from me?"

Are they gonna ask me about Leslie? she thought to herself. She knew that *she* had not done anything to warrant an investigation. However, she did have marijuana on her at the moment, and that made her nervous about them searching her or taking her in for anything. So she planned to go lightly and answer what they wanted.

"You live here with Bridget, Yula, and Leslie?" the black officer asked her.

Ayanna answered, "Yeah," and left it at that. She had a right to remain silent.

The black officer smiled to try and loosen her up. "You're into rap music, aren't you?"

Before Ayanna could answer him yes or no, he added, "Do you smoke marijuana? You know, weed, or blunts?"

She nearly swallowed her tongue as her heart jumped.

The young white partner smiled and said, "You don't have to answer that."

It was the good cop/bad cop routine, but Ayanna was in no position to challenge it.

The black officer pushed the question aside and said, "Well anyway . . . what can you tell us about Kaiyah Jefferson from Tulane University? She was over your house a few times with a video camera, right? You even freestyled on tape a bit," he commented.

His young partner smiled again, as Ayanna grew more apprehensive.

How much do they already know? she asked herself.

She answered, "Yeah, she . . . she wanted to tape us for a documentary."

"And *all* of you wanted to do it?" he asked her.

They both stared into Ayanna's face for her every answer. But she could read through their trap, deciding that her careful honesty would be the best policy.

"*Everybody* didn't wanna do it. *Bridget* wanted to do it," Ayanna hinted, taking the heat off of herself.

"What about Leslie? Did Leslie want to do it?" the young white partner asked. He had this . . . normalcy in his tone, but Ayanna knew better than to fall for that. She trusted neither of them.

She answered, "Everybody don't wanna be up on camera like that. I mean . . . *I* wanted to do it. But . . . you can't force people to do what they don't wanna do."

"At least not Leslie, right?" the young white partner commented again.

Ayanna took that and ran with it. "Well, ask *her,* then," she said, and headed for the front door.

The black officer said, "Where can we find her right now? We hear that you're the closest to her."

Ayanna shot them a look of doubt and asked, "Who told you that?"

They try'na bullshit me now! I am not the closest to Leslie, she argued to herself.

"From what we understand, you knew Leslie more than the others. You could pull her strings a little harder," the young white partner instigated.

"That's not true," Ayanna told them. *Nobody could pull that girl's strings,* she mused.

The black officer wrote his number down. He said, "Well, if you remember anything you might want to tell us, you make sure you give us a call."

She took the number and didn't budge until they had turned their backs to her.

"Have a good night's sleep," the young white partner said as they left.

Ayanna took a deep breath before she entered the house. As soon as she made it inside, she wanted some answers. She marched right up to Yula, who was sitting at the dining room table, and asked her, "Who told those cops that I was the closest in here to Leslie? I was never the closest to her. Bridget was the one always sweatin' that girl."

However, Yula didn't look the least bit moved by Ayanna's usual tirade. Yula said solemnly, "Eugene got killed last night."

Ayanna paused and said, "*Bridget's* Eugene?"

Yula nodded to her. "Yup."

Ayanna thought about it and said, "Damn. I didn't know he was out there like that. I just thought he was . . ."

"A pretty boy," Yula finished for her.

"Is that why those cops were here?" Ayanna asked her.

Yula shook her head. She said, "The black and white cops who wanted to talk to all of us were here for that girl Kaiyah from Tulane. But there were two other white cops that came here first, who wanted to talk to Bridget about Eugene."

"What, they thought she had something to do with it? She loved that boy," Ayanna stated.

"No, they were jus' asking her questions about him to try and figure everything out."

Ayanna just stood there inside the dining room. "Damn!" she finally repeated. "So how did Bridget take it?"

Yula shook her head again. "She went off. Then those second cops came here and started asking about that girl Kaiyah while the first two cops were still here. And when they started asking about Leslie . . . that's when Bridget jus' . . . she jus' lost it."

Yula looked into her roommate's face and concluded, "Something funny's goin' on, Ayanna. And I think . . . a lot of it has to do with Leslie. I mean . . . we don't have any proof, but . . . shit is just weird, man."

Ayanna found it hard to breathe at that moment. *Should I tell her what I know?* she asked herself. It was the moment of truth. She asked Yula, "Um . . . what do *you* think about Leslie?"

Yula took a deep breath of her own. She answered, "At first, I just thought that she was hardworking and private about herself. But now . . . I jus' don't know about her, man. I don't know who she is, really. She's just startin' to scare me. Because . . . some of the things that she says . . . I mean . . . it just don't seem like she's the same age as us."

Yula looked to Ayanna for understanding and asked her, "You know what I mean?"

Ayanna did know. Leslie had an old soul that was not at all playful. Ayanna took another breath and decided to finally tell what she knew. She was ready to reveal what Leslie had told her, even though she had been warned not to. So she opened her mouth to Yula and answered, "I know exactly what you mean. She—"

The kitchen telephone rang right on cue and scared the shit out of Ayanna!

"Shit!" she cursed out loud as she jumped with the ring of the telephone.

Yula looked toward the phone and said, "That's her. That's the same thing that happened the last time we tried to figure things out about her."

Yula was even terrified to ask the question, but she asked it anyway.

"You think that voodoo stuff is real?"

The phone rang a second time before Ayanna could answer.

"Get the phone, Yula," she responded to it.

Yula refused to be afraid. She stood right up and walked over to it. *I'm not gonna be afraid,* she told herself. *I'm not gon' be afraid of anything anymore. I won't live my life that way. Leslie was right about that. So I can't be afraid of her either.*

Yula answered the phone bravely. "Hello."

The caller on the other line listened for her voice before hanging up on her.

Yula paused and hung the phone up herself.

"What happened?" Ayanna asked her.

"They hung up."

"You think it was her?"

Yula thought it over. She doubted it. "That wasn't her," she answered. "Leslie's not the hang-up type. If she doesn't have anything to say . . . then she's not gonna call."

Ayanna nodded her head and agreed with Yula's logic. Leslie spoke her mind, or not, and that was that.

"So who do you think it was, then?" she asked.

"Her sister called here twice today. Her boss, Jake, called from the restaurant after the cops asked him questions about her. And her father called too. But I doubt if Jake or her father would hang up on me," Yula assumed.

"So you think it was her sister, then?"

Yula nodded and answered, "Probably. But I know one thing, Leslie's out there doing something . . . and I guess it'll all come out soon."

Ayanna nodded and thought, *Good. So I'll jus' keep what I know to myself then, and let it all come out on its own.*

≈≈≈

Laetitia walked away from the telephone at her place in the Desire projects in a fit of nerves.

Damn! Where is she? she continued to ask herself of her sister.

Jurron continued to watch her as she paced through the house, long after the girls had been put to bed. He asked her, "Yo, ah . . . what's wrong with you t'night?"

Laetitia heard his question loud and clear, but she ignored it.

Jurron became irritated and asked her more forcefully, "Tees . . . what da fuck is goin' on wit you?"

That's when Laetitia expressed herself to him. "Don't you curse at me," she told him. "Because if your ass would have shown me some respect in the first place instead of runnin' around wit all these bitches out here, then I wouldn't be thinkin' shit right now."

Jurron was floored by it! He had been good for weeks. And for what, to still be reprimanded for what he had done in the past?

He nodded his head and said, "Aw'ight, den," and stood up to walk out the door.

"Don't you leave here," Laetitia warned him.

"Well, what the fuck am I stayin' here for, if you don't appreciate me bein' here?" he snapped at her.

"I said, don't leave here," she warned him again.

Jurron studied her steel demeanor and told himself, *This bitch is crazy now. And I don't know what's goin' on wit her family and all but . . . I'm jus' gon chill.*

He calmed himself and told Laetitia, "I'm jus' goin' out to smoke me a cigarette, and you told me not to do it in the house, right?" And he waited for her approval.

Laetitia took a breath and huffed, "Yeah, okay. Go kill yourself, then. That's all those cigarettes are doin'. They're not making anything better for you. It's jus' slow poison."

Jurron said, "Yeah, well, let me go poison myself then," and he strutted out the door.

Laetitia thought about it and softened her approach.

"That was wrong," she told herself. "He's been trying lately."

But that's all he's been doin', she countered to herself. *We need more than that!*

Yet she still wanted him there with their young family. So she ran out to find him.

"Jurron! . . . *Jurron!*" she yelled from the project hallway as she approached the stairway. Her heart began to race as she sped up her step to track him down. *What if something happens to him because of me gettin' mad at him like that?* she panicked to herself.

"*Jurron!*" she screamed even louder as she ran down the stairs.

"I'm right here, girl," he finally answered from the bottom of the stair-case.

Laetitia took a deep breath and thought, *Thank God! Thank God!* She told him, "I'm sorry about that. I'm jus' worried about my sister right now, that's all."

Jurron took a drag from his cigarette and asked, "What's goin' on wit her?"

Laetitia knew that she couldn't go into any details with him.

"When I figure everything out, I'll tell you then. But I still don't know right now."

Jurron nodded. He said, "Leslie's smart. I'm sure she's all right."

Laetitia stared at him. She thought, *Yeah, I know she's smart, but being 'all right,' I don't know about that part. And I'm partly to blame for it. So I jus' . . . I jus' wanna tell her I'm sorry.*

But it was too late for sorries. Leslie realized *that* long before she made it back to her hotel room. Sorries never changed a damn thing! Either you were forgiven for your transgressions or you were forced to suffer the consequences of your actions.

Leslie planned to suffer the consequences. There would be no escape, and she would not choose to run from her punishment.

"Get ready to crucify me," she told herself as she lay back on her cheap hotel bed. *I just hope they learn something from it,* she told herself. *But most likely . . . they won't. They'll just make me into . . . another monster. So be it. I'll just be that monster, then . . . Fuck it!*

Outside on the corner of Beaucoup's hotel room where he lay cold and murdered in his blood, his soldier had finally given up on him. "Aw, fuck dis, man. He jus' gon' have to be mad at me, den. And I'll get my cell phone back from him t'mra," he told himself as he walked away.

He thought, *That nigga prob'bly embarrassed that she ain't show up anyway.*

≈≈≈

After the cleaning lady had screamed bloody murder and thrown up in the hallway, the three investigating officers could not believe what they saw in Beaucoup's hotel room when they arrived that morning.

"Christ! I've never seen a job done this . . . professionally from a woman," one of the officers commented.

"You call that professional? I call it insane," the second officer countered.

"So what did she do first, his throat, his arms, or his heart?" the lead officer asked rhetorically.

"Well, she left his main piece intact," the second officer joked of the bloodied and naked man.

"That's how she got to him," the lead officer responded. "So she probably slit his throat first, then his arms, then finished him off with one to the heart."

"Then she took a shower to wash away his blood," the first officer added as he looked into the bathroom at the used towel and washcloth.

"He was probably so damn high in here that he couldn't even feel it," the second officer said, as he inspected the marijuana that was left in the room.

"Oh, he felt it, all right. He just wasn't able to do anything about it," the lead officer countered. He said, "Well, what we do know is that our victim checked in here last night with cash under the alias of Butch James. Now let's find out who was working here last night when he checked in, and who came to see him."

At the end of their report, they came back with the description of a black hooker, wearing all-black lingerie, with long, dark hair, and dark eyes, wearing a colorful Mardi Gras mask.

"Well, I guess we start with the hookers then," the first officer commented.

"Hmmph," the second officer grunted. *Why even waste our time with this trash? Then again, I would love to meet the woman who did him in. She seems very . . . creative.* And he walked out with a slight grin on his face before the New Orleans news reporters began to barge into the hotel to break the story.

≋

Pierre Beaudet sat wide awake and was watching his color television set that morning when the news of Beaucoup's murder broke. However, Pierre was not watching the local news. He was watching the ESPN sports channel for the latest on college basketball. March Madness had begun in college hoops, marching right up to the Final Four tournament. It was a great way of taking his mind off of the recent events.

But Leslie wanted to make sure that he *did* watch the local news that morning. So she paged him as soon as the news hit the airwaves. She had been watching and was ready for it that morning.

Pierre called her back with hesitancy, but he did manage to catch her this time.

Leslie answered the hotel lobby pay phone where she had paged her brother. She responded, "Look at today's news and figure out how you protect your li'l sister."

That was all she planned to say before she hung up on him.

Pierre scrambled for his remote and clicked on the local news channels.

A black woman news reporter was at the hotel scene with live cameras rolling.

"Investigators say that we're definitely looking at a plotted homicide here. However, they've also stated that they don't have much to go on. Evidently, the woman suspect covered her tracks meticulously, which the investigators say would be unusual for a common, ah, hooker."

That was all that Pierre needed to hear. He clicked the television off and snapped, "Damn!"

Did Leslie *do that shit?* he asked himself. He remembered how terrified the Creole boy was the night before, when he had left Leslie alone at the hotel room.

"So, what did you tell his ass before he left?" Pierre remembered asking his sister that night.

And she looked into his face and said, "I told his ass that I would pray for him. Because if he really does that shit . . ."

"Damn!" Pierre snapped to himself again. He had always realized that Beaucoup had a crush on his sister. He could tell by how Coup talked about her.

So he tried to pull one over on Leslie after . . . they killed that boy . . . and then Leslie killed his ass, Pierre theorized. He knew that his sister had it in her. Just like their father, Jean, had it in him. Pierre still wondered how everything had been settled so smoothly years ago after his sister had been . . . violated on account of him.

"She got real close with Dad back then," he reminded himself out loud. *I mean, she had always been closer to him than the rest of us, but . . .*

"Damn!" he told himself one more time. It was just . . . unbelievable to him. But yet it fit Leslie. She had kicked ass constantly for Laetitia, to the point where girls in the neighborhood were afraid to even look at Leslie too hard. Not even many guys wanted to deal with her, regardless of her attractiveness. Only the boldest guys even asked about her, street generals like Beaucoup. And look where it had gotten him.

The next thing Pierre knew, someone was calling him on his cell phone.

He checked the number and saw that it was one of Beaucoup's soldiers.

Should I call these niggas back? he questioned himself. He knew they wouldn't have anything good to say to him. They had never liked him much anyway. And now Beaucoup was no longer there to protect him from them.

However, Pierre was curious. He needed more answers about what had gone on with his sister. So he called the soldiers back to act innocent about her.

"Yo, whassup? I jus' saw the news," he told them right off the bat.

"Yeah, and we need to talk to you about that shit, man."

Pierre hesitated. He didn't like their tone.

"Talk to me about what?" he asked them nervously.

"We'll tell you. Jus' meet us at the spot, man. We think we know who did it."

"Oh," Pierre uttered. "Aw'ight. When y'all want me to meet y'all there?"

"In a hour, man. And don't be late, either, nigga. This shit is serious. We need to handle this shit. So don't start actin' all scary on us. Ya heard?"

"Yeah, I hear you," Pierre responded. But when he hung up his cell phone, he knew better.

"Them niggas ready t' kill me," he mumbled to himself. *They must know that Leslie did it. Beaucoup must have told somebody. And they think I'm stupid. Or . . . they must think that Leslie wouldn't tell me.*

He pondered the whole situation. *I wonder if they would try t' kill Leslie for this after they got me?* he asked himself. *And why wouldn't they?* he concluded. *I don't put nothin' past them niggas. They'll do anything!*

He told himself out loud, "But you know what? . . . I ain't plannin' on runnin' no more. From nobody." And he began to make his own plans.

On the other end of the phone call, the four soldiers gathered to discuss their fallen general.

"So, you say that Coup was waiting for Pierre's sister last night?" they asked of the trusted soldier who was there.

"That's what I'm tellin' y'all, man," he answered in guilt-ridden disbelief. It was his fault for missing the setup. He said, "That bitch is wicked, man. I mean, I saw the hooker in the mask, and . . . you know, I blew the shit off. I thought it was jus' some ugly whore try'na hide her face out dere."

"Yeah, you couldn't have known that shit, man. She was jus' crafty," one of the others responded.

Will, the trigger man who had shot Eugene, was more thoughtful about exacting revenge.

He asked, "So, what do we do now? Kill Pierre first, and then hunt down his sister?"

The trusted soldier answered, "Naw. We call her up on my cell phone, 'cause I know she got that shit. The police would have answered my phone calls by now. And they found his gun. So we jus' wait for her to answer my shit. Then we tell her that we got her brother and try'da kill 'em both at the same time."

One of the other soldiers grimaced at the idea. He said, "Aw, man, that shit ain't gon' work. You think she gon' go f' dat shit? This bitch a killa, man. She prob'bly don't even care about her punk-ass brother like that."

"We'll see," the trusted soldier responded. "Seriously, though," he commented, "this girl Leslie ain't no joke. Coup was try'na do that same old okey-doke shit on her that he does on everybody, and she wa'n't goin' f' dat shit."

Will grinned and said, "You sound like you admire her."

The trusted soldier didn't speak on it, but he did admire Leslie. She simply did what she had to do to stop Beaucoup from owning her. That's what he would have done. Ownership was his way. It was the law of his jungle, to rule or be ruled. And Leslie had proven that she was the bigger beast.

"Anyway," the trusted soldier went on, "first we gotta catch up to this nigga Pierre, because I don't think he gon' show. But I think we'll find his ass before we find his sister. For all I know, this bitch could be dressed like a Gypsy next time we see her. Because I know she saw me out there."

The other soldiers laughed at it.

One of them asked, "Yo, but they *are* from Haiti, right? You think she did some voodoo shit on Coup last night?"

Will was the first to answer the question. He said, "Yeah, she did some voodoo on 'em. She sliced his ass up like a blood stew, that's what she did. But we got guns. So jus' don't let her get too close to ya' ass," he joked.

The trusted soldier said, "Coup had his gun wit 'em last night too. And that shit ain't do him no good."

Will said, "Yeah, 'cause he wanted some pussy from her and put his gun down. But I'm not try'na put my gun down. I'm gon' blow dat bitch head off like a voodoo doll."

They laughed again, but nervously. They realized they were not going up against an average, around-the-way girl. Leslie was extra. And they planned to treat her that way.

≈≈≈

Ayanna Timber saw the news report on Beaucoup while she was at the house on a break from school, and she immediately rushed into the bathroom to hurl.

"Oh, shit," she muttered over the open toilet as her stomach muscles contracted.

She killed him! she thought to herself. *She killed him!*

Her stomach forced her breakfast out of her. *"Uuuuggghhhh!"*

Bridget heard the commotion in the bathroom from behind her locked door, where she had remained in her room since receiving the jarring news on Eugene's death. She had become practically hypnotized by the new wooden voodoo doll that she had purchased during the Mardi Gras celebration. She continued to spin it left and right as she asked it through telepathy, *Come on, Leslie, tell me what I need to know. Tell me what I need to know, dammit!*

Bridget was too embarrassed by her possession to tell anyone what was on her mind. Leslie Beaudet, the voodoo girl, was behind it all. Bridget was certain of it. Eugene had been possessed by Leslie just like everyone else had been. He had asked about her constantly. Bridget knew in her gut that the two of them had been together. And when Eugene came crawling back to her and to leave Leslie behind . . . she had him killed, just like she had Kaiyah Jefferson killed. However, Bridget didn't have any proof of anything. And all of her wild assumptions had driven her to the edge of sanity, as she continued to curse the wooden voodoo doll.

Come on, you bitch! Tell me what I need to know! Tell me!

Outside of their house, the two plainclothes officers staked out for Leslie's return.

"You actually think she's gonna come back here, Gil, if she's guilty of something?" the young, white partner asked with a strawberry Danish to his mouth.

"You'd be surprised what people do sometimes, Brian. You'd really be surprised. That's why we're able to catch so many criminals. Humans are creatures of habit, just like the rest of the animals. And if she left anything here . . . eventually . . . she'll be back to get it."

He smiled and added, "That's if she hasn't left town already."

Brian smiled himself. He said, "I have this wild idea in mind right now that I don't think I should mention to you. You might think I'm racist for it."

Gil looked at his young, white partner and said, "Spit it out. I got over that white/black shit a long time ago. Criminals are just criminals, and that's all they are."

Brian nodded his head and said, "Okay, then . . . Well, this new murder on the news about this alleged hooker with long black hair and dark eyes . . . Let's just say . . ."

Gil beat him to it and said, "No way. That's not just racist, Brian, that's space invader X-Files shit. What have you been smokin', brother?"

"See, that's why I didn't wanna mention it," Brian responded with a chuckle. "But it fits her description, and what we saw of her on the video. I mean, we could at least show her picture down there at the hotel."

Gil looked at him and joked, "So, I guess you wanna blame this one black girl for the crash of the stock markets too."

Brian shook his head and said, "I should have known better."

"You damn right you should have known better."

"Well, she *was* missing last night, with no alibis."

"Yeah, but we're talking about a college girl, and not a damn hooker, Brian. We don't know that this girl has done anything yet."

Brian eyed his veteran partner and countered, "I thought we were talking about a murder suspect who just happens to go to college."

Gil countered, "Well, how about this one, Brian? Let's call her a college girl, who may have been an accomplice to a murder on the streets where she grew up?"

They both paused for a stare-down before they looked away at a female student walking up the street toward Dillard's campus. Once they realized that it was not Leslie, they allowed themselves to have private thoughts about each other.

Gotdamned white boys think that every black person is guilty, Gil thought to himself. *And I'm not saying that this girl is not, but let's prove it first.*

Brian thought to himself, *Yeah, he thinks I'm racist. I should have just kept my big mouth shut. But I'll know for the next time. Then again . . . this would be a lot easier if I had a partner who I didn't have to play the politically correct game with. That stuff just gets in the way of police business.*

Miles away, Courtney Taylor made his own conclusions about the recent murders.

He smiled broadly while thinking it all over. Then he rubbed the naked scar on his left side.

"A hooker wit long black hair and dark eyes, hunh?" he repeated to himself from the news reports. "Mmm hmm. I was right not to fuck wit dat girl again," he mumbled to himself.

Looks like Bo-coup *ran into her blade now,* he mused. *But he didn't survive the shit like I did.*

"I guess he musta thought she was soft like her brother," Courtney commented out loud. "But he didn't know . . . Leslie a bad bitch!"

He chuckled to himself and said, "I guess that nigga know now. And it's too late for his ass."

≈≈≈

Beaucoup's soldiers waited for Pierre to show up at their meeting spot on the east side of New Orleans.

"Man, that motherfucka ain't gon' show. He know we 'bout to kill his ass. He ain't that damn stupid," one of them commented impatiently.

The trusted soldier was the lead thinker now. He said, "We gon' wait a li'l longer anyway. And then we gon' go lookin' for 'em. And when he don't show . . . that'll give us more a reason to kill his ass for bitchin'."

Will, the fast-trigger man, smiled and began to laugh. He said, "Yeah, I like that idea right there. And I'ma be the first to shoot 'em."

The trusted soldier looked and thought, *This nigga must think we in a Western movie or some shit. This ain't Clint Eastwood.* But before they left the area in search of him, Pierre showed up wearing a heavy dark jacket.

"Speak of the devil," Will commented with a sinister grin.

Pierre didn't seem too jovial at the moment. He asked them, "So, who y'all think did it?"

No one commented immediately. The lead soldier suggested, "Let's take a ride. We'll talk about it."

"A ride to *where?*" Pierre asked him, standoffish. He realized how close the trusted soldier had been with Beaucoup, and Pierre wasn't budging to take a ride with them. So they all watched him in his stance to see how they could gain his trust. He seemed to be on guard with them.

Will finally spoke up and said, "Look, nigga, if we wanted to do sump'in to you, we wouldn't take you for no ride, we'd jus' do the shit right here."

Pierre looked him dead in the eyes with newfound courage and said, "Do it, then." He opened his jacket and revealed two black nine-millimeter pistols that were jammed into the left and right sides of his waistline.

"Aw, nigga, you ain't gon' *use* 'em, so what you pullin' 'em out for?" one of the soldiers dared him.

Pierre took a quick breath before he pulled out both of his guns and aimed them. He then fired four shots into the soldier's chest with the steadiness of an assassin.

BOP! BOP! BOP! BOP!

"Shit!" The other soldiers reacted and moved for cover.

Oh, this nigga came out hea' for war, in broad daylight. I like dat! Will thought to himself as he dodged behind their car and pulled out his own gun.

Once Pierre had felt the rush of adrenaline from shooting the first soldier,

he aimed at the second soldier as he began to run, and gunned him down in
his back.

BOP! BOP! BOP!

The fuck has gotten into him? the lead soldier asked himself as he scrambled behind the car with Will. *I guess he jus' woke up this morning and got ti'ed
of bein' a punk!*

"You had your Wheaties this morning, hunh, Pierre?" he yelled, trying
to lighten the mood.

Will laughed at it himself as they both crouched low behind the car for
cover.

Pierre responded, "You can say dat. Some ma-fuckas jus' won't let you
live in peace. I know that now."

The lead soldier listened to Pierre's logic and was convinced of his
assumptions. *This boy gon' kill all of us. I guess he got his sister's blood in him after
all,* he thought.

Then he realized that it was broad daylight. They couldn't just have a
shoot-out there without anyone reporting it to the police. Maybe that would
scare Pierre off long enough to get the hell out of there. So the lead soldier
began to shoot his gun recklessly into the air for someone to report it.

"What the fuck are you doin'?" Will asked him.

"Look, man, we need to regroup. This nigga serious. I wasn't expectin'
that. Neither was you," he responded to his trigger-happy friend.

"Aw, man, he's just one nigga, man. Fuck dat! He a punk! The same
punk that was afraid to shoot two nights ago."

"Yeah, well, in case you ain't noticed, this ain't two nights ago. And I'm
gettin' the fuck outta here," the lead soldier refuted.

Will snapped, "Aw, fuck dat. This nigga ain't gon' *punk me.*" So he rose
up from behind the car with his gun and aimed to fire at Pierre, and missed
all three shots.

POP! POP! POP!

But Pierre didn't miss. He stood as steady as if he had a shield around
him and continued to fire without any cover.

BOP! BOP! BOP! BOP! BOP!

The lead soldier looked up and witnessed Will's body jerk in five different
directions. All five of Pierre's bullets struck their mark, hitting Will in the
shoulder, chest, face, head, and then his neck as he fell backward and hit the
ground.

Gotdamn! the lead soldier panicked. He desperately fired two more shots
into the air.

"Hey, Pierre," he called out, "it's jus' me and you now, man. We don't have to do this. The cops are gonna be comin' soon anyway." He could already see cars and bystanders beginning to gather in the short distance.

He said, "Yo, man, your sister jus' did what she had to do. Ya heard? I mean, that's just part of the game, man. Beaucoup got fucked up last night, but I can go to the grave wit it, man. That's the code of the streets; you win some, you lose some."

Pierre said, "It's too late for that, man. It's too late for all of us."

The soldier stopped and listened for the police sirens approaching.

He said, "Look, man, we still got time to get outta hea', Pierre. You go your way, and then I'll go my way. Come on, man, before the cops get here."

With that, Pierre opened fire on the car from where he stood on the other side of it.

BOP! BOP! BOP! BOP! BOP! BOP!

Glass and debris were flying everywhere as the bullets got closer and closer until the remaining soldier gave up on his plea.

This nigga's gon' stone crazy! he told himself of Pierre as he gritted his teeth.

"Aw'ight, den! You really wanna go out dis way? Well, let's do it, then!" The last soldier leaped to his feet and aimed his gun, only to meet the onslaught of Pierre's bullets that were already aimed in his direction.

BOP! BOP! BOP! BOP! BOP!

The New Orleans officers arrived at the scene in their squad cruisers just in time to witness Beaucoup's trusted soldier join him in death from the unleashed fury of the Beaudet family.

"Christ!" one of the officers cried as they climbed out of their cruisers and took cover behind their own cars.

"Put the gun down and walk away with your hands up!" they told him.

But instead, Pierre aimed both of his guns at his own temples.

"No way," one of the officers commented.

Pierre mumbled to himself in French as he took deep breaths and contemplated his fate. *"Je suis désolé ma belle sœur."* I'm sorry, my beautiful sister. *"Pardonne-moi je t'en prie."* Please forgive me. *"Je ne t'ai pas protégée comme un frère."* I have not protected you like a brother.

"What is he saying?" one of the police officers asked in confusion.

"It sounds like French," the other officer responded, as several more cruisers rushed to the scene.

However, Pierre continued as if there was no crowd watching him.

"C'est pour toi, Lez." This is for you, Lez. *"Je peux mourir comme un homme maintenant."* I'm able to die a man now.

One of the officers had a desperate thought in mind to shoot the young man in the leg to stop him from his madness. But Pierre pulled both triggers of his guns before the officer could execute his plan. And the gathered crowd watched the scene in horror as it ended dramatically.

BLAUWW!

. . . The
Tragedy. . .

While the two investigating officers, Gilbert Hines and Brian Willard, continued to stake out their assignment into the early afternoon, Bridget finally decided to make her move from the house.

She called her father at his office in Ann Arbor, Michigan.

"Dr. Chancellor's office," the receptionist answered.

"Hi, Gloria, it's Bridget."

"Oh, hi, Bridget. How is everything at school? You'll be coming home soon for spring break, won't you? Or are you going on vacation at the beach or something? That would be nice, right?"

Bridget was not really up for the chattiness. She thought, *Yeah, if I still had someone to share it with.* She responded, "We'll see. But can I speak to my dad, please?"

"Oh, of course. I'll get him right on the line."

Her father answered the phone with concern. It was the middle of the day, and fortunately, he was not busy with a patient at the moment.

"Hey, honey, is everything all right?"

Bridget paused. "Um . . . I'll tell you about it when I get back home. But I'm calling to tell you that I need my own apartment down here. Things are not working out."

"With the roommates?"

"Yeah."

"What are some of the issues you're having?"

Bridget sighed and answered, "I really don't feel like going into all of that right now, Dad. I just need you to send me the money as soon as I find out how much it'll cost me."

"You mean, how much it'll cost *me*," he corrected her.

"Dad, please. Trust me on this. It's worth it. I just . . . I just don't feel like talking about it right now. I don't even know if I wanna finish going to school here," she added.

"Wait a minute," her father responded, "is it all that bad?"

"Yes," Bridget answered without hesitation.

Her father thought it over. "Okay, I'll wire you the money or overnight you a check, but I really want to talk to you about this. Okay? Have you spoken to your mother yet?"

"No, but I'll call her. I just wanted to make sure that you would help me first."

"Well, of course I'll help you. Especially if it's going to affect your studies down there. And I only have one daughter. I love you, honey," he told her.

Bridget was able to smile again.

"Thank you, Dad. I'll call you and Mom later on when I'm ready to talk about it."

"I'll tell your mother to expect the call."

When they hung up, Bridget felt spirited enough to finally come out from her room. She walked to the bathroom, where Ayanna had locked herself in, and asked her what her problem was.

"You're not pregnant are you?" Bridget assumed, speaking to Ayanna through the locked door.

"No," Ayanna answered her weakly.

Bridget was not in the mood to continue the conversation, so she went on about her business and walked downstairs for the first time that day to try and eat something.

Outside the house in their unmarked car, the two officers continued to wait, until Gilbert came up with a stretch of an idea.

"You know how to catch a fox in a hole?" he asked his young partner.

Brian looked at him blankly, and was uninterested in playing guessing games.

So Gil finished his punch line himself. He answered, "You let the fox run *in* the hole first," and he ignited the car engine. "Let's take a ride around the block and get some Arizona iced tea or something."

Brian smirked and remained silent.

Sure enough, as soon as their car disappeared around the corner, Leslie, who had been watching them from down the street, wearing a dark jacket and a fisherman hat, quickly made her way to the house and pulled out her key.

Bridget turned her head from the dining room table, where she tried to force down a bagel smothered with cream cheese, and a small glass of orange juice. When she saw that it was Leslie, her eyes grew wide. Yet she was too surprised by it to budge. She didn't expect to see Leslie at the house again. She hoped that the police would catch her first.

"Hi, Bridget." Leslie spoke good-naturedly.

Bridget just . . . stared at her and didn't know what to say.

Ayanna heard Leslie's voice from upstairs in the bathroom, and she froze herself.

Oh shit, she's here! She panicked, while holding her stomach tight.

Downstairs, Bridget finally managed to open her mouth to Leslie.

She asked her, "*Why?* Why are you *doing* this to people?"

Leslie took off her jacket and fisherman hat to reveal a deep blue, off-the-shoulder blouse to complement her blue jeans. She appeared as if she was ready for a hot date and hadn't harmed a fly.

She looked at Bridget with confusion and asked her, "What are you talking about?"

But Bridget was determined not to be swindled by her anymore. "Cut the bullshit, Leslie. You know what you've been doing," she snapped at her.

"And what *have* I been doing?" Leslie questioned her as she approached Bridget at the table. She didn't appear threatening at the moment. Nevertheless, Bridget stood and moved away from her.

"I know what you are," she responded. "You're one of them people. Voodoo. You're one of them. That's why you want everything to be a secret. It's a part of your sect. People like you always want things in secret. That's why you speak French around us when you do. It has nothing to do with the language, it has all to do with who you are. And the cops are going to find you."

Leslie looked at her terrified roommate with pity in her eyes.

"What is wrong with you, Bridget? What are you talking about? Are you sick or something? How come you're not dressed for school?" She continued to move toward the poor girl as Bridget rounded the table to stay away from her.

"Bridget knows what she's talking about. You're a priestess. You told me so with your own mouth," Ayanna revealed. She descended the stairs with every bit of courage that she could gather.

And Leslie stood still . . . and silent.

She spoke without facing Ayanna and changed her light tone. "I told you that I would hurt you, too, right? Well . . . I'm gonna *keep* my promise."

However, when she turned to face her housemate, Ayanna pulled out a blade, six inches long.

Leslie looked at it and smiled at her. "I don't even need anything to deal with *you*."

"Well, come on then, *bitch!*" Ayanna screamed, forcing herself into a fight.

Leslie approached her with her hands down. "Do you even know how to use that?"

"We'll see," Ayanna answered. Nevertheless, she backed up as Leslie came near her.

"Use it, then," Leslie challenged her.

Bridget continued to watch them from the dining room.

Ayanna took a breath and talked herself into charging Leslie with the knife. But Leslie sidestepped her amateur stroke with ease.

"Stupid," she told Ayanna as she grabbed her knife-wielding hand at the wrist with her right hand. She then began to slug Ayanna in the face with her left fist.

"Ahh!" Ayanna yelled as she struggled to free herself from Leslie's grip. *"Bridget, help me! Help me!"*

Bridget was not used to much physical combat. She had used only her words, her family wealth, and her intellectual cunning with the white girls of Ann Arbor. But this was New Orleans, and Ayanna and Leslie were both from the hard-edge streets of more urban territory.

So Bridget charged without much skill involved, only to meet Leslie's left foot to her stomach as she tumbled backward and into the dining room chairs.

"Unnhh!" she moaned as she crashed to the floor.

However, Bridget's clumsy attack was enough of a diversion for Ayanna to drop the knife and twist her hand free to strike Leslie with her own fists. And as soon as she was free, she rushed Leslie into the sofa and began to whale on her as if her life depended on it. And it did!

"Bitch!" Ayanna yelled out as she struck out at Leslie again and again against the sofa.

Leslie seemed only amused by it. She blocked the majority of Ayanna's wildness with her shielding arms. She raised her right foot and kicked Ayanna in her stomach, sending her flying across the room.

"Uugghh!" Ayanna panted as Leslie forced the wind out of her with her kick.

"Is that all you got, Ayanna? I thought you was from the southwest side of Houston. Y'all ain't shit, then, if you really representin'."

Ayanna became inflamed, even without the proper oxygen filling out her lungs, and she charged Leslie again, only to catch a right fist to her mouth, a left fist to her head, and an elbow to her back before she violently hit the floor.

Shit! Bridget thought to herself as she watched the ass kicking that Leslie was giving to Ayanna.

"You've been wantin' this for a long time, haven't you?" Leslie taunted as Ayanna squirmed across the floor in pain.

I can't let her do this, Bridget told herself. So she climbed back to her feet and fought with what she was good at, her use of clever words.

"This won't make you feel any better about yourself, Leslie. You'll still be miserable! Even if you kill all of us. Have you thought about that? It won't change anything for your sorry ass!" Bridget hollered from her safe distance.

"Neither will all your father's money, bitch!" Leslie spat back at her.

"You wish you *had* my father's money, don't you? That's what your problem is. You're just a *broke bitch* who's mad about it!" Bridget countered. "And I don't have to bust *my ass* to get *mine!* Is that why you hate me so much?"

And Leslie . . . began to laugh. It was humorous to hear Bridget tell the truth for once.

Leslie shook her head and said, "That's how you've felt all along, ain't it? You wanted to do good by taking in some li'l ghetto girls to make you feel like you were worth something. But you ain't worth shit, Bridget. And you know that. That's why you hung on your li'l Creole man so much.

"You really wanna be white, don't you, Bridget?" Leslie asked her. "Or as light as you can get. Because you're ashamed of being black. And you're always trying to find a way to feel better about it. Well, guess what, bitch . . . you ain't never gon' *be* white, no matter how much you *try!*"

Bridget felt a deep mourning inside as Leslie beat her at her own game. And when she found nothing else to counter with, she shouted, "Fuck you! I know you killed him. Because nobody loves your evil ass! And I hope God sends you straight to hell! You *witch!*"

Ayanna finally gathered herself from the floor and reached to grab Leslie's legs in the distraction. They both tumbled to the floor in a mad scramble for a position to strike. And instead of waiting again, Bridget jumped in the middle of it to try and help Ayanna out in battle.

Meanwhile, Yula Frederick headed on her way home from campus with determined thoughts on her mind. *I don't care what's going on with Leslie, I'm gon' keep doin' what I need to do,* she told herself. *These are the best grades that I've had in my life, and not Leslie or no one else is gonna stop me from keepin' them! So if Bridget and Ayanna wanna let this affect them where they stop going to school and whatnot, then that's* their *problem.*

Yula had no idea that Ayanna and Bridget could use her help at that moment. They were both getting their asses kicked at the house.

Leslie catapulted Ayanna into the wall with the force of both of her legs from the floor.

BLOOM!

"Ahhh!" Ayanna squealed as her back hit the corner of the wall between the living and dining rooms.

Leslie then wrestled Bridget into a choke hold where she could beat her face and smash it into the floor. "I'm gon' give you a ass kickin' like you've never seen before!" she snapped as she began to beat Bridget with her right hand, while holding her down with her left.

"Ahhh! Help me, Ayanna! Help me!" Bridget pleaded desperately.

Leslie sent the girl's delicate face into the hardwood floor and busted her lip open against her teeth. And Ayanna was helpless to assist, while she squirmed from her own injury.

"Ahhh!" Bridget continued to holler as fresh blood ran freely from her mouth.

Yula felt something stirring as she reached the house, and she quickened her pace to get in.

The two police officers rounded the corner of the block just in time to see Yula hustling up the patio steps with her keys in her hands.

"You see that?" Brian asked Gil.

"I'm right on it," Gil told him. He slammed the squad car into park out in the middle of the street, and his young partner beat him out of the car as they both scrambled toward the house.

Yula made it inside just in time to witness Leslie sending Bridget's face to the floor again.

Yula didn't hesitate for a minute! She rushed straight for Leslie and sent a violent forearm to her head, sending Leslie flying from Bridget's back and into the same dining room chairs that Bridget had knocked over earlier.

"You wrong, Leslie. You wrong!" Yula told her as she continued to rush Leslie with her superior weight, size, and strength.

Leslie tried to figure out how to counter Yula's size, but there was not enough room left to escape her. So she desperately clawed at Yula's eyes with her nails.

Yula blocked it with her left arm, and slammed the entire force of her body into Leslie's, sending both of them into the dining room wall.

BLOOM!

Leslie's head slammed into the wall, as Yula refused to give her any space to fight back with. She held Leslie there against the wall with her left forearm, and came down with a right-handed fist, pounding Leslie's head into the wall again, right as the two officers forced their way into the house.

"You *wrong!*" Yula continued to yell as she smashed Leslie with her powerful blows.

And when Leslie's head hit the wall a third violent time behind Yula's determined force, she slid to the floor unconscious . . . and the fight was over.

Seeing Leslie knocked out cold, Ayanna grabbed her knife from the floor and attempted to finish her off before she awoke.

The young officer, Brian, grabbed her arm before she could stab Leslie with her knife.

"What the hell are you doing?" he reprimanded her. "Do you wanna spend time in prison? The situation is in hand."

"No-o-o!" Ayanna screamed at him in a rage. "You can't take that bitch to jail! You gotta kill 'er. You gotta kill her! She can still get us from jail!"

Yula looked at her hysterical friend and understood what she meant. None of them really knew the extent of Leslie's power. Nevertheless, Gil was already securing his handcuffs around Leslie's wrists before more harm could be done to any of them. He then looked to Bridget, who was still conscious. Her bloody mouth had bled all over the floor. She appeared to be in shock.

When the police backup arrived with an emergency ambulance, Brian was given more breaking news from the police station dispatch.

Gil looked toward his younger partner and awaited the news.

"What is it?" he asked, as soon as Brian had received the details.

Brian answered, "A Pierre *Bo-day* just shot and killed four armed thugs on the east side, near the Intracoastal Waterway." He paused and added, "Before he blew his own head off with two nine-millimeters."

Gil winced and said, "Her brother."

"And the plot gets thicker," Brian responded to him.

≈≈

Over the next few hours, Gil and his partner created a hypothetical scenario of events regarding Leslie Beaudet's case for their superiors at the station, while armed policemen guarded over their injured suspect at the hospital.

"Okay," Gil addressed everyone. He had written the names and dates in a tree of events on a white board with his black marker.

He began: "Our suspect's mother, Anna-Marie *Bo-day,* dies of AIDS, and she's obviously ashamed of that, so she doesn't tell her roommates how her mother really died. Then Kaiyah Jefferson comes along with her documentary project from Tulane and hounds the roommates to share her personal information. Our suspect finds that out, and sends Kaiyah Jefferson into a death trap in her old neighborhood in the Seventh Ward. Meanwhile, Bridget, the roommate, unknowingly competes with the suspect for the affection of Eugene Duval from Xavier, and when the suspect loses the fight for him, she has him killed by our group of dead thugs, led by Mr. Beaucoup, and accompanied by the suspect's brother, Pierre."

Brian smiled, happy to know that he was not off on his earlier hypothesis.

Gil continued at the white board: "Well, after killing Eugene Duval, Mr. Beaucoup wanted his ah . . . payoff inside the bedroom. So our suspect shows up at his hotel room dressed as a hooker, and she gives him a little more than he had bargained for."

"I thought they found a gun at the scene," one of the superiors questioned.

Gil answered, "Well, with the group of guys that Mr. Beaucoup ran with, he's likely to always have a gun near him, business *or* pleasure."

The superiors nodded.

"Okay, continue," they asked of Gil.

Gil said, "Well, after Mr. Beaucoup's group of thugs heard the news about him being turned into a spaghetti and meatball sandwich with plenty of sauce, they knew exactly who did it, and they wanted to let the brother know. The brother, Pierre, who was not known on the streets to be, ah . . . of a violent nature, showed up with a surprise for them, and took them all out to protect his sister. Then he decided to kill himself rather than to be taken in, which of course . . . would have incriminated himself and, more importantly . . . it would have eventually led to the incrimination of his sister, and our suspect . . . *Leslie Bo-day."*

The superiors nodded their heads and were impressed with it.

"Well, now you have to go back out there and prove it," the chief concluded. "Did you do a second questioning of the roommates? They should be ready to talk now. Everyone heard about the big catfight you guys broke up over there."

Brian chuckled with his superiors and answered, "That's next on the menu. But that's the one thing that I still can't figure out," he commented. "Why would she come back to the house, and to the only people who knew enough to convict her?"

"She wanted to be caught," the chief answered immediately. "This doesn't look to me, or to you, as you just explained to us, to be a case of, 'Oh, God, I killed someone! Let me cover up my tracks.' This is a case of deliberate and plotted murder. She's out to make a statement. 'Don't fuck with me, or I'll kill ya!'"

They all shared another chuckle to lighten the load of their hard-line work before the lieutenant raised a question of his own.

"Now, what about this voodoo crap we're hearing about, Gil? Can you substantiate any of that?"

All eyes were directed toward Gilbert, the only black man in the room.

Gil answered hesitantly, "She has a Haitian immigrant father, *Jahn-Pierre Bo-day,* who stays at a New Orleans homeless shelter, and a younger sister, *Lateesee-ah,* who lives in the Desire projects with two young children and their father. Her family has been known to speak fluent French. But the only voodoo that we're able to substantiate from the interviews we've conducted about Leslie is that she's highly intelligent, introspective, and driven."

The three white men in the room—including his partner, Brian—all listened to Gil's calm explanation, but they were honestly unsatisfied with it.

Oh, spare us the poverty excuse and this intelligence crap, Gil. We didn't ask you for that. Is there such a thing as voodoo, *or what? That's what we wanna know. You're black, aren't you? So tell us what you really know about it,* they all wanted to follow up and ask him. But instead, since Gil was a respected professional on the force, they decided to leave him alone about it and maintain their own professionalism with a nod of political correctness.

And as Gil stood there in front of them with his hypothesis still on the board, he thought, *Every morning I wake up and ask myself,* Whose side are you on? *And I honestly still don't know sometimes.*

. . . and Legend

Gil and his young partner followed up on their case by questioning the roommates again at the station. But with Bridget Chancellor's injuries, and the immediate contact she had made to her father, who was already en route to New Orleans with a lawyer, there was a slim-to-none chance of speaking to her that night. However, Ayanna and Yula didn't have the same protection and counsel that Bridget could afford. So they sat nervously at the New Orleans police station behind a rectangular table, awaiting their next line of questioning.

Neither one of the girls was sure of what they wanted to say, how much they wanted to say, or if they should say anything at all with Leslie still alive.

Brian sat across the table from them as Gil stood and cleared his voice to speak.

"Now, we all understand that this has been a very . . . difficult experience for you with everything that's happened. But we still have some questions that need to be answered, and we cannot help you to feel, ah . . ." He searched for the right words to use and came up with, "Safe from your fears, unless you tell us everything that you know."

The officers already knew some of the information, but the roommates would know more of the details that were still crucial to tie all of the loose pieces together.

Yula looked to the young partner, who remained seated and silent across the table from her. He took in her reaffirming look and nodded to her. It was okay to talk. However, Yula still did not know how much she would say, and Ayanna remained unconvinced that talking about Leslie would do any good. It seemed that it would only irritate the matter, as if picking at an unhealed wound.

However, Yula took a deep breath to overcome her fears. She told herself that it was the right thing to do to unravel the whole story from point A. And she looked at no one in particular when she commented, "Leslie always liked to challenge people. It was like . . . you know, she wanted to see if she could break you down all the time. She always tried to test you to see how strong or weak you were."

Yula looked into Gil's eyes to see if he understood her. And he did. In fact, he had to force himself not to look at his partner when he thought, to himself, *Just like white people. No matter how much I prove myself, they still feel a need to test me. And I'm not saying that I'm a perfect investigator by any stretch of the imagination, but neither are they.*

However, he kept his personal thoughts to himself, and continued to listen to Yula.

"In a way," she continued, "Leslie made us all stronger by it. I know she made *me* stronger."

Ayanna had heard enough already! They were there to help convict Leslie and to put her ass away, not to compliment her character. Yula seemed to be going in the wrong direction.

Ayanna cut her off and said, "She was a fuckin' control freak. She always had to have it her way. And when she couldn't get it, she'd always try to fuckin' scare you with something."

Yula countered, "Everybody wants their own way. You're gonna tell me that you don't."

"Yeah, but I didn't act like she did about it."

"Because you're not her," Yula responded.

Brian sat there listening to the bickering between the two girls and thought to himself, *This is gonna take all night unless Gil asks them exactly what we need. Where was Leslie during the murders? How did she get along with the victims before they were killed? And did she make any disparaging comments about them prior to their deaths?*

That's what Gil needs to be asking them, Brian snapped to himself.

He became so distraught about it that he decided to ask his own question.

"Do either of you believe that Leslie was capable of killing someone?"

And the room became . . . silent.

The girls were hesitant to voice that kind of truth, especially to a police officer.

Gil immediately sized up the situation. He realized that his young partner had made a false move. He said, "Anyone is capable of killing under the
right circumstances." He didn't want to shut the girls down by asking them
the obvious. They would have to take things slowly.

Eventually, the officers got around to asking the girls more specific
questions. They received some of the answers that they wanted. However,
Leslie had still been too meticulous to leave more convicting clues, and the
voodoo comments that Ayanna Timber made were so . . . far-fetched that
the officers figured that it could hurt their case more than help it, depend-
ing on the views of the judge and jury, which left too much to chance.
They wanted to convict Leslie on premeditated murder, period, and leave
all of the other spooky business out of the courtroom.

"So, what do you think?" Brian asked Gil after they had allowed the girls
to leave.

Gil paused for a minute. He said, "This is going to be one of the
more . . . interesting cases in the history of New Orleans. There's just a
whole lot of elements going on here."

Brian paused himself before he chuckled at it. "I think you're going a
little overboard there, Gil. We're finding what we need to know, slowly but
surely, and this girl will eventually trot off to jail for a long sentence like the
rest of the criminals who get caught. Shut and closed."

Again, Gil kept his thoughts to himself. But one thing was certain for
him . . . American law had always been unequal. And he had served enough
years on the police force to know.

≈

With so many murders all in proximity, and the hypothesis floating around
of their connection to one female suspect, Leslie Beaudet (a Dillard University sophomore studying in international business), as the ringleader, the
New Orleans media became desperate to jump the gun on whatever story
angle they could create to stay ahead of the competition, and long before all
of the facts were in. Once the white-owned and -operated mediums of
human sensationalism caught on to the whispered rumors of voodoo, with
the suspect's Haitian heritage, and her spiritual position as a young priestess,
reporters ran with the story and sparked the New Orleans local news into an
explosion of national headlines that erupted through the news wire services:

YOUNG VOODOO PRIESTESS SUSPECTED
IN 8 DEATHS IN NEW ORLEANS

Leslie's brother, Pierre, was included in the mix, where reporters correctly assumed that he had carried out his murders to protect his sister, and then killed himself as the connecting evidence. And the majority black city of New Orleans was aflame with the news.

"You hea' 'bout dat voodoo girl t'day?"

"Yeah, chile, dat stuff is crazy. That's why I'on mess wit dem voodoo dolls and stuff. That stuff ain't no game. It's for true. And if people ain't know it befo', they know it now."

"Dey damn sure do."

All of the boys who had ridden the bus during Leslie's travels noticed her picture in the paper and on the local news and were scared straight.

"Shit! That's that black girl on the bus before, man! That's her! She coulda killed us."

"Damn, yo! I ain't pickin' wit no more girls on the bus as long as the day I live, man. For true! Or at least not no black ones like her."

And they laughed again . . . nervously.

However, the passengers who had ridden the bus during the fatal accident where the boy had fallen under the wheels and was crushed to death didn't joke about her. Some of them even thought about trotting down to the police station or calling in to tell what they knew. But most of them had changed their minds and figured that it was none of their business to get involved in it.

The boy who had fallen on Leslie that fateful day noticed her face in the news and kept his thoughts to himself as well. *Oh my God!* he panicked. *What if I wasn't pushed on her, and I fell into her by mistake? She could have had me run over that day.*

The old priestess spoke about it with a trusted friend in her home.

"Is she the one?" he asked calmly of the priestess at her table.

She took a sip of her drink and smiled at him before she gave her short response.

"We shall see."

"Did anyone else know?" he asked her.

The old priestess paused with her drink in hand.

She said, "I've not yet met her father. But I've met her younger sister."

Her company nodded. "And is she in the knowledge?" he asked, referring to the sister.

"She's not," the priestess told him, "but she wants to be. And we shall see about that when she must hold up to the outsiders on her own, and without the protection of her sister."

The trusted friend nodded again. "Is the younger sister as . . . prudent?"

The priestess answered, "No, but she is eager to learn."

Her company thought about it a minute. "And will you teach her?" he asked curiously.

The priestess laughed out loud and answered, "Of course not. Only if she never seeks me again. She has too much of a need to be loved. But if I could teach Leslie . . ." She laughed with her words before she could finish. "Oh, what I would *learn* from her."

"So you believe that she *is* chosen," her old friend pressed her.

The priestess took another sip of her drink and answered the same as before. "We shall see." She added, "When we ask the ancestors." And she held out her hands across the table to his.

A few miles away at the Desire projects, Jurron Chesterfield's head was whirling. The police had been there three times, and had found nothing but the last of his sanity. However, when they had left the third time, they had taken the rest of that.

This shit is crazy, man, Jurron told himself, anxious to smoke another cigarette outside. *And I'm scared to fuckin' leave! They might think that I did something. Especially with me fuckin' wit dat girl Phyllis before she died. I knew something was funny about that shit.*

Nevertheless, he refused to ask Laetitia more about it while inside of their apartment. He figured the police may have bugged their apartment on the sly.

Laetitia was amazingly calm throughout the whole ordeal. She only desired to see her sister face-to-face and eye to eye, no matter where they held her. So she was busy calling the police stations to find out where they were holding Leslie.

Jurron slipped outside to have that cigarette that he was craving, and he noticed two officers sitting in a squad car parked across from their building.

Aw, man, I can't even smoke a cigarette now. These motherfuckas are sweatin' us! he panicked. His hands shook so badly when he tried to light a cigarette that he decided against it. *If they see me shakin', they'll think I did somethin' then too.*

So he felt trapped and didn't know what to do with himself. *All this shit jus' because this girl had some good pussy,* he mused. *Boy, I swear to God, if I could do it all over again . . . I would have never said a word to this girl.*

The employees at Popeyes noticed Leslie's face on the news reports as well.

"Oh, my God! That's that girl that Phyllis was helpin' right before she got hit by a car that week."

"Yup, that *is* her! Oh, shit! You think we should tell the police?" one employee asked.

The rest of them looked at her as if she were nuts!

"Girl, you gotta be outta your damn mind. Phyllis was fuckin' wit dat girl. And I told her ass to stop. But you know how Phyllis was. She did whatever she wanted to do. So, shit, I ain't gettin' involved in that."

Someone else commented, "Yeah, you right. 'Cause if she killed Phyllis like that, then how you plannin' on sleepin' at night after you drop dime on her? I hear that them priestesses don't play that shit! You see how she tricked us into thinkin' she was a bum. Then she fronted the role like a hooker to kill that guy at the hotel."

"But that girl in her second year of college," the employee concluded. "So she obviously knows what she's doin'."

The girl who questioned it toned down and shut her mouth. They all went back to work in hushed silence as the next wave of customers began to flood in.

However, Leslie's employer, Jake, was not as fortunate to blow things off so easily. He could barely think straight when he had heard the news.

My heart can't take this shit, he thought to himself, while remaining at home alone. *Jean probably knew this about his daughter all along,* he pondered.

"Talkin' 'bout how damn proud he was that she was in school," Jake snapped out loud. "I bet he knew this shit. That's why they kept calling me. They all knew it!" he assumed.

"See if I ever hire another Haitian in my life again!" he exclaimed in his uproar. He mumbled, "And to hell wit 'em! They can say what they wanna say about it. 'Cause I don't need this shit."

My heart, he thought again, while grabbing at his chest at phantom pains.

Jake got so incensed that he looked up the phone number of the homeless shelter again to call Jean and give him a piece of his mind while he was still piping hot.

"Hel-lo," a woman answered the phone there. She had obvious irritation in her voice.

"Get me Gene *Bo-day,* will ya?" Jake told her.

"Gene is not here. Okay? And he has not been here today." The police and concerned citizens of New Orleans had been bothering them all day long about Jean and his family.

"Well, where is he, then?" Jake demanded.

"I do not know. Okay? Thank you for calling."

Jake said, "Yeah, thanks for nothing," and hung up the phone on her. And there was no way in the world that he could stomach being at his restaurant that day. Jake was thinking about taking a whole week off.

Back at the homeless shelter, Ray overheard the commotion on the phone inside the office, and he knew exactly what it was about. He took the news straight to Freddie and Clarence, who were watching for further news updates on Leslie Beaudet's case inside the recreation room.

Ray looked over and smiled at Clarence. "You see that?" he asked him. "And you were fuckin' wit dat girl's father, like you ain't know no damn betta. I bet you won't fuck wit Gene no more. And you lucky you back to bein' healthy now!"

Clarence looked and didn't say a word.

The only thing that Freddie said was, "You think Gene ever comin' back here?"

Ray stopped and thought about it. "I don't know. But I'll tell you one thing, if he ever do, I don't think I'm gon' be eatin' his gotdamn food no more. I'll jus' be a hungry and homeless motherfucka around here!"

Freddie chuckled at it. And although Clarence didn't comment out loud, he thought to himself, *I hear you on that. I ain't eatin' his damn food anymore either!*

When the three New Orleans universities of Dillard, Tulane, and Xavier circulated the tragic news that they all shared around their respective campuses, the students there were all in shock.

You never know who may be in our classrooms and in our dorms, the majority of students questioned. The administration, teachers, and staff were all terrified. But there was nothing any of them could do to screen students who may have . . . suspect histories and go on to carry out such horrific actions as Leslie's . . . if what they reported about her was true.

Professor Marcus Sullivan believed now that the reports were true. He didn't need any more proof. Nevertheless . . . he didn't plan to condemn Leslie for her actions. He still wanted her story. Who was she? And why would she do it? He wanted to understand her fall from grace.

However, the administration of Tulane wanted to understand *his* fall.

"Did you know about this?" Professor Sullivan was asked more times than he cared to be. Even Kaiyah Jefferson's parents in Little Rock, Arkansas, called the school to give the professor an earful, and to bring charges up against the university. This professor and his special assignments had sent their daughter to her death.

So Marcus packed up his things for the day and snuck away from campus, not, however, to return home to Algiers, but to figure out a way to have a word with Leslie. And while he went about his desperate search for the answers that he seemed destined to find, the citizens of America were captivated by the news, and they began to discuss the madness of voodoo, poverty, love, education, class, racism, and murder all in one big gumbo meal from Miami, Florida, to Buffalo, New York, to Chicago, Illinois, to Phoenix, Arizona, and all the way up from Seattle, Washington, to Minneapolis, Minnesota.

The news of Leslie Beaudet in New Orleans, Louisiana, had created American gossip at its best! And everyone had something to say about her. So at the New Orleans police stations, the phones were ringing off the hook with anonymous tips and outlandish questions about everything.

"I tell ya, I hate those damn news reporters sometimes. Seems like their job is to make our job more difficult most of the time," an officer commented from his desk.

Brian Willard moved through the office on his way out with Gilbert Hines, overhearing the various complaints that had gone on from the wildly popular newsbreak that day.

He looked back to Gil and said, "I guess you're right about this case."

"We'll see," Gil responded with a grin. They were headed on their way for their first interrogation of the suspect, who was being moved into a private holding cell after spending a precautionary night at the hospital after her concussion.

"So . . . what are you expecting to hear from her today?" Brian asked Gil as they reached the squad car outside.

Gil thought about it and had some ideas.

"Well . . . if she's as smart as we think she is, I doubt that she'll say much of anything."

Brian listened. But he disagreed.

I'll get her to talk, he convinced himself. *I know just what to do, politically correct or not.* And he climbed into the passsenger seat of the car.

≈≈≈

Leslie kept her eyes wide open as three officers led her into her holding pen with handcuffs around her wrists and shackles around her ankles.

This is where they always wanted me to be anyway—chained or dead, she thought to herself cynically. How else would you expect her to think in her situation?

As soon as they released her from her handcuffs and shackles to lock her into a small, private cell, Leslie thought of her remaining family members, while the other women prisoners stared at her through the bars that separated them.

Now they're gonna go after my father and sister, she assumed. *That's the most fucked-up thing about it! I can take what's gonna happen to me. But . . . I don't know about them. And Pierre . . . I still love you, big brother. I'll probably be joining you and Mom soon anyway . . . It's better than livin' in this fucked-up world.*

But I'm not going down without a fight! she told herself. *I'm gon' give them something to remember me by. All of them!*

One of the women in the neighboring cell wondered why everyone was sneaking peeks at Leslie. They seemed to be in awe of her.

"Who she? What she in hea' for?" the curious woman asked from no one in particular.

They all looked at her as if she were a Martian.

"You ain't heard?" the boldest woman decided to comment. "That's that voodoo girl. She's in here for multiple murder."

The curious woman looked back at Leslie and became excited.

"Hell yeah! That's right! We ti'ed of takin' this shit!" she exclaimed through the steel bars in Leslie's direction. She even offered the young woman her support with a raised fist.

"Go on, girl! Do that shit! You beat me to it."

Leslie ignored her. Unperturbed, the woman nodded.

"That's all right, li'l bit. I feel you anyway. I *feel* you!" she emphasized with her right hand over her heart.

Leslie continued to ignore her. *I'm not in here for that ignorance. And I don't need no friends in here,* she told herself. She refocused on her thoughts about her father and sister.

Papa, ne t'inquiète pas, she meditated in French. Dad, don't worry. *Je vais être okay.* I will be okay. *Laetitia a besoin de ton aide maintenant, et tes deux petites-filles.* Laetitia needs your help now, and your two granddaughters. *Aide-les maintenant.* Help them now.

Jean already knew it. It was only logical. Laetitia and his granddaughters were all that he had left. He had realized that Leslie had chosen her own way even before he was hit with the confirming news that morning. However, getting to Laetitia and his granddaughters without being noticed would be the hard part. The police would be everywhere, and they would be ready for questions and answers that were all obvious to Jean.

America was separate and unequal . . . and therefore, some of its unincluded citizens were forced to live by their own rules. Nevertheless, the societal rules of the unincluded were never recognized by the American law and those who judged within the courtrooms.

So Jean-Pierre concluded to himself, *There is no way out for my daugh-ter now. They will slander her like a witch of Salem. This has al-ways been the way of the Wes-tern world. They only care to unda-stand themselves.*

Jean remained in hiding within the dilapidated ghetto buildings of interior New Orleans, where he knew that no one would search for him. And within the dim light that shone through the boarded-up windows, he wrote Laetitia and his granddaughters a letter of explanation concerning his views of American hypocrisy, and what he felt they must now do to survive it.

≋

No later than Jean had finished writing his two-page letter to his daughter and her young family, the salt-and-pepper police team of Brian and Gil showed up at the holding pen to question Leslie inside of their interrogation room.

Leslie sat across from them at the small square table in handcuffs and shackles again, as if her freedom could harm them.

Gil stood as Brian sat again. And Gil began with the line of questioning.

"So, why did you do it, Leslie?"

And Leslie said . . . nothing.

So Brian wasted no time in executing his plan of interrogation.

"Forget about why she did it. Why did she come back to the house and get into a silly fight with her roommates, who knew everything? That was stupid," he spat into Leslie's face to provoke her. "I just can't figure that part out."

And Leslie said . . . nothing.

Before Gil could ask his next question, Brian added fuel to his own fire. "You know you're gonna fry for this, don't ya? You're not gonna get away with it," he told Leslie.

Leslie looked up into Gil's eyes to see what his response would be to his partner's line of questioning. And although Brian was indeed stepping out of line, Gil knew that he could not befriend Leslie in any way. Leslie was looking to play the color card, so Gil rebuffed her.

"What are you looking at me for?" he asked her sternly.

Leslie looked away.

Brian asked her, "Who taught you to use a knife like that? Your father taught you? We hear that both of you guys are, ah, *chefs*. So, who has your *father* sliced up?"

Gil had to take a deep breath on that one. However, he didn't want to reprimand Brian in front of their suspect. And Brian knew as much, continuing with his own method.

"You think that just because you're poor that you can take justice into your own hands? Well, you can't. And frankly, I don't care what they did to you."

Finally, he got a rise out of her.

Leslie asked him civilly, "What did I do to you?"

"*I'm* asking the questions here," Brian snapped at her.

Leslie looked away and thought, *Fuck him! He's being a typical white man. And his partner is being a typical nigga! He's letting this white man say whatever he wants to me while he stands over there like an asshole. That's why I don't count on America to help me. They don't give a fuck about people like me. They just want us to stay in the 'hood and out of their fuckin' way!*

"What are you thinking about now, Leslie? You wanna kill me, too?" the white officer asked her.

Leslie couldn't help herself anymore. His approach was starting to get to her.

She answered, "White people don't die. They rise up again like the phoenix." And she turned away from him again.

Brian humored her. He said, "So you only kill poor, defenseless black people, then. Is that it? Because they'll stay dead."

"They're already dead," Leslie countered. "You white people didn't give them a chance to live."

Gil finally spoke up and said, "Your small opinions don't apply to everyone. You chose to do what you did. And white people didn't have a thing to do with it."

With that, Leslie stared up into Gil's brown face again.

How dare you front like that, you motherfucker! You know what time it is with white people. I know you do, she snapped to herself.

Then she spoke on it. "I bet your small opinions don't mean much to your white bosses, unless you have the same opinions that they have. Let's talk about *that*."

"No, let's talk about your murders," Brian told her, redirecting the conversation. He said, "White people are not gonna be on trial here, *you* are."

Leslie responded immediately, "White people are never on trial for fuckin' with black people. Ain't that right?" she asked the black officer specifically. She had her own method in mind, since they wanted to try and play emotional charades with her.

Gil decided to unleash on her.

"Who the hell do you think you are? You're not the judge and jury. You're a suspected murderer."

"And you're an Uncle Tom in here to capture a runaway slave for your white master," Leslie responded to him.

Gilbert became so humiliated that he launched himself at her across the table and nearly grabbed her by the throat.

He shouted, "I live my life correctly! Which is a lot less than what I can say for you!"

Brian was even shocked by it as he pulled Gil away from her.

Leslie continued to sprinkle on her spices. "You see that, white man? That was more black-on-black crime. Only this time, you were here to stop it."

Brian looked at the cunning black girl while she sat at the interrogation table in handcuffs and shackles, and he thought to himself, *We're gonna have to regroup. She is highly intelligent. And I'm gonna need to do this by myself. She figured out how to get under Gil's skin.*

So he led his veteran partner out the door to speak it over with a superior who waited outside of the room.

"Are you okay, Gil?" the lieutenant asked him. Gil had usually kept a cool head.

He nodded and was embarrassed by his outrage. "Yeah, I'm all right," he mumbled.

Brian still figured that they had a job to do.

"Do you mind if I finish up with her on my own?" he asked his partner.

"Go on," Gil told him. Brian didn't hesitate to return to the room.

"Where's your partner?" Leslie asked him as soon as he walked back in.

"Like I told you before, I'm asking *you* the questions."

Leslie turned away from him again. She said, "I need a black interpreter, because a white man wouldn't be able to understand me."

Brian paused a minute and responded, "Try me."

Leslie looked into his face and said, "I want a lawyer."

Outside of the interrogation room, the lieutenant shook his head and commented to Gil, "She's tough. We're gonna have to be real careful with what we allow in the media with this case. They've already made this thing into a national circus. And we don't need any . . . big fish coming down here and getting involved in this thing. So we're gonna have to keep her quiet."

Gil listened to him and didn't like what he heard. He faced his superior and asked him, "What are you saying? She can't say what she wants to say? We still have a solid case on her."

"Yeah, but you know, if she can get you all riled up with some of the things she says, Gil, then who's to say that she won't be able to do it with more African Americans?"

"But she's still a murder suspect," Gil argued.

"A murder suspect who's a college student, with fine grades, who is very attractive, speaks fluent French, cooks, and knows what to say and how to say it," his superior summed up.

"And is that a problem?" Gil asked him.

Would he rather have a poor and ignorant black girl in there than an intelligent one? he asked himself. The lieutenant's comments made Leslie seem right in her assumptions about race and injustice, and that bothered Gil.

The lieutenant caught on to Gil's angle and decided to keep the rest of his thoughts to himself.

This is gonna be a hell of a case when this thing all pulls together. And an ugly one! I can see it now. We'll have to keep the television cameras away from her as well, he mused to himself as he continued to listen in on Leslie's responses.

"We have enough evidence on you right now to make this thing a clean and cut case in the courtroom," Brian lied to her. They were still trying to piece everything together.

Leslie looked straight into his face, and her eyes told him everything . . . and nothing.

She repeated, "I want a lawyer."

And that was it. Brian even realized it. So he gave her one last comment to think about before he left the room. He said, "You're gonna pay for what you've done. I just want you to realize that."

Leslie thought to herself, *I've already paid for it . . . before I even did it. That's what you white people will never be able to understand. Because you're not forced to pay the price for your skin.*

When Brian walked out of the room, he shrugged his shoulders to the other officers and stood silent for a moment. He mumbled, "I guess it's up to the courtroom now."

That much was obvious. No one bothered to comment further on it.

"Ah, Lieutenant Blocker," one of the desk officers called to their superior.

"Yeah, what is it?" the lieutenant grumbled in the middle of his business with the suspect.

The desk officer told him, "Ah, the younger sister has been calling all of the police stations trying to track down the suspect to see her. She says it's her constitutional right."

"Her constitutional right?" the lieutenant repeated with a smirk. Then he looked at Gil and Brian, and had a curious thought in mind.

"What do you guys think about that idea?" he asked them.

Brian caught on immediately. "We put her sister in the room with her and see what we can get out of it," he stated. "She's not gonna talk to us. So let's see what she has to say to her sister."

Gil was still trying to figure out whose side he was on. Now they were working to entrap the suspect's remaining family members. Nevertheless, Leslie was suspected in several murders, and Gil was a police officer, so he had no choice. He had to go along with things.

He nodded his head to the other officers and agreed to it. "Let's do it."

≈≈≈

Once the younger sister arrived with a police escort, Officer Brian Willard walked back out to Leslie's private cell and told her that she had a visitor to see her.

Leslie was apprehensive about it, but they forced her to return to the interrogation room anyway. However, this time, they allowed her to speak or not to speak without the shackles or handcuffs. And as soon as Leslie spotted her sister, Laetitia, sitting inside of the interrogation room, she thought, *Shit! This is the last thing that I need right now. These assholes are gonna try* anything! So she sat down on the other side of the table and shot Laetitia a look of reprimand.

Don't you know they're just waiting for you to say something stupid in here? she questioned her sister with her eyes. But with her mouth, Leslie sighed deeply and said, "I'm so glad to see you. This has all been crazy. Make sure you give my love to the girls when you go back home."

Laetitia took in her big sister's look and her words, and she understood them both.

I'm not here to help them out. I'm here to support you, Laetitia suggested with the warmth in her eyes. And with her mouth she responded, "You *know* I will. This has been crazy for all of us."

Leslie paused for a second to feel her sister out. She was impressed by Laetitia's poise. She had matured a great deal over the last month. A year ago, she would have been bawling all over the floor and filling up a bucket with tears.

But just when Leslie began to admire her sister's new maturity, Laetitia made a mistake that proved that she still had some learning to do.

"Je t'aime," she told Leslie in her French.

Leslie responded back in English, while shooting her sister another stern look across the table.

"You know I love you too, girl," she responded with her words. With her eyes, she told her sister, *Do not speak French in here. That only gives them more reason to suspect something. And you don't want to appear too smart in here either. That could be dangerous for you. They don't like smart black people unless they can use you. Ask Daddy.*

So Leslie decided to help her sister to play the innocent fool. Out of the blue she said, "You need to go back to school and finish your GED. That's the only way your daughters'll have a chance in this world. *You* need to be educated so *they* can be educated."

Laetitia responded accordingly. She frowned and asked, "Why are you thinking about school at a time like this?" Laetitia hated even the thought of school. Leslie knew that already.

"Education is power," she told her calmly. "Or that's what they say."

Laetitia read through it. She thought, *Yeah, I do need more education. Voodoo education, like you got . . . from Daddy.*

So she nodded her head to Leslie and agreed with her. "Okay."

"And you never give up on your dreams," Leslie added to her. "You gotta keep hope alive."

The three officers looked at one another outside of the room and collectively shook their heads.

"This is a bunch of nonsense." Lieutenant Blocker responded first. "They're in there playing a friendly game of volleyball."

Brian smiled, amused by the girl. Leslie was indeed a character. He asked out loud, "Did we really expect anything more?"

Gil was still having trouble trying to understand where his place was in all of it. And he hated himself for it . . . for still having a black conscience. It had not been successfully erased in his American police force training.

He spoke up to convince himself that he could still do his job.

"It'll all come out in the end," he told them. "All we have is time now."

Leslie returned to her private cell and was satisfied with how she had handled the situation. As Laetitia prepared to return home, she was satisfied with their meeting as well. Leslie was still her big sister, ahead on every game, and she still was able to protect her. One point Leslie had made certain to establish with Laetitia before she left was that "A lack of income is a terrible thing to have in this new world. Because without money . . . you basically can't afford to live."

I love my sister to death! Laetitia thought to herself as they led her to the awaiting squad car for the return trip home to Jurron and their two daughters. She understood her sister loud and clear in their talk. Laetitia needed to find a way to become prosperous, by any means necessary. And she was convinced that her sister had all of the answers that she sought.

Meanwhile, Professor Marcus Sullivan had finally tracked Leslie down at the holding pen himself. When he saw the police officers leading the younger sister away to an awaiting squad car, he continued in his desperation to get Leslie's story in any way that he could.

He pulled out a business card and scribbled his home telephone number on the back to hand to the sister through the police officers.

"Please, call me. I want to discuss this with you. I would like to get her full story," he told the sister.

The police quickly shoved him away, but Laetitia had already received his card with his number, and she wasn't planning on giving it up. She flipped the card over and read his Tulane University title on the front, and she wondered how much her sister's story would be worth to a college professor.

≈

Back at the light-blue-and-white house near Dillard's campus that night, Bridget Chancellor sat with her father and their lawyer. She reflected on all of the recent events with a guilty conscience. She had searched so diligently for more substance in her life, but once she had found it and it had proven to be too much for her to handle, she chose to conveniently run away.

Leslie would think that was typical of a rich girl to do, she mused. Ayanna and Yula were not running. They could not afford to run, and they had no high-priced lawyers to advise them on how. So Bridget became hesitant to follow through on her hasty plans to leave them.

"What are you thinking about, honey?" her father asked her while they sat at the dining room table. Bridget wanted them to talk about the case

while there at the house. She refused to separate herself from her roommates. Ayanna and Yula listened in from the living room. They were naturally curious to see what Bridget would do.

Bridget looked to her father and their well-dressed, light-brown lawyer,
and she shocked everyone with her response.

"Leslie needs proper representation," she mumbled through her still-
swollen mouth.

Ayanna and Yula looked at each other in the other room and froze.

Did she just say what I think she just said? Ayanna asked herself. *I hope she's
not planning on defendin' that girl.*

Yula continued to listen.

Bridget's father responded, "She'll have representation appointed from
the court."

Yeah! Ayanna thought to herself from the living room.

"I said 'proper' representation, Daddy," Bridget countered. "Regardless
of what she's done, she deserves a fair trial like anyone else."

Ayanna thought to herself, *Is this girl crazy!* She was nearly about to
voice her opinion out loud in there. But Yula was impressed by Bridget's
courage.

That's interesting, she thought. *I didn't think that Bridget . . . had it in her.
But I would be even more impressed if her father and his lawyer agree to do it.*

On cue, Bridget's father responded, "You don't need to worry about
that right now. That's her problem."

Bridget looked back to their observant lawyer and said, "But that's
always been the case for her. No one has ever tried to help. Not really."

"Look, Bridget," her father cut in on her, "I've been telling you again
and again that there's only so much that you can do to help."

Suddenly, Ayanna was . . . reminded of the separation of wealth, power,
and representation in America. So she found herself stuck in the middle of
the argument. She still didn't want to defend Leslie, but she understood
Bridget's point. Poor people were always underrepresented, and that
included herself and Yula in the situation.

Bridget's father went ahead and dropped a bitter pill on all of them. He
said, "Bridget, if this girl is guilty of all of the things that she's being
accused of, including the murder of your friend Eugene, then it's just a
waste of money to try and defend her. And I don't see why you would want
to."

Yula looked to Ayanna with obvious disappointment. And Ayanna was
incensed with anger and confusion. She no longer knew which way was up,

right or wrong, left or right, top or bottom . . . So she rushed outside of the
house to try and gather her thoughts alone.

"Motherfucker!" she cursed, as soon as she made it out the front door.
She was still trying to understand what she felt inside, as a wave of tears
flooded into her eyes and rushed down her face. "I'm tired of this shit!" she
whimpered to herself.

By the time she tried to wipe the first outbreak of tears away, Yula had
joined her outside.

Ayanna looked into Yula's sympathetic face and cried, "I'm confused,
Yula. I don't know what t' think anymore. I don't know what to do. I'm just
fuckin' tired of this shit. I mean . . . people are always actin' like you ain't
worth shit jus' because you don't have no money. It was the same way in
Houston. That's why I wanted to rap so bad, because I wanted to get some
money to get away from this shit. Ain't no guarantee we gon' get no good
jobs out of college."

Yula said, "I know how you feel, Ayanna. Trust me, I know. But we
don't have no choice but to go to school. We can't all be rappers and singers
and entertainers all the time. We have to be lawyers and doctors and teachers and everything else to defend ourselves, make ourselves healthy, and
teach ourselves. That's the only real way we can fight back."

"But I'm sayin', them motherfuckas still don't care," Ayanna responded
as tears continued to roll down her face. "You hear what he said, 'It's a waste
of money to defend her'? I mean, if he gon' say shit like that, then he makes
Leslie seem right for what she did. No matter how hard that girl worked,
who gives a fuck? So you might as well say, 'Fuck it! *Fuck it!* I might as well
kill somebody. They don't care about me any-fuckin'-way!'"

Yula said, "And you end up right where Leslie is now, in jail with no
defense."

"Who defends us anyway?" Ayanna asked her.

"We have to defend ourselves by doing whatever we have to do to keep
our freedom," Yula countered. "Nobody made Leslie do what she did. She
chose to do it. So now she has to deal with the consequences."

"But she still needs what the Constitution says she should get. And
that's a proper defense from a capable lawyer," Bridget stepped outside with
her roommates and stated. She said, "And if I have to save up my own
money to do it, then that's just what I'll have to do."

Ayanna and Yula stood silent for a minute while Bridget said her piece.
She said, "And I know y'all may not like me anymore or whatever,
but . . . I'm hurtin' *too* right now," while fighting back her own tears. "It

would be real easy for me to just . . . go on back home to Michigan like nothing ever happened. But that would be a lie. And whether y'all like me anymore or not, I'm gonna do what I feel is right."

And tears rolled down Bridget's face.

She said, "I just . . . wanted to feel like I was doing something. Can y'all forgive me for that? I just . . . wanted to do my part."

That's when Yula cried.

She said, "Yeah, girl. I forgive you. Because you didn't have to do nothin' for us. But you chose to." And she embraced Bridget in a hug.

Ayanna nodded her head . . . and gave up her love.

"Yeah," she mumbled. "I can't front on you. You got our back . . . so I got yours."

And Yula pulled them all into a hug under the porch light in the dark.

Time Will Reveal

Laetitia called the eager professor from Tulane University and set up a time and place for them to meet for a private conversation about her sister. But when she was ready to leave, Jurron was a little fed up with having to watch their girls at home by himself again.

"Where you goin' *now?*"

"I'll be back" is all Laetitia told him before she grabbed the front door handle. Even her daughters were getting used to her new coming and going. They began to cry less about it as their father cried more.

He said, "Naw, I'm not gon' keep hearin' that shit. You gon' tell me where you goin'."

Laetitia stopped to look back at him. "Well, if you must know, I'm goin' out to try and get us some money. Can *you* do that?" she challenged him.

Jurron paused and asked her, "Get some money *how?*" He had the wrong idea on his mind.

Laetitia grimaced at him and read his insecurities.

"No, I'm not out there ho'in'. You were out there doin' that, and that didn't bring us *no* money. In fact, you took money away from us. So I'm goin' out there to use my *brains* now." *Like my sister did,* she kept to herself. *But I'm not gon' kill nobody. I'm gon' start outsmarting them for money. And I'm gon' be a priestess too,* she convinced herself. *It runs in my family blood. I jus' wasn't usin' it before.*

Jurron saw how determined and fiery Laetitia was as she stood there at the door, and he backed down from her again. However, when she had left, and his two daughters invaded his lap for his daddy love on the sofa, he mumbled to himself, "I'm not gon' take much more of this shit. I'ma tell you that right now." *Voodoo or not,* he kept to himself as he caressed his daughters.

Laetitia wore a dark hooded jacket and snuck to an avenue spot where she could catch a taxi to her meeting place with the professor without being noticed by the police officers who had begun to limit her family's privacy, or the privacy that they had left in the rumor-infested projects. They had their own ghetto newspapers, called gossip, innuendo, and pure, unadulterated bullshit! Laetitia had it in mind to start using some of that ghetto bullshit to her advantage.

If anybody wanna act scared of me and my family because of this shit . . . well, then . . . let 'em, she pondered as she waved for a driver. *And I'm gon' open up my own voodoo shop, make up a bunch of spells and shit, and charge them whatever the hell I wanna charge 'em. Then I'll tell them assholes that I'll have them killed for givin' up any of my family secrets. You watch! That's all that old priestess is doin', talking a bunch of psychology and shit. I can do that shit too.*

I felt a whole lot of pain in my life, she reflected. *And like that old woman said, if I used my own pain, then I can relate things to a lot of people. Because I know what life is about. I lived through this shit! My family's been rich and we've been poor.*

"Where you goin'?" a driver finally pulled over and asked her.

Laetitia climbed into his backseat with the excitement of confidence and told him where to drive. But when she arrived at the meeting place, the professor looked a bit irritated.

"What's wrong?" Laetitia asked him, reading his pale face. She dropped her hood to display her blotchy skin with no more need for makeup. She *wanted* to look special now. She figured she could use it to strengthen her presence. Her vitiligo made her hard to ignore.

The professor responded to her by looking down at his watch.

"You're thirty minutes late. I thought you had changed your mind."

Laetitia heard him out and thought before she spoke. She had to train herself to make every word count, like a priestess would. Like the old woman . . . and Leslie.

So Laetitia opened her mouth and answered, "There is no limit of time for information. And I'll come when I'm supposed to arrive. Now let's talk," she told the professor with authority.

I can't ever let anyone think of me as being young anymore, she told herself.

But the professor cut straight to the chase and asked her, "Is there any way you can put me on the visiting list to see her?" Leslie was his interest, and not her little sister.

Laetitia read through that and told him, "We're more concerned right now about putting together a defense team for her trial. My father and I," she hinted.

The professor took the bait. He became immediately interested in the father.

"Can you also arrange for us to meet with him? I would love to speak to your father as well."

Laetitia thought again and answered cleverly, "My father is busy pulling together all of the finances that he can get while researching lawyers. He has no time for this. But if I could tell him that it would help us economically for what we must prepare for, then . . . maybe he would listen."

I'm gonna work his white ass to the bone! she insisted. *Watch me!*

However, the professor was no fool. People had always asked him for money whenever he sought out answers to his many questions. Reciprocity was the way of the world *before* capitalism.

She's trying to get herself a paycheck out of this, and I can see her coming at me a mile away.

He responded, "This isn't about money. This is about telling your sister's full side of the story. And I can't help you with the lawyers."

Laetitia paused a second. Her mind was still working on overdrive. She said, "Well . . . let me ask you something, Professor. What the hell is the difference in tellin' my sister's 'full side' of the fuckin' story, or even my side of it, for that matter, if it won't help to change shit? I mean, what are we talkin' about here?

"You want my sister's story for free?" she asked him with conviction. "And what are you gonna do with it? Get paid for some fuckin' voodoo research. And write a book or some shit on it? Because I know that's what you're here for. That's all everybody's been talkin' about. 'The voodoo girl.' You think I ain't heard it?

"You don't give a fuck about my sister!" she cursed at him. She had lost the cool head of her plans. She said, "So if you want her to tell you about some voodoo magic, then you talk to me first! And I'll speak for her, because I know her, and I love her. And Leslie is telling me *right now,* because I can *feel* her in me. And I can feel my *mother* in me from the grave. 'If you want my story, mother*fucker,* then you show me *your* magic! You get me the fuck out of here! Can you do that, white man? Where's your magic?'"

The professor came right back with his response to it all, even through his flushed red face of embarrassment.

He said, "Wait a minute, I didn't put you there. I didn't put any of you there."

"You didn't?" Laetitia asked him on cue. "Are you sure?" she added with hard, dark eyes.

And the professor froze. He was amazed by it. And he *was* sure. He was sure that he felt hundreds of years of pain emitting through her dark eyes at that moment. *He* could feel it.

Wow! he thought to himself. *How many thousands of black souls are speaking through her right now?*

In his hesitation, Laetitia knew to end their heated discussion with less instead of more.

She said, "Yeah, so you think about how much it's worth to you, Professor. And then you come find me. You know where I'll be. I'll be right in the projects."

And she walked away without another word.

≈≈≈

As another summer of muggy New Orleans heat approached, new, young brown souls played out in the streets, on the sidewalks, and at the ragged playgrounds that surrounded them in the various housing tenements, while they enjoyed the only life that they knew, and sang along with the new songs of survival that they had learned from the fortunate superstars of hope, while bobbing and weaving to the catchy lyrics of "My Baby," from the young rap star Lil' Romeo:

"They call me Little P / I represent the CP-3 / Calliope, you heard me / straight from New Orleans . . ."

Kids will be kids. And as they jumped rope, and played ball, and laughed, and ran, and joked, and smiled, and dreamed, they still loved America. Dearly! However, they had no idea how many blues they would have to suppress from their daily lives in less than ten years when they began to turn teenagers and understand the weight of poverty and despair. And how to hate the same America that they *used* to love. But for now . . . they knew no better than to love America unconditionally, including love for Leslie Beaudet, whose trial for multiple murder was still pending with a date set for early 2002, while she waited behind bars in seclusion with no money for bail.

So the little brown girls of New Orleans formed a circle of four and held hands together as they chanted out her name and spun around in a circle.

"Lezzz-leee . . . Lezzz-leee . . . Lez-lee, Lez-lee, Lezzz-leee . . ."

The parents who heard it scrambled to their children to snatch them up and stop them from their blind insanity.

"Stop it! What the hell are you doin'? You don't talk about that girl! Do you hear me? You are never to talk about her. It is not a damn game!"

And the children were bewildered by the hypocrisy of their parents. *Why can't we talk about her? Everyone else does,* they asked themselves. But it was more grown-up stuff that they could not understand until they were much older. Or at least they were told so. But the truth was that their parents would never be able to explain who she was, and why she did what she did, without facing the lies of America themselves, those painful lies of color . . . and *his*-story, and how *his*-story continued to affect *their* stories, while he and his children played the role of the innocent, until the ghetto decided to snap, like *she* did.

However, the kids did understand something. They understood that they would stop at nothing . . . to find out who Leslie really was, and what had driven her to do . . . what they claimed she had done.

IN MEMORY OF BARRY A. MURRAY (1951–2002)

"May the truth *always* be revealed!"

ABOUT THE AUTHOR

Omar Tyree is a *New York Times* bestselling author, a journalist, lecturer, poet, and recipient of the 2001 NAACP Image Award for the best work of fiction. His bestselling novels include *Flyy Girl, A Do Right Man, Single Mom, Sweet St. Louis, For the Love of Money,* and *Just Say No!* He lives in Charlotte, North Carolina.

To learn more about Omar Tyree, visit his Web site at www.OmarTyree.com.